ALSO BY KE

<u>Blade of Traesha Trilogy</u>

Daughter of War

Weapon of Rulers

Speaker of Fates

<u>Supernaturals of New Brecken</u>

The Maker

The Alpha's Den

UNMOURNED

KELLY COLE

For Allison. Nothing prepared me better for the world than having a big sister

PROLOGUE

THREE YEARS AGO...

Nook darted between the dark trees, listening carefully. Oblivious to the rumors drifting in from the cities, the birds sang and chirped and hopped on the branches above as they did any other day. Nook felt as carefree as they did. Now wasn't a time to worry about death, conquering royals, and complex politics she couldn't possibly solve. Not after the note. A distraction was welcome, especially this one. Nook couldn't quite smother the creeping smile on her lips. Her breath kept escaping on a nervous laugh. She'd never experienced this before—the tightness in her chest as her heart worked frantically to soar. At fifteen, she didn't particularly like the sensation, but those older than her spoke of love around smiles, so Nook supposed it was a feeling that grew on you.

To steady herself, Nook paused and filled her lungs. The forest air was moist, and the scent of the fallen leaves turned to mulch tickled her nose. Still lovely. Still familiar. Nook's hands drifted in the breeze, one reaching to pluck the hard, red berries hanging above her head. Mourning trees didn't often grow this close to the road, just as Nook rarely ventured so near. She lowered her hand and shook her spoils in her palm. The red berries glistened. She loved the sound of their beady bodies knocking against each other. The juices within ready to burst. So much power in such a small, unassuming package. Nook loved them. She loved that she'd been told her entire life not to love them. With a wry smile, Nook tossed them into her mouth, relishing the tart juice as they burst with pops only she could hear inside her head.

Nook laughed again. Feeling steady with their taste to ground her, she resumed her uphill trek. She crossed a stream by climbing a felled tree, weaving effortlessly between limbs that jutted toward the canopy of brightly colored leaves clinging to their branches overhead. Once on the forest floor again, she veered right when a hatter squawked a warning from the opposite direction.

Finally, she reached the thick wall of vines surrounding Lover's Meadow. The woven thorns reminded Nook of home, where she was likely being missed after leaving early this morning without word of where she was going. Or maybe they hadn't noticed her absence. The older Unmourned were probably too busy discussing the situation in Factumn and whether it warranted exposing themselves... but that was only Nook justifying her actions. Her mother would know she was gone, and she'd worry even worse because of the tension between the cities.

She tried to feel guilt for causing her mother worry, but excitement was too quick to overshadow it.

Nook had never been to Lover's Meadow, but it held the memory of her people. The Unmourned always spoke of this pocket in the forest with wiggling eyebrows and dancing smiles. Nook's breath shook with nerves. She didn't know what would happen beyond these vines, but if she trusted anyone, it was River.

Strong River. Braver than anyone else. He smiled at Nook's

antics when others snapped for her to stop. He was two years older, and Nook had been terrified he'd never grow to see her as more than Bough's younger sister. The message Nook found in the dirt by her family's home said otherwise. Nook had covered it with leaves before she left. Nothing was permanent in their forest, but she wanted to stare at River's message as often as she could. It still didn't feel real that he would want to meet her here.

Nook reached to part the vines and was gripped by a moment of indecision. Partnership was a big deal. She'd always watched and admired River, but the idea of partnership... that would take some getting used to. She'd have to tell him she wasn't certain she was ready for a full commitment. It would take some more time, but she'd get there. River was worth it. It was basically friendship with more responsibility. Nook winced at the thought. River, Bough, and her had been three of the few children raised below the Valley. With River and Bough coupled as best friends, Nook had grown used to sneaking through the forest alone. She *liked* it even. She liked breaking rules. Doing things none of the other children dared. She liked the few glimpses she'd had of the outside world. Her wildest dreams took her there. To the cities. Not to partnership.

If she wasn't old enough to give those fantasies up, was she old enough to answer to someone other than her mother or her increasingly bossy sister? Would River even want the future Nook did? Would he want to take up trading with her? Guarding the outskirts? Rarely visiting the monotony of the High Valley? Nook found it strange that out of all their conversations, she didn't know River's hopes for his future. But she did know River was serious about duty. About their people and family. Would he be as amused when Nook's behavior became a reflection of their partnership? Or would he become embarrassed and dismissive like her mother and Bough?

But this may be her only chance. She'd longed for a closer

relationship with him for the past year, ever since she realized he could be more to her than Bough's best friend. Ever since she started noticing his long, slim fingers and the soft warmth of his brown eyes. Ever since it had become difficult not to reach to push his hair out of his face so she could fully see his determined expression. Nook nodded to herself and tightened her grip on the vines, ignoring it when a thorn slipped into her palm.

She was young, but River could help her grow. She'd been sheltered, she knew that, but it was time for her to make her way in this world. It was time to think about the future, not about dreams.

It was time to think of duty and tradition with something other than dread.

Nook burst through the vines, smiling.

A shriek greeted her. "Nook! Get out of here!" Her sister's furious voice rang in Nook's ears. All she could do was gape at Bough without her coat. Her tunic was rucked up by long, slim fingers. By River's fingers.

"But..." Nook sputtered out of words, and River lowered his hands. Even in doing so, Nook could see how much he let his touch linger. How reluctant he was to let Bough go.

Bough picked up her coat and hurled it at Nook, hitting her full in the face and making her stumble back, tripping over the roots and landing heavily on her backside. She felt the skin in her right palm tear again, and embarrassed tears welled. Nook scrambled to untangle herself from the fabric, roots, and vines. Her ankle cracked when she yanked it free. River winced and made to stand.

"Are you all right, Nook?" he asked.

Bough stilled him with a hand on his arm. It pierced how easily he heeded her. Bough's face paled, but she clung to her glare. By the time Nook got to her feet, embarrassment had boiled into an anger of her own.

Nook hurled the coat back at her sister, searching her mind desperately for anything to say to sway the moment in her favor. "I'm telling Mother!"

"Oh, grow up!" Bough shouted back, but her voice hitched with anxiety, and Nook smirked as she pushed her way out of the meadow blanketed with golden everblooms and disappointment.

She lost them quickly in the trees. Or they never followed. That thought made her even angrier as Nook stomped through the forest, thinking little of where she was going and ignoring how her twisted ankle wobbled. Of course the message had been for Bough. Of course beautiful, clever, dutiful Bough would be the sister who gained River's affection. Bough was already being primed for leadership. Their mother watched *her* with pride, never embarrassment. Bough didn't avoid her chores. She didn't make their mother bite her lip with worry when she said she was going to take a walk.

No. Bough just went to meet with River in Lover's Meadow.

"*Gah!*" Nook threw up her hands, trying to think of anything besides the skin of her sister's back and River's hands caressing it as they kissed. She would not cry. She would not cry.

It had taken her all morning to get to Lover's Meadow, and it would be a long walk back. Sighing, Nook turned toward the heart of the forest, only to come face to face with a knife.

"Are you serious?" she asked in exasperation, more to Fortune than the dark figure pointing the blade.

The figure hesitated, her question catching them off guard. "Give me your coin," the voice behind the black mask was rougher and deeper than Nook was used to, but still young. A boy, if she had to guess. Nook shifted back, distrust edging its way in through her anger. His hand was gloved. His body was entirely covered, the large hood and tied triangle of fabric pulled up over his nose, leaving only his cheekbones and eyes visible.

Nook glared into them until the knife lowered slightly.

"I don't want to hurt you," he said, sounding tired. "Just give me your coin, and you can rejoin your party."

"My party?"

"On the road."

Nook glanced toward the road on instinct. She must be closer to it than she realized for a bandit to have found her. They were common these days, making her people even more wary. The peace was disrupted, and the road between cities dangerous. Her mother would be furious if she knew Nook was here.

"This is just my luck today," she muttered, giving in and untying the small bag of coin on her belt. Jal had just given it to her for her birthday, and she'd carried it as if she were a city dweller.

It hurt to hand it over, but she would have no opportunity to spend it anyway. Carrying it was childish. Like a game of dress up. And there was something about the bandit's weary voice, the holes she now noticed in his worn clothing, and the shadows around his eyes that made her want to help.

She tossed the coin to the boy's feet. He didn't lower his gaze as he knelt to pick it up. Nook tilted her head when the stream of sunlight revealed the color under his hood. She'd never seen eyes like his. They held the entire forest: brown and green and every murky color in between. The skin of his nose and cheeks that she could see was spotted with freckles.

One glimpse under the hood, and he seemed even younger than she first thought. Maybe even her age.

He froze where he knelt, eyes flicking down. "Where are your shoes?"

"Umm..." Did travelers on the road never go shoeless? Nook gestured vaguely behind her. "I took them off over there."

"But the stream is that way."

Nook saw it then, the clever gleam in his eyes. Assessing. Widening as he looked more closely at her outfit. She stayed silent, swearing a few choice words in her head that she'd picked up from Jal.

"You didn't come from the road," the bandit said slowly. It wasn't a question.

Nook swallowed. But the clench in her stomach didn't last long. She was still angry, and she was tired of hiding between the trees. She lifted her chin and reached for the knife in her belt.

Never in her life had she seen someone move as fast as the bandit did then. Her people trained, learning to defend themselves against the beasts of the forest and wanderers in their trees. But they prepared knowing they wouldn't get hurt. They didn't move like him. Like it was second nature. A skill developed of necessity, the same as cooking or breathing. He slipped the knife from her belt with his free hand before she could even touch it, spun her, and kicked out one foot so she ended up on the ground, defenseless between one breath and the next.

"Uh..." Where had her words gone?

They stared at one another; wariness and anger right at the surface. Nook was embarrassed now on top of everything. She longed to charge, to let him try to hurt her, but she couldn't betray her people so completely.

"So, what happens now?" Finally, words. And they came out steady and sharp, cooling some of her humiliation.

He hesitated again, knuckles whitening on her knife hilt. Then he blew out a breath, mask filling with its force. "Go."

He stepped back and lowered the weapon.

"I want my knife back."

He raised an eyebrow as he slid it into his belt. Nook balled her fists. Why couldn't one good thing happen on this day? Huffing, Nook got to her feet and turned, smacking a branch out of her way with more force than necessary. She wasn't paying attention to her surroundings. The birds were silent and gone

7

with an outsider present. There were no hatters near to warn her.

She was taken completely unawares by the furycat that lunged from the trees and yowled in her face.

LEV DIDN'T THINK. He just moved. A childhood of training to go on the offensive didn't vanish over a moon cycle. When the beast appeared, Lev was close enough to pull the strange girl out of reach of its swiping claws. They toppled backward, the girl making a sound of protest even as the claws barely missed her face. Lev didn't give the beast time to try again. With a grunt, he drove his knife into the monstrous, catlike creature's ribs. The girl was silent where she sat in the forest mulch, watching the beast die. Its weight became too much for Lev to support, and he let it fall sideways. Confident it was dead, he pulled out his knife.

Lev turned to the girl. She had a smudge of dirt across one cheek. She wore loose pants and dirty feet. Her tunic was long and patched, but her cheeks were full of better health than even the merchants on the road. Even those wealthy traders had suffered from the quick and brutal war. Lev marveled at the utter lack of fear in her eyes.

"Are you hurt?"

"No," she snapped, getting back to her feet. She frowned at the dead beast, bending closer to look at its stomach. "Oh, shame. I love furycats."

Before Lev could respond, the girl dropped and crawled into the bushes. His mouth dropped open when she grunted, scooting back with her prize, hands and knees now fully coated in mud.

"Look what you've done," she said, holding a baby furycat tucked close to her chest. Her eyes blazed with anger. Unrestrained and untempered. Not even trying to hide her emotions.

Lev had never seen anyone like her. "She was just protecting her kitten."

"It would have killed you."

The girl rolled her eyes. He could read her every thought. "Don't put this on me. I've had enough bad luck trailing me today. I don't want this, too." She shoved the yowling creature into Lev's arms. He held it awkwardly.

The girl pointed into his face, the dried dirt on her cheek contrasting sharply with her pale blue eyes. "Don't let it die."

"I'm not keeping it!"

"Fine!" She threw up her hands, taking a step back. "Let it die. Then it *and* its mother will haunt you. They say killing a furycat is six years of poison luck. You can suffer it. I want no part."

She turned to walk away.

"Wait!"

"*What?*"

He didn't entirely know what. This was the longest conversation he'd had in a month. He didn't want it to end. "You can't leave me here with this."

"Then let it die! But get away from the bodies. There are bigger things than furycats that will want the meal you provided."

"You can't be serious!" As soon as the words left Lev's mouth, he realized he was echoing her from earlier and scowled.

"Enjoy the coin," she called over her shoulder with a wave.

She was quickly swallowed by the trees, leaving Lev alone with the rustles and cracks that he still wasn't used to after four long weeks of hiding in the poisoned forest. The furycat in his arms squirmed, and Lev began rubbing its chin as he'd seen women around the castle do with their pets. Even as a baby, the beast was larger than any of the cats he'd seen there. The kitten began to emit a low rumble, drawing Lev's eyes away from where the girl had disappeared.

9

It really was cute. Lev knew he couldn't leave it. He glanced at the mother's body with regret. Her blood was cooling and sticky on his hand, turning his stomach. He'd seen enough death. He'd been alone too long already. He missed his brother. Missed having a duty. Lev sighed and adjusted his grip on the kitten, instinct overcoming his awkward hold as he tucked the little beast in close.

* * *

ONE YEAR AGO…

Lev woke slowly, head pounding and eyes too large for his skull. He groaned and clutched his forehead as he forced them open.

Only to see the girl. He sat abruptly, forcing a glare to match her smirk. But he was distracted almost immediately from his summoned anger. "He's letting you touch him."

The smirk widened. Coin stretched his neck as she scratched the spot behind his ears. "Of course he is. He knows who saved his life."

"You pulled him out of a bush. You didn't save his life." Lev was half convinced this interaction was only a fever dream.

She quirked an eyebrow, the look reminding Lev painfully of his brother. "Maybe, but I saved yours."

Lev couldn't deny that. He'd thought it was over the moment his stomach turned and kept turning until he was dry-heaving and too weak to stand. He couldn't remember anything after that. The girl tossed him her waterskin. He drank greedily without question. It was the most trusting thing he'd done in years.

"What happened?" he asked. One had to learn from every mistake in these trees.

"You drank from a river that had a fallen mourning tree in it upstream. Luckily, there wasn't enough poison to kill you, but it wasn't pretty."

Lev frowned. "How long did I sleep?" It was semi-dark now, and his last memories were of the morning.

"Just a few hours."

"How is that possible? How am I..."

"Alive? I gave you some antidote. But don't let it happen again. This stuff isn't easy to make."

Lev sat forward, heart jumping into his throat. "Antidote? There's an antidote?"

The girl tilted her head, looking faintly amused. That expression on anyone else would have made Lev's skin crawl. Too patronizing. Almost smug. Yet, even with their few passing interactions over the past two years, Lev was fairly sure this girl would never be able to elicit such a response from him. His heart was too busy pounding for his skin to crawl.

He pretended it bothered him anyway and met her look with a flattened stare.

The smirk reappeared. "Yes, city boy, there is an antidote."

Lev could only blink at her, head spinning with the possibilities. Since he'd gone into hiding in this forest, he had come to love it grudgingly. But only so much was safe for him.

This antidote opened corners of this hidden world he never would have dared to explore.

"How effective is it?"

The girl shrugged and pulled a tin container from her pocket. She twisted it open to reveal a raspberry-red gelatinous salve. "As long as someone doesn't directly eat the berries, this can save them." She put the lid back on, twisting it back and forth between her palms until she reached a decision. "Here. This time of year, a lot of berries are dropping. It's a wonder you made it through last fall."

Lev took the container gingerly, fighting the urge to refuse it. To refuse her help. He recognized the container now that he held it. Many of the wealthy traders traveled with it on hand. Lev felt a twinge of nausea, wondering how many of them he'd cast aside when he'd raided their packs.

"How much would this cost?" he asked.

The girl's expression hardened, and Lev realized only then how much she had dropped her guard. He cursed himself for asking.

"What, are you just going to sell it?"

Lev only shrugged. Things were easier when she was glaring at him.

"It's not cheap," she admitted, eyeing the tin in Lev's hands as if she wanted to snatch it back. "I don't know what Jal is asking for it these days. Midhaven sells it cheaper, but I know Lilstrom doubles the price. It's nearly impossible to pay for it in Factumn. And illegal." It would be. Queen Vasca wouldn't want any of her conquered subjects making a run for the forest. Their labor was too valuable.

"Jal sells it?" Within the last two years, Lev had gone to the other trader far too many times for help. None of the other city people hardened enough to travel between the mourning trees could be even remotely trusted.

"He has... connections."

Lev pressed his lips together. She likely meant her people, but they'd never come close to discussing how she survived in the forest. How she seemed to know so little about the cities. Her entire lack of fear as she sat on the forest floor beside him.

He wouldn't ask her now. He didn't trust himself with that information. He could only guess what horrors would happen to her people if the cities discovered the Unmourned were more than a folktale. If Queen Vasca discovered her.

The silence stretched, the girl watching him as warily as always. She was looking at him closely. Eyes sweeping his entire face... his mask wasn't on.

He looked around, waiting for the flare of panic. It didn't

come, and Lev knew then that this girl was dangerous for him. "Where did you put it?"

She rolled her eyes at his sharp tone and gestured behind him. His coat and mask hung drying on the nearest tree. She'd cleaned them after saving him. He buried the feelings the image brought forward—such a mix of gratitude and exhaustion. After two years of surviving the mourning trees, Lev knew he wanted to live. He just hadn't figured out how to do so happily. He couldn't reconcile his past with the idea of a less-than-dire future. One day, they would find him or the forest would take him. So, he survived one day at a time. If that ever became easy again, he would maybe figure out the rest.

There were so many reasons he stayed in the forest. One of the main ones was the need to focus on the simple act of surviving. There were no spare moments to plan escape. Another reason was the proximity to his brother. Coin's presence at his side another.

And when the night was truly still, and the fear ebbed briefly, the possibility of seeing this girl again was much easier to focus on than the future.

Yet, despite all this, Lev realized how close he'd brushed against death. Fatigue tugged at his spirit. It could have been over.

Lev stood and approached his clothes. Resigned to keep fighting.

NOOK DIDN'T TRUST the bandit. The flat look in his hazel eyes. The tight grip he kept on the salve. The lack of a simple thanks. Not that she expected one. But still.

She scoffed as she stood. "Well, I'll leave you to it. Be more careful. Boil your water, and don't expect me to show up next time."

He finished tying the ridiculous mask over his face, eyes bored above the cloth as he flicked a glance her way and turned back to his coat. Nook swallowed a sigh and gave the furycat one last scratch. She'd only heard of a few others who had successfully tamed one of the forest's beasts. What made this boy so special? Nook had nearly believed him invincible before the furycat had led her to his fallen form.

Nook's hands had only stopped shaking after she forcefully scrubbed the vomit from his clothes, the labor relieving the strange, nervous energy that had flooded her at the sight of him nearly dead. It wasn't fear, not for him. Not for an outsider. It couldn't be.

Nook slipped between the trees. She ignored the furycat's protesting yowl as she took off at a run. She'd stayed too long. Anyone following her markings could have found her with him. Her mother would have been furious. It could have ruined everything she'd worked for silently this last year. All the duties she'd performed without complaint. All the hours she'd remained in Thornwall even when she longed to escape the confining vines. She'd been good. Great. A model citizen.

Tomorrow, her mother would decide if she wanted to remain the forest leader another year or retire to High Valley. If she chose to retire, she would place her vote for her replacement. Everyone knew she would choose one of her two daughters to lead the trade. To be in charge of trips to the city, to travel the forest and gather enough coin and supplies to keep the Unmourned hidden in the mountains, high in a shallow valley, comfortable.

Nook was young to be a leader. She knew if her mother chose to wait another year, it was a good indication that all Nook had done to prepare herself for leadership would pay off. All the times she resisted the urge to go off on her own. The hours she spent asking her mother about the trade whenever Meadow was in Thornwall for her bleed.

It was funny to her that since Bough and River partnered, Nook and her sister had switched. Bough was almost always gone now. Even passing her bleeds in hidden pockets of the forest that were far less protected than Thornwall. Nook had caught River and Bough with Jal multiple times. Meadow always insisted on being present for any interactions the Unmourned shared with the trader. If Nook were to tell their mother about her sister meeting with him, there was no way Meadow would put her support behind Bough.

Nook was the best option. She was strong. Maybe the strongest ever. She wasn't afraid. She would do exactly what it took to keep her people safe. She would never back down or give away their secrets.

She would leave the forest. See the cities. Just one more year. One more year of listening and sneaking away without their mother knowing. One more year of checking on all her people scattered through the forest. Of avoiding High Valley. One year until the threat of being moved there was removed.

If Nook ruined all that progress by saving the bandit, she would never forgive herself. Convinced he wouldn't wake up, she'd stayed late into the day. She should have been in Thornwall hours ago. It would take her the night to get back. Nook pushed on, owls hooting their greetings as she went. Creatures rustled in the bushes, but they quickly identified her as Unmourned and scurried on.

Exhaustion pulled at Nook as she finally reached her childhood home. As always, she gulped in a lungful of forest air before entering the curtain of vines. The poison coating the thorns and the mourning trees nearby gave off a sweet odor. Nook couldn't resist turning and grabbing a handful of berries, popping them in her mouth and letting the flavor steady her before she pushed her way in.

Fortune was with her. She wasn't the last one to arrive at the meeting in the village center. Hardly anyone noticed as she slid into her place on the thick wooden benches surrounding the fire pit in the heart of their spiraling homes. Nook was shocked when Bough slid in next to her, even later than herself. She gave Nook a quick, nervous smile, and Nook tried to return it. Her sister wanted leadership almost as much as Nook did. It was something they knew about each other, but both only ever discussed separately with their mother. At the end of the day, it was Meadow's choice. Her daughters would only ruin their chances for the position if they fought each other for it. But Nook was determined. Bough had River. Bough had the fastest run and was the most successful with arrows and knives. Nook's sister was the best hunter and should get assigned *that* position. Bough didn't need to lead trade; she could feed the Unmourned by providing them all meat.

Nook had her love for the cities. Her luck against death. Her burning desire to see the world beyond the poisoned forest. She would learn trade and customs quickly. Their mother would see that. Nook had to believe it.

The sun rose, its rays reaching between the trees in teasing orange strips. Nook tipped her head to take them in, imagining an open sky. Sunlight without interrupting branch shadows.

Meadow stood as the last of the forest Unmourned settled around the fire pit. Nook's mother looked different today. Her short hair, often in disarray, was brushed back and neatly trimmed. Her features were relaxed. She, Nook, and Bough shared the same blue eyes, a color that contrasted beautifully with Bough's dark skin. Bough's father had been a merchant, traveling the road. He'd quickly lost his curiosity for the treacherous forest, but a night in Midhaven was all it took to conceive Meadow's firstborn. Their mother said no more about him and only that Nook's father, a man likely from Factumn given Nook's pale coloring, had been kind and fond of raspberry cake.

It didn't matter. Some Unmourned partnered for life with people from the cities they met during rare trips within. Some went for an occasional night of pleasure. Some never wanted to see the world beyond their trees at all. None of them longed to experience the world outside like Nook did. They listened closely to their history and didn't dare question it.

Nook knew the world outside could be cruel. She'd heard horror stories her entire life. Nook just wanted to judge them for herself. And a massively egotistical part of her thought the Unmourned, or even just her, could help.

"Thank you for gathering today," Meadow began, "We hold this meeting every year on my birthday, and I am still honored you look to me to lead you in our life here on the forest floor."

Was there a but coming? Nook saw something new on her mother's face, making her stomach flip.

"I have served as the leader in the forest, conducting trade and ensuring we keep our families above well-fed and supplied for the last thirty years. My daughters have known nothing but forest life, and I have nearly forgotten what it's like to watch the sunrise between the mountain peaks. I have decided, finally, that I miss the sight. This time next year, I want to celebrate another year passed with my mother and her partner. I want to tell the rest of our children about life in the forest and warn them about the cities. I am ready to pass my next years in safety, unworried, and surrounded by my family."

Nook's heart was pounding. She and Bough exchanged an alarmed glance. As much as she'd hoped for it, Nook hadn't actually thought Meadow would retire. That she was doing so this year was worrisome, but it didn't mean she wouldn't recommend Nook. She might be young, but everyone had to know Nook was capable.

"I am so grateful to all of you for following me these last too-many years. As I step down with the hopes of retiring surrounded by my family, I am willing to leave behind a member. I have paid careful attention to my daughters' educations over the years. No one would lead you better in my stead than..." Meadow turned, eyes meeting Nook's. Her heart raced briefly, only to shatter as Meadow looked away and held out a hand for— "Bough."

Rustle, the oldest member of the forest Unmourned, called, "We'll hear her case."

Bough smiled and stood. Nook knew from that look, the easy stance, that Bough had never once doubted this moment would come to pass. She'd known. Just like she'd known River's love, she'd known their mother's confidence. "Of course. As many of you know, this last year, I have shadowed my mother on her trades. I've learned everything I could from her and have plenty of ideas of my own. The most significant being my alliance with Jal. Partnering with him, a man from Midhaven and a trusted forest trader, I have learned more about the cities and the war between them than even my mother knew. No disrespect, of course." Laughter. Nook thought she might be dying inside.

"With him as our figurehead, we have sold many of our salves and remedies without fear of exposing our people. River and I have gone into the cities with him often, always blending in and monitoring him as he conducts business. The price for his services is fair, his manner is completely trustworthy, and he asks for nothing more than I have offered. Since beginning trade with Jal, our profits have tripled. Life in High Valley has never been more secure, and trading has never been less risky. I have already proven I can provide for our people. I will continue doing so under the next leader's rule, but I know I am fit for the position. It is only up to your vote."

And so, hands were raised. Nook, too young to even vote, watched as Bough was unanimously given the position Nook could only dream of. She watched her mother's pride as she and Bough shared a long, uncomplicated hug. She watched Bough and River kiss, a sight she thought she no longer found painful. The music started on new instruments Bough's coin had provided.

Nook stood and turned from the fire. Escape was her only goal.

"Nook!" Meadow caught up with her. She grabbed Nook's arm and tried to pull her into a hug, but Nook shrugged her mother off. She refused to look into Meadow's eyes. "I'm sorry, Nook. I have to do what is best for our people. Bough is the better fit."

Nook nodded. She couldn't speak, or she'd expose the tears she was fighting.

"I love you, Nook. You are incredible. But... you don't belong in the cities. You, you aren't careful. You're reckless. Passionate. Too fascinated by the outsiders. It is time to outgrow those things and focus on your people. On duty. You are perfect as a gardener. I'm hoping you'll agree to come to High Valley with me and—"

Nook stumbled back. "Do you know me at all?"

Meadow's eyes hardened. "I know you too well. You need structure, guidance, protection—"

"I can take care of myself. I always have. While you've been off preparing Bough for—" Nook's breath caught, her mother's words repeating in her mind as everything became clear. She'd lost the chance to become forest leader the moment she'd been found after falling out of that damn tree. Her mother had never looked at her the same since Nook's broken body had been carried back to Thornwall.

"Nook. Things are too dangerous. Honey and Current died. They were killed. By outsiders. The same people you are so curious about."

"The same people Bough is working with."

"She trusts Jal, and I trust her. Jal has always traveled the forest with respect, nothing like that bandit we've seen you following—"

"*What?*"

19

"Nook. We can't trust your fascination with them. You're coming back to the Valley with me."

Nook hated her mother then. She hated the bandit for getting sick. For needing help. For his strange eyes that tempted her to get too close. She hated Bough for getting chosen over her once again.

"I won't go. I'll stay here. The forest is my home. I'm allowed to stay." If Bough said it was fine.

Nook turned from her mother before Meadow could respond and left the wall of vines. She would have to return in a few days. She hoped by then Meadow was up high in the mountains.

1

THE PACKAGE

S lipped between the Mourning Forest and the ocean waves, bustled the city of Lilstrom. The Lilstrom Port was located conveniently among the protective cliffs of the coast and in the center of several large countries to the north, south, and across the ocean. Rivers flowing from the forest provided fresh water, though it needed to be boiled and checked for berries. The nearest trees were free of those poisonous berries, some ancient people having cleared the area for the city and a decent patch of land for farming.

The port was a chaotic stretch—a never-ending flow of ships docking, resupplying, and vanishing on the next tide. For ages, kings had taxed these ships and grown fat off their products. The cliffs and poison forest made any risk of attack trifling. The city was content and bustling but never ambitious.

Until Queen Vasca stepped into power upon her husband's death.

The stories and rumors about the first queen of Lilstrom were as chaotic and ceaseless as the ships moving in and out of port. The first was the story of her arrival. One cold winter day, a grand ship from the Kingdom of Eer docked. A woman like no other stepped into the city. They say she had one eye green and one brown. They say her hair was fire and gold. They say the moment she took them in, a hush fell over the docks for the first time. The first time ever.

They say the waves paused as everyone held their breath.

The queen was grim. She was the last of seven children. The afterthought. The empty ring finger that was key to the King of Eer's access to the port and discount on the docking tax. She didn't try to look happy to be moved from her father's sprawling and successful land to this condensed city. But her father was expanding his reach and needed the port within his grasp. Vasca took in the city that her father wanted so badly.

She decided she would take it for herself instead.

Her new husband didn't cooperate but also failed to pay attention. When the new queen asked for the right to build her own guard, he shrugged. He didn't understand that his wife was patient. That her vision expanded for years. That was what a woman like her had to do. A man like him only knew instant gratification. The ambitious and the content. Lilstrom would learn which trait won in the end.

The queen put out a call. Every male child born that year would be taken to the palace. The streets were swept. The king was confused. The people were unsettled but unaccustomed to protest. The queen's future army was plucked from the homes of the quickly. From the servants of the castle. From the merchant wives with husbands at sea and even the minor nobility. She declared this to be the way of things every three years. The people protested. The queen threw them money and convinced her husband to ease the grip of law on the city, to allow them pleasures once tabooed and more profit off their trades. The queen carried and lost a child, claiming she knew their pain and yet the sacrifice was *still* necessary. Her citizens settled. Every three years, the process occurred again. The people of Lilstrom hoped for daughters.

Seven years after the second round of children were taken, the king died. There were rumors of an heir, but the queen assured the people she knew what she was doing as she stepped forward and took the throne. The people were quieted. They were living better than ever before. Their children were spotted training, healthy and strong. A child army, the likes of which never seen before. Not even in the tales brought in from distant lands. Parents still longed for their children, but those unaffected carried a sense of pride in this new militia. The parents were in the minority, and their voices swallowed in the excitement of change.

Twelve years after the children were first plucked, they began patrolling the street in groups of two. They upheld the queen's laws, which were already generously lax. They always came to the defense of the people of Lilstrom. The first time a foreign sailor dared test the young army, the city was shocked to see how their sons wielded their swords. How ruthlessly they killed to protect Lilstrom. To honor the queen. They were expressionless. They were cold. They were lightning fast and hard as stone.

They were named the Queen's Swords. A single man had trained them from the beginning. A slim, quick man. His name spelled death. He led the Swords and was called the Queen's Dagger. In less time than anyone could have expected, the queen had an army and ruled the city without question.

Lev watched two of the Swords now. He hid behind a tattered curtain on the Red End of Lilstrom. These streets were fully debauched. Filled with near-naked bodies, brawling, and drunken laughter. The Swords only patrolled here often enough to let merchants and sailors know not to misbehave toward the people of Lilstrom. It was bad luck for Lev to run across a pair.

He tugged up his face covering. Straightened his hood. He wore Queen Vasca's colors, a burgundy cloak and bronze pants, marking himself as a citizen of Lilstrom to avoid suspicion.

Hopefully, they wouldn't look twice. The falling rain and clouds above darkened the streets. It hid Lev further, and he marveled at how the Swords didn't flinch from the cold water. They let it soak them, heads never ducking, discomfort never shown.

Lev grimaced as if to prove to himself he still could. He eyed the swords strapped to the patrolling men's waists. Clever, wicked blades. Just like the woman they served. As soon as the Swords passed, he continued down the muddy street.

He found the tavern he wanted and ducked inside with great relief. He hurried to find a seat at the bar. The pub buzzed with the noise of Lilstrom. The queen held a tight leash in many ways but understood the merriment found in Lilstrom drew merchants and sailors nearly as much as the prime location of the port. Queen Vasca's formidable reputation, her Swords, and the tales of life in Factumn meant she was rarely crossed, and her people were treated with respect even on the Red End.

Lev still preferred the fearfully exhausted tension that hung over her other city. Factumn was dangerous; robberies, murders, and masks around every corner. Lev fit in better. Here, he *had* to hide his face, a necessity that only drew more attention to him, even in the most illicit tavern. The Red End was the only place smugglers dared trade in the city, but it was still too risky for Lev's liking. It wasn't a good sign that the Swords were nearby.

It amused Lev sometimes that the people who dared venture off the forest road were more fearful of Queen Vasca and her guards than the mourning trees and beasts that lived among them.

"There you are, boy. I was beginning to think you drowned in the rain," Jarles said, sitting on the stool beside Lev. His wet leather clothing squelched unattractively.

Lev turned enough so the older man could see his raised eyebrows under his wide hood. He'd been waiting for five minutes at least.

"You up for another job?" Jarles asked, gesturing to Helen, the barkeep.

Lev didn't bother responding. He and Jarles met here the first of every other month so the former smuggler could give him the newest goods that needed carried off-road. Often, it was for the stilted rebellion happening in Factumn. Other times, it was for Queen Vasca's lower guards in Factumn who couldn't get their hands on the luxuries they were so used to finding in Lilstrom. Pleasure drugs and top-shelf alcohol mostly. Once, a pair of boots from a famous cobbler who didn't want their shoes sold in that "dirty city."

Jarles and his contacts paid well. He was among the few forest smugglers who had survived long enough to earn the money needed to settle and had developed connections that kept him comfortable in Lilstrom.

And Lev's prices were steep. He traveled the fastest. Never lost product and never stayed in either city long enough to gossip and get himself caught. Lev was grateful for his dealings with Jarles. His days of robbing caravans on the road were behind him. Too many close calls, one with the Queen's Dagger even, had set him looking for other ways to make money in the forest. He patted his pocket now, feeling the tin of antidote within. The girl had been right. Jal's product wasn't cheap. If Lev wanted to disappear deep into the trees and escape these gods-forsaken cities, he'd need way more than the tin he'd used sparingly over the last year.

Three more jobs, and he'd have the money to buy enough antidote to last him at least five years. Maybe by then, his face would be forgotten. Perhaps he would be able to grow a full beard. Be just unrecognizable enough to pass the queen's men on the docks and sail far away from here. Unlikely, but at least he'd have five years without a mask and hood with only Coin for company.

It sounded like bliss.

Helen approached. She took in Jarles with her hands firmly planted on her hips. Jarles grinned and winked at her. He was a large man but possessed the grace and skills to survive the trees. He was beginning to gray at his temples, but his features had softened since living in the forest and conducting business in ale houses. He was aging well into his new life and acted like he knew it.

It mattered little. Helen did not look impressed.

"You just going to stand there looking pretty or actually serve me a drink?" Jarles asked, eyes glinting.

"Depends. You going to sit there getting drunk and loud or actually pay your tab?"

Jarles barked out a laugh. "Helen, my dear, you are a treasure."

"And you aren't worth shit," she said. But her expression broke into a fond smile as she passed a tanker to Jarles. She raised her eyebrows at Lev, but he only shook his head. He couldn't risk lowering his mask to sip watered-down ale.

Helen moved on with a wink cast his way.

"The job?" Lev prompted before Jarles could stray off task again.

Jarles's expression shifted, more wary than Lev had ever seen it. "I have a package that won't get past the checkpoints on the road."

"Clearly." Few braved the Mourning Forest. Fewer did so off the road where Vasca's guards patrolled, protecting the merchants with permits by killing the forest beasts. Those trying to travel the road without buying an expensive permit or being granted one by the queen were killed just as quickly.

Lev and his fellow smugglers avoided all that by traveling the trees. He brushed his fingertips against the tin in his pocket again. He would love to say he'd figured it all out on his own, but of course, the mysterious forest girl was the reason he was alive today. The reason he so successfully smuggled for a living.

"Can you do it?" Jarles asked.

"Can you pay?"

Jarles smirked. "Of course. Double. Half of it when I meet you in your room with the package, half of it when you get it to those waiting in Factumn."

Lev's eyebrows drew together. "Double? What's the package? I have to be able to carry it through the forest, you know." Despite his hesitation, Lev's heart picked up speed. That was one less trip. He could buy the antidote weeks sooner than he originally planned.

He could taste freedom. It was bitter with a sweetened after-taste like the salve in his pocket. He had to go. He wanted to go. But his thoughts went to his brother, and he swallowed down the feelings associated with further separation from him. His brother was likely dead. If he wasn't, he hated Lev for abandoning him. Lev needed to focus on himself, on hiding, even when it hurt to leave his brother even further behind.

"That won't be a problem," Jarles said. "Do we have a deal?"

Lev considered long enough to make Jarles lick the sweat from his upper lip. He didn't like the nervousness on the older man's face. This was obviously a risky job, likely for the rebellion if Jarles was being so shifty about it. They could pay when they had a job but didn't often risk sending things through the forest. If they did, it was usually a coded letter containing sensitive information.

Jarles liked sending those with Lev, thinking he couldn't read. But Lev didn't bother opening them anyway. He was finished getting involved with the politics between the cities.

But double the pay...

Lev nodded and stood. "I'll see you upstairs in the morning." He wanted responsibility of the package for as little time as possible within the city limits. He and Jarles never traded in public, and people who frequented establishments like these knew to keep their eyes to themselves on the upper floors. The agreement made, he nodded to Helen and made his way upstairs.

Once in his room, he bathed and washed his clothes. There would be aspects of city life he would miss. Tubs of hot water and mattresses of down among them. Hanging his things to dry, he turned to the bed. He hadn't slept in a bed in weeks. This one sagged, and he could hear the revelry downstairs through the floorboards. Still, it would be better than the hard forest floor.

Or not. Lev woke continuously through the night. He missed the forest quiet. He missed Coin's watchful presence. Whenever he thought of his furycat companion, he felt a curl of anxiety. What did the cat do when Lev left him at the forest edge to enter the cities? How much was Lev missed? As much as he missed Coin?

When dawn's light cast a soft glow on the curtains, Lev pulled himself from the musty bed and winced from a headache likely brought on by the odor. He dressed. His clothes still smelled like the forest, a welcome distraction from the sickly scent of the tavern. It was comforting. He'd be back in his trees and alone again in less than an hour if Jarles arrived on time with the package.

Lev sat before his fireplace and waited for Jarles's knock, mind shifting through the possible routes he would take to leave the city undetected. As always, avoiding the Swords would be the most difficult task. He knew their patrol routes well enough to be confident in his escape, but with their skill, he could never feel entirely safe.

Jarles's quick rap on the door sounded right on time for once. Lev opened it and stepped back to let him enter, freezing when a girl about Lev's age walked in behind the older man.

"What's this?"

"This is a girl. I assume they have those in the forest. Well, if the stories are true, they have plenty—"

"Just stories. You know that," Lev said quickly. "What is she doing here?"

"I'm going to Factumn with you," the girl said, stepping inside and pulling the door out of Lev's hand to close it. "We're paying you more than enough to get me out of this shit hole city."

Lev snorted. This girl looked and sounded like a Factumner. She was slight and done in light shades and soft pink. The people there didn't have the diverse coloring of this port city. Lev was sometimes amazed by the uniformity of the people in the city deep in the forest. "You think Factumn is better than this? You must not have been there the last three years."

Her face paled further. "I have information that will help them."

"I'm not part of the rebellion, and I don't smuggle people."

"It's double the pay, Lev," Jarles stepped in when the girl drew a breath to retort. "If you can't do it, I'll contact Remi. Or maybe Jal will enlist the bleeders to help him smuggle her to Factumn."

Lev scowled. "*Just stories.* Jal will charge you three times my price doubled. Remi will probably—" Lev barely stopped himself from saying what Remi would do to a pretty young girl like the one glaring at him now.

Remi would take that glare as a challenge and do his best to teach this girl not to meet his eyes.

"Jal may be expensive, but he's good. Maybe even better than you, with those lady friends—"

"Those. Are. Just. Stories. The Unmourned don't exist." Lev glared at the other smuggler.

"Just because you're jealous they show themselves to Jal and not you doesn't mean they aren't real."

Lev only let his scowl deepen in response to Jarles's teasing. The older man's smile fell, nerves replacing cheer. Lev knew what lurked behind his eyes when he didn't stifle his expression.

Lev was capable of horrible deeds. He had to be to survive as he had all these years. He let it show until Jarles took a step back. The man was careful. He knew a threat; it was how *he'd* survived all these years.

The girl didn't. "They kidnapped me after killing half the palace in Factumn. My brother. All my friends. They murdered them right in front of me. I have to help my que— people there. You don't have to be a rebel to lead me through the forest. I'll do whatever it takes to keep up with you."

"Can you swim?"

A reluctant head shake. No.

"Hunt?"

"No."

"Fish?"

"No."

"Make a fire?"

"No."

"Can you even identify a Mourning Tree or the berries?"

"Of course I can. I traveled the road to get here. I saw plenty. Vasca is cruel. You have no idea what I have gone through working as one of her maids these last few years. No idea what I'm willing to try, to learn, to risk, to get away. You don't get to stand there looking at me like I'm an idiot for fighting for myself. You get to take the job or move along. Your opinion is unnecessary. And if no one takes the job, I suppose I'll see you in the forest. I can figure it out on my own, just like I'm sure you did." If she rose her chin any higher, she'd be staring at the ceiling.

Lev pressed his lips together under his mask, fighting back a rebuttal. A defense.

Jarles stepped forward again. He looked slightly amused now that the girl made Lev hesitate. He took advantage of the pause. "She's connected to important people in Factumn. People willing to pay. I'd much rather give the job to you. I like you, Lev. You remind me of myself at your age. I don't trust Jal, his gossiping mouth, or his swagger. No one in their right mind would trust Remi. There aren't any other smugglers skilled enough to do this. I know you can and I know you won't blab about it after."

"I don't smuggle people."

"You'll smuggle this one. Come on, Lev. She's a fighter. She's smart. But if she's caught in Lilstrom now that she's abandoned her position, you know what will happen to her." Jarles raised a hand when Lev made to protest. He pulled a bag of coins from his belt. "Double the price now. *And* when you get her to the other side." Jarles shook the heavy load. The man's upper lip was sweating again. He didn't like having this girl in his charge.

Someone passed outside the door, pausing when they heard the unmistakable shake of coins. Lev reached for his knife. The three of them held their breath until the creaking of floorboards marked the person continuing on. Likely to hide out in the stairwell, hoping to catch the owner of the coin unaware. Jarles pulled his knife, rolling his eyes.

The threat gone for now, Lev couldn't pull his eyes from the bulging leather sack. He tasted bitterness. Sweetness. He smelled the forest without a mask to catch his breath and heard the rustling trees without a hood to muffle the sound. Felt Coin's silken fur between his fingers uncovered by gloves.

"Please," the girl bit out the word. She didn't want to beg. Lev cringed at the Factumn accent she hadn't learned to conceal. "Please, I need to go home. She—they need me there."

"Who? Who is willing to pay so much?" Why it mattered, Lev didn't know. It all seemed too good to be true.

Jarles shot her a warning look. She dropped her eyes, but her lips thinned. "Double the pay now and on the other side," Jarles repeated. "Take it or leave it, Lev. You need to get out of Lilstrom before daylight either way."

Lev thought quickly through his route through the forest. Could he take another? Would Coin warm to company? How much time would she add to the journey? This girl wouldn't know which berries to eat and which to hold her breath around. She wouldn't know how to climb to safety or when to run downhill or to read the claw marks in the dirt. If they got separated, she wouldn't know which way was up. She wouldn't know what to eat. Where to drink. When to sleep and when to pretend to sleep, so creatures passed by. How to build a fire that kept most beasts at bay. If she died, it was another life on Lev's shoulders.

It took constant work to keep himself alive in the poisoned forest. And still, he nearly failed all the time. Could he possibly manage to protect two people?

"I can learn," she repeated as if reading his thoughts. "I won't slow you down. And when I get across and help them, then maybe someday soon I'll help us all. Reopen the road to travelers, not just the ones who can pay or Vasca approves. It'll help you, too."

"So you plan to use some knowledge you have to kill the queen?" Lev couldn't keep the doubt from his voice.

Her chin jutted in response to it. "You don't know what I'm capable of."

"Apparently I don't know a lot of things." But Lev did, and he knew better than to hope alongside her. He must have seen what happened in Factumn in a completely different light.

One that shuddered out light from that moment on.

Queen Vasca and her Swords were unbeatable.

"Appealing to his better nature won't get you far," Jarles cautioned. "He doesn't have one. But he'll take the money. Won't you, boy?"

Lev's hands itched toward it. He wasn't even sure how he'd conceal such a large bag. The fact that he was already thinking about that proved Jarles right. He sighed. "Fine. We leave now. Stick close to me from this point forward and pray to whatever gods you believe in with your every breath."

"Best save your air," Jarles said with a wry smile. "They'll be expecting her three weeks from now. You'll have to make the journey quick."

Lev sent the older man one last glare and snatched the heavy bag of coin. He took the girl's arm to lead her from the room. Her grin was maddeningly smug.

The coins were a satisfying weight, but what had he just agreed to?

Jarles left first. He found the man on the stairs and loudly invited him for a drink, acting boisterous. As if he had just had the good fortune of obtaining a large sum of money. The man went along readily. Jarles would be able to handle him when the time came.

Lev nodded to the girl. He was pleased to note she followed him on near-silent feet down the stairs of the inn. She was used to sneaking and going unseen. Moving quickly and monitoring her breathing. That would help. They reached the streets, and he checked both ways. The sun was just beginning to rise. He quickly ran through the patrol routes. They were behind the schedule he usually kept when escaping Lilstrom. Their path would wind more than usual, but he was still reasonably confident they could avoid the Swords.

"Stay close," he hissed.

She muttered a response, but the rain had picked up again, and he couldn't hear over the sound of it dropping on his hood.

Lev set off at a brisk pace, the girl practically running to keep up on her short legs. His every step was nearly two of hers. Lev wasn't bothered by this. The girl's small stature would be an asset to her in the trees, especially once she'd learned to climb and spot the gaps in bushes to slip into. She'd be able to tuck herself away and hide in nooks easily. Yet, judging from her already labored breathing, she wasn't used to physical exertion like running. That may cause problems for them. Lev didn't let up. If she couldn't manage rushing through the city to avoid patrolling guards, she would never survive the poisoned forest.

They cut through the streets without incident. As they neared Lilstrom's edge, Lev raised a hand, and they slowed. He squinted over the field and to the distant trees. They called to him even from here. He'd grown used to the forest. City air was difficult to breathe.

The Mourning Forest was a sight to behold. Most of the trees were as common as any other in the land. Brown, rough bark. Green, rustling leaves. Only deeper, further from civilization, did it begin to live up to its name.

Mourning trees were easy enough to pick out. Fully grown, they were much taller than their harmless counterparts. Lev had ventured close enough to the forest heart to see some grew nearly double the size. Yet even the samplings as tall as Lev's knees grew the red berries strong enough to kill a man. When the juice made contact with broken skin from an injury as minor as a removed splinter, it could be fatal. To bite into a mourning berry was certain death. To breathe near a cluster of the trees gave one a headache. Lev knew to fear the trees. Anyone would, catching a sight of the stark, vivid green leaves veined in red set against the unnatural smooth black bark. While most of the forest trees bled together into monotony, the black trunks noticeably swallowed darkness.

Sometimes, Lev swore the black glowed.

"What are we waiting for?" the girl asked when she'd caught her breath enough to get the words out.

Lev didn't answer. He pressed himself closer to the nearest home and waited as the girl did the same.

In seconds, the ambling steps of sleep-deprived, soaking-wet guards passed without noticing them. These weren't trained Swords. Just regularly employed guards. Queen Vasca would be furious to see how they kept their heads down against the weather. She would be even more furious to see how easily two figures slipped out of the shadows and across the field, confidently entering the forest without paying for a permit.

Under the canopy of leaves, rain still broke through, creating a loud patter that Lev usually enjoyed. He was too tense now. Sharing his forest path with a stranger felt wrong, no matter how right the weight of coins on his belt seemed. Lev continued their brisk pace. These first acres of harmless trees were patrolled nearly as well as the road. He wanted to get through them as soon as possible and back into the safety of the poisoned tree terrain.

Lev fixed his eyes on the branches above and blinked through the rain, anxious for the rustling that marked Coin's presence. Coin was wary of strangers and unlikely to reveal himself to the girl for hours. Lev wanted to see him sooner and ensure the cat had been fine in his absence. If a patrol came near, the furycat would reveal himself to warn them. If he was fine.

"What are you looking for? I thought the beasts were deeper in the trees. Jarles said I shouldn't fear until we were a few days in."

"What's your name?"

"Felicity." She seemed pleased to give it. Or maybe she was just pleased Lev had eased their pace alongside the rough tone he'd taken with her thus far.

"Felicity, you should always be afraid in the forest."

She seemed unsatisfied with his answer but held her tongue.

"What do you remember of your journey to Lilstrom?" The road was dangerous, but nothing like the actual trees.

"Not all that much. We traveled with Vasca's army. Hardly anything went wrong. They kept us in the back of a prison wagon and only let us out a couple times a night. Once, a furycat attacked a servant girl, and another man drank bad water. They both died."

Lev winced. "So you can identify all the mourning trees?" This was the most important to her safety.

"The black is easy enough to spot. Even children in Factumn are told to avoid black trees with red veins."

"Good. But it's easy enough to avoid a tree." Lev stopped and crouched. He pushed aside a tangled bush, revealing the sapling growing in its midst. The mourning trees were creeping ever closer to the cities. "If you were to step on this or fall into the bush, it probably wouldn't kill you, but you'd get sick enough that the forest beasts would smell the poison in your blood, know you were weak, and come for you."

Felicity's eyes widened. "How did you know that was there?"

"It's killing the bush." Lev pointed at the dried leaves barely clinging to the bottom. "Any time you see death, be wary of what is growing nearby." Lev straightened and brushed off his gloves. "Mourning trees aren't the only deadly plants in the forest."

Felicity scrambled to follow as Lev maneuvered himself over a fallen tree. Ducking under it, she asked, "What other plants do I need to watch for?"

"There are vines with thorns that will leave your arm or leg numb if you prick yourself, others that will kill you. Short bushes with leaves that come to five and a half points will make your body break into a rash and have closed people's throats and eyes with swelling. I once came across a patch of flowers in bloom that had a smell so sweet I don't remember falling asleep. I only woke when night fell, and the petals had sealed shut. I'm lucky nothing killed me in that time."

"What did the flowers look like?"

Lev considered. He'd made up names for most plants in the forest and had them well categorized in his mind, but he didn't know enough about plants outside these trees to compare them to anything. "They have pink petals, a lot of them fanning out."

"Like a rose?"

"Sure."

"My lady keeps a rose garden. They're her favorite. I wonder if she could grow those flowers. Do you think they could be brewed? Make a sleep drought of some sort?"

Lev narrowed his eyes at the girl over his mask. "My lady" clearly didn't refer to Queen Vasca. Her voice was too fond. Who in Factumn was her benefactor? "I wouldn't play with what we find in the forest."

"Yes. I suppose we would risk the flowers spreading if we lost control of them." But Lev could see she was still mulling over the idea.

Lev shook his head and pressed on. The forest was calm for now but too quiet. Where was Coin?

"What else?"

"Hm?"

"What other plants?" she asked.

"Weeds that grow in still waters. Never eat those." Lev shuddered at the memory. "Also, avoid bird droppings. They can eat nearly anything in these trees, and the poison is just as deadly after passing through their bodies. Also rats and other rodents rub themselves through the juices to protect themselves from predators. Don't let one touch you."

"I always wondered about the animals in here. How do you think they learned to survive?"

"By becoming more dangerous than the plants."

"Dangerous how?"

"I don't have time to go through all the beasts." Nor did he want to share the names that had stuck in his mind for them when he named them as a fifteen-year-old. "With the animals, you will just have to trust me. When I say climb a tree, you climb. When I saw run, run. When I say stop moving—"

"Stop moving." She grinned hesitantly. She was watching him more closely now. He realized he'd dropped his gruff attitude almost entirely. Her eyes lit with the excitement of freedom, and he was the provider. He didn't like the smile. The warmth in her gaze. The sense of safety she was hesitantly welcoming. No one had looked at him like that since his brother. Lev had failed him so terribly...

Lev jerked a nod. The humidity in the trees was clinging to his skin. Felicity was sweating and flushed, still recovering from their dash out here.

"And... the people?" she asked after an all-too-brief pause. Lev's stomach sank. Was she going to keep up this chatter the whole time? He quickened his pace, hoping to tire her.

"The smugglers and thieves don't go as deep into the forest as I do. Well, Jal does, but he's harmless." He'd share his wares before stealing from anyone. Lev had given up trying to figure out how the gentle man survived the trees. He wouldn't consider the possibility that the stories were true.

The strange girl's face flashed in his mind. Blue eyes filled with emotion. Wry lips and long, dark, messily braided hair. Breathtaking. He pushed it away. However she lived here, it was a secret that wasn't his to dwell on or share. She'd saved him enough times that he owed her that.

"I don't mean smugglers and bandits like you. I mean the people who learned to live in here. Did they have to grow as dangerous as the animals? Are the stories about the women who bleed the mourning poison true?"

Lev glanced back at Felicity. She'd stumbled already and had mud on her dress where her knees hit the earth. "I don't believe in the stories."

"But both the cities talk of them. It can't be a coincidence. Women who are impossible to kill, who bleed out the poison every month and eat the hearts of men who venture too close to their—"

"It's nonsense."

The girl. How little she said about herself. The way her eyes shifted, checking the trees. He knew what it looked like when someone was wary of an outsider. He'd felt the same way plenty of times growing up, knowing his only role in this world was to keep his brother safe. He'd failed his brother, but he would keep this girl's secret.

Lev cleared his throat. "Let's save our breath now. We have a long way to travel and don't want any guards to hear us. I want to be out of their patrol path before we break for the night."

Felicity glanced at the trees, just now lit by the full morning sun, and sighed.

2

FINISHED

There were stories in the cities about the people who lived in the woods. The Unmourned. To most, these stories were folktales. Others blamed the existence of the rumors on those who survived the berries, believing they had seen visions of beautiful, strong women while in the throes of the poison's side effects.

It was said in distant years past, oppressive laws and the threat of being thrown into the forest spurred most Factumn girls to agree to submission and marriage. Still, many braved the trees. Criminals were forced outside the walls to fend for themselves as punishment. Young children lived in fear of disappointing their parents and losing their place in the city. Only when the farmlands surrounding Factumn couldn't support the growing population did the threat dissipate for unmarried women. Only the most devious of criminals were banished into the trees in the decades before Vasca's attacks.

The Unmourned had their own story, passed down enough times to feel as much like a folktale as the people in the cities believed their existence was. The only point always agreed on was that Factumn had rejected them. The mourning trees had chosen them. There was a force in those bleeding black hearts that made those trees kill most and save some.

It was a poison too strong not to be magic.

Death. Magic. Fortune. Whatever the speaker chose to call it, it had granted those capable of giving life the ability to survive the berries. Arguments took place about the names of the forces. Life was stronger than Death. Magic favored those oppressed by manmade power. Fortune blessed them because of their goodness. The Unmourned always smiled during these debates. It didn't truly matter because they knew one thing for certain: they had a home, and the life they created in the forest was simply a gift.

The mourning forest was a wide, sprawling valley that took two weeks on foot to cross from city to city by the direct path of the road. The mountain peaks to the west tapered into steep cliffs against the ocean, ending with the Lilstrom port to the south. To the east, the proud peaks grew taller and taller until snow and high altitude defeated even the mourning trees. The Unmourned didn't know what lived past their height. They settled in a raised portion of the valley between the mountains, pruning the mourning trees around their small city and existing in the comfort provided by their people who lived in the heart of the forest.

The forest-dwelling Unmourned had continued their duties even as war shook Factumn and Lilstrom. Despite the safety of High Valley, some would always prefer to live in the forest their people first called home. They hunted, traded, and hid in the walls of vines, called havens, scattered through the forest that only they knew about and could enter. The war between the cities had led to a time of fear and uncertainty, but under the latest forest leader and her alliance with Jal, the Unmourned had yet to suffer. The salves and dyed threads and seasonings they produced using the mourning berries were continuously in high demand. Rumor had it the queen preferred the red shade of their lip balm over any other product. The flour, corn, and other city products that made life convenient never ran out.

The Unmourned had retained stability despite the unrest in the cities.

All but one, it would seem.

Nook woke and knew it was morning, though it was permanently shadowed inside the wall of vines. Her back was stiff, and she twisted her hips to release the tension with a series of audible pops. She always felt heavier, slower, and much older than her eighteen years during these days of bleeding. Her head held a constant ache above her left eye. She rubbed at it as she tidied her bed and left through the thick flap of fabric that was the home's door. The grass was dotted with homes within the haven her people named Thornwall. The Unmourned called their dwellings tents, though the structures were far more stable than the name implied. They contained rooms sectioned off, washing basins, and fire pits sunk into the wood floors for cooking and warmth. Nook stayed in her family home near the heart of Thornwall when she was in the grips of her monthly bleed.

Greener was in the very center of the village, stoking the fire pit. Her time had begun earlier than expected, but Greener could rarely count on her body to be consistent and had been safely within the vines when she started. Yet, for how inconsistent Greener's start always was, her time rarely lasted over three days. Nook was steeped with jealousy when she saw Greener turn and finish packing the small bag at her waist, set to leave already.

Nook approached and sat with her lower back to the fire they kept burning at the center of camp. Most forest creatures had long ago learned to fear the Unmourned and associated them with flames. Fire had become a true deterrent from most threats. The constant smokey smell meant the Unmourned were protected from any animal brave enough to test their vines.

Greener fed the flames branches from a redash tree. Exposure to this particular smoke throughout Nook's childhood had led to an immunity to its sense-deadening aspect, but it still worked to relax her muscles, even those cramped and strained in her lower abdomen.

"Are you leaving today?" Nook asked the obvious simply to break the silence.

"I am," Greener said. "I have lots of meat to pack into High Valley. I could wait, though, if you want to come." Greener didn't sound all that hopeful, but everyone always hinted that Nook needed to spend more time with their people there. Lingering loyalty to Nook's mother prompted suggestions whenever Nook had to retreat into the vine walls.

Nook ignored the offer. "Where are you going after?"

"I plan to gather more pelts before winter. I'll go meet Ash and Bower near the grazing grounds."

"I thought Ash was due back here in a couple of days?" Nook had been looking forward to seeing her cousin. She always loved it when their cycles aligned.

Greener shook her head, a smile curling her full lips. "Ash went into Lilstrom, remember?"

Nook gasped. "It took?"

"It took!" Greener laughed, but worry dimmed the amusement in her eyes. Ash hadn't yet reached her third decade. It was early for her to risk pregnancy. However, Ash looked forward to spending more time in High Valley. She performed her duty, hunting in the grazing lands to provide meat, but she was already ready for an easier life surrounded by their community. Now, there would be no guilt when she left her duty as a hunter. The honor of motherhood was far greater.

It was their people's way to give birth in High Valley, where it was safest, surrounded by the elders who would help her.

Nook sighed. It would now be months before Ash was forced to hide in the vines for her own safety. The blood and pain of childbirth was the price she would pay for that freedom. Nook debated going to the grazing grounds to ask Ash about her experience but quickly shook away the thought, cheeks warming. She wasn't ready to face the reality of losing her cousin to High Valley like so many others. There was a chance Ash would choose to return to the mourning forest to raise her child like Nook's mother had, but this was rare.

Greener beckoned Nook closer. She kept her long fingernails clean, and Nook's eyes always caught on the sight. Her own nails were perpetually broken and dirty from digging up mourning trees. Nook settled to the ground before Greener, sighing as the older girl began working those long, gentle nails through her hair.

"Do you think you'll see Bough and River?" Greener asked.

Nook's shoulders stiffened. "I don't think so. Last time, I left right before they showed up."

"You won't wait for them?" Greener sounded saddened by the thought. There was a time when Nook clung to her sister's company, but that was before Bough was given leadership and River's heart. Now, their relationship grew more strained each time they encountered each other. Bough hadn't followed their mother's request to have Nook sent to High Valley, and for that, Nook was grateful, but Bough also hadn't made it easy on her sister to have her around.

After their mother had recommended Bough for leadership over Nook, Nook's dreams had wandered. She ventured closer and closer to the forest edge and the road. She watched the outsiders who entered their trees with growing intensity. In her most bitter moments, Nook considered leaving. If she couldn't live in service to her people the way *they* wanted, maybe she could just go. Maybe she could explore the curiosity that had tugged alongside her desire for leadership. Maybe she hadn't wanted leadership, just a path into the cities. Maybe this was the very reason their mother hadn't given her the position. Nook had always been dangerously fascinated with the outside world. Too prone to risking herself to explore it. This flaw never failed to make their mother frown. But their mother had let Nook down. Nook felt more freedom than ever to disappoint the woman who raised her even with Meadow far in the mountains.

Only loyalty to her sister had kept Nook within the trees.

Yet the resentment Nook couldn't seem to quell grew every time she resisted the urge to step onto the road. Resentment led to avoidance. Nook had no desire to see her sister or mother. Among a people that valued loyalty and family above all, none of the Unmourned understood Nook's self-imposed solitude.

"I don't think so. I left off in a spot thick with mourning trees. I need to clear it quickly before they fully take root."

Greener's response was a heavy sigh. The hair braiding that usually relaxed Nook now felt like Greener holding her captive. Nook itched to leave the fire's stifling warmth. As soon as Greener tied off her hair, Nook gave her a quick hug and left for the cleared area of grass they used for training. It was early yet, and her people rarely worked with weapons while they were vulnerable with the bleed. Nook pulled out her knife and winced. The break in her forearm from two weeks ago proved irritating to heal. She hadn't thought the injury would be this bad at the time, but soaking it in the cold river was all that eased the sharp pains of the bone rapidly fusing back together.

When Nook arrived at camp, Fawn had seen the splint and teased her carelessness. Nook had refused the numbing salve the older woman offered then but since lived to regret the flare of pride. She switched to her non-dominant hand. The practice with her weaker side would be good. After several throws at the straw target, the unfamiliar burn in her muscles mirrored her thoughts.

Nook missed how easy it used to be for her to spend her days at Thornwall, River and Bough by her side. Now, the walls had a way of creeping in too close. Even the trees outside the wall of vines loomed above her, the branches swaying like a beckoning hand. Nook daydreamed about city streets, open skies, and conversations with strangers breathing stories she'd never imagined.

Nook wondered if Fullbloom was set to bleed soon. If she and Jal would return to Thornwall with Bough and River. The four of them traveled together often since Fullbloom and Jal partnered. Maybe it would be worth seeing Bough for a conversation with the trader. Nook hadn't heard news from the cities in weeks, and Jal was her only source of information—the only one who still indulged her and her questions.

Nook's thoughts shifted to the other smuggler she had met in the trees. Her movements slowed. If she was honest, she'd been resisting the urge to seek him out more and more. The draw toward the boy with the freckled cheeks and scars was as dangerous and persistent as her desire to leave the forest. She'd stopped leaving marks in the trees that would let her people follow her and ventured as close as she dared to his camps. But every time she considered stepping out of the shadows and greeting him, she remembered the mistrust in her mother's eyes. How disappointed she'd been that Nook had interacted with him. How it had cost her the position of forest leader. Anger flared, and she directed it back to the masked boy with the ease of practice. She wouldn't be where she was today if he hadn't needed her. She would just speak with Jal when she saw him next. It wasn't worth finding the other boy. Nook had learned her lesson. Only Bough could leave the trees. Only her sister could make friends with outsiders. Only Bough got her way.

Nook should just forget the boy and the world he represented before she found out if her mother's fears were valid.

FOUR DAYS LATER, Nook emerged from the river water, pushing back her hair as she broke the surface. She felt good. Stronger. More like herself. But she had yesterday, too, and had still been bleeding. Nook swam over to the vines dangling over the slow-moving current. Reaching up, she pricked her thumb on one of the thorns. When she lowered her hand, there was no pain, no blood. Only a tiny hole that wouldn't bother her for the next few weeks. She likely wouldn't even notice the slight itch of healing skin during her next bleed.

Satisfied, Nook left the river and dried quickly with the blanket she'd hung. Her freshly washed clothing was still too damp, so she walked back to the center of Thornwall wrapped only in her blanket. Her steps were light with escape within her grasp.

Nook's stomach dropped when River came into view on the dimming path. His eyes were pinched, and he pressed a hand to his lower back. Although Nook usually felt the bleed pulling at her lower stomach, she had experienced the breath-stealing ache that came with lower back pains and didn't envy him.

He looked as surprised to see Nook as she was to see him. "Are you finished?" he asked, taking in the lack of pain on Nook's face and the light color of the blanket she'd chosen to dry herself with.

"Yes, just today. You only starting?"

He rolled his dark brown eyes toward the leaves above, affirming the answer to her question. "Go check on your sister, would you? She was worried we wouldn't make it back on time for me. I don't think she's calmed down yet."

"You know how Bough loves to worry."

River huffed a laugh and ruffled Nook's drying hair before continuing to the cold water and the promised relief. Nook smiled at his back. Despite all her reasons for avoiding him and her sister, she missed them.

Nook continued up the path and spotted Bough between the

nearest tents almost as soon as she cleared the incline. Bough was unstringing River's bow, her eyes darting constantly toward the path he'd taken to the water. When her gaze landed on Nook, her eyes narrowed even further. Nook swore under her breath. She should have known Mint and Greener would tell on her. Both had lingered past when they'd finished to "spend time with her." By that, they meant wait to report to their leader.

Nook lightened her tone and plastered a smile on her face. "Hello, Branch."

"Nook." The lack of nickname belied how upset Bough was.

Nook sighed and gave up on her smile. "Look, I got distracted."

"*Distracted?* You came inside the vine wall *after* you had already started? What were you thinking? *And* you were out there alone? Again!"

"Time just got away from me! I'm fine!"

"That's just it, isn't it? You're always *fine*. You think just because you survived—"

"Bough! Stop worrying so much! We're here. I'm done and safe, and it won't happen again." Nook moved forward and wrapped her arms around her sister's solid build. Bough had only grown stronger since she'd taken up leadership of their people. Nook hated how even their different statures made her older sister the better choice. "You have bigger issues to think about than my tardiness. Get your priorities straight."

Bough laughed, though it sounded forced. At least she relaxed into the hug, pressing her cheek into Nook's wet hair. "I'm glad you're safe. I can't believe you broke your arm. You should be more careful. I missed you."

"I missed you, too. How did it go in Lilstrom?"

"Good. We go to Midhaven next."

Nook pulled back. "Are Jal and Fullbloom here?"

"Yes. Fortunately, we're basically synched. Fullbloom and I will start bleeding in the next couple of days, and after we finish, we'll set out." Bough hesitated a beat. "You should hang around and come with us, Cranny. You can wait outside the town while we do business. Then, we'll be going to High Valley with the supplies. Mom always says how much she misses you."

"I miss her, too." They both knew Nook wouldn't be joining them, even with Bough trying to tempt her with proximity to Midhaven. The grueling trek into the mountain alone would have Nook complaining long before they arrived. "How long will you stay there?"

"We're just going to drop the supplies off. I worry about the havens and you too much to stay up there for long."

Nook swallowed her annoyance. "You should certainly hurry back. You don't want to know what I have planned."

Bough stepped back with a smile so familiar Nook knew a moment of regret for all the time she spent away. "Fine, Cranny. Let me braid your hair."

Nook let her sister draw her into the fire pit in the middle of the village. There were several walled areas like this one throughout the forest called havens. Safe places for their people to hide if they didn't time their bleeding well enough to make it to Thornwall. All secured for the Unmourned to go and heal. Thornwall was deepest in the forest and closest to High Valley. It was the biggest and safest and the only one with individual homes within the vines—a miniature version of the city where the rest of their people lived.

Jal was seated on one of the logs surrounding the fire. Full-bloom sat on the ground, leaning against his legs. She had a basket of stones at her side and was chipping them away into what would make the points of arrows. Jal was in the midst of a story that took place in the Lilstrom fish market. Nook settled onto the ground to listen, and Bough worked at her hair.

Bough was firmer with her hair than Greener was. This braid would stay longer like their mothers' braids always did. The way Bough clicked her tongue and asked how long it had been since Nook brushed out the knots also reminded Nook of their mother.

Bough was turning into her completely.

Nook had to admit Greener had been the last to brush it days ago. Bough laughed and used her pinkies to part the wet mess down the middle. She began weaving it into two braids down her scalp the way Nook liked. River joined them, his short hair still dripping as he took his place at Bough's side. Surrounded by stories of the outside world with her family so close, Nook felt her body softening in a way it rarely did at Thornwall. For the space of a heartbeat, she considered going with them to High Valley. Maybe enough time had passed. It could be good to see her mother; perhaps Meadow wouldn't try to convince Nook to stay out of the forest.

But then Jal finished his story. He and Fullbloom left for their tent. The quiet descended, watchful and stiff. The usual restlessness Nook felt within the walls took hold and she itched to wander the trees now that she was incapable of being hurt once more. She ached to hike in the night world, daring the nocturnal forest beasts to test her. To bed in the nearest meadow where a break in the trees would allow a view of the stars. There was no place in Thornwall where one could see them. The vines pressed in, woven together too close to the branches above to let their light in.

Nook ran her hands over her braids to check her sister's work and made to stand. Bough stopped her with a hand on her shoulder.

"We need to talk, Cranny." There was a forced sweetness to Bough's voice that set Nook on edge.

"I don't think I want to have this conversation."

"Mother sent word again. There are enough of us patrolling and trading here in the forest. You've claimed no real tasks." Bough paused and took a bracing breath. Nook's body was yet again stiff with unease. "You can't just wander the trees—"

"That's not what I do! I've been clearing the mourning tree saplings around our havens and—"

"Don't interrupt me, Nook!"

Nook drew back as if she'd been struck. Bough was using her leader's voice. The command in it hurt more than Nook wanted to admit. She felt like a small child again, excluded from Bough and River's complicated games and more mature discussions.

"You risk yourself too much. I know you're trying to help, but it's not enough. You have to grow up, Nook. Mom and I have let you play around longer than we would anyone else. You know as well as we do that the position in High Valley suits you best. It's what you claim you're doing in the forest, but there, you'd actually be helping our people. You *know* all of this."

Nook clenched her jaw. She did know what her sister meant, but Bough would never get her to admit it.

Bough sighed. "You know your limits better than anyone. They need someone to tend to the mourning trees protecting our High Valley. It's the most dangerous job, Nook."

"It's boring. It's confining. And I'll be stuck there as soon as I agree to start."

"You'll be protecting our elders. Our mothers and children. Our people who don't bleed. I'll be able to see you often when I bring supplies. You *need* a purpose, Nook. You can't just go about wasting your strength playing in the trees. Breaking your arms and putting us at risk watching the road with your body in splints."

Nook froze. "Are you having me followed?"

"No, but Willow did see you. You have to be more careful. The fact that you didn't know she was there proves how unfit you are for a life monitoring the outsiders. You *have* to stay away from the road! You're going to give us all away after we've worked so hard to stay hidden. Generations of work. You know how dangerous the outsiders are, Nook. How much they fight and kill and don't care about their fragile lives. They've murdered two of our people! We cannot get any more caught up in that. Your curiosity is too dangerous. You need to stay away. You need to go to High Valley. It's where you belong."

The words were all too familiar. Nook stared at the ground so her sister wouldn't see the rage reddening her vision. "It's where Mom can watch me so you don't have to keep worrying and can focus on our other people. So you can travel through the forest without thinking you might run into me. So you can keep going into the cities with Jal, *an outsider*, without worrying I'll keep trying to follow you around like I did all our childhood. But I won't go. Making your life easier isn't a good enough reason for me to trap myself up there where I'll never be happy."

"Nook—"

Nook leaned away from her sister's warmth and got to her feet. "I'm tired."

"Nook, stay here awhile at least, won't you?" River bid with a tinge of anxiety in his voice. "We really have missed you."

His hopeful gaze was enough to ease some of the anger. Bough reached for his hand, grateful for his interference. Nook envied their silent communication. The mutual support.

Nook's chest tightened, straining her breath. "Sure. Maybe until you all head out."

Bough's eyes dimmed. She could always tell when Nook was lying. But short of forcing Nook to stay or ordering her to accompany them, there was little she could do.

"Sleep well, Cranny," Bough said, sounding defeated.

"Goodnight," River said, still sounding hopeful.

"You too, Branch. Goodnight, Stream."

Nook ducked away. Their family tent was only a short walk from the fire. Made of mourning tree twigs treated in oil to stay pliant and breathable but woven together tightly enough to provide privacy, it was larger than the other tents within the walls. Bough would be staying in River's tent, away from the responsibility of leadership and their mother's legacy for the night. Nook was undisturbed as she packed her bag. Their mother's presence pressed in from every twig and item around her. When she was Nook's age, Meadow had been bringing supplies to High Valley for two years. Meadow had a gift for dealing with outsiders and avoiding suspicion that she was certain Bough inherited and Nook lacked. She'd been trusted to trade without revealing secrets, to travel the road while looking like any other traveler. Since Vasca's triumph, this task had become more complex, but Bough's quick thinking and befriending of Jal had saved them. Meadow had retired with the knowledge she was leaving her forest dwellers in capable hands. Trustworthy hands.

Not with Nook.

Nook shouldered her pack and checked her belt. Her water skin was full, her knife sharpened, and her emergency bag of coins padded enough to stay silent as she walked. Her small red pouch holding her supply of mourning berries was low, but this would be quickly remedied. Nook peeked out the fabric flap that served as a door. Bough and River still sat in the heat of the fire. His arm was wrapped securely around Bough's waist, his lips pressed into her sister's loose, tightly curled hair. Nook was far from the anger of jealousy she used to experience watching them love each other. She couldn't be happier for them. Yet the hollow reminder of her own solitude rang at the sight.

She ran on silent feet to the river and the gap in the vine wall. Hawk was guarding the entrance and nodded to Nook as she slipped away. They would report Nook's absence to Bough but made no move to stop her.

Free from the confinement of the walls, the weight on Nook's chest lifted like a sigh. Nook smiled as the forest welcomed her back. She set off in the direction of the road.

3

REBEL

F elicity rustled under her blankets, beginning to wake. She moaned as she rolled to her side, hand reaching under her back and flinging away a rock she must have slept on. Four days in the forest, and she had yet to complain. Lev tried to swallow it, but he was impressed.

He'd only had to slow his pace the first couple of days as Felicity grew used to the rigorous hiking. The sound of her heavy breathing behind him had eased day by day. Now, as they packed their sparse camp and ate the remaining rabbit hanging over the fire and the strawberries they picked from a nearby patch, she seemed almost excited to venture deeper into the forest. The trees had mostly been harmless thus far, but Lev had warned her the night before the real dangers would begin that day, starting with the presence of more mourning trees. She'd accepted the news almost eagerly. Lev watched her close as she adjusted the pack on her back, eyes studying the forest as though waiting for it to reveal all the secrets it contained.

Just before they set off, Coin crept into the small clearing they'd camped in and approached Lev for a scratch. Felicity stumbled back a step, and Coin shot her a look. Neither of them had warmed to the other. Coin was too wary of strangers, and Felicity had told Lev the details of the furycat that attacked the caravan that transported her between cities. Eventually, the story came out of how she'd watched a lifelong friend bleed to death from the furycat's claws raking her stomach. Felicity's bleak expression as she described the scene made it clear it was only one of the many horrors she had witnessed in this war.

That Lev could listen without blinking at the details probably said just as much about his experiences.

Felicity relaxed once Coin was satisfied with his morning scratches. The furycat jumped in a powerful lunge onto a branch to Lev's right and vanished in seconds. Lev sighed, missing the steady company of his pet. This job couldn't be finished soon enough. He shouldered his pack and waved Felicity forward.

They hiked for an hour before Felicity broke the silence— ages, by her standards. The sun rose steadily, and the day grew warm even under the shade of the trees. "You're walking slower."

"It's more dangerous."

"Because of the trees?"

"And creatures." Hadn't he already described the entire forest for her? How she always had more questions ready was beyond his understanding.

"But your furycat will warn us if anything gets close, right?"

"Usually, but he's not here now, is he?"

Felicity rolled her eyes. "It's not like it's my fault. I can't help that he scares me or that he doesn't seem to like me much, either. How did you tame him?"

"I didn't." Coin had terrified Lev with his ferocity on multiple occasions, attacking nearby threats before Lev even knew they were there. Yet the cat had never so much as batted Lev without his claws fully retracted. This wasn't something Lev had taught the cat. He couldn't explain it any more than he could say exactly what he'd done right to keep Coin alive as a kitten. It had been an anxiety-ridden first few months, but they'd come out of it and had never separated for more than a night since.

"But how did you get him to travel with you and protect you?"

"Maybe it's just that I travel with him and protect him."

Felicity snorted. "Could you give me a straight answer, just once?"

"Fine." Lev was reluctant to share the ins and outs of his forest life. His ability to travel deep in the trees was how he made his living, but he doubted his bond with a furycat could be replicated. The closest he'd seen to it was the mule the trader Jal had trained to carry his goods without getting spooked or eating the mourning berries, but the mule wasn't of the forest. Lev was the only person who traveled peacefully alongside a forest beast.

"When she attacked, I killed his mother and found him in the bushes. I couldn't let him die. We've taken care of each other ever since."

Felicity nodded, expression thoughtful. "What is that?" she asked, pointing to a tree sprouting indigo berries. Its bark was a faded, ashy maroon.

"That's a..." Lev winced. Another embarrassing name that he'd made up years ago came to mind. "...tree that I believe survives by mimicking the mourning trees. It's not poisonous, but the berries look similar enough that they get avoided. All they do is make you tired if you eat them. It's very flammable, even damp from the rain, so it makes a great fire if you're willing to risk sleeping more heavily than usual for the warmth. The smoke is... strange."

Felicity smiled. "See, it's not so hard to give a straight answer. What about those little white flowers?"

Lev shrugged. "Those are just pretty."

She laughed, delighted. "So it's not all death and mourning in the here?"

"Of course not."

56

"And you're not all death and mourning? You actually like it in here?"

Lev didn't answer that. Felicity let his silence slide with a satisfied smirk. "What other trees and plants should I look out for now that we're further in?"

"I'll point them out as we go. There's too many."

"Fine. Where are you from? Sometimes you say words like a Lilstromer, other times like a Factumner. Sometimes with no accent I recognize, making it seem more likely you're from Lilstrom."

"I was raised by people from all over."

"Where?"

"Doesn't matter."

"It *does* matter."

"Why?" Lev narrowed his eyes at Felicity.

"Because I need to know how loyal you are to Vasca."

"No more loyal than you."

"You're wrong," she spat the words. Lev stopped, facing his companion, head tilted in confusion, his mask hiding his frown.

"Why do you say that?"

"Because you're *here*." Felicity gestured vaguely to the forest around her. "You aren't fighting or doing anything to help those of us under her thumb."

"I've transported plenty of objects to help the rebellion." A poor defense. He'd made it clear on many occasions that he wasn't a member of the group.

"And have you ever transferred anything to help Vasca's supporters?"

Lev's hidden lips twisted in a wry smile. "They don't need anything dangerous smuggled. Only comfort items."

"So you only help the rebellion?"

Lev shook his head. He'd carried messages and aid for plenty who claimed no alliance to either cause. Who were too scared to risk death going against the queen but still wanted

57

their loved ones on the other side of the forest to know they remembered them. Lev had learned to spot the fearful, and they'd learned to look for his mask. Their despondent expressions always got to Lev. They didn't have anyone's support and only knew to keep their heads down. They had seen what happened to those who risked rebelling. They were the ones who were so close to giving up that all it took was sending a letter to lost family to make them smile and kindle an ounce of hope.

Helping them felt just a bit like atoning for his past. But he'd never told anyone about these letters, these people who learned to seek him out. He wouldn't start now just to try to sound like a better person to Felicity. He didn't know why he bothered to get defensive to begin with. He didn't help those oppressed by Queen Vasca. He did nothing but serve his own needs.

"But you're helping me, so you must not support her. You must know what she's doing is horrible and evil. I'm going to the rebellion. I'm going to help them end Vasca. You can help, too. With your knowledge of the forest, you can help immensely."

"I don't support Vasca, but I'm not part of that hopeless rebellion. I'm getting paid by them. That's it." That's all it could be. Lev would only cause more harm than good if he strayed from his path.

Felicity huffed. "How can you say that? How can you not care? Forest knowledge and smuggling aside, it's obvious you're a soldier. We need people who know how to fight."

Lev stiffened but didn't break his stride. He fought the urge to look at her and give her the satisfaction of knowing she'd hit a nerve. "Why would you think that?"

"I was raised in castles, remember? I watched the Marked Men and how they trained. I saw boys formed into men who walk like you, who hold knives like you, and always have a weapon within reach. I also know that when Vasca's army attacked, they targeted the Marked Men so the royal family would be defenseless. I know they were so hunted that many had no choice but to run to the forest. *Some* of them probably went back to join the rebellion, to continue fighting for our royals as they were trained to. They're good men."

Silence.

"Well?" Felicity pressed. She looked at Lev's arms as though she could see through his sleeves and know whether or not he bore the tattoos of Factumn's most elite soldiers.

Lev forced the emotion from his eyes, making his expression and voice entirely flat. "I'm not a good man."

Felicity wasn't put off. Lev's jaw clenched behind his mask. "Do you support Vasca, or don't you? So maybe you won't fight. You could—"

Lev ignored her. He picked up his pace and turned their path north and the incline of the trees. He usually avoided this steep route, but Felicity fell quiet and concentrated on keeping up. That was by far enough questions for one day.

Hours later, even Lev was sweating under his hood. Pulling air through his mask was difficult. It sucked into his mouth with each inhale. He stopped and leaned against a tree to rest. A thought had been nagging at him, and he turned to Felicity. She was wiping off her sweat-dampened forehead.

"What information do you have that you think will help the rebellion so much? That made you risk leaving in person rather than sending a letter?"

Felicity's eyes sparked. "You don't answer any of my questions, remember?"

Lev nodded and forced down his curiosity. He turned away to drink so she wouldn't see his face.

He was surprised when Felicity spoke. The words rushed out of her like it had taken all her will to hold them back. She'd only needed a little nudge to free them. "I was tying her grace's dress when I heard." Sometimes Felicity slipped and referred to Queen Vasca with titles and compulsory respect as she had when she was the queen's servant. It always softened Lev towards her to remember what life she had escaped to join him. "The messenger told her the Swords weren't content. They were spread too thin and needed more members." Felicity's eyes were alight with excitement and hope. "She told the messenger to return to the cliffs and remind them who they served."

Felicity pressed her clasped hands to her chest. Despite himself, Lev's body hummed with tension at the news. At the implications.

"The *cliffs*, Lev. I know where Vasca hides her army. The Swords. All those monsters that murdered my lady's family and gave Vasca our city. I know where they sleep when they aren't on duty. Where they'll be their weakest. We finally have a place to strike."

Since first mentioning her plans for the rebellion, Felicity refused to stop pressing Lev about her ideas. She was smart. Too smart for Lev to relax around her. Not only did she think he could help by fighting for the rebellion and using the forest secrets against Queen Vasca, but she also convinced herself he knew more about Lilstrom as a city than he let on. That he could help them get to the caves in the cliffs when the time was right.

"I only know the way to Red End and back to the forest."

"Horse shit. But let's say that's true—the black market holds the city's secrets. Doing business there, you must have heard a lot about other places in the city. I wanted to question the barkeep, but Jarles convinced me I was safer keeping my head down until I got out of Lilstrom. He didn't answer any questions either." She was still clearly disappointed by this. "So, what have you heard?"

"I've heard men convince me to bring things into the forest for extravagant prices, and then I stop listening."

60

"But the rebellion—"

"I'm tired of your constant talk about Factumn's damned rebellion!" Lev felt instant regret for snapping, but still, he was proud of himself for lasting a week before doing so. He softened his voice, "Please, Felicity."

Felicity halted and pointed a finger in his face, a gesture he found as annoying as her constant talk. "It is not *Factumn's* rebellion. The people of Lilstrom are just as tired of Vasca's reign. How else do you think I escaped the palace?"

"How many?"

"What?"

"How many in Lilstrom are truly opposed to her? Enough?"

Felicity huffed. "Not as many as there are in Factum."

"Anyone powerful?"

She crossed her arms. "Some! But not many." The admission clearly hurt. "The powerful are only powerful because they support Vasca. A few in secret oppose her, but... not enough to risk their wealth and titles."

"So, it's mostly the poor and hungry. There are very few of those in Lilstrom. She keeps her people happy. It's not shocking those who are against her don't prosper."

Felicity nodded reluctantly.

"And they'll be kept poor and hungry as long as they oppose her. Those aren't the allies you want."

"There are a lot of poor and hungry people. And they're angry and—

"It's not enough."

"So what will be? Who do we want? How do we get the rich to back us?"

"You're asking the wrong man."

"But who do you think might help?" she pressed, stepping closer and peering up at his eyes shadowed by his hood.

Lev stepped away and threw up his hands. "Maybe you should start with the powerful who aren't rich. Maybe you should start with the highly trained army you plan to kill." Lev winced when the words left his lips, especially when the calculating look flashed in Felicity's eyes.

She shook the thought away, lip curling in disgust. "There isn't hope for those monsters. The Swords would never cross to our side. Vasca took away their ability to think for themselves and replaced it with bloodlust when they were babies." She shuddered. "You didn't see them attack the royal family. It was awful." She started walking again. "If only we still had the Marked Men. They were the only army trained enough to go against the Swords." Another hopeful look cast his way.

"A different army trained since childhood to kill for their royalty?" Lev muttered the words, but Felicity possessed uncanny hearing.

She turned back to him with a glare but at least kept her hand at her side. "The Marked Men were recruited for the skills they showed early. They were trained and lived alongside the royalty they swore to protect by their own volition. The Marked Men had a choice, and their loyalty was given, not beaten into them. They died fighting for something they believed in. They were brave and honorable. Good men, like I said."

Lev put his hands up in surrender. "I told you I was the wrong man to ask."

Felicity rolled her eyes, agreement hanging in the pause. But as always, she wasn't done. She always needed to have the last word. "We'd have better luck recruiting Vasca's courtiers than her dogs. *Or* men who know the forest well enough to give us an advantage." She went off again, explaining how Vasca's rule of the road weakened Factumn and how much Lev could help their cause. They needed to get a small army to Lilstrom to attack the cliffs. Lev drowned her out for the most part, focusing on the forest again, searching the shadows for beasts and the plants for signs of death. When they stopped to make camp, she fell silent as they collected wood for the fire. She was quiet enough that Lev nearly relaxed.

Felicity did speak again, but softly. "Half the reason I wanted to travel with you and not Jal was your reputation. I can't see you having any qualms against collecting the berries to kill Vasca's d—"

"Stop." Lev had heard enough. He threw down the branches he'd collected. "I'm going upstream to wash off. I don't want to hear any more about the rebellion when I return."

He stalked into the trees, ripping off his mask to draw in full breaths of air. Coin happily slipped through the bushes to circle his legs. Why couldn't she just let it go? Why did it always turn to death and war? Killing. He couldn't do it anymore. All this talk... Lev's skin crawled with memories. Circling, spiraling. Blood. His brother's paling face. The bodies he passed. Lev stumbled, Coin sniffing up close, knowing what was next.

Lev dropped to his knees, gasping, hands over his eyes as if it would block the sights haunting him. It didn't help. Nothing helped. Lev ripped off his gloves and wiped his hands on his pants vigorously, certain they were wet and sticky and warm. The blood would crust and stain the wrinkles in his knuckles and edges of his nails. It would always linger. He couldn't ever be clean of it.

Losing the battle entirely, Lev heaved the sparse meal they'd eaten into the bushes, and the panic consumed him.

Eventually, he became aware of Coin pushing his head into Lev's chest, centering him and easing the harsh breaths he couldn't fully draw back in. Lev felt the rumble of Coin's purr, the soft breeze sending the leaves surrounding him into a flutter, the muted roar of the stream nearby. He let the forest sink into his bones and forced the memories away with deep, shuddering breaths.

Queen Vasca's rule was harsh and complete. The forest was the only place she didn't have ears. The rebellion had probably remained a minor enough threat in her eyes that it didn't need quashing, but if anyone reported Felicity's words back to her... Lev shuddered. Even the forest suffered the last time the queen sent her men down the road to quash Factumn's last attempted uprising. Many with permits had died when their trade was requisitioned, and they were left with nothing among the trees. Queen Vasca's soldiers had burned the few farms Factum had grown on the sparse lands between them and the forest and bordering mountain. Trees were consumed, and animals ran deeper into the forest, upsetting the delicate balance.

For Queen Vasca to show her strength again, growing as it has with Factumn's gold to back her, would be devastating. Princess Amalia, the last of Factumn's royalty and Queen Vasca's appointed figurehead, would never survive. The queen would jump at any excuse to flaunt her power. To solidify it completely. The people of Factumn adored their princess and had to be grateful to Queen Vasca for leaving the girl alive. Now, Amalia had to carry out Queen Vasca's rulings, slowly driving a rift between her and her people. In time, not even the rebellion would support her. The queen loved such games, and no one played them better. Princess Amalia's life was just a power move. She would be removed in a heartbeat if Queen Vasca thought the girl brought the people too much hope of returning to independence.

It was all so complicated. So delicate. Lev had no place in this rebellion. In the cities. Lev doubted Felicity would last long once he left her in Factumn with what she knew. The thought nearly made him sick again.

By the time Lev calmed himself and finished washing up in the cool water, it was far later than he'd expected. Dread filled Lev when he noticed how dark it had grown.

When her scream pierced the forest, Lev was already cursing himself for leaving Felicity alone with the beasts of the night.

4

A SCREAM IN THE FOREST

Nook had been enjoying the rains, but she could tell from the first rays of dawn it would be a hot day. Rolling up the blanket she'd thrown off in the night, Nook looked around for her stone and flint. She'd fallen into a bad habit of discarding them after starting her nightly fire. Twice, she'd had to double back to her camps after realizing she'd left them behind. The birds sang in the branches above her. The day too calm and bright. Nook already felt tedium building.

Nook had muddied both her tunics an embarrassing amount and would need to make her way to a stream soon to do her washing. She pulled on the dress Jal had gifted her for her eighteenth birthday two months ago. The cream color wasn't practical, the length and lace even less so, but Nook loved it. She wore it over her black pants and laced up her boots.

Nook couldn't resist swaying in place and watching the dress fan out. Jal had told her its uneven hem was a current style in Lilstrom. The fabric was soft under the lace, and the long sleeves came to a point over her hands, held in place by small loops she pulled over her middle fingers. Frivolous beauty. Nook loved it. What must it be like to exist where a skirt didn't constantly catch on the world around you?

Ready, Nook sighed and faced her day. She had to pass it somehow. Temptation itched. The longing for her usual haunts flared. Nook tried to resist. She really didn't want to cause more of a rift between her and Bough. She wanted to interact with her people without them watching her warily. Without them feeling the need to follow her and report to their leader. When Nook made herself stop and think, she didn't want to be drawn to the cities. To the road. To the boy in a mask who seemed so lonely and silent.

With no plan forthcoming, Nook wandered. She cleared out the saplings attempting to grow too close to the nearest haven. She found a path a smuggler was trying to form and planted said saplings in their way, visible enough to deter the smuggler without causing them harm. In a moment of weakness that took two hours, she ventured close enough to the road to hear a merchant and guard discussing a large party making its way from Lilstrom. If it was big enough for discussion, it must be enormous. The news filled Nook with dread. She carved warnings in the trees for her people but never signed her name so no one would know it was her peeking at the road again.

The pull to see the procession for herself was strong, but Nook fought it. It would take her days to reach their point in the road, as they were likely traveling slowly with so many. Whoever it was, it wasn't the Unmourned's concern... although, if they went through Midhaven, they might run into Jal and Bough. That would be a problem. But Nook couldn't warn her sister directly without giving away how close she'd gotten to the road. Nook assured herself Bough was careful, and with the party being so large, her sister wouldn't miss it. She'd be fine. Nook could let it go.

Nook dismissed the road and doubled back into the forest. She won *that* battle within herself, but the restlessness didn't let up.

Giving in, Nook did the least dangerous of her vices. She went to find the bandit. To follow him just far enough to make sure he was okay. To see the furycat and give him the scratches he loved. The poor pet always seemed anxious. Sometimes, he sought Nook out when the boy was in the city. Nook always stayed too close to the forest edge when that happened. It meant a night of the furycat following at her heels, warming her side as she slept. Then, he slipped away to find his companion when the time came. The furycat seemed to possess a sixth sense for the boy's location.

It took her most of the afternoon, but she found the bandit's path by checking a trap he left in a small creek. The fish had been emptied, proving he'd passed recently. Nook turned toward Factumn and began to follow his route, looking for the furycat to sniff her out before she got too close.

The furycat found her within minutes. Nook smiled. She clicked her tongue, and the beast, so black it was purple in the light, came alive at the sound. Prancing forward, it collided with Nook hard enough to knock her off her feet. She let out a laugh and wrestled with the bulky feline until she had gained the upper hand. The play turned to belly rubs, which set the furycat to purring, a sound Nook would never get used to after a childhood of hearing only hissing and yowls from its kind.

She sat with it in the dirt until his head popped up in the direction of his companion. Nook watched him go without surprise. When the bandit was in the forest, the furycat never left his side for more than a few minutes. That he'd stayed with Nook as long as he did was her first sign something was off.

The second sign shifted into hollowness in her chest. The bandit was always careful with his steps, rarely leaving evidence of his passing. But there, alongside his nearly indecipherable trail, was a set of smaller footprints.

It appeared to be a woman's boot.

Did he have a companion? In the three years Nook had been aware of his presence, he'd never once traveled with another human. Occasionally, he and Jal crossed paths. Nook was nearly discovered once by River as he, Bough, and Fullbloom scrambled to hide when they came upon the two smugglers talking. Nook remained hidden, watching their faces as Jal and the bandit shared a meal and peacefully went their separate ways. They had been stunned. Nook had felt smug about the interaction as if it should prove she wasn't a poor judge of character and that her speaking with the bandit wasn't so horrible. But then, as soon as the boy was clear, Fullbloom complained about how much meat he'd eaten from their stash, and Bough looked disgusted by Jal's generosity.

In the years that had passed, Jal made a point to interact with the boy when he could, ignoring the Unmourned's distrust. He and Nook shared a curiosity about the bandit-turned-smuggler who was clever enough to survive the trees on his own. He had suffered so many close calls Nook and Jal were amazed he hadn't quit the lifestyle. Yet Jal brought back stories of the bandit's equally risky time among the outsiders. There was a bounty on his head and stories about his miraculous evasions of capture.

Nook suspected Jal and Fullbloom may have played a role in the last stories. She knew when Bough wasn't around, Fullbloom had grown far more sympathetic to the outsiders throughout her relationship with Jal. Neither would admit it if they ever had helped the boy for fear of their interference getting back to Bough. Technically, Jal was free from Bough's rulings, but his relationship with Fullbloom was something Bough could end with a few threats. Fullbloom was too loyal to her mothers in High Valley to risk losing her standing among the Unmourned, no matter how much she might love Jal.

But aside from herself and Jal, Nook didn't know of the

bandit interacting with anyone else in the trees. She frowned at the footprints, fists clenched. The unexpected anger reminded her of the day she'd met the bandit, how she'd been reeling from what she saw in Lover's Meadow. But this wasn't *that*. It couldn't be. Jealousy made no sense here. She didn't even like the thief. What did it matter to her if he had company now?

Nook turned to go the opposite way. Let the bandit's new friend scare off the longclaws at night. Let *her* check the streams he drank in for berries. Let her be chastised by her family for stupid, ridiculous fascinations born from loneliness. Let her leave behind conveniently placed animals and uncover harmless bushes of berries so he didn't have to hunt when his strength was failing. Let her strip the lower branches of mourning trees so he didn't brush up against the berries when he had to pass through their groves. Let her...

A scream chilled Nook to her core. She turned back to where the furycat disappeared.

"Don't go," she whispered to herself. Bough would kill her. Jal assured them the bandit wasn't a talker. He'd never mentioned Nook or indicated he cared she was an Unmourned. For whatever reason, Nook had trusted him from the start, even when her family warned her away.

This new girl, though... she could destroy Nook's family if Nook revealed herself. It would be reckless to help. To interrupt the natural order of the forest. This was the way of the trees for the outsiders.

The bandit was never without a weapon. He had the furycat. He was intelligent and quick. Nook had seen it with the furycat's mother and later with other beasts he'd had to go up against through the years, always a carcass left with knife wounds or arrows in the exact perfect places to leave killing blows. The girl was his problem, and he was capable.

Nook chewed her lower lip. Everything in her wanted to

help. Especially when her gaze shifted, landing on the marks in the trees. Surely, they would have lit a fire before nightfall to keep the longclaws at bay... but there was no orange glow that Nook could see. The scream had been so near.

There was no more time to hesitate now that Nook knew what had happened. Her heart was a wild, desperate thing in her chest as she set off at a run. The boy was in so much danger. Maybe the girl, too, but chances were higher she'd be safe.

Keeping her head low, Nook darted forward fast enough for her skirts to get in her way. She came to the camp, then froze. It was empty. There was no blood. No one laid to waste by the longclaw.

Heart in her throat, Nook tried not to hope when she spotted the boy's footprints and followed them. They were spaced like he was in a hurry but not running. Had the longclaw picked the girl over him? Hadn't the smuggler been with her? Thoroughly confused, Nook followed his footprints, jumping and ducking more clumsily than usual with her hands holding her skirts. She should have just worn her muddy clothes.

A figure in black suddenly burst from between the trees, directly into her path. Nook dropped her skirt and lunged sideways to avoid him, catching herself on a tree. Relief flooded, sharp and sweet at the sight of the masked boy unharmed. She tried to even her breathing and calm her racing heart. Tried not to show him what seeing him upright did to her.

"You!" The boy's eyes over that stupid black cloth went wide.

"Me," Nook said, mind blanking on a better response. He stared at her, then flicked his gaze back to the forest, worry knotted between his brows.

She thought he might speak again, but another form came down from the trees. The boy's furycat hurtled toward her as if they'd been separated for days, not less than an hour. Despite the scream ringing in her ears, Nook smiled and let him crash into her, sending them both onto the forest floor.

"Coin!" the boy jumped forward, voice cracking in panic. Nook couldn't stop a laugh at his reaction. The boy halted, tilting his head when he heard his pet's purring. Nook could barely make out his eyes under his hood, the smattering of freckles across the top of his nose.

Nook scratched the beast under the chin, smiling harder at how it made the cat's eyes unfocused.

"I forgot how he likes you," the bandit said.

Nook couldn't tell if his words were a question. "I did save his life, Freckles. You should probably be purring, too."

"Hmm." Nook figured he must be frowning behind his mask. She didn't know if it was from the nickname or her taunting. Then he shook his head and squinted at the ground, muttering too quietly for her to hear through the cloth.

"Dammit!"

The outburst startled Nook enough to sit up. "What is it?"

"My companion. A... creature took her. I lost the tracks."

"Which creature?"

He glanced at her, hesitating. "The big one. With six legs and long claws for digging their dens."

"A longclaw." She'd read the trees correctly.

"Yes." His hands went to his hood, tugging it lower. "Usually, Coin warns me, but we were both away. He's too wary of her..."

His eyes went to the animal now as he pressed his face into Nook's knee, rubbing his cheek possessively. The boy dropped his hands.

"I can help you find her," Nook said. She pushed Bough's face from her mind. "If she isn't on her monthly bleed, she should be fine."

"Why should that matter?" His voice belied his panic of the subject.

71

Nook rolled her eyes. "Where did you lose the path?"

He turned and led her back the way he came. Nook followed him as he crossed a shallow stream and pointed to deep scratches in the dirt.

Nook nodded. She'd suspected as much. "See how deep the marks are? It jumped." She pointed at the branches above them. "Longclaws hate the water. It'll have taken to the trees. Climb up there. You'll find scratches in the bark to get back on the trail."

He didn't hesitate before pulling himself onto the nearest branch. He was well-practiced at climbing, a skill that had likely saved his life on more than one occasion in the forest.

It also revealed the muscles of his arms and shoulders under his tight black shirt. Nook dropped her eyes quickly.

"It turned that way," he said. Nook could barely hear him over the mask and height.

The furycat, Coin, left her side to follow his owner through the trees. Nook opted to stay on the forest floor, following the sound of their movements until they came to a clearing. On the opposite end was a slight hill crowned with three mourning trees graying with death and a hole dug into the base. Another mourning tree had already fallen; its brittle leaves turned brown, and berries shriveled into tiny balls of maroon.

It was a longclaw den if she'd ever seen one. The beasts preferred to live underground. Once, when they were very small, Nook and Bough had come across a seemingly abandoned den. Nook could still remember the cloying scent inside. The smell of gnawed mourning tree roots. They were still damp to the touch and rank with poison, saliva, and the mold the longclaws grew to attract small creatures to eat. Bough had insisted they leave as soon as she realized how fresh the teeth marks were. Nook would not be persuaded, exploring deeper and trying to uncover the secrets of the roots with her child's eyes. The beast showed up, yellowed curved claws raking the dirt as it snarled. It had sniffed the air around them, tiny, beady eyes pinched in the skin furrow. It shuffled back with a hiss. Nook had discovered then how it felt to hold power in this forest. She and Bough crept around the cowering beast toward the exit, Nook barely containing her giggles and her sister looking back at her as if she'd gone insane. They had made it out unharmed. Unmourned.

Lev slipped to the ground and crouched behind the bushes next to Nook. He eyed the dying mourning trees. Nook wished she could see his face to read his expression. She had the urge to pull his mask down as she had when he was unconscious that one time. She didn't know how worried he was for the girl or if he even knew what the cave was.

"It has her in there," Nook whispered. She could hear its wet snuffling as if it moved among its roots. "I can draw it out, but you'll have to shoot it."

His hand went to the bow on his back. "My arrows only made the last one I came across angrier."

Nook considered the den and the trees surrounding it. Did she dare? She turned back to the boy, now noticing the crease between his eyes, his fisted hands, the tightness in his shoulders. Was he even breathing?

His fear decided her. Bough may never forgive her, but Nook could help. And despite every warning, every horror story, every act of violence the outsiders had committed in her trees, Nook trusted him. "Wait here."

She circled the clearing and climbed the hill to the healthiest of the mourning trees. The boy nearly gave up their hiding place when he jumped up to stop her from grabbing a handful of the still-ripe berries. Nook jostled their familiar shape in her hands, pausing to look before she turned to join the boy again. The roots of the mourning tree were not deadly. The closer one got to the poison of the berries, the more poison the tree held. Branches could make someone incredibly sick to the point where they may not recover, while the bark of the trunk caused intense nausea and vomiting. The roots made a pleasant tingling and stiffening. Some in High Valley even rubbed them on their faces to help with wrinkles.

Nook pushed the boy back into the bushes with her free hand and plucked two arrows from his quiver. She shushed him when he began to protest and squeezed the berries, freeing their poisoned juice. He cringed away from her, eyes wary.

The power of the forest.

Nook pressed the tips of the arrow into the juice cupped in her hand. Even this probably wouldn't kill the beast, but it would take it down long enough for them to free the girl. Finished with her task, Nook used her water skin to clean off her palm. She placed the arrows carefully in the dirt at the boy's feet. "I don't need to warn you not to touch the tips."

He nodded. Nook let herself study him for a moment. The moonlight reached their hiding place, and she could see under his hood. It had been a long time since they were this close, and his eyes were so intent on her. The forest colors, brown and green and even flecks of gold, were grounding. Nook tried to look her fill but realized soon that such a thing may not be possible. Her desire to stare at him was bottomless. She cleared her throat and tore her gaze back to the den. This was bad. This was why she wasn't a leader. Nook summoned her anger and held onto it, letting it seep into her voice when she spoke. "Do not leave the trees until you've shot it. Can you do that, Freckles?"

He didn't answer, but she figured he'd nodded again.

She readied to stand but stopped when he grabbed her arm, touch light and fleeting. "Lev. My name is Lev."

Warmth spilled over Nook's nerves, making it hard to keep her tone sharp. "Nook."

Lev moved for a better view of the clearing, and Nook found herself face-to-face with his mask. The skin under his eyes looked bruised. He was tired, panicked, on edge. She had a feeling he'd been like that even before this situation. It bolstered her spirits, realizing he hadn't been enjoying his time with his company. She immediately felt guilty. The girl was in *danger*.

Calling herself every kind of stupid, Nook stood to face the beast. She heard Lev's muffled warning as she pushed through the forest and let out the call of a highland elk.

It worked to draw the longclaw's interest. The beast peeked from its den and snarled at the sight of Nook. She let out a snarl of her own and pulled her knife from her waist. The longclaw cautiously entered the clearing. It knew not to try feasting on an Unmourned in the forest unless they were bleeding, but long-claws were known to be patient. They'd trapped Unmourned before, waiting for days until they became vulnerable with their bleed. Chances were high that the girl was still alive.

The longclaw's coarse, sparse hair was raised along its spine. It crept forward on all six legs, claws digging into the earth as it decided to run or fight. Protect its find in the cave or run. It bared its yellow teeth along its long, hooked snout, the rounded nose scrunching. Nook swallowed her disgust. There were plenty of beautiful sights in her forest. The longclaw was not one of them.

If it would just run, the situation would be far simpler. Nook kept her readied position, knife in front of her as she'd been taught, and balanced on the balls of her feet. It was foolish to plan on the longclaw making this easy. She held her ground in front of Lev and waited. If it ran, she wanted it to go in the opposite direction of the bandit. Longclaws knew non-bleeders were always vulnerable in the forest and wouldn't hesitate to attack. Once again, Nook wondered how the boy had survived this long alone.

Coin's hiss reminded her he'd had help. The furycat was crouched in the bushes before Lev, the two of them creating a line of defense.

The beast sniffed the air when a breeze carried her scent,

and she could almost hear its disappointment at learning she wasn't bleeding. Nook feinted forward, trying to get it to take off. Instead, it hunched lower to the ground and fully exited its den, ready to defend. Nook made a face at its long naked tail, her least favorite part of these beasts. Of course it wouldn't run, not with her luck.

Nook stepped to the side, clearing the way for Lev to make the shot. River would have taken it, but Lev hesitated. The beast watched her close and mirrored her movement, lining them up again. Nook heard the wood of Lev's bow creak as he pulled it. She took another step to the side. Why didn't he take the shot?

It was then she saw his companion. She had the light skin of the Factumn natives, yet her hair was a red Nook had never seen before. Even covered with dirt, it flamed. She looked terrified as she stepped out of the den and edged away from its entrance. Nook winced as she crept toward the fallen mourning tree without noting it, her eyes fastened on the longclaw. Nook needed to finish this before the girl reached the potentially poisonous branches. The girl's progress put her in line with Lev's shot. Nook wished for the first and last time that longclaws were bigger, big enough to block the girl from a stray arrow tipped in poison. Lev wasn't willing to risk it.

Nook made a sound to draw the girl's attention from the beast. She deliberately cut her eyes to the fallen tree, and the girl glanced that way but didn't seem to realize what a threat it was. Her attention quickly went back to the longclaw.

The beast's tail flicked, and the girl let out a yelp, jumping out of the way and moving again toward the tree. The beast turned and snapped its hideous yellowed teeth. The girl was so desperate she scrambled, tripped, and fell into the branches of the tree with a series of cracks. Nook saw no help for it. She lifted her knife and charged. Lev shouted as Nook drew the longclaw's focus.

The longclaw rushed Nook rather than the girl. Rearing

back, the beast shifted the front of its body and swiped upward. The sharp, curved claws caught Nook in the stomach, hooking up and under her ribs and lifting her off the ground.

Only then did Lev finally let his arrow fly. Nook rolled her eyes while in the air.

5

THE LONGCLAW

Lev's emotions always traveled to his hands. It had taken years of harsh discipline to swallow feeling enough that they wouldn't shake while wielding a weapon. Years of flexing his fingers to get heartbreak and guilt out of the tingling in his palms. His brother always looked at Lev's hands when he was reading Lev. They were his tell.

His training was the only reason the bow didn't dip. The only reason his aim didn't falter. The arrow slipped between the beast's ribs, the slight indent he'd known how to spot on man or beast since he was five. It was instinct now, though he would rather have had a clear shot to the throat or an eye to be sure it was fatal.

His hands numb with cold, Lev watched the girl with despair. Nook. How had he only just learned her name? She was lifted into the air, curved claws hooked into her stomach. She seemed so small in that mortal moment as she and the beast crumpled. Lev couldn't breathe.

Only when he saw Nook squirm under the weight of the giant-clawed-rat-pig did he move. Tossing his bow aside, he leaped over the bushes and ran to her side.

"Don't try to move," he told her.

"I'm fine."

Lev let out a sound that could only be described as a laugh, but there wasn't anything funny about the sight of the claws stuck in her stomach. With a grunt, Nook tried to pull the dead giant-clawed-rat-pig's paw off her, sitting up a bit as she worked to free herself from the claws.

"STOP!" Lev's voice was too high.

"Really, Freckles. I'm completely fine."

His hands hovered uselessly over her as she struggled. Shit, they were shaking badly. She freed herself with a shove that sent her flat on her back. Lev pressed his hands into her stomach, applying pressure as his mind raced for some remedy to an injury this dire. He could rip up his cloak for bandages. His supplies were too low. He had no salves to help the bleeding or prevent infection. Maybe the mourning berry salve would help. The best he could do was somehow get her to a clean stream. But how to move her without her bleeding out?

Coin sniffed at the giant-clawed-rat-pig, hackles raised enough that Lev knew it wasn't dead. He should get his knife and finish it, but he couldn't take his hands off Nook's wound. Not while she was still breathing, and there was a chance.

He'd seen too much death. Panic was blacking the edges of his vision again.

Nook took his wrists. "Freckles."

He kept his focus on holding his hands where they were and breathing.

"Lev!"

Startled, he looked into her eyes. Only to look away. He didn't want to see how the light dimmed as the shock wore off and she passed. His palms ached with the hurt radiating from his chest. He'd seen this so many times; it shouldn't get to him like this still.

"Lev," Nook repeated, more softly now. Her grip on his wrists was firm. She gave them a tug. "Lev, I'm fine. Look."

He shook his head. He was breathing too hard now, his mask dragging toward his mouth with each inhale.

"Please." She sounded annoyed and let go of one wrist only long enough to pull the mask off his nose, tucking it under his chin. It startled him out of his spiraling thoughts. "Just look."

Reluctantly, he let her lift his shaking hands. And stared in disbelief. She held his wrists and waited while he dragged his eyes from the rips in her lace dress and back to her vibrantly alive face. No dimming in her blue eyes, only a hint of smugness.

"Th-there's no blood," he finally got out.

Nook's lips curled into a smile. His eyes always went to her mouth. That was what had first captured his attention when he saw her all those years ago. He'd never seen lips as expressive as hers—full and dipping and twisted with intent. Lev's thoughts were chaotic as he tried to process what he was seeing.

"It will come," she said casually, "but not for a few weeks."

"I don't understand." There were holes where the giant-clawed-rat-pig had sank its claws, but the flesh was pink underneath, slightly puckered. No red. No pulsing gush that Lev had seen from similar injuries.

He had thought maybe... but seeing this was different. This proof of the Unmourned's fabled powers. It was too unbelievable.

Nook studied his eyes. Reading all the confusion there, she laughed. "Don't tell me you've lived in our forest this long and haven't heard the stories."

The confirmation was condescending enough that he realized how close they were and sat back on his heels. They were never this open with each other. Nook's expression became guarded as she waited for his reaction. He tried to match her walls, but it was far too late to appear truly apathetic as he should. Indifference was uncomplicated, but Nook had just saved their lives. It felt cruel to act like he didn't care. "How does it work? Does it hurt?"

Nook looked to their left. Felicity was getting to her feet, shaking her head to clear it and swaying dangerously. Nook let go of his wrists, the warmth of her touch lingering. Warm, not cold and ashen. Not stiff with death. Lev finally took a normal breath, body relaxing as the danger passed.

"Later," she said.

He frowned at her but nodded before pulling up his mask back up. Lev hurried to Felicity, unable to resist checking over his shoulder. There wasn't a hint of pain in Nook's features, no extra effort as she stood. She even rolled her eyes when she caught him staring. Lev turned back to Felicity.

"Are you hurt?" he asked.

Felicity frowned. "My ankle. A few scratches from the tree and bruising from when it carried me." She shuddered, eyes falling on the giant-clawed-rat-pig. No. His mind was clearing from the anxiety, and he remembered Nook had called it the longclaw. A much better name than the one he'd assigned it at fifteen.

"Is it dead?" Felicity asked.

"I don't think so," Nook called. She was crouched by its mouth, fearless as she stuck her head close to listen to it breathe. "The poison will make it sleep for a while but won't kill a long-claw. They build immunity by chewing on the roots in their den. I recommend you get far away before it wakes."

Lev ducked his head slightly, hiding his eyes under his hood. He didn't like that she planned to leave again, though of course she would. It unsettled him how disappointed he was. He clenched his fists and swallowed the feeling, reminding himself every reason why he was alone.

At his gesture, Felicity lifted the skirt of her simple green dress, now torn and covered in a layer of dirt. He knelt to examine her ankle. She rested a hand on his shoulder to bear the majority of her weight. That told him more about the pain than the swelling did. Thus far, she'd been careful to keep her distance.

He touched the bones and bent her foot gently, turning it this way and that while watching her face closely. "Just sprained," he finally decided. "Badly."

"You'll need a crutch," Nook said. She sprang away from the longclaw and plunged into the trees, murmuring to Coin when he joined her. So full of energy. Life. It was like the relief of a summer breeze ten times over to watch her.

Felicity turned to Lev with wide eyes. "Where did she come from? Who is she?"

Lev shrugged. "I met her years ago, but she just appeared. She does that."

"Is she..." Felicity didn't finish. The question of whether the Unmourned were real was too ridiculous to voice.

Lev didn't like the focused curiosity in Felicity's eyes. It was the same look she got when asking him endlessly about the forest's dangers, especially the poisons. Calculating and deadly. "Some people just live here," he muttered, hoping she would leave it at that inadequate answer.

Felicity showed him the scratches along her forearms as Nook came bounding back into the clearing. She carried a branch and sat on the ground to carve the joint where she'd pulled it into a handle for Felicity. Nook looked up as Lev turned Felicity's arm to wrap it. Out of the corner of his eye, he watched Nook's hand slip with the knife, nicking herself. There was no blood where the blade should have sliced the base of her thumb. She didn't even seem to notice what she'd done.

"Are those from that tree?" Nook asked of the deep lines on Felicity's arms. Her expression carefully neutral. Lev's stomach squirmed to see his anxiety mirrored. The wounds were too dark, almost purple rather than red. He looked at the fallen mourning tree. Apparently, being dead hadn't made the poison in its branches less effective.

"Yes." Felicity didn't seem to think anything was amiss, glancing at the tree as well but not recognizing it with its colors dimmed in death. Lev finished bandaging the wounds, resisting the urge to share a look with Nook. His thoughts went to the precious antidote in his pocket. There was so little of it left.

Nook kept her voice light. "You'll just have to keep an eye on those. It's hard to keep wounds clean here."

"How often do you come to the forest?" Felicity asked with forced indifference.

Nook let out a laugh. "Often enough." She stood and offered Felicity the newly fashioned crutch. "Can I talk to you, Lev?"

He nodded and followed her into the trees, lifting a hand just in time for Coin to come to his side and press his face into his palm. They stayed close enough to keep Felicity in sight. "The mourning tree is still poisonous, isn't it?" he asked in a low voice.

Nook worried her bottom lip. "Yes. The color of her wounds is too dark. If her skin turns black in the next few hours, you'll know for sure."

Lev shook his head and paced away, Coin at his heels. "People survive as long as it's not the berries, yes?"

Nook nodded. "She'll get sick, though. Very sick. She needs the antidote. Dehydration could be as much a problem as the poison once she starts vomiting."

With a clenched stomach, Lev pulled out the tin and opened it, staring at the small amount that had become his symbol of freedom. He could buy more. He had the money now.

Nook hugged her stomach, anxiety clear on her features. "That won't be enough. It might hold off some of the symptoms, but you need to get her to Midhaven."

"You don't have any?"

"No. I don't usually carry it. That was just Fortune's hand." Nook's eyebrows bunched, and she stared distantly into the forest. Lev stared at the concern etched deep in her face. She didn't even know Felicity. Hadn't seen her before minutes ago. "Freckles... her ankle is already hurting. It's only a matter of time before she starts..."

"I know."

"Can you get her there?"

Lev sighed, his mask fluttering with the breath. Could he? Possibly. It was two days of travel cutting through the trees. The forest was relatively flat in these parts, with fewer mourning tree patches to navigate. But could he get into the village? That was the real issue. Too many warrants were out for his arrest. Too much strange activity along the road. He didn't know what he'd find. For the most part, he'd avoided the village and its hardened people. The guards that hung around there often patrolled the forest trade route. Before his smuggling, he'd often stolen from them and their charges along the road. It was best to elude them.

But he could go without a mask. It was unlikely anyone in Midhaven would recognize him. Lev pulled at his sleeves. It had been years since he'd revealed his face, and this issue aside, he still lacked a permit to travel the forest. Entering and leaving the village was risky without one.

Lev glanced back where Felicity was warily eyeing the fallen longclaw and testing her new cane. She hobbled along and winced. Lev knew the pain would only get worse. He had little choice.

Yet all these worries shifted to a dull roar when he glanced back at Nook. He still couldn't believe she was here.

He could do it. But he heard himself say, "I could use some help."

Nook thought for so long, frowned so hard, that he braced himself for the no. She hugged her stomach again, and he fought a bizarre urge to reach forward and free her from herself. She looked so torn and sick over it that Lev changed his mind. He opened his mouth to assure her he could handle the journey when Nook came to her decision. She straightened and dropped her arms with a resolute nod.

"I'll come."

"You sure?"

She rolled her eyes and left his side to join Felicity again.

Lev allowed himself a small, relieved smile behind his mask.

NOOK DUCKED into the trees to collect firewood. She'd picked the spot where they now camped. It was as though she had a map of the forest imprinted on her mind. She'd led them true west as far as Lev could tell. Lev could only imagine how quickly Nook could maneuver the forest on her own. Especially if she truly didn't have to look for threats or berries as she traveled. *If.* It was true. Lev had to stop questioning his own eyes. Nook had been impaled. She'd survived without a wince.

The legends were true. The Unmourned existed.

One was here helping him. *Him.*

Lev was surprised that Felicity seemed more comfortable using his arm for support. Too often, Nook paused and tilted her head. Mostly, her eyebrows would knot in frustration over what she heard or maybe didn't hear, but sometimes Coin would duck under the brush, and they would exchange a warning glance before Nook turned to Lev and asked him to take out his bow. She'd step forward to take Felicity's weight and push them on.

During one of these instances, Felicity asked, "Why does he suddenly need his bow so much more?"

Nook gestured toward the north. "There's a lake that way and fewer mourning trees between here and Midhaven, which means a lot of animals that haven't built a resistance to the poison live here. Which means a lot of predators live here. Which means, as with every part of the forest, we need to be careful."

Lev was fascinated by the way Nook moved through the trees. She never once stumbled or lost her footing. She never appeared to tire, even after an entire day of offering Felicity her arm. When she sensed Felicity flagging, she would ask the other girl about city life. Nook seemed as interested in the cities as Felicity was in the forest, just without the rebel's ill intent. The constant conversation exhausted Lev, and he didn't even participate.

"How do you bathe?" Nook asked casually at one point.

Felicity started at the intimate question. Her cheeks warmed when she glanced back at Lev. He hoped it was from embarrassment and not the fever that was coming in only a matter of time.

"We draw water from the well and use it to scrub. For the nobles, we heat it over the fire and carry it up to their private chambers. We help them scrub with flower-scented soap."

"Soap?"

Lev was glad his mask hid his smile. Felicity stumbled and let out a laugh. "Yes, soap. It takes away the dirt."

"How? Like using a pocked stone?"

"I would guess so. I haven't used one of those."

Nook was satisfied by that answer. Her mind skipped to the next issue. "Where do you relieve yourselves?" Felicity faked a coughing fit, now red up to her ears. Nook seemed oblivious to her distress. "And when it's your time to bleed—"

Felicity fell then and effectively cut off the conversation. Lev moved to take his turn supporting her hobbling steps, and Felicity mouthed her thanks. He tried to hand Nook his bow.

"There's a reason I asked you to take it out. I couldn't hit the widest tree in the forest." Nook pulled a knife from her belt and wiggled it at them. She flounced away then, occasionally whistling or muttering about heated water for baths. Every once in a while, he caught sight of her snapping a branch or carving into the trees with her short knife. Lev heard her address Coin and wondered again at their familiarity. He'd never seen Coin willingly approach another human. As he watched them in the break in the trees, he felt sure they were both equal parts forest. He rarely felt like an outsider in these trees, but Nook moved through them as though the mourning poison truly pulsed in her blood as the stories claimed.

When she picked the place for them to sleep that night, it was darker than Lev usually liked. Nook had pushed them as far as she could while Felicity was still able to walk. After Nook left to collect wood, with an unnecessary warning for Lev not to leave Felicity again, Felicity lowered her voice.

"She *is* one of them, isn't she? Do you think they bleed poison during their monthly time?"

Lev felt his cheeks heat at this second mention of the woman's time in one day. "Does she seem like she bleeds poison?"

"Well, she certainly knows how to use that knife. I've never seen anything like it. My lady used to sneak into the Marked Men's training. She wanted to learn what they know so badly, but I've never heard of a woman being trained." Felicity's voice was full of wonder. It saddened Lev to hear it. Such a thing should not set their worlds so far apart. It was no mystery why the Unmourned had vanished into the forest rather than live in the oppression of Factumn and its traditions.

Coin shuffled at the edge of their camp. Lev clicked his tongue and tried to draw his pet closer. Felicity stiffened beside him. He couldn't tell which of them was more fearful of the other.

"Why didn't he protect me from the longclaw?" she asked, accusing.

"We were deeper in the forest. Neither of us heard it get to you." Guilt clawed yet again at Lev's throat. He clasped his hands together, squeezing hard through his leather gloves.

Felicity crossed her arms. "I don't see the point of keeping such a beast if it can't keep you safe."

Lev forced his jaw to relax. "He keeps *me* safe."

"He would keep her safe, too, no doubt. Why does he like her and not me?"

Lev just shrugged, listening to Nook's whistling deep in the trees. He stilled. Over the sound of their footsteps and Felicity's heavy breathing, he hadn't paid much attention to Nook's strange melodies. Now, he heard clearly how her whistle echoed through the trees. Eerie notes that carried on the wind and slipped between the branches. The birds in the distance picked it up. Or maybe she picked it up from the birds. Lev had never heard them chirp and sing like this. His heart broke a bit, knowing that if he ventured closer, they would stop. The birds were even more distrustful of outsiders than Coin.

Nook slipped back through the trees, and Lev hated how the sight calmed him. It wasn't something he should grow accustomed to. Only, he'd spent so many hours wondering if he'd imagined her, it was all too reassuring every time she revealed herself.

Nook hiked up her tattered skirt before crouching in front of them. She moved so effortlessly. Unhindered by society's standards and trained by the forest. Those who instructed him to fight would even envy her. She didn't kneel with the practiced dignity of city women but quickly dropped to curl over the balance she kept easily on her toes. She leaned to listen to the trees, sitting back on her heels. Lev, trained to move with awareness of every muscle and forced to balance and shift into countless stances, was sure he'd have fallen if he tried to mirror her. She was natural. He was trained. That grace couldn't be beaten into a person.

Nodding, Nook resumed striking the flint and stone, hands steady with the forceful blows. In little time and with patient blowing, she coaxed the sparks to flame and tossed the tools aside. Lev didn't even think before he picked them up and put them back in Nook's pack.

Felicity sighed and held her hands up to the heat. Lev shook his head and moved to get the dried meat from his pack. He was staring at Nook too much. It was time to get over the shock of her presence. He needed to focus. To stay distant and prepared for when they inevitably parted ways. Nook never looked happy to see him. Aside from words required to travel the forest, she hadn't spoken with him all day. Hadn't she made her distaste for him clear? Nook was only doing this for Felicity, whom he wouldn't know again after leaving her with the rebels.

He distributed the meat. Nook took a strip and wrinkled her nose after nibbling on it.

"Why is it so bitter and dry?"

"Salt."

"Salt?"

Felicity froze upon hearing their exchange. Lev didn't like how little interest she showed in eating or how she looked paler in the fire's orange glow. "You really have only lived in the forest."

Nook laughed and shoved the meat in her mouth. "That was actually a joke. I've had better dried meat, though. I'll be right back."

"It's dark." Lev felt foolish as soon as the caution left his lips. Nook smirked wryly, her lips pressing together and twisting up on one side. He pulled his eyes away from the arresting movement. Even chewing and with her cheeks full, he struggled not to stare. He'd been alone too long.

"It sure is, Freckles." She vanished between the trees.

Alone once again, Felicity dropped her voice. "What is she to you? Really?"

"I don't know what you mean." He busied himself, pulling blankets from his pack. It was a clear night and warm. They wouldn't need cover. Coin and the fire would keep most animals from disturbing them. He had no plans to leave Felicity alone again.

"You've been staring at her like you've never seen a woman before. I'm beginning to feel insulted," Felicity said, her tone teasing. But there was a tightness in her voice that sparked concern in Lev.

"I need to check your scratches."

Felicity nodded and held out her arm as she settled back onto her small pack. She looked ready to sleep. She stared into the flames, only wincing slightly when he picked at the tucked cloth to free it.

Lev's stomach swooped painfully, palms tingling with aftershocks, as he unraveled the bandage. The scratches had turned black. The sweet scent coming from the wound turned his stomach harder. Without thinking, he pulled off a glove and pressed the back of his hand to Felicity's forehead. She was too warm but not yet burning with fever.

She jerked back from his touch. "What is it? What are you not telling me?" She freed her arm from his grasp and gaped at the black scratches. The black would spread in her veins as she grew sicker. If they didn't hurry to get the cure, it would reach her heart. Unlikely to kill her, but the damage could last for years.

"The tree that scratched you was a mourning tree. Its branches don't carry the same strength of poison, but they do carry it."

Felicity swallowed hard. She looked dazed, and her voice shook. "What's going to happen to me?"

"You'll get sick. But we're going to get you a cure. This should help for now." Lev took the tin from his pocket. It wasn't as hard as he thought it would be to spread the remaining salve over her wounds.

Her eyebrows furrowed. "You knew? Even before?"

"Keeping you calm will keep it from spreading as quickly."

"Where is the cure?"

"Midhaven. It's another day's travel from here. Maybe two." Depending on how well she could keep up.

"Can't we keep going?"

"Not in the dark. No one should go into the forest after dark."

Felicity shot a pointed look to where Nook vanished between the trees. Lev only shrugged. He wouldn't be the one to confirm she was Unmourned. Nook was safe.

The image of the giant—the longclaw impaling her flashed in Lev's mind. His hands chilled at the memory, and he pushed it away. He bandaged Felicity's arm and kept watch as she succumbed to her exhaustion.

6

LATER

Nook hesitated, dead rabbit in hand. Out of Lev's presence, her head was clear enough to think. She leaned against the nearest tree. Harmless with sturdy brown bark. It smelled of sap, not poison. Nook almost wished for mourning berries, her strange addiction to eating them making her mouth water.

Lev needed help getting to Midhaven. Felicity would get sick. Nook wanted to help them. She knew she could. She could help them more than anyone. But what would Bough say? Were the Unmourned watching her now? Nook hadn't seen any recent marks in the trees, but she couldn't be sure.

Bough wouldn't want Nook to abandon people in need of help. But if Bough were in her position, she would have thought of some way to do so without risking their people. Somehow, with the fall and her fear, Felicity seemed to have missed Nook's exhibition of her unmourned strength. Nook could tell the girl was suspicious, but she was also getting sick. She'd begin to vomit soon, her body giving into aches and her mind succumbing to fever dreams. At that point, if Lev truly could be trusted, he might be able to convince her she'd imagined the girl of the forest when Felicity was healthy again.

Maybe.

It was a flimsy argument that Bough wouldn't buy. Nook tried to think what Bough would do in her place. The answer came to her. Jal. He could help Lev. Load Felicity onto Dorris, his mule, and get Felicity to Midhaven with the Unmourned making sure they reach the village safely while staying out of Felicity's sight. Jal could make sure Felicity doubted her memories of Nook.

It was what Bough would do. It was a good plan. Jal was even close. Nook would just have to find a mark from Bough, River, or Fullbloom and follow the trees to him. They were on their way to Midhaven. Away from Lev, Nook could almost imagine going through with it. But... he'd looked at her and admitted he needed help. It was the trust in his eyes that had made her agree. Lev was as wary of others as his furycat. As the Unmourned. Jal told her the boy never gave him any details about who he was, where he was from, or why he was in the forest. He never asked for help and never stayed the night in Jal's camps.

But he asked Nook for help. He'd looked at her like he'd been hoping she'd stay. And when he thought she was hurt... Nook couldn't shake it. That panic he couldn't hide. The way his hands had trembled until she was trying to hold them still instead of pulling them away. It warmed her core even now. He was forbidden and dangerous and guarded in the extreme. Nook was playing with fire. She'd shown him too much. Bough would be beyond angry.

And yet...

Nook pushed off the tree and rubbed at the bark's impression on her forehead. She continued to their small camp. Lev trusted her, and she knew he'd never tell anyone what he'd seen. Lev had *trusted* her. He wanted her opinion. He was confident Nook was Felicity's best chance. He didn't think she was reckless. Didn't think that she would ruin things or that she wasn't responsible enough for the task. He wanted her at his side. The way he looked at her, Nook was confident he wouldn't have picked anyone else. Not Jal. Not River. Not Bough.

He saw Nook as capable, and damn if that didn't stroke her battered ego. If that didn't make her stand taller under his beautiful eyes. She should hate him, should want to do what was right. Those desires wilted to nothing under his confidence. That was what she wanted. To be looked at like that.

And to leave the forest. Lev would show her Midhaven. Felicity would answer all her questions. These two were everything she'd wanted to experience. She never would have wished the poisoning on anyone, but this was precisely the type of task she thought herself suited for.

Nook pushed Bough from her mind and stepped into camp, noting the relief Lev couldn't immediately hide from his eyes. Relief she'd returned. He was happy to see her.

It felt so nice.

"It's later," he prompted gently. Nook understood so much from his sparse words. He was referring to their conversation near the longclaw den. Asking for answers in a way she could pretend she didn't understand. He was curious but would never force her to reveal her secrets.

She nodded and set to skinning the rabbit. Only once it was roasting did she turn to face him, drawing her knees up to her chest and resting her chin on them. He continued to stare into the fire. She wished she could see his face. His eyes didn't tell her enough. She wanted to tug off his mask again, heart skipping at the memory of doing it before. She loved his freckles, the soft end of his nose. She wanted the full effect, no hood or mask or darkness.

"It is later." She sighed. Where even to start? "What do you know of us? The stories?"

Lev snorted, the fabric of his mask shifting. Nook was washed with fresh longing to see what face he made beneath it. "They say the women in the trees bleed the same poison the mourning berries hold. That they only bring death and are the most dangerous creatures to haunt the forest. Some say once a month, the women of the forest transform into the beasts themselves to protect their land. More flattering tales say you were blessed by a long-forgotten goddess who allows the women of the forest to live in their youth for as long as the trees themselves."

Nook felt herself smiling, and Lev glanced over in time to see it. He didn't turn back to the fire, his pupils slowly growing as he watched her face, eyes dipping to her lips.

"What do you think?" Nook asked, curiosity hitting like thirst. She wanted him to reveal his mind to her so badly.

"I think your people were smart to learn to live in the trees. I think if I had a family here, I'd never leave them either. Before today, I suspected maybe that's what you were, but I didn't believe the stories. But then..."

"But then the longclaw got me."

Lev nodded.

Nook pulled in a deep breath. "Were you not afraid of me? If the stories say such things?"

Was he smiling? "No. I wasn't afraid."

"Will you take off your mask?" Her own blurted words caught her off guard, but she couldn't share her people's secrets with a man who didn't even trust her with his face.

His hand went to the cloth as he contemplated her question. The seconds passed, and Nook became sure he'd tell her no. She'd seen his face but wanted him to show her this time. Willingly. Nook looked away. Such thoughts weren't useful. They made her feel fifteen again, running to meet with River only to learn what disappointment was.

She saw Lev move in the corner of her eye. When she turned to face him again, his mask was rumpled under his chin, and he was pushing back his hood. She let herself drink in the sight.

His hair was flattened from living under his hood for so long, but the curls fought violently to keep their spring. It was mostly the color of a dried path closer to the road, light brown. But in the firelight, she could see a hint of the other shades hidden throughout. Reds and pale yellows and darker, muddy browns. She had the urge to pick the strands apart and look for all the colors the curls hid.

Instead, Nook's gaze dipped lower. His familiar eyes stared back. Like his hair, they couldn't decide on a color. Green and gold and brown, all shimmering together. Nook laughed, noticing how his freckled, tan skin was noticeably lighter under the line where his mask usually sat. It made her wonder why he wore it so much, even when traveling the forest alone.

Maybe the reason was on his right cheek. Nook reached slowly and pressed her fingers to the four lines of scar there. Anger built in her throat as she traced their path from his ear. The longest reached the corner of his mouth and skipped to end on his chin. The shortest began just under his eye where his tan line began. As she traced the scars again, she realized they aligned perfectly with her fingers. A human had marked him like this with their fingernails. Nook struggled to swallow the taste that left in her dry mouth.

"Who?" she asked.

He looked back at her, multicolored eyes searching. She knew what he was looking for. She was looking for the same.

Trust.

"It doesn't matter," he finally said and pressed his lips together. Fine then. The trust wasn't there yet for him. He would show her his face but save his stories. Maybe later they would come.

Nook lowered her hand. "We don't get injured for the majority of the month. Well, we do. I'll bear the holes from the longclaw, and if I were to break a bone, I'd have to splint it so I could still move with ease. But I wouldn't feel pain, and I don't bleed until my time comes. We bleed from any injury we would have received as our monthly blood. Our bodies heal as it happens. So with these," Nook pressed a hand to the punctures the longclaw left in her stomach, "it will hurt and itch, but I won't bleed except for below. We can survive in the forest so well because of this ability. Not even the poison can kill most of us, though it makes the cramping nearly unbearable."

She smiled, seeing the color bloom on his cheeks. He suddenly couldn't meet her eyes. "Every human born female does it, even your queen," she reminded him. Jal had explained long ago how embarrassed the city people were to discuss monthly blood. She still found the idea amusing. "How can you live alone in the forest yet be afraid of something so common?"

"I'm not afraid. Just uncomfortable. It isn't spoken of."

"We're speaking of it now."

It took him only a moment's effort to meet her eyes again. She nodded to encourage him, seeing the questions there.

"Can anything kill you?" he asked.

"Yes. Once, a woman lost her head; she couldn't heal from that. Hunger, thirst, drowning, the cold... things like that can kill between bleeds. And just as blood comes in different intensity for all of us, some of us are stronger when it comes time to heal. Some have died from stabbings they experienced earlier that month, bleeding out completely when the time comes. Some of us can survive much more. It makes us cautious. Many are unwilling to test their limits."

His lips pressed together, pulling at the scars on his face. "Could you die from the gia—the longclaw?"

"No. I've tested my limits more than most. Not on purpose, but I know I can survive much worse." To prove her point, Nook reached into the pouch she kept next to her coins on her hip. She had refilled it at the longclaw's den. Nook pulled out some berries and tossed them into her mouth. Lev's hand shifted in his lap as though he fought the urge to stop her. She smiled, and his expression tightened, seeing the berry juices on her teeth and lips.

"How?" he asked. Nook cocked her head. She was usually better at following his blunted conversation, but his face distracted her. "How did you test your limits?" he clarified.

"Oh." Nook hesitated. She didn't like reliving those weeks. Or the pain of surviving them afterward. She opened her mouth to answer, but he held up a hand.

"It's alright. Later," he said.

So he imagined there being a later, too. Nook should hate the idea of it more.

Nook fought a smile. It seemed too revealing a response, but her traitorous lips still curled at one corner. Turning to look at the fire, she caught sight of Felicity's fresh bandage. "Has it gotten worse?"

"It's black."

"We don't have much time."

Lev didn't respond, but that was agreement enough.

"Why is she here with you?"

"I'm being paid to escort her to Factumn. To the rebellion."

Nook's heart sped dangerously at the thought. Jal had told her about those who opposed Vasca's cruel reign. They sounded brave and exactly like the type of organization that could make the differences she imagined the world needed.

But if she started asking questions, she may never stop. And Lev didn't need that right now. "You should sleep. You look exhausted."

He seemed startled by her observation, his hand going to the mask around his neck as though he'd forgotten he had taken it off. After a moment's pause, he pulled it back on. The hood went up after, and he settled back against his pack. As he drifted to sleep, Coin crept out of the bushes. Nook scratched his ears. When an owl hooted nearby, she hooted back. She let the peace of the darkness fill her. She loved her forest at night.

FELICITY WAS WORSE in the morning. So much worse that Nook regretted the night of rest. She hadn't wanted to push the girl too hard for fear of the poison spreading faster from the effort, but now thin lines of black webbed up her arm, and Felicity was too feverish to care. They got her to hobble for half the morning, but in time, Lev lifted her on his back and did his best to follow Nook's brisk pace. She was glad she'd gotten him to save his strength yesterday, using his bow as an excuse, but still hadn't expected Felicity would need to be carried so soon.

Nook glanced back at Lev's tall build and broad shoulders. So far, he didn't appear to be struggling, but it was only a matter of time. Nook eyed the slight girl and wondered if she could carry Felicity. Probably, but not for long. Her muscles wouldn't hurt, but her body still grew tired. When it came to it, she would try, but she wasn't looking forward to it.

"My lady. I'm sorry. I'm coming," Felicity murmured. She'd been calling for "her lady" nearly all morning. Lev told her she'd been one of Vasca's maids. Nook had heard enough stories of the woman for the information to chill her bones. She couldn't imagine the nightmares plaguing Felicity now.

Jal was a great storyteller and Nook's primary source of information on the outside world. He'd been the one to explain strife between the cities to Nook one night by firelight, Full-bloom laying with her head in his lap, Bough turning a rabbit on the spit, and River nearby keeping watch.

"We all know you think you understand the forest best, Nook, but you know nothing of the cities," he'd begun. "Their story is bloodier than most and filled with unrest. Years and years ago, they didn't know of each other. Factumn was a steady place, a small land lined by the mourning trees and mountains ruled by a family that favored hierarchy and keeping traditions. It's said they fled another land that valued progress by traveling through the mountains and landing in the Factumn clearing. They struggled as the years passed to feed their growing population, cutting into the poisoned forest more and more and risking the wrath of the creatures within. They put a wall against the trees when they got too close, extending their farms in the opposite direction but running out of land at the mountain base. One Factumn prince, the youngest of five, longed for their father's attention. He decided he would venture into the forest and look for a food source. He'd hunted outside the wall enough that he was sure he could avoid the poisons and hidden terrors. The queen wept, sure her favorite son would never return. They say a queen's tears hold power." Bough snorted at that. Jal turned to her. "If blood can, why not tears?"

Bough had nothing to say to that, so Jal continued. "They protected the young prince and his party as he pushed deeper into the forest than any had traveled since the Unmourned vanished, as the stories go. He followed a river and realized the friendlier trees followed its path. The mourning trees stayed away from the cool, clean water. This path would eventually become the road that traders follow now."

"He was shown the path," Bough impatiently cut in. Jal looked at her in surprise. "It wasn't that long after we found our home in High Valley. Enough time for the fear and anger to fade back into curiosity about the city they left behind. A few Unmourned came forward and helped the prince. It was the last time we showed Factumn any loyalty. It was a mistake. He betrayed them by building the road, inviting in too many strangers, and spreading stories about us. We've cut all ties since." Bough shot Nook a look, reminding her of the lessons their people had learned when curious and helpful.

Jal nodded and continued. "However it came to be, the road led to the meadow that became Midhaven and eventually to the discovery of the trading port of Lilstrom. This was considered great luck, for though Factumn needed the food products grown and traded in Lilstrom, the Lilstrom people had an eye for beauty. They bought and traded the gold from Factumn's mountains in their ports. For years, the cities both prospered from the alliance. There was peace along the road and between the cities. Midhaven became a town of diversity and adventurers. The inn was popular. The people hardened by life in the forest."

"Your home," Fullbloom cut in, smiling fondly up at her lover.

"Of course," Jal said. "I am forest folk just like you."

They shared a laugh at his claim, and Jal slipped back into his story as they quieted. "The peace didn't last. Factumn only traded what gold they needed to feed their people. They restricted the number of children couples could have, not wanting to risk expanding deeper into the forest. They were careful when extracting gold, and the dangers kept them from growing greedy with the mountain's treasure. They found stability and depended on Lilstrom less and less as the years passed. Then, the king of Lilstrom died. Many say by his foreign queen's hand, and I tend to believe that judging by her actions since. Queen Vasca grew dissatisfied. She wanted more gold, but the Factumn royal family refused her. So she sent in her army, the army she had built modeled off the Marked Men but honed to be crueler and sharper and more obedient. And they were young. She took the babies from her land and fashioned the Queen's Swords. Unfeeling. Unquestioning. Unflinching. They knew nothing but a life of training and following the queen. She paired them, using them against each other to ensure loyalty. They surpassed the abilities of the Marked Men and had swords rather than wooden staffs. The Marked Men were hesitant to fight mere boys. Factumn could not defeat her—"

"Enough," Bough cut him off. "Nook doesn't need to hear all the bloody details. We should go to sleep now."

Nook had sighed. Bough didn't know she'd pestered Jal for all the details already. She couldn't believe humans were capable of such acts. She couldn't imagine a world so much bigger than her life in the trees and her family within.

Nook knew enough for goosebumps to prick her flesh every time Felicity told the queen she was coming, panic rising in the girl's voice.

They took a break as evening set in. Felicity groaned as Lev lowered her to the ground.

"No more," she whispered. "Just take me to my lady."

Nook brushed Felicity's hair away from her face. Her skin was clammy and hot. The strands of red stuck to her forehead and cheeks. "Please, drink."

While she held the water skin to Felicity's mouth, she glanced up at Lev. As if reading the desire in Nook's mind, he pulled down his mask and knelt on Felicity's other side. His expression was pinched. His own hair stuck to his skin with sweat, and his cheeks flushed from the exertion. "What are we going to do?"

"We have to keep going. She doesn't have enough time for us to stop. Soon, she won't keep the water down."

Nook could feel his exhaustion in the air, coupling with her own. She corked her water skin.

"I don't like traveling the forest at night," Lev admitted.

Nook nodded and tilted back her head. Through the branches, the colors of the setting sun broke over them. "I can keep us safe."

Lev studied her for a long moment before he nodded and went to pick Felicity back up.

"Let me take a turn," Nook said.

Lev shook his head. "You're keeping us safe, remember?"

"Right." Nook stood. She listened for a long moment to the distant forest calls, the gentle hooting, the twig snapping where Coin crouched on a branch, the hush of wind through the leaves. She drew her knife and let out a nervous whistle. A hatter answered in the distance, but otherwise, they were alone.

All her favorite forest allies had fallen asleep or avoided the outsiders she traveled with. All but Coin. He would be enough. "Stay with me."

Lev didn't reply, but she felt his warmth as he stepped in close.

7

TEMPTATIONS

F elicity weighed more with every step. At one point in the night, Nook had to tie Felicity to Lev's back when she kept listing to one side or the other. They had to scramble each time Felicity began to gag, but the vomiting had evolved to dry heaving a few hours ago.

Lev tried to relax his muscles as they hiked. Holding tension was a waste of energy when carrying Felicity was strenuous enough. But he'd learned early it was too risky to travel at night. A fire was needed to keep the creatures of the dark at bay. Coin stayed close, eyes flashing in the moonlight. Nook carried Lev's bow for him but never reached for it as she listened intently. At one point, she told him to wait and darted into the bushes. Coin had paced the path in front of him as Nook took care of whatever threat had appeared. Lev forced his mind to stillness. Made his hands relax under Felicity's knees. Nook was fine. She couldn't be hurt.

The relief the knowledge brought felt like magic. He'd always lived in fear of those he loved being hurt by his mistakes. It happened too often. Nook felt safe to be around because she was simply always safe. It freed his mind for a level of attachment that was foolish, but he was unable to quash it. He could feel the desire to stay in her presence swallowing him with each minute they spent together. This, too, felt like magic. He almost laughed at the thought. Lev had experienced enough of the forest to know that was exactly what this was. The Unmourned, the berries, the creatures, and his fascination with it all, especially Nook. It was magic. There was no other word to describe the forest.

When Nook came back, steps silent and deliberate, Lev searched her face and found it calm. She noticed he had lifted his mask out of habit, and she tugged it off his nose without comment. As soon as she turned to pick their packs back up, Lev let himself smile a bit. Focusing on Nook, her every glance and action, distracted him from his shaking muscles and the pain of carrying Felicity.

He couldn't tell if her braids were messier than before or if her dress had any new tatters, but she moved easily, and her face revealed nothing of what happened. Lev moved, focusing on Nook's back for as long as he could. Another hour later, the exertion pushed his mind to that deep, swirling place where thoughts didn't hold. Where he acknowledged every pain and aching muscle and let it float away. He found himself in his memories of training, where he'd first learned to disappear in his head. His body knew well how to continue through the burn of tired muscles. He stayed steady. He'd survived worse than this. Nook replaced his brother as the silent encouragement at his side. He wouldn't let her down. He wouldn't drop the girl hurting on his back. Breathing in, breathing out, he let himself become a means to an end—the pain second to the success of the mission.

The sun rose, turning the forest vibrant and orange, and Nook halted. Lev stumbled into her back. Worry flared when Felicity stayed silent behind him, even with the jolt. Her labored breathing didn't change. Lev longed for her constant chatter.

Nook turned around, grabbing Lev's shoulders to right him.

He might not have been able to do it without her help. "Sorry. It's just, we're here," Nook said.

Alarm slammed into Lev, lifting the fog of pain and exhaustion.

Nook saw it clearly in the dawn light. "What is it?"

"I can't be recognized. I..."

"Oh. The thieving?"

"Among some other things." Lev squinted through the trees. To their left was the estate that had held Midhaven's leading family, first descended from the Factumn prince who founded the town and now one of the queen's trusted nobles. Lev could already spot a couple of Queen Vasca's Swords walking the estate's wall. The navy blue uniform stirred fear wherever it was spotted, despite the simple make. The Swords weren't meant to look flashy, nothing like the intricately tattooed Marked Men in their golden breastplates. The sword hanging from the belt of one of Queen Vasca's men was enough. The empty eyes were enough. The stillness. The posture. The power of movement. The pairs that stood side by side, communicating silently. The Queen's Swords were raised in another world and thrust into this one to wreak havoc at her command.

Lev fought the urge to lift his mask back into place.

"So we need to get in unseen. How many guards are there."

Lev's brow furrowed. "Usually, there are only two at each checkpoint on the road and a pair watching the estate. Then, lower guards dressed in green aren't usually a problem. But it looks like there are more now." He saw such men walking along the river that cut through the center of Midhaven and standing at the bridges that allowed travel from one half of town to the other. One guard was walking away from them along the tree line. If Lev and Nook had arrived any sooner, they might have run into him.

"Must be for that big party going to Factumn," Nook muttered. Lev's hands went cold. Nook surveyed the trees around them with a frown. "It's still a few days out, though. Traveling slow."

"How do you know?"

Nook brushed a carved series of notches in the trees. "This is a warning for our people to look out for it. The party has a fancy carriage halting their progress." The mark did look like a carriage, now that Lev studied it closer. He'd seen those markings before. Being unable to read them had always felt like he was missing out on another layer of the forest. Another layer the Unmourned had access to. He was tired and hurting enough that his jealousy was more difficult to bury than usual.

"The Swords are here to secure the town." Lev stepped closer to Nook, grip tightening on Felicity enough that she murmured a protest. It took effort to relax his fingers. "The Queen is traveling to Factumn."

Nook nodded slowly. "You must be right. I've never seen this kind of preparation before. We need to get Felicity the antidote and leave quickly. And I need to warn our traders."

"I'll get Felicity in. You go tell your people."

Nook shook her head. She pulled out her knife and left her own markings in the tree. "We stay together. I said I'd help."

"If you're sure." Lev untied Felicity, and Nook took her weight without objection. He barely managed to pull himself onto a low branch nearby tree to tuck his black coat and mask against the trunk and out of eye-line. He needed to shed the bandit's garb. To the average person in Midhaven, it would reveal him. But a voice in his head screamed it wouldn't be enough. He was going to get recognized and caught. Coin watched him and crouched low, knowing it meant Lev was leaving the tree cover.

When he dropped from his branch, Lev's knees nearly gave out. Only a force of will kept him standing and allowed him to lift Felicity again.

"I know a place to go," Nook muttered.

"I thought you'd never been outside the forest."

"I know someone who has. Do you know of the inn on the west side of town?"

Lev nodded. He'd hid in their stables once. It was an inn slowly falling into disrepair. Queen Vasca's guards and wealthy traders avoided it because of the poor-quality ale and small rooms. But it was situated close enough to the trees and river that Lev liked the idea of it.

He started in that direction. "Wait." Nook stooped and came up with a handful of mud. She reached and brushed it over Lev's scars on his cheek. He froze under her touch. She brushed at it until she was satisfied. "If you don't want to be recognized," she said.

"Thanks."

Nook smiled and wiped her hand across her forehead and Felicity's chin. They made a downtrodden and dirty group as they picked their way to the lower part of the town and slipped out of the trees between rounds of patrols, sticking to shadows cast long by the rising sun. Lev glanced back once to see Coin vanish into the trees to wait. His heart squeezed as it always did when they separated.

The inn was on the opposite side of town from the keep. Although Midhaven lacked any proper form of royalty now or even before Queen Vasca took over on her way to Factumn, the inner workings of the village clung to the wall of the keep and profited plenty from traders passing through. However, they had taken a hit under Queen Vasca's rule. Lev had learned the anti-dote salve could only legally be sold to guards and permitted travelers. Products were often searched, and the citizens carried identification to ensure no one fleeing from Factumn had landed there. The small population wasn't enough for Queen Vasca to concern herself with regularly, but she kept plenty of rules and threats hanging over their heads.

The owner of the grand keep was now one of her men, the

previous lord murdered when her Swords first traveled the road. He maintained Queen Vasca's decrees and profited from the trade she allowed in Midhaven. Likely, he was preparing to pay the small village's tax when the queen passed through.

Businesses near the keep wall were clean and flourishing, the village gradually shrinking and sagging as one traveled further out. The inn they approached now sported cracked windows and multiple locks on the back door Nook led them to. She paused in front of it, mouth slightly open. She touched the doorknob lightly, marveling.

Lev's chest tightened as he reached forward and knocked. The sound made Nook jump. If she thought this dingy place was so amazing, he couldn't imagine her reaction to the cities on each end of the road.

An older woman answered the knock. She quickly assessed them, eyes lingering on the blue-black hue of Felicity's pale skin. Lev carried her cradled in his arms.

"Are you Siana?" Nook asked, voice low.

The woman looked at her more closely, holding out a hand. Nook put hers in it, nails dirty and short. Siana squeezed. "You know it took me three weeks to make that dress."

Nook's eyes widened comically, looking down at the dirtied and tattered garment. "It took me much less time to ruin it."

The woman's smile spread slowly, seeming all the more genuine for the careful way she allowed it. "I see why Jal likes you, Nook. Come, come."

As soon as the door was shut and bolted behind them, Siana hurried about the room. She crossed to the pantry, crouching and prying up a floorboard within. "To your left, there's a hall. The family rooms are down there. Take the last two, and I'll start this brewing for tea." She stood with a small canvas bag in hand. Nook must have recognized it. Relief lightened her features.

They turned for the hall, but Siana's voice made them pause. "Did you mark the trees? Warn them who was coming?"

"Yes. We know."

Siana nodded. "The girl won't be able to move for a couple of days at least. Does Bough know you're here?"

Nook's eyes shifted. "Yes." A lie. Lev kept his face clear, but he tucked away that insight into Nook's personality. She wasn't a good liar.

But the woman nodded again. "Good. I know she worries about you. She wouldn't want you here with what's coming. We'll get this girl moving in no time."

Nook nodded, jaw ticking.

Lev stepped forward before the innkeeper saw her annoyance. "Thank you."

His voice was enough for Nook to clear her features. She put a hand on his arm, leading him to the hall. Not a moment too soon. He put Felicity down a bit hard on the bed, arms giving out at the last moment. He swayed into Nook, and she took his weight without appearing to notice.

When Lev straightened, Nook bent to brush Felicity's hair away from her sleeping face. "You can go next door. Rest and clean up. I'll help Siana brew the tea."

Lev didn't want to leave Nook's side in this unfamiliar place. He reminded himself again she couldn't be hurt but knew that wasn't precisely true from her guarded features after Siana's last comment. He made himself go. These stirring feelings of attachment would only lead to harm.

It felt like hours passed as Lev paced in what must have been Jal's childhood room. It was strange to be in here, but it also had an air of the familiar. He liked Jal, and Nook must know him well to have heard of this inn. To have a dress made by the woman Lev assumed was Jal's mother based on resemblance. Even with several pairs of Queen Vasca's Swords patrolling the village and more on the way, Lev relaxed like he hadn't in a long time. The stress of monitoring his surroundings faded until only concern for Felicity filled his thoughts. But the hushed murmuring of Nook and Siana next door was not panicked, and the smell of the antidote wafted into the room. Felicity would be fine.

Lev stilled, his mind filtering through the events that had led him here and snagging on the memory of the pried floorboard. He swallowed hard.

The antidote was within reach. Likely enough of it to keep him safe for years, the only reason he'd agreed to this risky job in the first place. Enough that the bag of coins at his hip and its twin waiting in Factumn didn't matter. He could leave. Vanish right as Queen Vasca's activity on the road heightened. Her appearance could only mean more war and death for the forest he had come to call home. Best to disappear into its depths.

Lev stepped toward the door. Jal was close by. He knew the Unmourned better than Lev ever would. They would give Jal more antidote for his mother. Jal could get Nook back with her people. He could escort Felicity to Lilstrom. Collect the rest of Lev's promised money to compensate for all the inconvenience.

Lev's mind had been trained to filter through possibilities like this. Look at every situation in a way that benefited him most, disregarding others. Lev hated that half of his brain. It led to his loneliness. His failing his brother. His hiding.

Yet Lev knew with certainty this was his way out. His best option. He'd already failed the people he loved most. At the end of the day, he barely knew Felicity or Nook. What did he truly owe them? Lev put a hand on the doorknob, forehead thudding as he rested his head against the frame. He should just do it. Walk down the hall, grab the antidote, and find safety. He owed himself a chance to breathe.

His hand refused to turn the handle. Lev stilled, reconsidered. He should think this through. His body was too exhausted, and if he stole the antidote, he wouldn't have the strength to run.

And this might be his last opportunity to sleep a full night on a mattress for years. Relief was a gentle brush as he realized it would be foolish to act now. He needed to rest. Later, when everyone was busy or sleeping again, he'd make his move and leave. In a few hours.

Lev woke with a start when the door to his room burst open. Nook flounced in without so much as a greeting and collapsed at the end of his bed, head resting on his ankle. Lev didn't know it was possible to go from sleeping to blushing so quickly.

"She'll be fine. She's resting, but we cleaned her up, and she kept some food and water down." Nook's words were reassuring, but her expression rigid as she stared out the window. She looked spent, and Lev regretted disappearing by himself to sleep. He wasn't a healer, but he should have at least offered to do something. Instead, he'd plotted how to steal from the innkeeper who helped them and planned his escape before taking advantage of the provided mattress.

This was why he didn't deserve to grow attached to people. Why he should hurt them in the short term when it would be so much better for them in the long. Better for everyone that he be alone.

Lev swallowed a sigh and followed Nook's gaze out the window, desperate to keep his feet still so she wouldn't move. Maybe he could do something now to make it a little better. An apology in advance.

"Have you ever left the forest?" he asked, voice soft and low.

"Not before this."

Lev liked this, the quiet moment of them in a room together, her face turned so he could watch her freely. He gave himself a moment before he spoke.

"We can go out. Look around a bit." Words that could very well be the stupidest thing to leave his mouth. "I can wear some of Jal's things to fit in."

There was a brisk wind outside, a promise of cold. The long coat on the hook by the door had a tall collar he could pull up and hung beside a wool hat he could tug low. He'd risk this for one good memory with Nook before he left everything behind, burning it all down on his way out of her life.

"Why would you do that?" she asked, pulling her eyes from the outside world. Her entire focus landed on him. She didn't know to flinch away. Lev liked the trust and kindling hope in her blue eyes. She'd taken her hair out of its wild braid and washed it so it appeared darker than before. So deep a brown it was nearly black.

Lev shrugged. "I want to. I don't often have a chance to do the things I want."

"What would you want to do? If you had the choice?"

It wasn't a question he'd often considered before catching and halting the useless train of thought. It wasn't worth wondering. Every choice was made toward survival, toward avoiding discovery and the people of the cities. "I don't know. What about you?"

She studied him, doubtful of his answer. It surprised him when she supplied one of her own. "I would explore the cities until I could decide if they are worth helping. Then, if they are, I'd want to help."

"Help how?"

She frowned, shoulders pulling in defensively. He didn't like the way she made herself smaller, the way her eyes turned wary like she was already bracing for his response. "Small ways at first. Like Jal does when my—our leader doesn't know. He gives people money and supplies sometimes. But maybe, when I was sure what I was doing was right, I could help in bigger ways. I have such an incredible gift from the forest; it's hard sometimes, knowing I could do more."

"Why haven't you?"

"Because it would reveal that my people are real. Two of us

were murdered in one of our havens just months ago. Imagine how we'd be hunted and manipulated if the people knew. We aren't allowed to leave the forest without permission."

Lev nodded and squeezed his hands together. "So you're torn between helping strangers or your family. Helping strangers who may just turn around and murder you all."

Nook dropped her eyes, catching her bottom lip between her teeth.

"Or, you start small like you said and help differently. You would be a great smuggler. Carry messages or..." He paused, wary of letting Nook see too much into his past. "Could you murder someone, Nook? Poison the right person with your berries? Climb into the right room or remove the right guards to ready an attack? The dead can't talk. Can't hurt anyone else."

Her eyes widened. He'd taken this further than she had been ready for, Lev could see that. Good. Give her some insight into who he was. Who the people in the cities were. But then she surprised him by taking a breath and growing thoughtful. "I don't know. The people I'd have to consider killing, they would have killed too, right? And hurt a lot of people?"

"And will keep doing so, I have no doubt."

"Would that make it right?"

Lev couldn't answer that. He didn't know. He'd never known.

"But what if they're just doing what they were told?" Nook asked. "What if they have to do it or the people they care about get hurt? What if even Vasca thinks she's making the world better, justifying her actions like I'd be doing? In all the stories, few villains think of themselves as evil. Everyone is their own hero. If I killed, I would be a villain to some."

Nook sighed, and Lev stiffened as she pushed off his ankle and scooted to sit, looking at him closer, warm hip bumping against his leg. "I think I'd want to help by showing people it's possible to live peacefully. To learn to communicate. It's not as though we've never had a criminal born into our community, an Unmourned who believes they could use our gift to excel in the cities rather than hide in the forest. We have long talks about how to help them resist, and when that doesn't work, banishment is a heavy threat. Most banished leave, disappear into the mountains or board a ship bound for who knows where. They don't want to be in the trees and our quiet life there."

"Do you resent the trees?"

"No. I love them. I love traveling them and going wherever I want. I want to see everything, including the forest, but I know it so well now."

"So let's go start small." Lev rolled off the bed, his head clearing slightly with Nook no longer touching him. He didn't let himself hesitate before pulling on the coat, tugging up the collar, and donning the hat.

Nook smiled up at him. Her first real one, wariness gone. "You don't think it's ridiculous? That I want to help?"

"I have no doubt you would be the best person for the job." And Lev meant it. She'd helped *him* of all people. He could recognize his opposite. Where Nook was bright and clever and resolved in her beliefs, he floundered and turned dark. She'd been raised by the strength of the forest while he'd hid and cowered in its shadows. And would continue to do so.

Maybe he could redeem himself just the slightest amount by encouraging her. Take the tiniest sliver of the credit for her future accomplishments. Let a touch of her brightness infect his imprint on the world.

Nook watched, smiling on the bed. The sight warmed him, flipping his stomach and making his hands restless. He wanted to touch her. To make her keep smiling. She tilted her head, hair shifting forward. It fell in straight layers yet seemed to refuse gravity at the roots, framing her face beautifully.

He swallowed. "There is a shop I went to once. It may still be open."

"What did the shop sell?" she asked. Was he imagining the lightness in her voice? The edge of flirtation?

"Pastries. Breads. Cakes. It's a bakery."

"A bakery..." she tested the word on her tongue as though it were an incantation. She shifted up onto her knees suddenly. "Yes. Let's go. Felicity won't be moving for a while. We can bring her something back."

His heart tugged. Pulled. Broke. Lev offered her his hand, unable to return her smile as she scrambled off the bed and grabbed it.

It was worth the risk and more.

Nook ran down the hall and out the back door, gesturing for Lev to keep up. But after bursting into the outside world, she faltered as a carriage rumbled past. Nook tucked herself closer to his side, and Lev's soul soared. They'd been so focused on avoiding people and getting Felicity here safely that Nook hadn't taken in the village as they'd left the forest. Now, the streets were busier, but nothing compared to one of the cities or even the trading center in the middle of Midhaven, closer to the keep. The afternoon sun was bright. It was a very different world to that of the trees.

And for some reason, this made Nook reach for Lev. He held her hand gently, wonderingly. He was glad she wasn't looking at his face as their fingers interlocked.

He cleared his throat. Forced his mind away from her cool skin, slowly warming against his. He hadn't worn his gloves, trusting the coat's long sleeves to cover any identifying features. "This is just the outskirts of the town. We'll go toward the center where the shops are, and trade happens. Most cities and towns are busier in the middle. People gather there, so it's easiest to blend in. With so much chaos, people focus on their tasks rather than others. The bakery I know isn't too far into the village center, so you shouldn't be too overwhelmed."

Nook wasn't looking at him. She took in the streets and homes lining it. There was another inn, a blacksmith, and a tavern on the street, all spaced out and barely full.

He'd been ready for Nook's boundless energy and an outpouring of questions. Not the wide eyes or grip on his hand. Three men stumbled out of the tavern, already drunk just past noon. One pushed the other, making him trip dip in the dirt path to gales of laughter. Nook sucked in a gasp and looked ready to turn back.

"Are you sure Felicity will be fine?" she asked.

"We can go back."

Nook considered shot a glance over her shoulder to Siana's door. The men moved on without paying them any attention. Nook shook her head. She squared her shoulders and adjusted her grip on his fingers. "I want to see a pastry."

Lev couldn't help but smile, chest warming. He remembered he wasn't wearing his mask and forced it away. Nook reminded him of his brother in that moment. Always the first to try something. Fully capable of acknowledging fear and moving past it. It was those small moments of bravery that Lev admired most. The times when it would be easy and harmless to step back, but his brother stepped forward anyway. Just as Nook did now, though she stayed close to Lev's side and half a step behind.

It was a crisp day, and the wind worked in their favor. No one was in the mood to linger and people watch. They walked past him and Nook quickly, never noticing the girl openly gawking at them and their outfits and manners. The river nearby lent a layer of moisture to the air.

Closer to the center of the village, buildings were tall enough to block some wind, and the slight crowd warmed the street. Nook's gawking began attracting second glances. Lev pulled her along before she drew too much attention.

"Stop staring," he hissed under his breath.

"Sorry, they're just so..." Nook half turned to watch several boys run past with wooden swords. "Does everyone carry a sword?"

"Most men do."

"The smugglers don't usually have them in the forest."

"There isn't much room for sword fighting in the trees. They aren't practical. When given a choice of how much to carry, a bow is smarter in such an environment."

"Do no women wear pants?"

"Not usually. Some who work jobs that demand it do, but tradition usually calls for dresses."

"And no swords for them." This wasn't a question. There wasn't a woman in sight with a weapon visible.

"No. Things haven't changed that much since the Unmourned left. Women are rarely taught to fight. It's better, but not great."

"How is it better?"

"Women have more voice on who they want to marry and what they want to do with their lives. Any money they make, they can keep for themselves and use to buy property or expand business. Queen Vasca, for all her flaws, does want women to have more power in this world. But if she can keep half the population defenseless and unable to resist, she's willing to uphold some strict traditions."

"How did Vasca gain any power if she's a woman?"

They spoke quietly, in low voices that wouldn't be overheard. Still, Lev's arms pricked with goosebumps at the risk of discussing this in public. He scanned the surrounding area for listening ears. Now that Nook focused on him, they were attracting less attention. "Lilstrom is more progressive than Factumn and Midhaven. Many foreign countries hold women as equals, and that influence was carried to Lilstrom's port. As for how Queen Vasca gained power, her father is a powerful king across the sea. He wanted the port in Lilstrom but didn't want the hassle of sending an army. I think being sold off in marriage herself is the reason she rid the forest lands of marriage laws first. When her husband died, Lilstrom was ready to accept a woman leader, especially with her Swords. No one in Lilstrom was willing to fight her for power, not when their children were defending her. She continued building her army and brought the right people into her circle. The wealth she gained kept them loyal. It wasn't about her gender. It was only about the benefits her leadership provided, helping the powerful stay powerful. And through it all, the threat of her father's might was there in case her army should stumble. It's said her father is very proud of her taking Factumn and holding it."

"So that's why she does it? For power and money and her father's pride?" Nook halted and pulled her hand from his, crossing her arms with her brow furrowed.

"I suppose."

"I don't think that justifies the deaths." Nook didn't seem to understand the motivation in the slightest. Lev couldn't imagine those aspects of life being important in the forest. Did Nook have a father? Did the Unmourned believe in marriage? Did they have a system for money? A power structure?

"Me neither." Lev didn't have much to add past that, and it wasn't time to ask his questions. Not in the middle of a busy street. Not when it didn't matter what he thought either way.

Lev turned them down the next street, missing the feel of Nook's hand in his. The bakery was just a few doors down. Lev watched Nook's face as the smell of fresh bread wafted in their direction. All thoughts of Queen Vasca and her crimes vanished. The look on Nook's face made leaving the inn entirely worth it. The fearless enthusiasm he'd expected finally struck her. Nook took up his hand again and pulled him down the street to the glowing windows of the bakery. She paused to look at the cake on display, eyes wide and inches from the glass. Lev stared at her hand in his. Her skin was flawless, his nicked and scarred by years of training. She still had dirt from the forest under her nails.

With a gentle tug, Lev pulled her inside. The baker took Lev's order in a brisk manner, nearly shoving the pastries over his counter and holding out his hand as he greeted the next customer. Nook had turned shy again and stuck close to Lev's side as he paid. He never spent coin on something this frivolous, not when it was so important to save for the antidote.

Lev reminded himself he didn't need it now that he would steal Siana's stash. The thought dulled his light mood.

They left the warm shop with their wrapped pastries and wandered until they found a quieter street. Lev directed them to a low wall of stones to sit on. Nook settled facing him, crossing her legs as she balanced easily. Her improper position drew looks from the few who passed, but they weren't Midhaven guards or Swords, and Lev was finding it more difficult to care.

"You two talked so fast," Nook said.

Lev smiled. "You should hear the port in Lilstrom. City people just talk faster. Go on, try the pastry."

He watched closely as she took her first bite, making a muffled noise of surprise when the melted chocolate at the center dripped down her chin. She licked off the drip, leaving a smear behind, and laughed. "It's delicious! What is it?"

"The middle is chocolate," Lev said. He took his own bite and let his eyes slide shut. He couldn't remember the last time he'd enjoyed something sweet.

"It's life-changing," Nook whispered to her pastry, eyes slightly crossed as she beheld it inches from her nose. Lev laughed, and she smiled at the sound, lowering her sweet to watch him. He turned back to the street, attempting to hide his blush.

They sat and ate. Nook savored her pastry and watched the townspeople's progress. "I always dreamed of coming here, but I was too afraid."

"I wouldn't have thought you were afraid of anything."

"My people don't trust the city dwellers. These huge buildings—" she gestured to the small candle shop behind them. It probably couldn't hold more than thirty people. Lev pressed his lips together to contain a smile. "The reliance on coin and clearing of the forest. I was told all the time not to get close."

"But you always wanted to?"

"The first time I felt curious was when I heard Bough talking about our fathers. Our mother met them in the cities. When one of us wants to have a child, we usually risk visiting the cities to meet someone for a night—always with approval and never alone. I look more like someone from Factumn, I've been told. But my sister has darker skin, like merchants from different lands. When I was little, the thought of Factumn's wall terrified me. And the stories of why we left. I convinced myself my father was from *here* instead. I used to imagine he was still here. That I could sneak into Midhaven and find a man with my eyes or nose or chin, and then I'd know more about why I am the way I am." Nook glanced at Lev, face flushing. "It was silly. Who he is doesn't matter to who I am. I know that now."

"If it matters to you, it matters to you."

"What about your parents?" Nook asked.

"I didn't know them well." Lev dropped his eyes to the pastry in his hands, picking off a flaky layer and eating it.

Nook's expression warmed. "I bet they were talkative. Incredibly social. Disliked hiking and the outdoors in general. Hated animals."

Lev couldn't stop his surprised laugh. Nook's expression turned so smug that he rolled his eyes and hooked his hand under her knee. With a quick jerk, he tilted her off the low wall and sent her into the tall grass behind them. His victory was short-lived. Almost immediately, Nook lunged and caught his shoulders, pulling him backward to join her. He dropped his pastry somewhere and couldn't care about the wasted coin.

Nook ended up crouched above him, her face hovering inches away. His heart stopped as he watched her eyes dip downward to his lips. He realized he was still smiling, his cheeks tiring. They were so unused to grinning. He held his breath. The wind shifted her loose hair, tickling his cheek. He didn't move.

"Nook."

She tilted her head, waiting, but he had no more words. "Lev," she agreed with a smile.

"Completely indecent," an older woman walking by scoffed in disgust.

Nook laughed and sat back, taking her warmth and the forest smell with her. Lev took a moment to catch his breath before he sat up, too. Nook remembered the pastry in her hand and took a huge bite, chocolate again spilling down her chin.

"Completely indecent," he said, echoing the woman's tone as he leaned forward to wipe it with his thumb.

The laugh Nook rewarded him with was sunlight.

8

CAUGHT IN THE NIGHT

J al's mother fed them dark, crusted bread and a chicken
soup that reminded Nook of the food she'd eaten visiting
High Valley. The reminder of her mother sat like a heavy
weight with each bite. What would Meadow say if she knew
Nook was here now? What would Bough do? Nook couldn't ask
Siana not to tell her sister she visited. Siana was part of Bough's
life, not Nook's. There was no way the innkeeper would stay
quiet. She would probably make them leave if she thought
harboring Nook and her friends would upset the Unmourned
leader.

Nook was in too deep to avoid any type of fallout. Yet when
she glanced up and met Lev's eyes, his face uncovered, though
guarded in Siana's presence, she couldn't hold any negative feelings. He was now, without a doubt, the reason she would lose
her people's remaining trust. When the time came to split up,
she likely would hate him again for it.

But he laughed earlier.

He sat close to her side.

He listened and asked the right questions, no hint of doubt
in her capabilities.

He watched her lips in a way that made Nook's heart skip.

His gaze shifted to Felicity often. Checking Felicity's color with the same concern Nook felt and looking slightly exasperated by the questions Felicity threw Siana's way as her strength returned. When he looked at Nook, she saw the cracks in his armor. It was a look meant only for her. A faith in her. Who knew a simple, bared glance could induce such pride and warmth? A connection that made her feel chosen? It was foolish and thrilling. It made her long to sit closer. To be alone with him again. To find out everything that festered behind his walls and see if she couldn't lighten his burdens, even just for a moment, as he did hers.

They retired for the night, Felicity talking to Nook as they went down the hall and even as she turned into her room. Nook looked toward Lev, pausing between the doors. She wasn't so unknowledgeable about city manners to think she could just choose to sleep with him. Was she really looking for an invitation? She didn't know what the hope in her chest was for, but it died quickly when he shut his door behind him without glancing back. She sighed and followed Felicity.

"So, you're not from Midhaven then?" Felicity asked, hedging. Siana had been careful not to reveal too much, only saying her son was a trader, and he was how Nook knew of the inn when Felicity asked.

Nook didn't respond, pretending to occupy herself checking if the clothing she'd washed and hung in this room had dried. She was tired of wearing the dress. The fond gaze Siana gave her while she wore it made her skin itch as the hours passed. Nook was lying to her. Bough would never allow Nook to come back and apologize. Siana had no reason to be so happy to meet her.

"Are you an Unmourned?" Felicity asked.

The room stilled. Nook tried her best to ignore the excited tension Felicity held behind her.

"I won't tell," Felicity pressed. "But I will try to convince you to come to Factumn with me."

Nook sighed. She wished she'd gone with Lev tonight. She wished Felicity had slept longer while recovering.

She wished she could just say yes and ask what Felicity thought she could do to help.

"Someone can live in the forest without being Unmourned," Nook said before climbing onto the bed. She blew out the nearest candle and tried to look relaxed as she settled under the blankets.

Felicity sighed and sat on her side of the bed. "Will you keep traveling with us?" she asked, voice hushed in the dark.

"No. I don't think I can." Bough, River, Fullbloom, and Jal would arrive soon. Even if they didn't find Nook at the inn, it would still be ruined. Siana would talk, and Nook would be in trouble. Banished to High Valley or, if Bough was generous, confined to Thornwall.

Certainly forbidden from speaking to Lev again. The thought nearly made her leave the bed and go to him. A last opportunity for them to be alone. A final chance to break through his walls and sate her curiosity.

"I wish you could," Felicity said. "I know you don't want to confirm it, and I understand, but I have questions about the Unmourned. I've heard about why the girls left all those years ago. How the forest accepted them and gave them certain freedoms... I won't pry, not until you trust me. I just think you should know Factumn has grown *so* much. We were planning to crown the princess as queen without her even marrying. Her parents had done so much to pave the way for her. The Marked Men patrolled the streets, ensuring everyone's safety. Women walked unaccompanied at night, no one was forced into marriage, and the schools accepted everyone, regardless of gender. Women had more opportunities. As a city, we have overcome so much together. We've learned in the centuries since the marriage laws. We were proud that we were making our way as equals. Then Vasca halted that progress. She ruined everything, but it isn't too late. Factumn is worth fighting for. It's worth loyalty. I just think the Unmourned—if they're real—would agree if they came back. It's not the same place their ancestors left. The girls forced into the forest were missed, even back then. The city *learned*."

When Nook remained quiet, Felicity kept talking. "The Unmourned have such a gift. They could use it to help so many. They could use it to put Princess Amalia on her rightful throne. Then, you would see what Factumn is capable of. My city deserves a chance. My people don't deserve what Vasca has done to us."

Nook rolled to face Felicity, sliding a hand to her under the covers. Finding Felicity's fingers, Nook squeezed. "Maybe that's true, but you aren't talking to the right person. I don't have as many freedoms as I wish."

"You have as many freedoms as you take."

"My family—"

"My family was murdered violently before my eyes. Do you know what I would give to have them mad at me if it meant they were alive? You do what you feel is right, but I'm doing this for *my* people, and from my perspective, you have as little to lose as I do. I saw what that animal did to you. You can't even get hurt."

Felicity let go and rolled away. Despite the new strain between them, her breath quickly evened out in sleep. Felicity was still recovering and would be tired for a few days. Nook hoped Lev wouldn't push her too hard as they traveled. Another fierce ache to go with them robbed her of breath. This one accompanied by guilt from Felicity's words. Nook tried to ignore the rolling in her stomach and get some rest.

———

NOOK WOKE WITH A START. She couldn't sleep well in the strange bed or the creaking of the inn around her, but these noises were new. She slid out from under the blankets and crept to the window, peering out.

Three men stood outside in the dark alley. Their low voices had woken her up. The hair rose on the back of Nook's neck when she spotted the weapons they carried, with more strapped to their backs. The only consolation was the lack of uniforms, swords, and the uneven number. These were Factumn men, not the queen's.

Nook held her breath and slid open her window to hear what they said. It creaked slightly, but these weren't people who'd grown up listening close to every forest sound. They didn't react.

A door closed, and Siana rushed into view. Nook frowned at the anger on her face.

"What happened?"

"That boy! I think he's the bandit. I don't know what he was doing with those poor girls, but he stole my stash and left them."

Nook pulled a breath in, quiet and slow and shaky.

"Those Swords might get in the way of him leaving with it," a man said, "but our hunters will find him first. This is Midhaven business—"

A patter of fast-approaching footsteps. Gasping words forced out between heaves of air. "Lord Marc... caught them. He.... made this grand show of thanking them for... finding the bandit, and then *his* guards took him. He wants... to give the bandit up to the queen when she comes. For her favor. Take the credit."

"So the Swords don't know he was caught?" a man asked.

"The lord wanted the bandit. The boy has a huge prize on his head, and Lord Marc thinks the queen will pay when she gets here. The Swords didn't see anything. They don't go as far into the trees as our hunters."

The Midhaveners fell silent outside Nook's window. She knew they were making a decision, one that could cost Lev his life. Nook squeezed her eyes shut, begging them to make the right choice even when she didn't know their options. Distantly, she knew she should be furious at Lev. But all she could imagine were the Swords. The stories about their viciousness. Lev tugging on his sleeves and reluctantly parting with his mask as he risked bringing her and Felicity into town.

All she could think about was the way she'd made him smile.

"Well? Siana?"

"My stash?"

"We got it first. We were able to hide it when Lord Marc and his men showed up. He only cared about the boy."

"Very well. Let the queen deal with him. Marc can have the credit. We should stay out of it."

Not even a moment of hesitation before the men agreed and took their leave.

Nook stood. Her next steps decided themselves without her giving much thought. She woke Felicity, a hand on her mouth in case she made a sound. But Felicity only opened her eyes, instantly alert and cautious. With a few gestures, they set to gathering their things. Even with the words they shared before sleep, Felicity followed Nook without question, curiosity brimming the trust in her eyes. She believed Nook was Unmourned and therefore worthy.

She pushed away the drop in her stomach Felicity's trust induced. Silently, Nook pressed a knife into Felicity's hands. The girl had gone unarmed far too long. They left through the window.

In a tunic and pants again, Nook moved easily. She slipped between buildings and began retracing the path they had taken to get to the inn from the forest. When Nook spotted markings of the Unmourned on signposts and pillars, she followed them through darker alleys and under a bridge. They took Nook to a lower section of the riverbank beneath one of the bridges. Staying on that trail, Nook and Felicity kept to the shadows of the plants growing above until the river opened again, and they had to continue through more alleys and nondescript passageways. Through all the strange turns, Felicity remained silent. Nook felt as though her mother was guiding her. Many of the markings were signed with Meadow's flourish—Bough's contributions mentioning Jal and his trusted locations directly below. Nook's family had spent so many hours in this village. So many sights they were familiar with and denied Nook.

The path led them true and undetected. Once they were back in the trees, Felicity relaxed. With a wince, she limped as the adrenaline slowed, and Nook remembered her wrapped ankle. She leaned against a tree, catching her breath and forcing Nook to halt. "What is it? What happened?" Felicity asked.

Stopping, even briefly, was like torture. "They captured Lev."

"Who? Why would that mean we have to leave?"

Nook paused. "Siana was the one who sent people after him. And I wanted to talk in private first. Do you feel well enough to help Lev, or would you rather wait for us in the forest?"

Felicity tilted her head. "Where was Lev? How did they find him?"

There were voices at the edge of the village. They weren't far enough away for this. Nook picked up Felicity's hand, moving them fast as if she could outrun the other girl's questions. Coin found them. His ears were pressed close, and his body hunched. His tail flicked angrily. Nook wondered how Lev convinced him to stay behind when he was captured. It broke her heart to imagine, and she ran a comforting hand over the furycat's spine.

She spotted a fresh marking in the tree to her left, one of Fullbloom's, and froze.

"What is it?" Felicity asked. She sounded truly frustrated.

"There are traps set. To catch animals, I think. Don't go near that tree." Maybe that answered the question of how Lev was caught. Especially since Coin continued to stick close, sniffing at the ground until he exposed a hidden rope. Nook crouched lower, taking in the intricate trap set to hoist the prey into the air and Coin's trepidation. His fur was rubbed off in lines she hadn't noticed along his stomach.

"He was freeing you," Nook realized. Coin must have gotten strung up somehow. Lev was caught while trying to free him. Maybe. It seemed the most likely course of events when Lev was clever enough to avoid evasion so far.

"What?" Felicity looked from the furycat to Nook as if Nook were insane.

"Nothing." Nook stood. "They're close."

It was slower going at this point. Like Coin, Nook was more familiar with the forest's dangers, not manmade ones. It took her longer to spot the traps. Seconds that added to valuable time for Lev.

"Wait. Just wait, Nook," Felicity grabbed her arm. "Maybe this is for the better."

"What do you mean?" Felicity didn't know Nook well enough to recognize her wary, impatient tone.

"He's a criminal, Nook. He's robbed along the road for years, even from Swords and Vasca's nobles and just normal merchants trying to make a living. If I had a choice at all in the matter, I wouldn't have gone with him. But, the man I had to go through to get out of Lilstrom said he was my best bet. But *you* are. You helped us and don't hide your face and you are kind. We don't need him. You can take me through the forest back to Factumn. Princess Amalia is waiting for me, and I must get to her as soon as possible. I have information that will aid the rebellion, that will save my people from starvation and Vasca's cruelty. Maybe you won't expose yourself to help us, but surely this isn't too much to ask. The sooner we get there, the better for all of them. If Lev has to face justice for his crimes, that's the world we live in. Please, Nook. You have no idea how horrible the queen is. She needs to be stopped. *Now*. I don't have time to worry about a bandit who hides his face."

Nook nodded and stepped out of Felicity's grip. She pointed to their right. "Factumn is that way."

Nook turned back to Midhaven. She was the only one Lev had. That had been the case since he entered the forest. Jal might have spared him a meal, but Lev wouldn't have even known there was an antidote if she hadn't saved him. Maybe he was a thief. Maybe he kept secrets. But he also had kindness in his eyes. He'd also raised a tiny furycat and gained its trust. He'd carried Felicity for miles on end, never stumbling, always holding her secure. He introduced Nook to chocolate. Nook knew little about the queen, but she knew facing her would cost Lev his life.

And Nook was the only person who cared. She couldn't betray that. Factumn and Felicity had the rebellion. Bough had the Unmourned and Jal. Lev had no one. Not a single person. It was a horrible, painful thing to imagine disappearing and thinking only a furycat would be bothered by your loss in the world. Nook had seen good in Lev's smile, heard it in his tentative, unpracticed laugh. He didn't deserve that. No one should have to be so alone.

A hard, unmovable weight in Nook's gut told her she was doing the right thing. It didn't let her consider Felicity's proposal. Didn't let her think about Bough's disappointment. Nook had to help Lev to live with herself.

Felicity stood frozen. "You won't help me?"

"*You* won't help *him*. I don't even know you," Nook said without looking back. She sidestepped a trap.

Felicity scrambled to follow. "But he's a criminal!"

"I know. He robbed me the first time we met."

"My people—"

"Are not my people. They have help. If they fight long enough, it won't depend on you or me if they succeed. Lev's life does depend on us." Nook ducked under a branch and spotted Bough's mark. She was always doodling them into trees, absently claiming the forest as she waited on River to hunt or Nook to finish rambling an excuse for why she'd gotten into the latest bit of trouble. Bough would probably get through four of her marks by the time Nook was finished this time.

"You can't leave me to die!"

Nook finally stopped and turned to face the other girl. "Yet you want me to do just that to Lev. You're breaking the law, same as him. You're planning a rebellion against the woman who made the laws you condemn him for breaking. You may go along with my plan to free Lev, or you can go on your own. He's the one you hired to get you through the forest. No one else will."

"There's a trader named Jal. He'll help me if I make contact."

"Will he?" a male voice asked.

Felicity whirled, hand going to her chest before she recovered enough to draw the knife Nook had given her from her belt. "Who are you?" she asked the man who appeared between the trees.

He shared a look with Nook, amusement flaring in his eyes.

"I'm the trader named Jal."

Nook scoffed at his dramatics.

FELICITY GREW MORE uncomfortable as the long silence stretched and thinned the air. Nook liked to think herself immune to her sister's intimidations and let the quiet linger to prove it before allowing herself to speak. "Just ask your questions."

"Why are you with an outsider?" Bough asked.

Jal fidgeted where he stood next to Fullbloom. He wasn't a fan of that term.

"Because she needed help, and now her companion does."

"And her *companion* wouldn't happen to be..." Bough let

Nook finish the sentence. It was eerie how Bough's voice could fill her mind without her speaking. *...the bandit you stalk?*

Nook crossed her arms and looked away.

She stiffened when Felicity stepped forward. "Lev can take care of himself," the girl began, "but I can pay for safe passage to Factumn. A large sum is waiting for Lev to escort me. We can pay you instead."

"And who is your backer?" Jal said.

Felicity's chin rose. "The rebellion and Factumn's rightful queen. I served Princess Amalia before the city was taken. She *will* bring her people to victory. I have information to help her. They'll be incredibly grateful to you for getting me back. You'll have a royal favor and coin for your trouble."

"They keep coin like that lying around while their people starve?" Bough snorted, ignored Felicity's outraged protest, and turned back to Nook. Bough probably didn't even realize how she leaned into River as she considered her next words. River had been watching Nook intently, letting Bough get her say, but Nook knew he was the one she needed to convince. "This is a new level of stupidity, Nook. I can't believe you went into the village. And to bring that bandit to Jal's mother..."

"What are you going to do about it?" Nook asked.

Bough's face tightened with anger. This expression was the one she donned before letting out the most cutting words. Nook braced, but River put a hand on Bough's shoulder. She glanced back at him, read something in his face, and reluctantly deflated.

"What do you need, Nook?" River asked. "What's happened?"

Nook loved him. She floundered with a sudden space to explain. If he would listen, maybe Bough would, too. She had to make sure her sister understood.

"I came across them in the forest right after Felicity got taken by a longclaw. I distracted the beast while Lev shot it with poisoned arrows, but Felicity fell into mourning branches and broke skin. Lev carried her to Midhaven. He knew what he was risking to save her. I could tell he was terrified of getting recognized, but he still did it and then he *did* get recognized and captured. We wouldn't have been here if it wasn't for Felicity or if I had just been carrying the antidote. It's our fault he got captured. I have to make it right."

"How do you know he was captured?" River asked.

"I heard them talking outside Siana's place. He... left without us, and the villagers went after him."

Jal's eyebrows rose. River frowned. They knew she was leaving something out, but she kept her face clear of the truth. She couldn't admit that Lev had stolen from Jal's mother and abandoned her and Felicity. She couldn't even think about that too hard. There were better ways to fix what he did than let Vasca have him. "The lord person took him. He wants the credit for Lev's capture when Vasca passes through Midhaven."

Everyone stiffened at the queen's name and the reminder of her proximity.

"She'll kill him. Maybe I don't know enough about the cities, but I can be sure of that." Nook crossed her arms. Eyes dropped, no one meeting her gaze. She tasted the first hint of hope. "So we help him. It isn't right, and we can do something. We don't have time to argue."

Felicity's brow furrowed. River was still studying Nook too closely. Bough looked torn, but Nook's shoulders sank, watching the decision form on her face. The hope on Nook's tongue dissipated.

Bough shook her head. "It's too risky. We can't rev—" she cut off and looked sharply at Felicity.

Bough's biggest concern would always be revealing themselves and proving the rumors true. As long as the stories about their people were just that, *stories*, few would tempt fate in the poisoned forest seeking Unmourned. Killing her people like they had Misty and Harrow in the haven they found.

Nook met her sister's eyes and took a fortifying breath. The chasm between them had grown since Bough made her vows to protect the forest Unmourned. Since their mother volunteered Bough and placed the rift between them. Nook didn't know if it could be bridged. Not after this. "I'm not asking for permission. I'm asking for help. I'm going either way."

A heavy beat passed. River sucked in a breath. Bough's lips twisted. Her fingers clenched, just to the first knuckle. Her sister didn't fist her hands like most people. Nook's heart squeezed at the familiar sight. She knew Bough better than anybody. Why couldn't Bough understand Nook the same way?

River moved then, stepping between them and turning to face Bough. He put his hands on Bough's cheeks and bent so their eyes were level. Nook couldn't see her sister's face, but her hands relaxed. Jealousy flared, this time directed at River and his closeness with Bough. While everything Nook did distanced them, River could bring Bough to his side with just a look.

"I'll go. I'll be careful, and I'll keep her safe," River said. "She'll do it anyways. She shouldn't go alone."

"She's just being foolish. That shouldn't mean you have to."

"Branch, she's family. We stand by family, even if they're chasing after boys you disapprove of," River tried for humor, but Bough was still stiff. "We'll be quick. They won't know what happened. The bandit is always getting away. They'll think it was just him again."

River let go of Bough and straightened, reaching for his bow on his back. Nook couldn't believe she'd convinced him. Gratitude left her speechless.

She couldn't remember the last time she'd felt this way.

"I'll go, too," Jal started to get up from his stump, but Full-bloom returned from hiding Dorris the mule away. It was almost like she'd been waiting in the shadows just to step forward and yank Jal back to his seat.

"No, you won't," she said. He wasn't protected like Nook and

River. Jal kissed her cheek and winked at Nook. Fullbloom leaned into Bough and told her the forest was clear, but they needed to keep moving.

Nook smirked at Jal while Fullbloom was distracted. She knew he would come. Nook and Jal tended to show unsettlingly similar traits. It was likely why Siana had warmed to her so quickly.

Nook felt a twinge of regret for leaving Siana without a word. It shifted into a pang. This mission would be far riskier for Jal. He shouldn't agree without knowing the whole story. Fortunately, Bough was arguing with River in hushed tones, and they weren't listening.

"He was stealing your mother's stash of the antidote," Nook admitted quietly, dropping her eyes. "That's why the Midhaven men went after him. You don't owe him anything, Jal."

He waved Nook's words away. "She didn't have much. There's a reason we were on our way here. To replenish her supply. He doesn't deserve to die for it, though we probably won't be friends after."

"You aren't going," Fullbloom reminded him in a surprisingly menacing singsong voice, wrapping her arms around his waist.

Felicity seemed to force herself to look away from Jal and Fullbloom. "But—"

"Stay here if you want," Nook said. "Or go on to Factumn. I don't care."

River turned from Bough with one last kiss. He checked his quiver and the knife strapped to his side. At his unspoken question, Nook patted her knives and the pouch of berries at her side. He frowned at the pouch. Nook was one of the few who carried the poison. It made even the Unmourned uncomfortable.

"Of course, she's staying here," Bough said.

Felicity looked affronted by Bough's dismissive tone, but

Nook was done with talking. She nodded to River and turned for the village.

"Wait!" Bough lunged and grabbed Nook's arm. "At least wait until nightfall."

"I'm not just going to stand here. We have to get closer to make a plan. Check the place out. If we think we can make a move, we will."

Bough's eyes narrowed. "You'll listen to River. You aren't in charge here."

River's eyes bounced from sister to sister.

Nook bristled at the patronizing tone. "I'm sure Stream and I can figure it out." She pulled out of Bough's tight grip and shot a look at Fullbloom. "Jal could come at least help us plan. He's the only one who's been in the keep."

"I have," Felicity said in a small voice. "They kept us in the dungeon on the way to Lilstrom." She hugged herself as if protecting her core from the memory.

Nook cocked her head. "And you hated it. You were still just going to leave him there?"

"He's a thief! And worse. The stories about him..."

"I don't concern myself with the stories they tell about forest people. Come on, River."

9

GOOD MEN

Before Lev opened his eyes, he took stock of his hurts. The men who had ambushed him while he freed Coin from the trap had been relatively gentle. A hit to the back of the head sent him staggering, and then there were too many bodies to fight at once.

Lev had yelled at Coin to run. His relief when the furycat listened had been so strong Lev barely reacted when the bag of antidote was taken from him. The rest had been a helpless blurring. The Midhaven hunters, only concerned with Siana's stolen goods, were replaced by keep guards that Lev had humiliated in the past. He knew then that his situation was dire. They'd handled him roughly, dragging him from the forest and throwing him in the dungeons of the grand estate. With promises to do worse if he acted out, they'd slammed the barred metal door in his face.

But at least they'd carried the poorly crafted swords of Midhaven. They weren't the queen's men, even if they served one of her lords. If they'd been the Queen's Swords, Lev would already be dead.

All told, his hurts were minimal. A few bruises. A gnawing

hunger from a couple missed meals. Cold from the damp cell as it rained outside. A stiffness in his left shoulder from the side he slept on. A numbness in his hands from the shackles on his wrists. He'd survived much worse but knew he couldn't get comfortable. Queen Vasca was on her way.

Lev heard talking outside the cell, his guards in conversation. He continued pretending to sleep so they would speak freely.

"And we're sure it's the bandit?" The guard sounded young and practically awed.

"Yes. They say he escaped even the Dagger once on the road."

"What kind of a man evades the Swords? He's young, too."

Their voices lowered, but as they were both staring at him, Lev had no trouble hearing. "He steals from nobles and defies the cruel queen's men. Are we sure he isn't a rebel?"

"Yes. He steals from Factumn traders, too. He's never done anything to help one side or the other that he didn't get paid for."

"He's just a kid. Maybe he doesn't understand what Vasca has done. Maybe we can get him to our side. He could be useful."

The other man made a shushing sound. "Lord Marc has ears everywhere, you dolt." They listened for a beat, but the halls of the dungeon were silent. "You know better than to talk like that in this house. Now isn't the time for heroics. Vasca will be here tomorrow. Best not risk our necks on a couple maybes."

One of them rapped on the bars. They looked unsettled when Lev didn't react; he only opened his eyes to let them know he was already awake.

"What's your name, boy?" the gray-haired man on the left demanded.

When only the sound of rain dripping onto the stone floor

answered, the young man on the right sighed. "We're here to clean you up. Vasca only likes dirty prisoners when it's her decision."

Lev didn't let the panic show on his face, but he couldn't stop himself from jumping to his feet and stepping away when they entered the cell. It didn't matter. In the small space, they easily crowded him, and with his shackles, he stood little chance against them. What happened next was inevitable. They called for more guards when they saw Lev's jaw stiffen and his hands clench. They weren't taking chances with the bandit who had evaded capture so many times.

With five guards, they succeeded in freeing Lev from his shackles. The blood rushing to his fingers only expounded the dread gathering in his chest, snaking down to his wrists and palms.

"What..." Lev's gloves were taken off, exposing a bit of his wrist. A burst of movement from the stunned guard and Lev was left shirtless.

"You—you—"

Stunned silence. Lev waited. Waited as they took in the marks tattooed along his arms. Berries, branches, swirling vines of sharp leaves in stark black, and the outline of a white rose.

"You damned *traitor*—"

"Coward—"

"Vow breaking—"

They had stumbled back in their shock, shouting over each other. Lev stretched his arms, staring at the marks that began at his wrist and wrapped upward, ending mid-bicep. Even after all these years, the strange black ink, said to be mixed with mountain gold, shimmered against his pale, freckled skin. Maybe if he'd left his arms uncovered more, the sun would have eased the stark contrast over the years.

When Lev still didn't talk, the most vocal of the guards

stepped forward. There was only the deepest of revulsion in his eyes. Lev braced himself. He'd seen that look. Lev knew what came next, but this was the type of man who felt the need to justify his anger. He spoke, voice low with venom. "If I'm not mistaken, that's the ink of the Marked Men. The Marked Men swore to protect Factumn's royal family with their *lives*. Only the most elite and *trustworthy* were granted marks. Most of the boys were raised right there in the palace like family. Some say that's where Vasca got the idea for her Swords in the first place, but the Factori family treated their Marked Men with respect. They lived alongside them and joined in their council. Looking at you, I'd say you're the princess's age, right? Even here in Midhaven, we heard how her father indulged her desire to learn to fight. She wanted to be the first Marked Woman, right? You two probably learned weapons side by side, went to the same tutoring sessions, and ate the same meals. At what point did you abandon her? When Vasca first attacked? When you thought Vasca might be winning? When you looked at the young girl beside you and thought her life wasn't worth the fight? That you'd rather hide in the woods living like a criminal than uphold your vows while your brothers kept theirs... how many of their corpses did you pass while you fled?" He paused, chest heaving.

Another picked up where he left off, voice tight with rage. "And then to not even join the rebellion alongside the survivors? None of *them* stopped fighting for their true queen."

"But even fighting in the rebellion, they believe desertion and breaking their sacred vows means death. Just like thievery means death on the road. You should have stayed loyal. I hope the years of freedom were worth it."

Lev slipped into that separate space in his mind. The space that could watch everything happening to his body and keep him distanced from the pain. He just wanted it over with, so he leaned into the first man's face. "They were."

"I hope wherever you're going, you see it when we win. When Vasca falls, the loyal will be rewarded."

"I'm sure I'll only see all the rebels who have already died for the lost cause. Ending up in the same place as me."

These were good men, Lev decided, to hold back for so long.

They didn't kill him. Despite the three years of helpless rage behind their fists, behind their kicking, behind their words. They shouted questions, demanding to know how he could have left the princess, the palace, the city, and lands to Vasca's conquering. As if he alone could have stopped it. They didn't even know how right they were. How justified their actions.

Lev never cried out and never responded. He was too well trained. Soon, even that separate place in his mind wasn't enough. He forced himself to think of the forest. Of what it had meant to be free, even for so short a time. He pushed away thoughts of the brother he left behind and focused on Coin. On the rare moments when he heard the birds chirping above. On Nook, dappled in sunlight and covered in dirt.

He clung to that as they beat his body. As they released their rage. As he heard the lord of the estate shout for them to get away from him. As they left him bleeding on the cold, wet floor.

When Lev woke next and took stock of his body, he grew bored categorizing the many hurts and bruises. The worst of the damage hung in the throbbing heat of his jaw, nose, stomach, and ribs. The rest were simple bruises. He was hungry and thirsty too. It was habit to note these things. When he was done, Lev tried not to think, but there was panic lingering, building. Queen Vasca was coming, and they'd left him alive. He hadn't escaped her. He had no idea how long he'd been sleeping. How close was she? How long before he faced the true punishments only she was capable of doling out?

This thought was enough to make Lev push himself into a seated position. He caught his breath, refusing to groan. The guard outside his cell stiffened and clenched his fists, hearing Lev move. Somehow, he hadn't counted on such loyalty to Factumn remaining in Midhaven, in the keep, no less.

There was a scuff down the hall. The guard reached for the sword at his belt, body shifting from angered to alert. Lev was distantly curious but still too far in his mind and away from the pain to do more than continue to sit and listen.

"Who's there?" the guard demanded.

Likely men from the village who heard of the deserter in the keep's dungeon. Maybe they would kill him before the queen arrived—a small mercy.

The guard pulled in air to shout, but an arrow embedded itself in his arm. He made a strangled noise and dropped. Lev frowned. A wound like that shouldn't have taken him out. But the guard's uniform didn't have sleeves, and Lev could see the black of mourning poison already spiderwebbing out from the wound.

"I'm here, Lev. It'll be okay."

Lev dragged his eyes from the fallen guard to Nook, standing over his prone form. She was here. She was really here. He was too shocked to respond.

He'd never felt this before. Just the sight of her made him want to cry. "What are you doing here?"

She rolled her eyes. "Just hold on. We'll get you out." She took him in—swollen eye, bruised jaw and chest and ribs and really everything. Lev itched to cover the marks along his arms. They hadn't returned his shirt. "They hurt you," she said, voice tight.

Lev shook his head. He didn't deserve anger on his behalf. "You need to leave. Now."

Another eye roll. Lev could barely process what was happening. Someone had come for him.

"How do I open the door?" Nook asked.

"I can do it," Jal said, coming into view. Another man was with them, bow held loosely at the ready. He was frowning at the guard he'd dropped. He knelt at the man's side, pulled out the arrow, and dabbed the wound with the antidote. He looked young, his face hairless and body slim. He was holding himself together well, but Lev was willing to bet that had been one of his first times shooting another human. It wasn't even a killing blow. Lev warmed to the man instantly. Growing up as he did, it was rare to spot those with genuine empathy. Those who understood what needed to be done but let it affect them. It was a breath of fresh air.

Like Nook.

"Lev," Jal nodded a greeting before taking out his picks. Lev sighed, ignoring the pain it brought to his chest. He didn't like owing Jal, but this situation was beginning to feel too familiar.

"Jal. I didn't know you were in this part of the forest."

"Didn't Cranny tell you?"

"Cranny?"

"Nook. Sorry, I guess you two aren't there yet."

Nook shoved Jal, making him laugh, and the other man shushed them both. Lev's attention caught on Nook's face. Her eyes darted to him with concern, but beneath it all, she was nervous, her hand spinning the knife she held between her fingers. Its blade was slicked with blood. Lev swallowed hard.

The lock sprang open under the coaxing of Jal's nimble hands. The trader nodded in satisfaction and pulled open the creaking door. The other man started at the sound, and Nook paused to squeeze his arm before she rushed into the cell.

Lev's heart went erratic when Nook took his face in her hands, frowning at the bruises. She brushed her thumb over his split lip. He couldn't breathe. There was a warm buzzing in his palms. He fought the urge to touch her back.

"Maybe they *are* there," Jal murmured under his breath.

The other man scoffed quietly, but Lev didn't look from Nook to catch his expression.

"Where else?" she asked.

"I'm fine."

Her eyes narrowed. "Where else?"

"Just bruises. And maybe a cracked rib. You need to get out of here."

Nook nodded. "We really do."

Her touch lingered on his skin as she lowered her hands. The archer stepped forward and cleared his throat. He'd found Lev's shirt where the guards had discarded it in the corner of the cell. Lev hadn't even noticed it was still within reach. Nook helped Lev into it and pulled him up. Lev didn't even let himself wince with Nook watching so carefully. He didn't need to stoke the anger he could read in her eyes.

"Back the way we came?" she asked her companions.

They nodded and fell into a formation that seemed familiar. The archer walked in front, Jal at his back. Nook pushed Lev forward and took up the rear. The archer glanced back as they started, but when he saw Lev was keeping up, he broke into a light jog, feet silent on the worn floors. They ran to the end of the hall and the last cell on the right. Lev was stunned to see Jal pull the bars from the window with ease.

As the archer listened for anyone approaching, Jal explained, "My father was a guard here. There's a reason this cell is always empty." He was wary and more distant than usual. Lev had a feeling he'd be more standoffish if Lev didn't look so horrible. The fact that Lev robbed Siana hung between them. The marks on his arms and Midhaven's loyalty could play a role, too.

Still, Jal had come. Nook had come.

"River." Jal gestured for the archer to go first. River pulled himself up and out with ease. Lev's hands chilled at the immediate twang of an arrow being released. Nook's hand again found Lev's, as if she could tell the emotions settled there. The comfort was an unfamiliar ease.

River ducked back into view and waved for them to follow him. Jal hoisted himself out, but Nook refused to climb through the window before Lev. There was a brief standoff between the two of them.

"Can you even get up there on your own?" she demanded.

A strange flare of panicked anger rose in Lev then. He wasn't used to the emotion and how difficult it made pushing out his words. "Just go, Nook. You shouldn't have come anyway. It's too much of a—"

Nook stepped forward, matching his glare. "Don't be an idiot. Say thank you and climb out that damn window."

"You could have—"

She cut him off again, this time by turning the knife in her hand on herself and shoving it into her stomach. Lev's air left him, and he rushed forward too late to stop her. She pulled the knife out slowly and waited for him to meet her eyes. There was no blood. No pain on her features. They stood toe to toe. In a movement so quick Lev could have imagined it, Nook rose on her tiptoes and pressed a kiss to his cheek. "Of course, I came. Of course, it wasn't too much of a risk. Nothing will happen to me. Now climb out the damn window."

Lev's head was still spinning when he turned and did as she said. If she kept stabbing herself to win arguments, he didn't stand a chance. With Jal's help, Lev stood up on the grass. Nook followed, and River pressed them forward. They crept close to the keep to avoid anyone spotting them through the windows above but kept their eyes on the wall across the lawn. The rain made it more difficult to spot the men patrolling, but it also meant the guards wouldn't see them.

They were moving along with confidence when the shouting started. River sped up. Lev ignored how his injuries protested as he matched the pace. His head pounded, and his hurt rib made it harder to breathe, but Lev had pushed through worse.

Eventually, they had to leave the shadow of the building. River found a garden path and attempted to use the bushes as cover, but they were quickly seen. Arrows rained from the wall and the turrets of the keep. The clanking of armor sounded over the rain, announcing the guard's advancing on them. Lev's only thought was a hope that none of those approaching were Swords. Nook's knuckles were white as she gripped her knife with one hand. The other rested on the pouch at her hip. Lev was comforted by the sight. She had steel in her soul and would use her advantages to escape. His eyes shifted to River and Jal. They were the bigger concern.

When the archer casually reached down and plucked an arrow from his leg, Lev realized he and Jal were the only vulnerable ones.

Dread curled in Lev's stomach as the guards rounded the corner onto their path. Death was coming. Not for the first time, Lev wondered what was wrong with him to remain so bothered by it. Or rather, what was wrong with the world he lived in that he was so comfortable with it.

"Stay close to me," Nook said between breaths. "Let me take the hits, and don't try any funny heroics." She pointed her knife at Jal. "You either. Fullbloom won't hesitate to kill me as soon as my bleed comes."

"Wouldn't dream of it," the trader said. His face was lit with the same sense of adventure Nook wore. Lev decided they were trouble when paired and turned as the first guard burst between the rose bushes.

River took the man down, and Lev's instincts grabbed hold. Whatever gifts Nook may be blessed with, Lev was raised for this. Heroics had nothing to do with his subsequent actions.

The guard had barely hit the ground before Lev had the man's sword in hand. He swung it and adjusted to the weight in time for the next man to join the fray. Their blades met, and the guard's eyes widened. It was a look Lev had seen over and over.

The look of a man realizing he was outmatched.

The movements of fighting came back to Lev as effortlessly as breathing, though he'd only carried knives and bows for the last few years. He'd been raised for this. Forged into a weapon. The man stood no chance against his palace training. Neither did the next. Lev's body twisted, and his arm moved with a second nature. He ducked and hacked and speared and resisted the urge to block with bracers he wasn't wearing.

Between him and River's bow, they cleared the first rush of guards and hurried on. Nook kept looking back at him, but Lev ignored her stares. The rush of the fight roared in his ears, but without an opponent directly in front of him, Lev's stomach was beginning to turn. He wondered if he executed a killing blow with the last guard too soon. He could have knocked him unconscious instead of going for his neck. Lev's hand was warm with blood. He silently begged the rain to clean it before the adrenaline wore off. Maybe that meant it was already wearing off. Lev's breathing turned ragged. His mind was fuzzing, spinning, narrowing to the blood on his hands.

Not now.

Lev focused on Nook's back. They made it through the gardens. The wall loomed before them, but River didn't slow. Rather, he sped up and ducked under his bow to sling it over his back. Lev's heart skipped a beat to see Felicity's head poke out over the top of the wall. She hurled a rope over the side, and River grabbed it. He climbed with stunning speed, hand over hand, feet running up the stones, taking mere seconds to get to the top and redrawing his bow to remove the guards gaining on them.

Jal took the rope and braced his feet on the wall. He climbed quickly to the sound of River's encouragement. When Nook pushed Lev forward, he did the same, though the effort made his head light. Jal and River pulled him up the last few feet, and Nook scampered up behind them. Guards had reached the base of the wall by then, but Felicity and Jal managed to pull the rope out of reach before they could grab it. They threw it down the opposite side, and before Lev could fully comprehend what had happened, they were down and sprinting to the forest. Nook's hand slipped into his and held off his panic as they ducked into the welcoming trees and ran to safety.

10

BRUISES SO DARK

Lev was still sleeping. Even unconscious, he kept himself still. Occasionally, his fingers would twitch and his frown would deepen, but he never made a sound. Nook stayed close. Coin had overcome his fear of all the strangers to curl up next to him. The sight of Lev's arm tucked into Coin's belly made Nook's chest flutter. Bough's looks were deadly, but Nook had no regret. Only the urge to sit closer to Lev.

They camped in a favorite spot of Jal's. Down the river where the water pooled, and an outcropping of rocks provided cover. Men from the village had come to them looking for Lev, and Jal went to meet them. He knew them each by name and promised to keep an eye out for the bandit, laughing that he had gotten away once more. "Seems like I'm always looking out for this man."

Somehow, Lev had reached the spot on his own feet but collapsed as soon as they settled and Coin came near. Bough watched him carefully, her blue eyes going back and forth between him and Nook, who was studiously ignoring her sister.

River had a proper fire going when Felicity and Fullbloom returned from collecting edible berries nearby. Bough and Full-bloom hadn't been able to sit still while the rescue was happening. They'd hunted the entire time. Their three rabbits were skinned and turning on a spit.

Felicity approached with the water. She and Nook hadn't spoken since Felicity initially refused to help. When the other girl made to kneel in front of Lev, Nook broke their silence. "Don't wake him."

Felicity responded in a careful voice, making Nook wonder how sharp her own tone had been. "Yes, he needs sleep, but if his wounds get infected, he'll be in way worse shape."

Nook swallowed hard and took in Lev's ruined face again. Freckles, scars, circles under his eyes, drying blood, and bruises so dark. Bough pulled a salve out of her pack. It was swirled with black. When the bark of the mourning trees was boiled, the water became poisonous enough to kill off the dirt in injuries that led to fevers but wasn't potent enough to harm a human. Coupled with herbs to aid healing, this salve and the antidote were the Unmourned's primary source of income. Only Nook's people could handle the mourning trees and knew the ingredients. Both had been banned by Queen Vasca when she couldn't get her hands on the recipe or learn its origin, but people needed it enough that Jal had never been turned in for selling it.

Bough handed the tin to Felicity. At the first brush of the wet rag across his face, Lev woke with a silent start that rose the hackles down Coin's back. Felicity froze when the furycat hissed but set her jaw and addressed Lev, calming the wild look in his eyes. "We have to clean your injuries."

Lev lifted a hand to his face, noting the absence of a mask as his eyes scanned the area around them for threats. "I'll do it."

He cleaned his face quickly and efficiently, probing the wounds without a wince. It was too practiced. Nook's hands bundled into fists. Had he cleaned the scars along his cheek the same way?

They had to change the bucket after he washed his face and hands. Most of the blood was not even his own. The hair rose on

Nook's neck, remembering the man he had become with a weapon in hand. She didn't know what would have happened if he hadn't joined the fray. Nook could admit now their plan had not been thought through. He'd saved them all.

When the clean water was placed in front of him, he bent, and his flinch betrayed the severity of the wounds along his stomach.

"Take off your shirt," Felicity told him. Lev froze. "Your arm is bleeding. Just take it off."

All eyes were on Lev now as he slowly did as Felicity said. It was Nook he looked to once the shirt was over his head. Felicity dropped the rag and scrambled away, jumping to her feet. Nook hated the look that entered Lev's eyes then. Almost satisfied with self-loathing as Felicity searched for words.

Nook ignored them all and kept her expression neutral as she took Felicity's place and picked up the rag.

"I'll do it," Lev said again. Nook ignored him, and he let her have her way. As soon as the cut along his bicep was cleaned of blood, it became apparent he'd need stitches. Nook grabbed Bough's bag and found the needle. Lev was staring at her, avoiding Felicity's accusing gaze. As she stitched his arm, his expression was reward enough for her inference. Perfect trust. Searching for a lifeline that she wanted him to know she was. She met his eyes, seeing all of him without reproach.

Because the marks that made Nook's heart clench weren't the tattoos on his arms. It was the four lines of his cheek, the other countless scars revealed now that his shirt was off, and the look in his eyes. He was haunted. Who cared what the marks along his arms meant? He was in the forest because he needed to be, same as the Unmourned.

"Why didn't you tell me?" Felicity found her voice. "Amalia wouldn't hold to the old laws. She'll let you come back. Especially if you bring me. It's not too late to make this right."

Felicity stepped closer again, and Lev pulled back. Nook shot him a look for moving his arm, but his focus was on Felicity. "It *is* too late," he said. "I'll take you to Factum if you still want, but that's it. Please, Felicity, don't tell anyone."

She froze as his words set in and struggled to collect her thoughts. Finally, anger won out. "Coward." She pointed a finger at his face. "I'm glad it shames you to bear those marks. You don't deserve them. You could make it right. You could stand by your vows and help so many people. But you're a coward."

Felicity left. Jal cleared his throat. "I'll just go check on her."

"I'll come." Fullbloom hurried to follow.

Even River and Bough couldn't handle the weight in the air. They mumbled excuses and slipped into the trees. Nook was relieved when it was just her and Lev. His eyes were down, staring at his arms with an expression Nook hated.

"Let me check your ribs," she said.

He sighed and nodded, relaxing into her ministrations. As the blood cleared, Nook could see all the other scars he bore. Skin that had been sliced and punctured. Evidence of burns and scrapes. Poorly done stitches.

And the bruises. So many and so dark that bile rose in Nook's throat.

She turned away and went to Bough's pack. Even more secret was the salve they made that numbed injuries. It was so difficult to make that few could afford it. Mourning berries were dried and crushed, mixed in with the other ingredients until the oily mixture turned a vivid red. It only took a little, but the salve sank into the skin quickly and eased most pains. The Unmourned used it sparingly during their bleeds because few of them liked working directly with the berries. It was yet another duty Nook's mother wanted her to go to High Valley to learn.

When Nook turned with the glass jar in hand, Lev was staring at his arms again.

"Stop it." His eyes snapped up to hers, and she continued,

"Nothing is different. I'll just put this on, and we can cover them again. It doesn't matter."

"It matters," he said softly.

"It matters," she allowed. She checked the raised skin on his chest, where she guessed an especially nasty bruise marked an injured, possibly broken, rib. He shivered. "But right now, we're fine. It doesn't have to matter right now."

Lev studied her. She gave him a small smile when he nodded. His shoulders loosened, and his attention turned to her hands.

"What is that?"

"It's a numbing salve. It'll help with the pain in your rib, just don't forget it's still hurt. If you overdo it, you could make it worse."

"Does it help with healing?"

"I don't think so. Just the pain."

Lev nodded. He crinkled his nose at the potent smell when she rubbed it into his chest, and Nook laughed. Only then did she realize how much tension he'd still been holding. He relaxed completely at the sound, his expression softening as he stared at her. He caught her hand, pressing it to his chest and keeping her close. She could feel his heart pounding.

"Why?" he asked. Nook stared at his hand holding hers, fighting the answer even in her own mind. "Why did you come for me, Nook?"

She swallowed, looking up. There was something breath-taking about holding eye contact with Lev. The intensity of his gaze yanked the response from her chest. "I needed to know you were safe. I couldn't stand not knowing."

He shook his head a tiny bit. "But I left you. I stole from Siana."

"If you feel bad about it, you know what to do. Don't make me explain *myself* when you have something to say but are too scared to do so."

Lev went quiet. Nook watched his eyes carefully and almost relented when she really did see fear there. Looking at his battered body, she couldn't help but feel he had been through enough. But she could also see the words he was keeping inside.

"Nook, I..." He took a deep breath, winced, and put his hand on his injured rib. "I let people down. The ones I let close. I'm dangerous, and being around me and with the choices I made, people get hurt. People *will* get hurt. I decided to take the antidote and leave so you wouldn't follow."

"That's how you justified it in your head, but you feel guilty because..."

Nook waited patiently while he puzzled that over. She thought of all the conversations with Meadow where her mother worked with her to express herself and get her feelings loose. Always patient, always asking the right questions. In the end, no relationship was perfect, but Nook had the tools to get to the core of herself when she wanted. Watching Lev struggle, she missed her mother. She wished she could give Lev a childhood of the same security.

"It's your decision if you want to be with me. I shouldn't have stolen or tried to decide for you." He couldn't meet her eyes.

"And I'm perfectly capable of thinking for myself."

"Yes."

"And you're sorry for leaving me?"

Was he sweating? A result of his injuries or the strain the conversation was causing him? "I'm so sorry I left. And stole. And that you put yourself in danger rescuing me."

Nook laughed a little. He was hopeless. "Not sorry for the last one. You're *grateful*."

Lev's lips quirked in a crooked smile. "Aren't I capable of thinking for myself too? Don't put words in my mouth. But... yes. Thank you for coming, Nook."

Mothers above, she wanted to hug him. Nook settled for squeezing the hand she still held. "I forgive you for leaving.

You'll have to apologize to Siana for stealing. I hope you talk to me more in the future about such decisions. And I can't make broad promises for the future, but you haven't come close to messing up enough that I would leave you to die." Lev smirked. "Also, Jal and Felicity were the ones who put themselves in danger. You don't have to worry so much about me getting hurt. Not for the majority of each month."

Lev lowered his head, pressing their interlocked knuckles into his forehead. "Can I be sorry your sister is mad at you for rescuing me and talking to me?"

"You can feel bad for me, but those were my choices and her reaction."

Lev pulled in a shaky breath. Then another. He lifted his eyes. "I don't want to leave you again."

Nook's chest warmed dangerously. She tried to summon the anxiety Bough's disproval brought, but the look in Lev's eyes felt more important. He needed her more than her sister did. Maybe even more than her people did. He had no one. Nook wanted to make change, to make the world around her a better place. Lev's eyes made her feel like she was doing that for him. The timid peace, the hopeful trust, the admiring sweep. Nook basked in his attention.

Nothing in the world had made her feel so centered. "I'm here," she said simply.

Lev ran her knuckles against his lips briefly. His following words were a breathless rush against her skin. "Andifyouwant-tostay,you'rewelcometo." Lev blushed.

Nook smiled and finished treating the bruises on his chest and stomach before moving on to his back. As she worked, she thought about his invitation. Bough was already so angry. Not enough to let someone die, but enough that Nook knew the rage was brewing deeper now that the danger had passed. What would staying with Lev do to Nook's standing with their people? What would Bough do to keep them apart?

She found Lev one of Jal's clean shirts and some food. By the time he'd eaten a bit, Lev's eyelids were drooping. It took little effort to convince him to go back to sleep. The next time his fingers twitched, curling in while he sucked in a quiet breath, Nook slipped her hand back into his. He grabbed on and went still. Nook traced the scar at the base of his thumb until the others returned. Even then, feeling reckless, she didn't let go.

LEV AND FELICITY WERE RECOVERING, sleeping heavily under River's watchful presence. Nook wouldn't have left them with anyone else. With a sigh, River read the look in her eyes and waved her away, a silent promise to make sure Bough didn't abandon the outsiders to the forest. Nook caught up to Jal, who patiently waited for Fullbloom to check if the path was clear for him to go to Midhaven and see his mother. The timing was getting tight. They needed to get on their way before the queen arrived, and Nook had set them behind schedule.

His expression turned suspicious, but a smile tugged. "What is it now, Cranny?"

Nook couldn't help but laugh. "I may or may not be thinking about going to see the queen."

Jal raised an eyebrow. It was broken by a scar in the middle, maybe the only characteristic of his face that betrayed the hard life he'd lived in the forest. "And I'm the only one you're telling?"

"Well, River knows I'm not at camp. Someone should know where I'm going. Have you ever seen her?"

Jal leaned against the tree behind him, squinting in the sunlight that hit his face in that position. "Yes. She's... I understand the curiosity. Stay long enough to watch her interact with someone. It's terrifying. Maybe that, over anything else the cities could show you, will be enough to convince you to keep safe in the trees."

They shared a smile, knowing it wouldn't be.

"I'm surprised Bough is letting you go into Midhaven."

"Well, it will have to be quick, but I need to check my mother is okay and make sure she's going to keep her head down when the Swords get there." Jal's jaw tightened. "There isn't enough room at the keep, so some will likely stay at the inns. Maybe they'll set up camp, but..."

But he was worried and couldn't stay to ensure his mother was okay. He was too recognized as an unpermitted trader.

Jal shook his head. "If Bough asks, Fullbloom and I will cover for you. Go. Stay high, and don't linger."

Nook kissed Jal's cheek and ran into the trees. She slowed only long enough to brace herself. She didn't tilt her head to look at the height she would have to climb. She didn't let herself hesitate long enough to feel the irrational fear that leaving the ground gave her. Grabbing the nearest branch, she pulled herself up quickly, stomach turning anytime she accidentally looked down. Heights always brought on harsh memories. But she wasn't alone. Should something happen, help was close.

"You are fine," Nook whispered over and over as she got high enough and began running, leaping from tree to tree, heart painfully lodged in her throat the entire time, though her steps were precise and practiced.

Birds hung close and chirped encouragingly. Nook focused on their sounds and kept her eyes on the next branch. Nook was fast. Her mother used to say she would have named her Flight if Nook had been as inclined to run through the trees as she was to hide in small crannies to avoid baths and the like when she was little. Nook outran the memories and her fear and knew only her rapid, silent path between the trees. Sometimes, she caught herself with her palms, skin scraping as she swung and landed on her next mark. Sometimes, she jumped so far it did feel like flight. It felt like true magic.

When she ran through her trees like this, Nook was the Unmourned in the stories.

The tamers of the forest and creatures of myth.

Catching her momentum hard against the tree trunk, Nook found the gap in trees that provided a good view of where Vasca's procession had made camp. The pair of Swords standing guard below exchanged glances and tipped their heads back. Nook hugged the tree and stayed silent in the shadows. She could barely see them and their crisp blue uniforms. They kept their hands resting on the hilts of their swords at their hips. A strap of knives crossed their chests. They looked tired, and one had a large welt under his eye. Nook couldn't imagine where it came from. They stood rigid and yet moved deliberately and with careful grace.

They lost interest and turned their attention back down to the forest floor. Nook heard one murmur something that made that other huff a stifled laugh. They glanced at each other, grinning. Their perfectly stoic masks broke for the barest second. Nook struggled to look away. They were a mismatched couple, one with hair so fair Nook had never seen such a white shade. The other was similar to Bough in skin tone, though his hair and eyes were a dark brown. These were people with heritages based in distant lands. Nook burned with such intense curiosity for the cities that lands across the sea seemed a surreal fantasy she didn't have room to wonder over. She barely let herself consider how vast the world was outside her forest and its road.

She'd heard how the Swords were paired, always traveling in twos and looking like strange mirror images in their matching uniforms. Somehow, she hadn't expected to see anything like friendship between them. A familiarity and fondness that came from being incredibly close to another person. It shifted and tilted her view of this army of Swords. It made them seem human, she realized. Not simply the weapons Vasca worked so hard to cast them as. Nook swallowed and moved on with more caution. She came to the tree line and stopped in full view of the camp.

Vasca was easy to spot. The queen stood frowning, with two women in plain brown dresses at her back. Heads bowed, they still watched the queen close. When her hand twitched, one was quick to step forward. After a command was uttered, the girl ran off. Out of nowhere, another girl replaced her. The Swords shadowed them, and at Vasca's side was the man Nook knew to be her general, the Dagger. Meadow had described him to Nook and Bough, warning them never to approach the tall, auburn-haired man who wore the black uniform with Vasca's symbol on the chest. A white rose. The same marking the Unmourned had carved into trees to warn each other of her arrival.

The queen turned, and Nook got a better view of her face. Hair the dullest shade of red, not quite blonde, made her look young in combination with the smattering of freckles across her cheeks. This did not look like the conqueror of lands. She stood with her mouth slightly open, breathing as though her nose was full. No one dared look too long at the strangely vulnerable characteristic. In fact, no one seemed to look at her higher than her shoulder. Only the Dagger had his chin in the air. They shared looks as if they were conspiring against every person around them.

There was a hush over the camp. No laughter. No forest sounds. The cook dropped a pan near the central fire pit and looked around with wide eyes. There was only the distance clang of steal as her Swords trained at the outskirts of the party.

The servant girl reappeared with a mug on a small plate. How she balanced it while nearly running was a mystery. She stepped up to Vasca with it, dipping her head even lower.

Vasca took it without looking at the girl and sipped its contents. When Vasca stilled, the entire clearing stilled. So silent that Nook could hear when Vasca spoke. "Why is it cold?"

The girl cringed. Nook saw Felicity in the poor girl's place so easily it robbed her of breath. Of course, Felicity left. Of course, she wanted to do anything she could to rage against such control. Without even realizing it, Nook reached for the pouch at her belt. She stroked its soft leather. Thinking. Watching. Wondering where the line was. If she dared toe it. If she could imagine crossing it.

She popped a berry in her mouth to settle herself, never once taking her eyes from the queen.

"Well? Get another, or you can stay in the forest. Maybe the Unmourned will take pity on you and bring you into their ranks." It jolted Nook to hear her people mentioned by the queen. Voice so cold, eyes so empty, there was no inflection in her words, though the Dagger chuckled like she'd made a joke.

This was what Jal wanted Nook to see. The vacant stare chilled Nook to her core.

Vasca kept talking, nearly bored. "Or maybe we will hear your screams as we leave you behind, and the forest claims you as it did the last girl who brought cold tea."

The girl nodded as though such a punishment was only fitting and ran to fetch another cup. Nook had seen enough. She went back in the direction she came, shooting a pitying glance down at the Swords on duty. They stood more relaxed than their counterparts nearer the queen. It said a great deal that they would rather be stationed this deep in the trees than at Vasca's side.

Nook traveled the trees more slowly as she thought on what she'd seen. When she neared camp, she came across Jal and Fullbloom also returning. Midhaven must have been tense for both of them to jump as they did when Nook dropped to the forest floor in front of them.

"She was..."

"Terrifying," Fullbloom finished, nodding. Jal gave an exaggerated whole-body shiver.

Bough shot Nook a frown as they returned to the small clearing where they camped but didn't say anything.

"Any news?" River asked. Lev was awake and sitting beside him, Felicity across the fire, scowl still fixed in place and meant for Lev.

Lev's eyes did a quick, assessing dip over Nook. He looked relieved. Nook realized he was making sure she was okay. Her people only looked at each other like that during their bleed. In a few steps, she was next to him.

Once they were all settled around the fire, Jal spoke. "There is a rumor as to why the queen has decided to travel the road now."

"What is it?" Felicity demanded.

"Marriage. They say she is traveling with her son, long since hidden from the public eye. He and the princess of Factumn are to be married, solidifying Vasca's power there."

There was a stunned beat of quiet. River spoke, voice soft. "I suppose that explains why the girl was kept alive."

Only Nook's proximity to Lev made her aware of his reaction. His hand fisted in the fabric of his pants, and his body stilled, face blank.

Felicity went pale and jumped to her feet. "But... no! She doesn't have a son! Amalia can't... she can't be forced into this... she..." Felicity fell silent, horror brimming her eyes as she stared at nothing and began to pace.

"That's the story. No one can confirm seeing this boy in her party, though," Jal looked to Nook, question in his eye. Nook shook her head once. No, she hadn't seen a prince. She felt Lev's eyes on her as she and Jal communicated silently.

"Well, a marriage sounds more peaceful than another invasion, at least," Bough mused.

Felicity drew in a sharp breath and shot her a glare. Bough shrugged. "The outsiders are barbaric. Forced marriage is horrible, but killing a city into submission is worse. I can't say I'm surprised. This is certainly in line with the history of the cities. I can only hope it'll bring some peace."

Felicity looked angry enough to cry. River stepped in, "Either way, the queen is near, and we should clear this section of the forest. Let's get a few hours of sleep so the wounded can travel further tomorrow." There was no arguing with River's calm reason. Felicity turned away from all of them, but the tension in her back made it clear sleep was far away.

Deep breathing filled the quiet of the night as they dropped into sleep one by one. Nook had settled down behind Lev, though he remained seated beside River in reach of the fire's heat. He'd insisted he slept enough and would help with first watch. Nook hadn't argued. River could only help Lev's tense shoulders. Nook often turned to River when she needed silent assurance. When she had been injured so long ago, and her mother left her side, it was River who was the most comforting in her place. He was so steady, so present.

Nook was half asleep when Lev broke the silence. Her ears pricked at the sound of his soft voice. River answered, his words easier to pick out as he explained the distance they hoped to cover tomorrow and where their group planned to go. Nook was surprised to hear River vaguely describe the path to Thornwall to an outsider.

Nook also knew River included her when he said "we," and her heart twisted. They would expect Nook to continue with them. To forget Lev and Felicity as the pair traveled on to Factumn. If Felicity still trusted Lev enough to stay with him after seeing the marks on his arms.

After a brief pause, Lev spoke again. "So, you're one of the Unmourned?"

Alarm tensed Nook's shoulders. She hated that River had to have this conversation.

"Yes," River said after a surprised beat in which he fully realized Nook had shared their secret. His voice wasn't tight with anger, but Nook couldn't relax. "I'm Unmourned."

"But you're..." Discomfort trailed off Lev's words.

"A man?"

A beat in which Lev likely nodded.

"And you're confused how one can be both?"

"I suppose I am."

River considered his words. Nook listened hard to his pause, wondering if he'd need her support. This conversation was one she'd heard enough to know River was willing to have it, but she could see how it wore on him afterward and prepared to step in.

"I'm sure people like me are more common than anyone realizes, and I take comfort from that," River began. Nook peeked under her lashes, relaxing slightly when she saw the calm on River's face. His head was tilted back, watching the moonlight through the shifting leaves above. He turned suddenly and looked at Lev.

"Strawberries are my favorite," River said. Nook fought a smile at the puzzled noise Lev made. "I can't tell you why I enjoy them more than the other fruit in the forest, but I know what I feel when I eat them. How my body lightens with pleasure at their taste. It's the same sensation as loosing an arrow and knowing it'll fly true. How I feel when the rain eases, and the forest smells like it does now. The way everything inside me brightens when I make Bough laugh." River paused, his eyes going to Bough's sleeping form. "I may have to bind my chest, and I may bleed with my sisters every few weeks, but at my core, where all these things exist and compose who I am, I am a man."

They fell silent. The fire crackled in the air. It became harder to breathe the longer Lev stayed quiet. Would he not respond? Could he think—

"Thank you. For explaining."

Nook released her breath. She pressed her lips into her blanket and let herself smile.

164

"Can I look at your bow?" Lev asked.

Nook nearly laughed at the question, and River was happy to hand over his favorite weapon. Lev traded his own, and the conversation shifted to the different builds. Lev was interested to learn River had made his and River asked about the market where Lev had purchased his. Nook was nearly lulled back to sleep by their easy chatter. Weapons and trade and hunting were light topics compared to the day they'd had. It was the most she'd heard Lev talk, and his voice was soothing in an unexpected way. She came back to attention when she heard her name.

"Nook said she doesn't shoot. I thought your people preferred shorter-range weapons after talking to her."

"Not necessarily. Nook is... impatient. She gave up on shooting early. She likes being closer to her target, to see the immediate results. Most of us avoid the unnecessary risk of short range."

"That makes sense."

A smile lifted River's voice. "You seem to understand her well for just meeting her."

"I've known her longer than these last few days," Lev said, voice even softer. It warmed Nook's chest, and she struggled to keep the pretense that she was sleeping.

"She's pretty, yeah?" River asked.

Nook was listening so hard she didn't let herself breathe.

Lev only hummed in response. What did that mean? Why so noncommittal... Had he never thought about it? Did he not look at her like she looked at him? So closely she felt she could count the freckles scattered over his face and enjoy every second of the exercise?

"You can tell she's awake too, then?" River asked, laughter in his voice.

Nook opened her eyes in a glare and threw the pack she'd been using as a pillow at River's head. Both men worked to stifle their laughter so they wouldn't wake the others. Nook's embarrassment couldn't live when Lev smiled like that.

River tossed the pack he'd easily caught back to Nook. "Well, Cranny, if you're awake, I'm going to get some sleep."

Nook rolled her eyes and stood. She wrapped her blanket around herself and moved closer to the fire, trying to tame her hair with her free hand as she stepped over Coin's curled form. He barely twitched at her presence. "Goodnight, Stream," she said, a grumble still edging her words. Her cheeks wouldn't cool.

River settled into his place behind Bough. Nook smiled to see how even sleeping Bough reacted to his presence, curling into his warmth and sighing with contentment.

Nook glanced at Lev as she sat beside him, heart skipping. He was smiling. The expression had to be painful under all his bruises. But they weren't what made looking at him difficult. The firelight played with his unmasked features, bringing his freckles and the gold in his hair to the forefront. She faced the fire and focused on breathing so she didn't reach for him again. The memory of him shirtless was impossible to push from her thoughts.

"Nook?"

She took a breath and turned back to Lev, hoping her thoughts were hidden. "Yes?"

"River said when we part tomorrow at the pond, you'll be going with them."

Nook looked toward Bough again. She'd barely spoken with her sister. She'd run to see the queen while Lev slept to avoid conversation with her. Bough's anger was simmering below the surface, and Nook could only guess River had kept it from erupting. But Bough wouldn't be able to let this go. Nook had broken far too many rules, and Bough's role as the forest leader meant enforcing the laws. But it also meant judging when to let things slide. Bough sanctioned Jal and Fullbloom's relationship, and everyone benefited from Jal helping their trade. Why couldn't they come to a similar agreement with Lev?

Nook knew this was a foolish hope. Bough was too protective, and Lev was a renowned criminal, not a trusted trader whose curiosity drove him too deep into the forest.

"Most likely," Nook said. "I just..." she couldn't finish the thought, but Lev nodded like he understood.

"Will you go back to hiding from me?"

The misery in his voice shouldn't have made Nook want to smile so badly. "I don't think so, no."

"Good." He didn't look entirely satisfied with her answer but didn't press her. Nook relished the easy quiet that blossomed between them until her eyes began to droop again. Shifting slowly to give Lev time to move away, she settled on her side next to him and rested her head on his thigh. He stiffened, and she nearly sat up again, but Coin moved to curl against her stomach. After a brief hesitation, Lev gently brushed his hand over her hair.

"You can play with it," Nook told him, silently begging him to do just that. She loved to have her hair brushed, her scalp scratched. Anything.

At first, Lev didn't seem to know what to do with her suggestion. He picked up a strand and let it drop. He brushed some finer hairs off her forehead. But then he grew more comfortable and began picking through the knots. As he did, her hair grew softer to touch, and he ran his fingers through it methodically.

Nook melted. She fought sleep long past the point where she was relaxed enough to do so, wanting to fully enjoy this moment.

Lev spoke, a smile in his voice. "Go to sleep, Nook. I can keep watch. I slept all day."

Nook shook her head.

"I'll be here when you wake," he promised.

She sighed and let the darkness claim her.

11

READING THE TREES

Nook's hair was in his mouth. Jal had taken over watch in the night, and Lev had positioned his pack under Nook's head in place of his thigh and laid down beside her. He was sure her hair had been flat and managed when he slipped into sleep, but now it was all the way over the pack, tickling his nose and sticking to the corner of his lips. His stomach dropped when he sat up and saw Nook's sister glaring at him from across the fire, knife in hand as she whittled a stick down to nothing. There was a whole mess of shavings at her feet.

Nook woke when he sat up. Her eyes narrowed on his face, and he wondered how badly his bruises deepened in the night. Still, when he tried a smile, she returned it and pushed off the ground, wishing him a good morning. Nook glanced about. The sight of her sister's fury quieted Nook in a way that made Lev's skin crawl. He hadn't seen her so cowed since their first steps into Midhaven. But from the interactions he'd seen between Nook and her people, he understood that he wasn't in a position to say anything. So he moved cautiously and spoke little as Bough scowled through the morning, not even gentle murmurs from River easing the furrow in her brow. They made a sullen group as they packed up and traveled, Bough setting a pace that had Felicity wincing from her ankle. Lev's rib ached, but he refused to let it show.

They would make it to their destination in only a few hours. A small pond that Lev often avoided. He knew other smugglers liked to camp there since the water was rarely compromised. Nook was still quiet at the front of their procession. Lev keenly felt the missed time with her. If Bough's mood had been better, Nook would have been at his side, laughing and talking with him and Felicity. Instead, Bough had kept Nook at her side and continued with a steady stream of hissed dialogue as Nook nodded and watched the ground. Lev constantly stifled the urge to go to her. He hadn't realized how accustomed he'd grown to positioning himself at her side. It was unnatural now to stay away. He sensed every inch of cold air between them and wanted to close the distance.

Felicity was dour today, too, still so angry with Lev for the marks on his arms and the betrayal they signified. She had agreed to continue traveling with him when faced with the option of returning to Midhaven or keeping to their original plan. Bough refused to offer Felicity or the rebellion Unmourned aid. So, Lev walked with Felicity's hard stare at his back and Bough's coldness in the front.

Lev distracted himself by talking with River or Jal, always keeping to the shallow topics that wouldn't make Bough glance back with a glare.

"We'll be right back," River called suddenly.

Bough looked ready to argue, but River pointed out some small droppings to Lev and tugged him off the trail to follow them, shifting his grip on his bow. Lev followed suit, grateful for the chance to take a full breath away from the group's strain.

They wove silently through the trees. Lev studied how River moved. Like Nook, he didn't have to watch the ground. He knew where to step, never stumbling or hesitating with his foot placement. River used the trees more than Nook did. She tended to duck under obstacles, but River climbed over. At one point, he took to the trees, jumping from branch to branch with more confidence than Lev could imagine obtaining after his few years of practice. When they'd found their prey and shot their arrows, Lev asked the question gnawing at him since he'd begun traveling with Nook.

"You look at the trees the same way," he said. "You and Nook. You look at the trees and listen the same way."

River smiled. "We're reading them. And listening to the birds. They sing differently for everyone, but our people have always had a special connection with them. They're quieter around you and Jal but still vocal. Other outsiders make them take flight or hide. I had to get away from Felicity. I don't know how Nook's been putting up with the silence."

"What do the carvings say? I thought they were warnings about the road."

River stepped to the nearest tree. It was old, scarred by fire, and towering above them. River hoisted himself up onto a branch just above his head and, once seated, pointed at a place in the bark above a knoll. Lev climbed to River's level to look.

"This is a more embarrassing example, but this is Tuft's writing. She's an aunt of mine. The dip here in her etching marks this as a place of significance for her. Likely, it's where her daughter was conceived, considering how close we are to the road." River cleared his throat and gestured to another symbol nearby, then at their prey. "This has always been a good place for rabbits. And this higher mark indicates there is water nearby. The pond where we're stopping is that way." River pointed.

"You can tell all that from a couple marks?"

"Yes. We leave them through the forest." River squinted, jumped down, and led them over a few trees. "Here. This one is Nook's. She's not as diligent about leaving them and rarely leaves behind information besides her name. She... doesn't appreciate being followed. But this curve is her family's; Bough and Meadow use it, too. The two lines show it's Nook, the second daughter. The three dots complete it. This was from a while ago. We look to the heights and how the tree has healed around them. Usually, we just pay attention to the fresh ones. This one is so low I'd say Nook was thirteen when she left it—before she turned sneakier with her rebellions."

Lev nodded and traced the mark, committing it to memory. They picked up their kills. On the way back, River pointed out a fresh carving of Bough's, proving they were on the right path, their group only a short distance ahead.

"How much can you read from that?"

River's fingers brushed the mark in the wood, a different, softer smile playing on his lips. "I can tell what part of the year it is. Which direction she's coming from and heading. That she has outsiders with her. And that she's furious."

"You can tell all that from the symbols?"

"Not all of it from the symbols. The last part I can tell because she really dug into the wood." River laughed, and Lev grinned uneasily, worry buzzing to his wrists for Nook.

"How bad is it? That Nook was with us?"

"It's not so bad. We'd be heartless not to help the occasional outsider. It's happened before. But that she was with you specifically and went into the village without permission... that's another problem. We have to be wary, and Nook has always been careless where you're concerned." The surprise showed on Lev's face. River laughed, knocking their shoulders. "I said she didn't like being followed. It's mostly because we've caught her trailing you too many times. She always insisted she was watching you to make sure you didn't try anything, but we could see it was interest. Nook dreams about the outside world. She's always been jealous of your freedom of movement. Jal always has to stop in Midhaven, and his relationship with Fullbloom and agreements with Bough means he can't go off alone. You travel as you wish, city to city. As

Nook wishes she could. It hurts Bough, feeling like we aren't enough."

"Why can't Nook just leave the forest? Don't the Unmourned usually?"

"Some of us do, yes. Not very often, but it's common to travel into Midhaven or the cities to try and get pregnant or do trade. Jal, Bough, Fullbloom, and I can't supply all our people on our own."

"But Nook can't do that?"

River shook his head. "She'd never been permitted. I think they've always feared she wouldn't come back."

Lev didn't have a response for that. What he knew of Nook, the tight hold they kept would be why Nook wouldn't return. They turned a corner and found the rest of their party just as the pond appeared. Lev looked to where Nook hiked beside her sister. She was silent. Her hair was annoying her. She kept angrily brushing it out of her face. Lev's protective urge flared yet again. Despite what Nook said, she could be hurt as easily as anyone. Whatever Bough was saying was proof enough in the way Nook flinched.

That Lev could ease anyone's pain was a sweet, unexpected rush. He wondered how far this power would go. If he ran to the front of their group now and took Nook in his arms, would she feel lighter? If he begged Nook to come with him, would she be better off at his side? He would do anything to keep her from hurting like she was now among her people.

Was it possible that Lev could make someone else's life better? That he could put in enough effort to make Nook happy? Could he deserve the interest she showed? Memories of the past bubbled, trying to drown the hope. Lev shoved them aside.

Nook looked back, and Lev offered her a small smile. Her shoulders relaxed, and her attention lingered. Lev brimmed with so much feeling he clenched his fists to keep it contained.

It was midday when they stopped at the pond—a soft oval of

clear water. Insects bobbed, and the ripples of fish dotted the surface. The dirt beneath their feet was soft from the rain and speckled with round, gray stones. They decided to rest and eat before heading their separate ways. Fullbloom and Jal started a fire for the rabbits Lev and River carried. Bough stepped close to River's side and helped gut and skin the animals, her movements unnecessarily vicious and her eyes constantly straying to narrow in her sister's direction. Nook knelt at Felicity's feet, checking over her ankle and frowning.

"I'll rewrap it and put something on to help the pain," she decided. "But you'll have to go slow."

"Do you think I could soak it in the pond?"

Nook twisted on her knees and squinted at the trees. Bough, River, and Fullbloom did the same. Felicity looked to Jal, questioning. He shrugged. "They do this a lot. You get used to it."

After exchanging nods with the other Unmourned, Nook turned back to Felicity. "The water is clear. You should be fine."

"Why wouldn't it be clear?"

"Sometimes water sources get poisoned, either by trees or growing things. Sometimes there are creatures in the water."

Felicity nodded slowly, but she waited until Jal had dipped his head in the pond and shook his hair out before she trusted it enough to put her feet in the cool shallows. She sighed in bliss at the water's touch.

Lev saw Bough take Nook's arm and pull her to the side as the rest removed packs and pulled out supplies for lunch. Apparently, she wasn't finished with her lecture. River glanced continually over his shoulder to check the sisters.

They spoke in low voices, Nook mostly avoiding her sister's eyes and frowning. She fidgeted with the hem of her tunic and nodded occasionally. At one point, she looked over to their makeshift camp. Lev caught and held her eyes and watched the decision settle in her features. She offered him a half smile with those twisting lips of hers and turned back to Bough. Unfathomable hope began to rise in Lev's chest. He found himself standing.

"No," Nook said the word loud enough for Lev and River to hear. River stiffened, eyes going wide.

"*What?*"

Nook dropped her voice, but Bough cut her off, nearly shouting. "You will come with us. You can't put off your duty any longer. It's time for you to go to High Valley."

"I said *no*."

"You... you're... Oh, I get it." Lev stepped in Nook's direction, distrustful of the sneer that took over Bough's face. "You want to go with them, don't you? You think they want you? No, they want your abilities. You've always been careless, Nook, but this is a new level of—"

"Bough," River was at the forest leader's side. Lev found himself halfway to the sisters as well.

Bough took a deep breath but let it out too quickly for it to have calmed her. "You know what? No! *I'm* the leader. I'm supposed to lead! Mother chose me. Our people chose me. We can't trust you, Nook! It's my job to stop our people from making stupid mistakes that compromise us all. You aren't leader because *you're* the person making those mistakes. The only Unmourned I even have to worry about. Nook, listen carefully. You are not to go to Factumn. I forbid it. I order you to go to High Valley with us. We'll go there now. It's where you will serve our people best and rid you of this ridiculous temptation and—"

"I said no." Nook's eyes were wide. She swallowed hard but shifted her stance and lifted her chin. "They need my help. Felicity is still recovering, and Lev is hurt. I'm going. And I'm going to see the city. "

A humorless laugh left Bough and made Nook flinch. "Nook," Bough's voice was low. River's strained features exposed his worry. Lev could tell this fight had been building for a long time. River had been dreading this moment. "I said it was an order. Our people obey my order."

"Maybe I'm not cut out to obey your orders," Nook spat the words.

"Nook," River turned his appeal to the younger sister. She shrugged off the hand he placed on her arm.

"You know I don't belong. You know I've never found a place in this forest. You took the life I wanted. You can't stop me from finding my own path."

"I can if it's for your own good."

"Really? How?"

"Nook. You know the power I hold. This is my forest. Our people are my people. All of it is my responsibility. You leave with this boy now, you break my command, you choose some masked bandit over your family, and I *will* banish you. You'll no longer be welcome in our havens. In High Valley. In our hearts. We will no longer speak your name."

Nook stumbled back a step. "You'd do that? Just because I want to see a city? Because I want—"

"It doesn't matter what you *want*. Grow up, Nook. Accept your role. It's that easy."

Nook's shoulders sagged. She took another step back. "I don't think you know who I am. Neither of you ever tried to know."

"I'm your sister. Of course, I know you. I know you so well that I know what's best even when you can't see it."

"What's best for you isn't what's best for me. I can't do what you're asking of me."

For the first time, Bough's confidence stumbled. "Be very careful what you say next, Nook."

Nook drew in a breath and straightened. Lev hadn't even noticed how much she'd hunched into herself as Bough spoke. "Banish me."

Silence smothered the clearing. River looked ready to be

sick. Fullbloom was close now, tears silvering her eyes. Jal remained by the fire, face pale, head shaking back and forth in denial.

Bough's face drained of color, the only sign she'd heard her little sister's words. "Nook. You'll never survive a bleeding on your own. You aren't careful. You need us."

"People survive every day without the forest's gift. I don't need the havens or our people when I'm vulnerable. I'll just be like everyone else. Like Jal and Felicity and Lev. I'll survive without you. I know my limits, and I know what I want. You don't trust me; I know that too. But I have to do this, or I'll never be able to *breathe*. I just don't know which of us is failing the other worse." Tears slipped down Nook's cheeks. She paused to steady her voice. "I can't do this anymore. I have to do what's right for me. Our people will be fine with or without me."

"You'll regret this," Bough whispered.

"So will you."

Nook was shaking. The tears were running continuously. Her hair needed brushing. There was dirt on her chin. She wasn't sure about her choice; Lev could see that. All she needed was some gesture from Bough. Some offer of compromise. Nook's eyes went to River and Fullbloom. She needed one of her people to be on her side and not her sister's.

But Lev was the only one there, closing the distance between them. Bough's eyes widened at whatever look was on his face. When River stepped forward protectively, Lev worked to clear his expression. They all stayed silent. The distance between Nook and the Unmourned stretched until she couldn't stand there any longer. Nook turned and left the clearing. In the direction of Factumn.

Lev heard Coin greet her and knew they would wait until he joined them to leave. The devastation was quickly burning into anger in Bough's eyes. Anger she leveled at Lev so thoroughly that River raised his hands to get her attention.

Lev didn't care much what either of them had to say. He turned to Felicity. "It's time to go."

Felicity hesitated by her shoes. She scowled at Lev's arms, covered by his shirt. She looked to Jal, a hope-filled question in her eyes. Jal put his arm around Fullbloom, his alliance clear.

"I'll get you to Factumn, Felicity," Lev promised. By now, she likely thought his word meant nothing. But Jal would stay with Fullbloom, and Fullbloom would stay with Bough, and Bough was running from the danger on the road. Lev had no desire to face it either, but he would finish this mission if only because Nook was determined to.

Felicity signed. She didn't like it, but she quickly laced herself into her boots, plucked one of the sticks roasting a rabbit in the fire, and came to his side as Lev shouldered his and Nook's packs before taking up his bow.

"Let's go home," Felicity said.

12

NO EXPECTATIONS

Nook stopped. She didn't know how long she'd been blindly walking. Pulling in gasping breaths that told her she'd been nearly running. Abruptly, she was consumed by the fear that came with being entirely alone. She longed to turn back. Go to her sister and beg for forgiveness, but her feet were rooted in place. Because Nook also wanted to demand an apology that she knew she'd never get. Her body was torn in multiple directions—heavy with guilt and flying high with relief. Banishment meant no duties. No expectations. No more chances to fail her people. Nook swallowed the relief down. She shouldn't be feeling that. Coin shifted at Nook's feet, drawing her attention from her whirling thoughts. He was listening to the forest. His presence was a steady warmth. Nook pressed the back of her hands into her burning cheeks and willed her body to match his stillness.

In time, Lev and Felicity came up behind her. Felicity gave Nook an uncomfortable smile, but Lev's face was so severe. How was it he knew exactly how to look at her? Meeting his eyes grounded her completely. Reminded her, at least for a moment, that she was a person outside her title as an Unmourned. He knew to offer her his hand and lead them onward without addressing what happened by the pond. Lev started up a conversation with Felicity about simple things. He just knew what Nook needed, and it was incredible. Was it because he knew *her*? How had he learned so quickly when Bough never had?

Lev began telling Felicity about how he met Nook and how they came across Coin. His soft way of speaking filled the forest and dulled the roar in her head. He never talked so much. Even in her anger, Felicity stayed quiet to listen. Nook's heart was soothed by his version of the events. She adjusted her grip on his hand, interlocking their fingers and stepping closer to his side.

The story ended, and Felicity asked, "So... you robbed and saved her?"

Lev stiffened, his hand tightening around Nooks. "Yes. In my mind."

Felicity was quiet for a bit. "Why do you need so much coin? Why did you steal from Siana?"

Nook looked up at Lev. He stayed focused on the forest ahead, face carefully blank. Sunlight passed over him in dappled beams as they walked, highlighting his tan line and freckled skin. His multicolored hair and eyes. "I was saving up to buy more of the antidote. I stole from Siana because, with that amount, I wouldn't have to keep smuggling. I just need enough to hide deeper in the forest for a while. To stay away from it all until people forget about me."

"You mean hide from the war even more than you already do."

Lev's eyes shuttered. He nodded curtly.

Felicity sighed and pressed on. "Is it that expensive to buy?"

"It sounds difficult to make," Lev glanced in Nook's direction. "Not many sell it."

"How well does it work?"

Lev paused. "I think very well. No one who has received the antidote has died from mourning poison that I know of."

Nook found her tongue, her throat no longer threatening tears every time she thought to open her mouth. "It doesn't always work." In High Valley, not all the children were born with the ability to bleed. There were partners and families without the gift, and a protective wall of mourning trees surrounded the small city. Those at risk all took the antidote regularly, but accidents happened.

"So, it comes from the Unmourned?"

Neither Lev nor Nook answered. It was obvious, and Felicity knew of the Unmourned's existence now, but still, the habit was difficult to break. Confirming anything about Nook's people felt too strange.

"How is it made?" Felicity addressed Nook, undeterred by the silence.

"With the mourning berries, everbloom flowers, and some other things," Nook answered. "I never learned the recipe." Out of a refusal to go to High Valley and be slotted into that duty. Now, it would never be an option.

"Watch out." Lev reached and steadied Felicity before she could step into a hole. She smiled her thanks before remembering her anger and jerking away from him. They were staying carefully away from the topic of his marks. For the first time, Nook noticed the softening he'd had toward the other girl. His hand where he touched her was gentle and ready. It differed from how he'd touched Nook, but there was caring there. Nook's heart broke, seeing how he had thawed only for the marks on his arms to cause a new rift in their timid friendship.

He looked Nook's way as she thought this, and his expression gentled even further. He hadn't even put his mask back on. Lev's eyebrows were still bunched upward as they'd been when she and Bough fought—the concern frozen on his features. Nook stepped closer to his side. Her thoughts settled. She'd done it. She'd left. She was going to see the cities—or at least Factumn.

Nook would see just how bad things outside the forest were, but also how good. Looking at Lev and Felicity, she knew there would be good.

That evening, Lev stopped them to build camp earlier than usual. They started a fire to boil water as they passed around the roasted rabbit Lev and River had shot earlier. The thought of River made Nook's breath catch. He worked so hard to make them all fit together. Nook never admitted the feelings she used to hold for him, but he seemed to know. He'd carefully tucked Nook into the outskirts of his and Bough's relationship so she never felt like she'd lost either of them.

But she had. Just as she'd lost her mother the day Meadow motioned to make Bough leader. It hadn't been to hurt her, but Nook realized now that moment had sealed her fate. She didn't want a life spent in High Valley. She wanted to stomp her foot at the childlike sense of unfairness that flooded her sitting here with Lev and Felicity. This was the only other option she'd been given.

Nook couldn't eat. Lev sat close and ensured a portion remained for her when she was ready. Felicity filled the space with chatter. Nook's distress temporarily easing the tension between the rebel and Lev.

"One time, Tack in the kitchens was angry because Vasca had turned her nose up to three meals in a row. She said he salted it too much. Then, she said that the carrots he'd used were bad. Then said the duck tasted like rabbit. Hardly anyone ever pushed back. She had such punishments... but he was *done*. He loved to cook and was proud of his skill. So, the next meal I carried up," Felicity had to pause to laugh. Nook loved how she couldn't get through a story without stopping to enjoy her memories. After seeing Vasca, Nook wouldn't have thought there would be a memory in her service to enjoy. "He didn't drop his eyes from mine as he ground the salt onto it. It was some kind of meat with carrots circling it. I asked him what I should tell her it was, and he said duck and carrots. I asked him what it really was, and he said he wanted to see if Vasca knew what rabbit tasted like. I was scared for him, but I also had to keep fighting a smile." Felicity paused again, grinning. Nook knew some of the joy was forced for her benefit, but she played along.

"And what did she do?" Nook asked.

Felicity's smile twisted mischievously. "She ate every bite. She loved it. 'Tell cook that's what I expect of him,' she told me." Felicity laughed again, the sound filling the forest and startling Coin. "I think that was when I realized she was just human like the rest of us. And if she was human and if Tack could be so brave, then she could be fooled, and I could be brave enough to do it. So, I started listening. I started watching. And I found the people who couldn't stop the displeasure from crossing their faces when Vasca made announcements. I learned the chinks in her armor, and I found a way to free myself. And here we are."

"What are you going to do now?" Nook asked. "Knowing the chinks?"

Felicity looked to Nook and seemed to age ten years in the firelight. Nook had never seen such hatred. So much determination. She shivered and found herself pressed close to Lev. He sat stiff, staring into the fire with an unreadable expression.

"I'm going to slip a knife in," Felicity told her, but her eyes were on Lev. There was a challenge, an accusation, a dare in her gaze. Some protective instinct rose in Nook, seeing the look and feeling the tension in his body.

"Then *you* should do it," Nook said.

"I'll be right back," Lev said, standing abruptly and vanishing into the trees. Not before Nook felt him start to tremble.

Felicity watched him go with pursed lips. Coin followed, and Nook debated joining him, but after the longclaw incident, Nook knew she couldn't leave Felicity alone. She pulled out her blanket and, after a moment's hesitation, Lev's. She spread it

182

next to her in invitation and settled down to sleep, staring into the trees where he'd disappeared.

"Aren't you going to keep watch?" Felicity whispered.

"Not this deep in the trees. Don't be afraid. Nothing is coming." Nook hadn't feared the forest at night in years. The creatures knew to stay from the Unmourned and their fires. They could smell when the Unmourned were vulnerable. They knew when the Unmourned were untouchable. Nook wondered if she was sacrificing this power by being banished. Her stomach dropped. What would she do when she bled next?

"I don't know if I can forgive him for leaving Factumn," Felicity said softly.

"You don't know what he saw or how he hurts. Maybe instead of judgment, you should work on understanding and support."

"No one offered me understanding and support after what I saw. The world doesn't work like that. It's too cruel."

"You have to be cruel too, then?"

Felicity went quiet. Nook was glad when Lev slipped silently back into camp. He paused by the fire, taking in Nook's setup. She only relaxed when Lev settled beside her, tugging up his blankets and rolling close so his chest pressed into her arm. He didn't reach for her but didn't pull away when Nook scooted closer to his warmth.

His sigh shook, and sweat beaded his forehead. Nook knew regret then for not following. She brushed the hair that stuck to his skin back and wiggled in closer still. Nook had always found comfort in small places. She'd been named after the habit of hiding herself between rocks and under lifted roots.

Lev relaxed and curled his arm around her. Holding tight. Nook smiled as her air warmed the space between her face and his chest. The blanket lifted to fully tent her from the outside world. The silent comfort exchanged between them meant more than any words spoken.

IT TOOK two days for the solemn mood to lift. Two days until Felicity tried to duck under a branch, got her hair caught, and comically whipped back with a sound that made Coin bolt up the nearest tree. Two days until Nook's smile broke through naturally and Felicity stopped shooting Lev betrayed looks, and his bruises could be looked at without Nook feeling the need to wince in sympathy.

The world wasn't righted, but they were apart from it all. The three of them moved through the forest that had become their home. When the choice was to laugh or cry, press forward or constantly look back, mourn or think about what was gained, two days made all the difference.

The forest rang with laughter. Nook pressed into Felicity's side as she caught her breath, clutching the girl's arm. They had stopped for a break by a clear creek.

"Eggs?" Nook clarified once she could speak.

"Hundreds of them. Once, I left a little shell in the tub, hoping she would sit on it."

"I'm so confused," Lev said, only to start them all laughing again. Nook couldn't look away from him, basking in his unmasked face and the rare smile playing on his lips. The genuine bewilderment there was adorable, and Lev could seldom be described as adorable. His laugh gave her goose-bumps. Low and cautious, like not even he was sure how it should sound leaving his chest.

"Did it work, though?" Nook had to ask.

Felicity shrugged. "I think her skin looks like any woman her age's would. Who am I to say?"

Lev was still smiling, relieved when Felicity met his expression with nothing but shared amusement.

"Do you have to stay in Factumn?" Nook asked, pressing her cheek into Felicity's shoulder.

She felt Felicity's sigh. "I do. My queen needs me."

"*Your* queen?"

"Um, yes. Princess. Amalia."

Something shifted enough in the other girl's tone for Nook to straighten. She raised an eyebrow. "Amalia?" Felicity ducked her head, and Nook laughed again. "Tell me about Amalia!" she demanded, shaking Felicity's arm.

"I started working as her maid before the invasion. That's all. I want to help her now."

Nook snorted. She'd seen this enough to know what it was now. The Unmourned loved freely and helplessly. They all shared these nervous, fragile smiles right at the beginning.

"That is *not* all," Nook said.

"What else?" Lev asked. He wasn't smiling anymore but watching carefully for what he was missing.

The blush on Felicity's cheeks and the lightness in the air inspired Nook to go to his side. She pressed close, and he barely hesitated before tucking her under his arm. "What else is there that would spur her to cross the forest with a smuggler she doesn't trust and still push on after nearly dying of the poisoning?" Nook said.

Felicity eyed her carefully before her shoulders sagged. "You see too much, Nook."

"I see what is in front of me."

Lev was still against her. Nook tipped her head back to see him staring at Felicity, understanding dawning. "You love Amalia?"

Felicity didn't respond. Rustling leaves punctuated the silence.

"Do you think she'd be a good queen?" Lev asked.

Felicity frowned. "Talking as if you don't know her, Marked Man."

Looking distinctly uncomfortable, Lev muttered, "I want to know your opinion."

After only a brief pause, Felicity nodded. "I think she could if she were given a real chance."

"But you haven't seen her in years."

Felicity sighed. "I saw enough in my time at the palace. Amalia was smart. Generous. She was close with all her servants, not just me. She was dedicated to her studies, not just the ones on politics, but fighting. Even without Vasca, she would have become the first woman to rule. She loved her family fiercely. And she loved her people. She studied them and questioned their decisions. I haven't seen her in years, but I have to believe she is still the same. We were very close and young at the time, but my feelings for her have only grown since we were separated. What she's done to help her people under Vasca's nose and the rebellion... She is the best person to lead Factumn."

Lev nodded, but he was frowning now. His fingers absently tapped against Nook's arm. "What do you think she'll do about the engagement?"

"I think I'll get there, and together we can stop it."

Nook admired the fierce conviction in Felicity's eyes. She felt herself smiling again. Nook ducked in closer to Lev's side and was rewarded with a reassuring squeeze. He pressed his cheek into her hair. Nook closed her eyes, drawing in the forest scent mixed with his essence. It had quickly become her favorite smell.

The forest was full of risks. Nook had never known those risks to be without reward.

Nook woke the following day under Lev's arm and cloak. A light rain had fallen in the night, leaving his hair damp and sticking to his face. As soon as she stirred, he startled awake. Life in the trees bred light sleepers, but the panic that flared on Lev's face each time he woke to a rustle or unfamiliar movement wasn't something Nook had seen in her fellow Unmourned. She rolled to hold him until he relaxed and his heartbeat slowed.

She eased herself from under his cloak and the blankets, smiling at him as he watched her. Coin was curled up on Lev's other side. The furycat rose when she did and followed her into the trees. They were close to the city. Closer than Nook ever ventured. Mourning trees lined the forest bordering Factumn. The only safe break was the road's entrance.

Nook knew Lev had maneuvered through the trees countless times before, but worry still pricked the hair on her arms as she came across the first mourning tree. Maybe Lev could pass with ease from practice, but how would Felicity fare?

Gulping in a deep breath, Nook took the lowest branch and pulled herself up. She didn't go far. Heights twisted her stomach more than anything else. Memories of a near-deadly fall made her vision swim. She forced herself on until she found a cluster of berries. To center herself, she popped a few into her mouth, relishing the fresh poison that couldn't touch her. A reminder she was stronger than most. She was daring. She was safe.

Comforted, Nook emptied her pouch of the now shriveled berries she'd been carrying and refilled it with fresh ones.

By the time she'd planted her feet back on solid ground, her fingertips were stained dark red. She found a stream and cleaned them as best she could but made a note not to touch her companions until her nails were safe again. She crouched by the water, soaking her hands, and listened to the forest stillness. This close to the city there were no hatters to be heard. Only the most dangerous and stealthy forest beasts dared to brave the mourning trees and the guards watching for their movement from high on Factumn's walls. A few rats rolled in the poison and tried to venture into the wall's gaps. Jal had told her of the deaths they caused. Unease stirring, Nook turned to hurry back to Lev and Felicity. The next leg of their journey would not be easy.

Lev was tending the fire when Nook returned. He offered a small smile as Nook sat. Felicity was on the other side of the flames, facing the bushes as she attempted to coax Coin nearer. Her fear of the furycat was finally easing.

"What is it?" Lev asked, sounding anxious.

Nook realized she hadn't returned Lev's smile. She cleared her throat and spoke softly. "I'm worried. About the next couple days. You sure you can get Felicity and yourself safely through the mourning trees?"

Lev nodded, but the hints of poison hanging in the air's sweet smell had already paled his skin. Both he and Felicity were moving slower than usual. Not enough that anyone else would have noticed, but the Unmourned paid careful attention to the effects of the poison. "We'll get through. I know a path."

The worry didn't ease. Nook drew in a breath as she forced herself to acknowledge her real concern. "And then?"

His hands stilled. He turned to look at her, the full force of his forest eyes disorienting. Nook's unease tightened her.

"We take Felicity to her people."

"And then?"

"And then, you and I will figure out what comes next."

"You won't just leave for the deeper part of the forest?" He'd have his money. Access to the antidote.

Lev thought harder than Nook would have liked. Finally, his eyes slid back to hers. She saw the conflict in his gaze. A large, hurting part of him still wanted to disappear. A large, hurting part of her wanted to beg him not to.

"You wouldn't come?" he asked.

"I don't think I would like that. Maybe for a bit, but I want to see the cities. If I can't go home, I want to do the things being an Unmourned kept me from."

He shook his head, and Nook's stomach dropped. The sensation halted when he put a hand to her cheek and dipped forward, giving Nook time to pull away. The kiss he gave her was shy and sweet and far too quick. Nook's first. From the look on his face, his too. Lev broke contact, but only enough to say, "I want to stay with you."

Nook knew he wasn't sure if wanting would be enough. He wouldn't make any promises. Not yet, at least.

Maybe someday.

"I want to stay with you, too." Nook pulled in a breath, still fixated on his lips. It took extra concentration to get her words out. "I'm scared. Scared you'll get poisoned. That you'll get caught in the city. That you'll be hurt. That I'll lose you. I don't usually have to worry about these things. I don't like it."

His features lit with amusement. "I must seem so fragile to you." Lev crinkled his nose and nuzzled it against her own, drawing a delighted laugh from her. His easy affection was new and beautiful. "I'm not, Nook. I can take care of myself. We just have to worry about Felicity."

"He says while covered in bruises." Nook traced the one along his jaw gently.

His eyes were so warm, so content, as he gazed back at her. The invitation was there. Nook slipped her hand behind his neck and tugged his face to hers. They reveled in each other's lips and breathless laughter until Felicity coughed roughly and forcefully from the other side of the fire. The sound broke their kiss and scared Coin back into the shadows.

13

SMUGGLERS ALLEY

L ev made quick work of fashioning face coverings for them. Nook pulled a face when he moved to wrap her mouth and nose, but if they came across anyone, he wanted Nook to blend in. And there was the way Nook still acted as if she weren't Unmourned in front of Felicity. She never talked about her people or answered Felicity's questions. Lev thought Nook trusted Felicity, yet he could understand why she held back. It was the calculating look Felicity got whenever Nook or Lev explained a different aspect of the forest. The way she'd eyed the mourning wood arrows in River's quiver or the water Nook told her to avoid. The comments she made, constantly urging Lev to stay true to the marks on his arms and reassurances it wasn't too late, that the rebellion would still accept him. Felicity had come close to looking at Nook like all the other potential weapons in the forest. It was enough to make Nook hesitate whenever mention of the Unmourned or her family arose.

Nook was quiet. She didn't like seeing him with the mask back in place. Her hands twitched when he talked, like she wanted to pull it down. But the face coverings were necessary where they were going. When they reached the stream they would follow the rest of the way to Factumn, he stopped them.

"We should move quickly. Queen Vasca is still behind us, but I want to be in and out of Factumn before she gets close and sets her Swords to patrolling the wall. We will be near the mourning trees, so if you begin to feel lightheaded, let me know. I've encountered more than one body of smugglers who didn't even make it this far into the forest. Stay close to me and pay attention to Coin."

Lev turned to follow the stream, turning often to help Felicity when the path began to dip and slope sharply downward. They slid into the narrow, muddy, and rotten-smelling ravine only the smugglers knew. Lev had come across some of the worst members of the forest within this tunnel-like path, but never Jal. Nook gasped when she looked up and realized how hidden they were. Only the barest amount of sun slipped through the small gap in the dirt and vegetation above.

"What if someone is up there?"

"They'd be long dead from the mourning trees." Or would have read the warnings he now knew were sprinkled throughout the forest. The path became darker as bushes and trees covered the rip in the earth above. Lev didn't know if the plants hiding the crevice had been planted by man or chance, but it hid completely what was referred to as the Smuggler's Alley by those who knew of its existence.

"How did you find this place?"

"I followed a smuggler out of Factumn when I first—"

Felicity interrupted. "Fled. Ran. Abandoned your duty."

Lev rolled his eyes.

"The smuggler just showed you the way?" Nook asked.

"Well. No. He discovered me and..." Lev didn't get the words out.

"You killed him," Felicity finished. It was too dark to see their faces, but Lev could well follow their thoughts. Especially Nook, who had seen him fighting up close.

"The Marked Men swore not to use their violence unless it was necessary," Felicity said.

Nook spoke with uncharacteristic venom. "Most smugglers in these trees *make* it necessary. You have to fight them back or they track you or kill you and worse."

Lev went cold. What had the Unmourned experienced at the hands of the hardened smugglers in these trees? Lev thought of Remi's cold stare when they came across each other. The other man hadn't hesitated before reaching for his bow and arrow. Only Lev's speed in throwing a knife directly into the other man's gut had saved him.

That was one of the few instances in which Lev was disappointed his actions hadn't led to death.

The cloying scent of mourning trees was less suffocating down in the ditch, but it was still enough to cause headaches and fainting without a mask. It was soon too dark to see. He took Nook's hand, she took Felicity's, and he pulled them forward, squelching in the mud as he tried to avoid stepping in the stream and keeping his free hand on the damp dirt wall to his left. As he moved, he explained that the left side of the stream was less treacherous; using it and listening close to Coin was the only way he'd avoided falling into the poisoned stream or coming across other smugglers.

"What about rats or other animals?" Nook whispered. She gripped his hand tight.

"Coin takes care of them."

"What do the others do?"

"They wear thick boots and carry fire to watch their path."

"And why aren't we carrying fire?" Felicity asked.

"Because the other smugglers are just as dangerous as the rats. I trust Coin more than a fire."

"Have you come across other smugglers down here besides that first one?"

Lev didn't answer that. It was a competitive business. Smuggling paid well—better with fewer people out there offering to do it. Lev has succumbed to the violence of the profession, but he often felt he and Jal were the only smugglers who actively worked to avoid the confrontation.

Usually, Lev and Coin passed through Smugglers Alley without meeting anyone. Of course, thinking about the forest violence with Felicity and Nook with him, this would be the trip they shared the path. Coin came close and growled. Lev knew the wall well enough to know they were approaching an alcove. He couldn't yet see the light of their company's flames, but he picked their pace up to a run. The fire was reflected in the water by the time Lev pulled Nook into hiding and pushed Felicity behind her. Nook grunted as he pressed his back into them, but the alcove's entrance was situated where the smuggler wouldn't see it unless he looked back after passing. If they could stay quiet, they should be fine.

After their dash, Felicity struggled to calm her breathing, but the scarf around her face helped dampen the noise. If he hadn't heard Nook's grunt earlier, Lev wouldn't have known for certain she was even here with them. Coin scurried up the dirt wall and into the forest above. There was nothing to do but wait.

"No, I thought I heard something."

Lev was surprised to hear a voice. A muffled and vaguely familiar voice. In all Lev's years smuggling alone in the forest, Jal was the only one he'd seen with companions within the trees. Smuggling was a solitary job.

"You didn't. What were you saying about this rumor? I didn't even know Vasca had a son. Why hide him? Do you think he's actually hers or just one of her Swords she's promoted to stick the little princess?"

Felicity let out a gasp, her foot slipping forward on the mud. Lev braced himself as she clung to his arm to keep from falling. Her nails dug into his skin through his sleeve.

"What was that?" the familiar voice asked. The hair on the

back of Lev's neck rose. Changed after three years, with a Factumn accent and muffled by a face covering, but a voice he would know anywhere all the same.

But it was impossible.

"Nothing. Just rain. You think she'll really fight back? Use this sorry excuse for a rebellion she's been gathering?"

The man snorted. The sound so achingly recognizable, but deeper, rougher. Lev told himself it wasn't who he thought it was. "You do remember I'm part of said rebellion. You saw the aftermath of the first invasion. Amalia is desperate, and she should be. She doesn't even have her Marked Men to protect her this time... You truly didn't hear that?"

The men were right at the alcove's entrance. Their firelight flickered and made shadows dance. Lev was steady enough to place a hand on the hilt of his knife, gripping it as the men came into view. He was dreading what he'd see. The resemblance was still shocking. Lev stiffened upon glimpsing his brother's profile. Even with a mask on, Lev's vision tilted from the wave of knowing. The face he had looked at every day for fourteen years and knew better than his own.

But it wasn't possible. It couldn't be his brother. Just someone, some Factumn rebel, who looked too similar. Only his strict training kept Lev silent. That, and the strength of Nook's hand as she realized something was wrong and grabbed his arm beneath Felicity's death grip.

"Just keep moving." The smuggler tugged the rebel's arm, urging him onward.

Not before he looked to the side. Lev could have sworn their eyes met, but the man's expression didn't shift. Not his brother. It was too unlikely. The two men pushed forward, squelching through the mud. As soon as they were out of sight, Felicity slipped the rest of the way with a yelp. She landed with her legs on either side of Lev's. Still, he couldn't move.

"Who was that?" Felicity asked from the ground, more

concerned with the men than the mud seeping into her dress. "Do you think he was telling the truth about being part of the rebellion? Why was he in the forest with a smuggler? We should have talked to him! Do you think Amalia is already planning to use—"

Lev shook his head to clear the memories. "We need to go. It doesn't matter what he claimed. Remi, that smuggler, is dangerous."

"But if he really is part of the rebellion, maybe they hired that smuggler to find me and make sure I get to Factumn. We *are* behind schedule."

Lev stepped out of their hiding place. He bent to help Felicity to her feet. His movements stiff. He had to keep reminding himself that wasn't his brother, but his hands and racing heart refused to listen. "If he's working with Remi, it's not a good thing." Why *was* the rebel here? It didn't make any sense.

Nook had thus far been silent. As Coin returned to lead them, she stepped forward to take up Lev's hand again. She gave it a reassuring squeeze. How did she know he was upset? Felicity remained oblivious.

It was unsettling to be read so easily. The only other person who read Lev had just been within arm's reach for the first time since Lev abandoned him. *No.* Not his brother. His brother was probably dead. This was just wishful thinking on Lev's part. A cruel trick of his mourning soul.

With an especially depraved smuggler at their back, there were no complaints about the punishing pace Lev set. He only slowed when he felt Nook jerk back with Felicity's stumbles. Nook helped the other girl regain her footing each time while still keeping hold of Lev. He wondered if her grip on Felicity's hand was as firm. If Felicity was comforted by it the same way he was, even as the darkness crowded and all he could see was the imprint of eyes uncannily similar to his brother's in the light of the flame. Smugglers Alley had never felt so long. Lev's thoughts circled and dipped, darker and darker with memories. The words echoed in his head. Queen Vasca was nearing Factumn. Remi and the rebellion were in his forest. None of this boded well.

Only Nook's grip on his hand kept him pulling in air at regular intervals. The panic barely held at bay.

This changed everything, yet nothing. He knew Felicity well enough now to understand she would be even more determined to get to Amalia's side, and he needed the funds for the antidote more than ever. He had to get as far away from Factumn and the rebellion and the smugglers as he possibly could. The sudden glimpse of his past made the forest he'd hidden in all these years feel like a stranger. Not a haven but a trap waiting to be sprung. Lev wished he knew what Queen Vasca was planning. He wished he knew why the rebel was here. He wished he knew why Nook hadn't said a word about any of it.

He wished his heart didn't squeeze painfully every time he imagined leading Nook into the danger within Factumn's walls. Felicity had come into this knowing the risks. The rewards. But why was Nook still here? Why would she leave her family for this? He should have told her who he was before she joined them. He'd thought their first encounter would be enough to show her he wasn't some prince. He wasn't someone who deserved her. She was better off with the family who loved her and could protect her. He'd seen Nook survive so much, but judging from the persistent worry that creased Bough's brow, the Unmourned weren't invincible. Lev wasn't worth the danger Nook invited by staying at his side—the risk she didn't fully comprehend.

He knew he should end this before it became too excruciating to do so.

He knew nothing had made him happier than the feeling of Nook's hand holding his.

The thought of leaving her at the forest's edge, the most

dangerous part of their path, was unbearable. Factumn was large, and Queen Vasca's reach wasn't all-encompassing. Lev decided he would show Nook Factumn. Hopefully, a glimpse of the downtrodden city would be enough to turn her away from city life altogether.

He would get Felicity to safety. He'd be careful. Then, he'd make himself do what was best for Nook. He'd buy his antidote and leave this all behind for an existence that would never make Nook happy.

Lev's hands went cold at the thought, but Nook held on.

DIMMING MEMORIES

Factumn appeared to be a good deal sturdier than Lilstrom. The people there had their own stories of their origins. Escape from a land on the other side of the mountains jutting to the north. Now, those mountains were considered uncrossable, and the forest loomed as a constant threat. Still, the people remembered their ancestors had survived and believed they continued to carry that hardened strength that allowed them to settle here.

Their buildings were built from stones of the mountains rather than the deadly trees surrounding them, so even the smallest homes could weather any storm. The streets were filled with cobblestones that lent the city a constant tap of noise. It was often cold in Factumn, and fashion reflected how even their stone houses were difficult to warm. The stretch of farms between the city and mountain drew enough prey to keep some in leather coats, but now most relied on the road and trade with Lilstrom. The heavy tax and lack of pay had them choosing between food and layers. They cursed Vasca's name as they lived off scraps. They tried to remind themselves who they came from. The strength of their ancestors. Their Marked Men and how they once danced in the streets, clicking heels as loudly as possible for warmth and laughter.

They tried. But it was growing more difficult each year. That was the time before, and the memories were dimming. It was now after. What use was thinking about before?

Before Vasca. Before their beloved king and queen were murdered so brutally in the throne room. Before their princess was forced to carry out Vasca's directives. It was well known Vasca had taken anyone the princess had shown affection for back to Lilstrom. Black days followed each of the princess's small acts of rebellion. News came of another advisor, Marked Man, or nobleman's child dying. The city had always been small, the people close and adoring of their royalty. They hurt with their princess. They wanted to fight alongside her when the rebels knocked on their door at night, but if the people fought back, Vasca would send her Swords. Their princess could die. Their city could only grow darker.

So, the Factumn people went to the mountains. They stripped the caves and mines of the once admired gold. They died in collapses or they died from exhaustion or they died from not meeting their quotas. The people died. Vasca got rich. The rebellion tried to grow, but it was dying too.

Now Vasca approached with her Swords and a son likely just as cruel as she. The people had tried to keep their princess safe with their compliance, but what would marriage mean?

It felt like the end.

It felt like the city had failed their ruling family. The family that led them across the uncrossable mountains and survived the deadly forest. Many hoped the princess was as strong as her ancestors.

Many more had forgotten how to hope.

———

Night had fallen by the time Lev, Nook, and Felicity climbed from the steep walls of the alley. They were still surrounded by mourning trees and would need to move quickly, but Lev made them wait in the tree line until the guards were scheduled to change up on the wall. It was a rugged structure surrounding the city. The widest entrance was on the opposite side, where there was farmland and a path to the mines in the mountains.

Lev squinted. It wasn't a tall wall. The one surrounding Queen Vasca's palace in Lilstrom was likely twice as high. From their vantage point, Lev could see how low the torches beside the guards had grown. The guard change would be any second now, bringing fresh, bright flames.

Felicity clutched Nook's arm to stay upright. He should have given her a face wrapping of thicker material. Finally, the guard nearest turned to greet the other guard, relieving him of his shift. The newcomer's fire burned bright, blinding the two momentarily. Lev bid Coin a quick goodbye and took off silently across the short stretch of grass between the forest and the city wall. He didn't breathe a full breath again until the three of them were at the base and out of view in the thick shadows.

Nook's mouth dropped open. Tipping her head back, she took in the sight of it for the first time. It was likely the biggest man-made structure Nook had ever seen. She grabbed Felicity's hand, and they shared a smile—a breathless laugh. Lev wanted badly at that moment to drag them both back to the trees and relative safety. But with his brother in the forest, there was no going back.

The wall was constructed of boulders from the steep mountains jutting over the other side of the city. When Factumn first settled, they had piled excavated rocks to protect them from mourning trees creeping in. The story said that was when the people first found gold. Some stones still have streaks of gold or other shining colors, but in the dark, it only looked like a jumbled mess of boulders. The top had a walking path of planks and ropes suspended a few feet above the unstable wall to keep watch. The footbridge was built, and the watch began on Vasca's orders in an attempt to fully control trade between cities.

Lev led Nook and Felicity to his favorite spot to pass through. Many smugglers risked walking the length of the wall to enter the mountain side of the city. This brought them to the edge of the royal family's grounds, a place Lev avoided religiously. Some smugglers made their way to the checkpoint where the road and Factumn met and entered the city clinging to the bottoms of wagons, using stolen permits, and the like. Lev wasn't sure if anyone else knew of his entry point or if they simply couldn't fit through the opening he found when he fled the Factumn at fourteen.

"We have to climb, not high, but there's a hole up here. Be careful." He placed his hands and ascended the boulders until he reached the break in the wall that one couldn't see from the bottom. It took more shimmying than it had a few years ago, but he came out the other side with only a few scratches, as usual. A short, precarious descent, and he landed in a crouch on the street. He watched for Felicity and Nook carefully, ready to slow their landing however he could if one fell.

His heart pounded with the exposure of standing still. He waited for Felicity and helped her down the last drop. Nook was right behind her, letting go sooner than he would have but landing effortlessly. He noted her flushed cheeks in the moonlight.

"Are you okay?"

"Fine. Just don't love heights. Where now?"

"There's an apartment I use when I'm here. Follow me." It was less an apartment and more an abandoned attic space. The streets were quiet this side of curfew. Lev led them up the narrow, worn gray stone steps carved into the side of an old building half an hour later. Neither Nook nor Felicity complained when they entered the small dusty space. There was only a pile of straw on the floor and a stack of Lev's spare clothing in the corner with a bucket for water. Lev waited until they were as settled as they were going to get. "I'm going to leave a message letting the rebels know we're here."

Nook bit her lip; the timidness of Midhaven had returned when she realized how much larger the city was in comparison. She'd stayed close to Lev's side as they ran through alleys and the lamplit cobblestones. It was a good thing they arrived at night. It eased Nook into city life without seeing the streets busy and suffocating. Nook's hand went to the pouch at her hip as she nodded.

"Don't stay long."

Lev kissed her cheek. He felt her absence as soon as he left, mingling with the gnawing guilt and anxiety that Factumn spurred. His hideaway wasn't far from the rebellion headquarters, but Lev went to the opposite side of the street where a tavern was emptying of the last patrons who were willing to ignore curfew for a few more drinks. The air smelled of sweat mixed with the dust of the gold mines. Men and women slumped over their tankers, choosing the release of alcohol over the bliss of sleep. If the barkeep was in a good mood, he'd likely let them stay the night rather than face the consequence of walking the streets so late.

Mathers was currently behind the bar. He caught Lev's eye and tilted his head toward the back room. Lev ducked that way, mask on and body fluid so as not to draw undue attention. The Nightscape was an old building, the floorboards softened by scuffing boots and spilled drinks. When Lev had a delivery for Queen Vasca's men, he met her guards in the back alley of the neutral alehouse. When he needed to meet with the rebellion, Mathers was always willing to communicate the details.

Yalla was in the back, brewing with her gray hair swept back from her face. "Lev! Survived the forest again, I see."

"Barely." It was their usual greeting. Yalla owned the

Nightscape and the building with the abandoned attic Lev stayed in. When he'd first deserted, she had found him hiding in an alley, hurt and starving, debating whether he should go back to the bloody aftermath of the palace to find his brother or continue on to save himself. She'd fed him, bandaged him up, and asked no questions. He'd left the next day, knowing he would only cause harm if he stayed. When he came back later and asked her to sell a small cache of weapons he'd stolen from a guard post, she'd done this without question. Lev suspected she knew of the marks on his arms. He hoped that wasn't the cause of her loyalty. Either way, he needed his contacts in Factumn, and Yalla and Mathers had yet to report him.

Mathers came into the back and shut the creaking door firmly behind them. "Delivery for the rebels or the dogs?" Mathers and Yalla may be willing to profit from the queen's men, but there was no love there.

"The rebels. Have they been busy?"

Mathers sighed and sat on one of the stools. Lev did the same. It had been a while since there was news from them, but it looked like change was happening in Factumn as well as the road. "You hear the queen is coming?"

Lev nodded, working to keep his face clear.

"Word has it she's suddenly got a son, and a marriage contract signed fifteen years ago by the late king and queen of Factumn. She's on her way to uphold it."

"No one has seen the son, though?"

"Not a one. Strange, right?"

Lev nodded again, unsure if he should feel relieved or not.

"Anyways, Amalia's been throwing herself into finding a way out." Mathers lowered his voice, and Yalla paused in her work, shoulders stiff as she listened. "She's hired a smuggler. A man who claims he's seen the Unmourned and knows where they hide. She sent a rebel into the forest with him to try and get the Unmourned on her side."

Yalla made a noise of disgust. "That smuggler is a murderer. Get him deep in his cups, and he starts bragging exactly how he knows where the Unmourned are. Well, if stories are true, they can't be killed as easily as he claims he did it. Self-defense my ass. He went into the forest and killed some women just trying to make a life for themselves."

Bough's wary face flashed before Lev's eyes. There had been real fear there. The Unmourned were vulnerable only at certain times, but something had happened recently to trigger Bough enough to threaten banishment. Fear made people irrational, and Remi was a good reason to be that fearful. Lev softened just the slightest amount toward Nook's sister.

"Even if they were Unmourned, as I think they were—and my mother secretly agrees but would never admit it for fear of the forest dwellers—the smuggler claims he discovered their weakness. Amalia hired him knowing this full well," Mathers said, grave.

It took a monumental effort for Lev to keep his hands still at his side.

Yalla scoffed. "She's a good girl. Always has been, but she doesn't want this marriage. She wants to free her people. That's what the whispers about her promise. That's what the rebellion says they're willing to do. Vasca's always had threats to hold over the princess's head, but I suppose this one is worth the risk of fighting back. There are two Marked Men across the street now, maybe the last two left. They've gotten almost careless going in and out with Amalia's messages. She will pull out all the stops to prevent this marriage."

To be desperate enough to believe the stories, to threaten the people whispered about almost reverently, Amalia must truly be finished bowing to Queen Vasca's rule. After all these years, something had finally spurred her to action. Lev wondered if it was the threat of marriage or the hope of Felicity's return. Maybe both. Maybe she knew Felicity was close, and this was enough cause to fight Queen Vasca over a marriage contract. And Felicity was finally safe from the queen, at least for now. Did this open an opportunity for Amalia to be more reckless?

Felicity would fuel the flames. She'd gathered information not only about Queen Vasca and her Swords but also about the forest between them. If Amalia asked, would Felicity tell her what she'd seen of the Unmourned? Would Felicity tell her about Nook?

What power was Lev giving Amalia by returning her love? What kind of danger was he putting Nook in? Should he continue with the deal?

Nook was safer without him. She wanted to make this choice for herself, but why wouldn't she choose to stay away? Lev needed coin. He needed his options. Then, if he were brave enough, he'd tell Nook everything. Then she'd leave him. What else could she do once she learned who he was? What he'd done?

"The queen is close. She was right behind us. I want to get out of Factumn as soon as possible. Will you tell the rebels to meet me at dawn? Same place. If they can't make it, I'll deliver their package after the queen has left."

"I'll go tell them," Mathers promised.

Their goodbyes were grim and hasty. Lev was anxious to return to Nook. When he climbed back up the steps into the attic, Felicity had fallen into an exhausted slumber.

She looked so young asleep, but the calculations had never left her eyes. Did Lev have a right to judge what Amalia was doing? If Felicity wanted to end Queen Vasca in the most violent way possible, wasn't she justified? Wasn't Amalia? The princess had watched her family slaughtered before her eyes. Felicity may be the last person Amalia truly loved. Maybe Felicity had enough information that Amalia wouldn't need to go through with her threats toward the Unmourned and would call Remi back in.

Lev settled onto the straw and reached for Nook. What would she do? Maybe Nook would agree to help Amalia if she knew the whole story. Maybe it wouldn't come to threats and more violence toward the Unmourned.

With his arm around her waist, Nook rolled to face him and went up on an elbow. She pulled off his mask and traced his tan line with the gentlest touch. Contact like this was unfamiliar. Seeking comfort something he'd never been free to do. Yet Nook provided it. "What are you thinking about so hard?"

He shuddered from the lightness of her touch, the weight of her knowing. "I don't know how to make things right."

Nook watched him, open and trusting. Free of judgment. But she didn't know. She wouldn't look at him if she knew. "Do you *want* to make things right?"

"I think I've done too much damage. If I tried, I'd only mess it up."

Nook touched his forearm. "Do you want to talk ab—"

Felicity stirred, and Lev shook his head. Nook sighed. She looked a little disappointed. Disappointment was better than disgust.

Still, she kissed the tip of his nose, making him smile despite everything. She tucked his head in close and curled tight around him. "We have to leave at dawn," he told her, lips brushing her collarbone.

"I slept a bit. I can wake you when it's time."

Lev nodded into her shoulder.

15
DROP OFF

Nook stayed close to Lev's side. Though it was early in the day and Lev assured her the streets were quiet, they still seemed crowded for her. Nook's lungs felt compressed as if all the people around her were stealing the air before she could draw anything in properly. Buildings towered over her, up to four stories, but they didn't provide the comfort of trees. They loomed, building menacing, immovable shadows. Only the forest scent clinging to Lev's shirt seemed breathable. She waited as she had in Midhaven for someone to recognize her for what she was. To know she didn't belong. She clutched her knife hilt at her waist and focused on the warmth of Lev's arm brushing her own. She was fine. They couldn't hurt her. But tales of Factumners locking the Unmourned up... waiting for them to bleed and then—

Nook swallowed and reached for Lev's hand. He stiffened as he always did when they touched but recovered quickly and gave her fingers a reassuring squeeze. He wore a scarf around the lower half of his face and had pulled up his hood. Nook missed his face. She wished his eyes weren't hidden. She wished she was enjoying this after dreaming of walking through a city for years.

Whatever hesitance Nook was feeling, Felicity was experiencing the opposite—practically skipping, eyes brimming with excitement and relief.

"It almost looks the same," she whispered. Lev had to take the girl's arm to keep her from following the streets she knew well. Felicity's eyes sought the palace in the distance, the longing stark in her features.

Lev turned them down twisting alleys with confidence. Dust clung to every building and person, coating Nook's tongue and making her long again for the clean air of her home. It didn't make sense to her until she saw the first cart full of gold that hadn't been rid of the mountain dirt. Lev leaned in to murmur in her ear, explaining how Vasca made the people of Factumn mine their mountain and supply her with riches. The vast majority of Factumn's people spent their days digging and sifting through dirt. They returned home covered in it. Coughing it up.

Nook's eyes went to the distance peaks, thoughts of High Valley and the red clay dirt she'd played with when they visited their grandparents. She turned away from the reminder of the duty she was neglecting.

She'd never seen people like this. Lev whispered for her three times to stop staring, but the sunken cheeks, the empty eyes, the downturned mouths were hard to look away from. Like coming across an animal corpse in the forest. It was so morbid and final and sad. Her head turned wildly as she tried and failed to take everything in, attempting to make sense of a life within walls. That storefront, a child watching her, a man and woman in the doorway shouting at each other. Nook was lost. Entirely reliant on Lev.

"We're meeting here," Lev said, bringing them to a stop. He sounded so tired after only a few hours of sleep. She'd felt him startling awake throughout the night. Reaching for Coin but finding Nook instead. He was too tired to keep the dread from his voice, to hide the slight tremble in his hand. Nook pressed closer. They were almost done. In a couple of hours, their task would be complete. They'd be free to go back to the forest. She could take him to Lover's Meadow, the closest haven, and they would be safe to plan what's next. Away from the queen who terrified him and the war he wanted no part in.

Nook had never been more certain her dreams were just dreams. No wonder her mother had scoffed, and Bough had rolled her eyes. What did Nook, one person, actually think she could do to help all these people? She wasn't capable of making a difference here. She was just so small. A girl from the forest who didn't know anything. Who had to rely on a man to keep her from getting lost. Nook hated the feeling. She wanted to go home.

"Is it safe?" Nook asked. She'd never seen Lev so anxious. She couldn't even read his face. He even dropped her hand as they approached. It went to rest near his waist, reaching for a weapon that wasn't there.

"It's what we came for. If you want to wait here, I'll find you after."

Nook didn't bother explaining it wasn't her she worried about. She only shook her head. Felicity was silent, heart in her eyes as she reached for Nook's hand again. They followed Lev down a short set of stairs. At their base, he knocked on a door four times. The slot at eye level opened, and a deep voice rang out.

"What's your business?"

"I'm dropping off a package. Sent by Jarles."

The man's eyes widened. "We specifically asked for Jal."

Lev shrugged. "Seems Jarles thought the man was too busy."

A grunt on the other side and the slot snapped shut. Nook worried that was the end of things, but the click of the lock sliding out of place followed. Lev pulled in a steadying breath.

Nook resisted the urge to reach for his hand again. She gripped the hilt of her knife instead.

The man held the door. "You didn't give them much warning. They're still on their way. I'll be upstairs if you need anything."

They could all feel Lev's frown, but he only nodded curtly in response. They went downstairs to wait. The dirt floor at the base of the creaking steps was packed in well, but Nook still envisioned it rising, clouding, and choking as it had outside. In this confined and windowless space... Nook swallowed. She had never felt further from the Unmourned. She missed her mother's presence. She missed River and Bough's ability to whisk away her problems. This was worse than the trees. Worse than Smuggler's Alley. Nook could walk the entire room in a handful of steps, yet she felt the panic of being lost.

Felicity paced. Lev stood with utter stillness in a way he never did in the forest. Posture straight and rigid. It was like he wasn't there with them, making everything worse. But then, Nook realized how much harder this was for him. Shut inside his mind, it had taken Nook this long just to begin to read Lev.

What she saw made her feel silly for her panic.

He felt her eyes and finally unfroze, looking Nook's way. Maybe later she would laugh at how he read her just as well as she did him. His brows bunched with worry that mirrored her own. They watched each other with deepening concern as the minutes ticked by. As the walls crept in. Nook couldn't take it. She started for the stairs, reaching to take Lev's hand as she passed. She would get them out. They could find another way to get Felicity to the princess, but she couldn't stand this basement cage and the dark feeling sinking her stomach any longer. The door swung open before her foot found the first step. Nook jumped back into Lev's chest. He steadied her and pulled her to stand at his side as the rebels filtered in, Felicity's breath catching audibly with excitement.

First to reach the basement room was a tall man wearing a protective layer of leather. A night-black mourning wood staff was tied across his back, and his bare arms were marked with branches, thorns, and berries like Lev's. The man seemed surprised, and the brief widening of his eyes as he took in Nook, Lev, and Felicity erased years from his face. He was just a boy. Maybe even younger than Nook.

Next came another older man armed with a bow. Then another. And then—

Felicity gasped and ran forward. "Amalia!"

The princess also sported a mourning wood staff, but the arms she opened for Felicity were unmarked. Amalia was tall and muscled, her hair tied into an unforgiving braid. Still, she buried her face in Felicity's neck and clung to her with a desperation that squeezed Nook's heart.

"I can't believe you are here," the princess whispered. At that moment, she sounded much younger than her nineteen years. It was easy to imagine her seeking comfort from Felicity, her maid, then trusted friend, then more.

The princess finally loosened her hold, stepping back slightly to frame Felicity's face with her hands. "You look exhausted. Was the journey horrible?"

"Not so bad, no. How are you?"

The princess opened her mouth to answer, but the Marked Man cleared his throat. "We must get back to the palace before you are missed, Your Grace."

Amalia nodded and turned toward Lev, eyes narrowing and hands straightening the skirt of her plain but impeccable dress, the only tell of her nerves. Nook had never seen such a clean garment. Lev remained perfectly still. His eyes were entirely blank, body at attention. He felt years away.

Nook wasn't even sure he was breathing.

There was none of the warmth Felicity received in the princess's voice as she addressed Lev. "You are not Jal. I am grateful you were honest enough to bring Felicity through the forest. I trust the trip went well?"

Lev didn't respond. He could have been made of stone.

"Well enough," Nook answered for him.

"And who are you?" Amalia asked her.

"Nook."

"Nook? That's your name?"

Nook didn't feel that question dignified an answer.

Felicity tried to soothe the growing awkwardness. "Yes. She helped us get through the forest." Felicity offered them both a smile. The princess's gaze shifted. Sharpened. Felicity seemed to be telling Amalia something with her eyes, something Nook didn't know her well enough to decipher. Lev didn't like it. He finally moved, stepping forward and gently tugging Nook behind him.

"My payment?" he asked.

"First, I need your word that you will tell no one about this. You did not see me. You never escorted Felicity. You were not here."

Lev nodded.

Amalia's eyes narrowed. "I said your word."

Lev cleared his throat to speak. Amalia crossed her arms and cut in first. "You would swear to the queen while hiding your face? Do you know nothing of vows and honesty, smuggler?"

"I confess I know little." Lev made no move to remove the scarf.

"You know some to return Felicity unharmed."

"Nearly unharmed."

Alarm flared across Amalia's face as she turned back to Felicity.

Felicity's cheeks reddened. Nook's stomach turned. She didn't like how Felicity turned meeker in the princess's presence. How hard she was trying to please. "It was a rolled ankle and a small amount of poison. The healer said it wouldn't even have killed me, but it was lucky we were close to Midhaven when it happened."

Amalia's lips pursed, and her eyes lingered on Felicity before turning back to Lev. "Remove your scarf, make your vows, and I will pay you. Please. I'd rather not linger here."

"Then just pass along the coin, and we'll be on our way."

A considering pause. Grips adjusted on weapons. "Why the reluctance?" the young Marked Man asked.

Nook's heart sank, and she *knew* what was about to happen. The sudden decision on Felicity's face. "He doesn't want to show you because he deserted. He was a Marked Man."

Lev's eyes slid shut. He shook his head. "I just need my coin."

Felicity stepped toward him. "Please, Lev. You could help so much." She reached for his hand. He pulled it away, hiding it behind his back. Nook noted how it shook. With a frown, Felicity grabbed his other hand and jerked up his sleeve. He could have pulled away, but Felicity's grip was tight, and Nook knew he was restraining himself. Lev appeared to have resigned himself to the situation. The distance was back in his eyes.

"See?" Felicity said, turning with a smile.

But whatever Felicity was looking for on the princess and Marked Man's faces, it wasn't what they showed now. Amalia was pale, her eyes glinting. "Remove your mask," she hissed.

Lev shook his head. He didn't notice Nook as she shifted from behind him and closer to his side.

"Amalia, you have to convince him to help. He knows all about the forest, and Nook is close with him. They can help."

"No. He won't."

"But—"

"You weren't there, Felicity." Amalia's voice trembled with rage, her blue eyes icy and focused on Lev. "You didn't see how Vasca murdered my parents. Did you ever question how she got past our Marked Men? How she got close enough to kill them? *She* didn't. Her Sword did. I still remember it so clearly. I was at their side when the Marked Man, hooded as they used to be, arms bare to show the marks, moved forward and so quickly, so precisely sliced both of their throats after Vasca's nod. He turned to me, and I realized I didn't know him. I knew all the Marked Men, but I hadn't looked close enough. None of us had. He glanced at Vasca, and when she shook her head, he didn't kill me." Amalia turned her full attention to Lev. "I wished so many times you had in those first days. You remember it? Do you remember killing them? Do you remember how I screamed? How you left me covered in their blood and returned to Vasca's side like a good little dog?"

The room was silent. Still. Strangely peaceful as Amalia's voice filled the space and painted the horrifying memory. The quiet allowed her following words to ring out even more clearly. "Kill him."

An archer drew his bow so quickly even River would have been impressed. Though he would have shaken his head to see what Nook did next. There was no thought. Her body didn't care about the crime Amalia had set at Lev's feet. All Nook saw was Lev's eyes under his hood, the wheeze of him struggling to breathe, how not even his clenching fists hid the shaking of his hands.

All she saw was the young boy in the forest, wonder in his eyes as Nook handed him a baby furycat. Looking back and seeing the pain on his face when he beheld its dead mother. All she saw were the scars on his body and the fear buried in his eyes when she touched him.

Nook knew she wouldn't regret it when she stepped in front of Lev—watched the arrow sink into her chest instead. Felicity's scream was a distant beast compared to Nook's anger. She deliberately grabbed the arrow shaft. She held Amalia's eyes as she ripped it from her sternum. No blood marked its tip. No pain followed its path.

Nook's fury buried deeper when Amalia's eyes lit with hope at the sight. "You're Unmourned."

And there it was. Confirmation of her people's existence. All for a boy. For a murderer. Confirmation was the promise of being hunted. Peace gone. The stories were true, and it would take another hundred years or longer before her people could be forgotten again. Nook had done exactly what her mother and sister always feared she would.

But Lev was still standing.

Nook twirled the arrow and narrowed her eyes at the princess. "We'll take our coin and leave now."

"He murdered my parents. He owes me his life." Amalia raised her chin.

"Your parents died three years ago. He would have just been a boy."

"He killed them."

"By choice?"

"No one was forcing his hand."

"Do you know that truly?"

"He killed them. It's unforgivable. Why does it matter?"

"Because I know him. I don't know you."

"You barely know him, Nook," Felicity put in gently. "I've been watching you get to know him. He hides so much, but I've only ever been honest with you. Please listen to Amalia. Fight for us..."

"You want to leave him to die again so easily?"

Felicity flinched. She wasn't able to meet Lev's eyes.

Amalia stepped forward again. Her men moved with her, protective despite their shock. "He was Vasca's favorite Sword. She ordered him to kill the king and queen, and he did it without blinking. She had his arms marked so they wouldn't know he was in the throne room. If you didn't know about that, what do you know of his past? How can you think you know him? As soon as he's in front of Vasca again, he'll turn back into her weapon. You haven't seen how well she controls them. I'm sorry you think him a friend, but he isn't. The Swords aren't capable of such feeling. Step aside. Now." Amalia let the steel enter her voice. Bow strings were pulled once more. Nook didn't falter, daring them to fire with her eyes. More than one arrow dipped with uncertainty.

As the moment stretched, Lev's breathing grew more shallow. He kept whispering "no" too quietly for anyone else to hear behind his mask. Nook reached for the bag at her hip, ready to be done. She just wanted Lev away from them. She just wanted to hear him breathe properly. She'd ask then.

She held up her palmful of mourning berries. Only Felicity didn't back away at the sight of them. Amalia was hauled behind her men, the Marked Man holding out his staff to keep Nook away.

Nook glanced back at Lev. He shook his head, just once, eyes wide. That was enough for her to be certain. He didn't want his would-be murderers hurt. He was good.

So good.

With fresh determination, Nook stared down the princess and squeezed the berries in her fist, letting the juices run between her fingers. She then placed the arrowhead in her palm, remembering when she'd first done this for Lev. To save Felicity. Nook closed her fingers around the sharpened end and pulled it from her fist, slicing the unfeeling skin. The Marked Man winced.

Amalia stepped forward, breathless. Still more hopeful than threatened by Nook's show of her gift. "Join us. Forget him, please. You could save us all."

"I know little of your wars. I know little of your laws, your road, and your history. But I recognize when an outsider thirsts for blood. I know such a thing can hardly ever be sated. The way you look at Lev, the anger in your eyes, that flash of pride when you gave the order to kill him." Nook shook her head, letting the disgust show. "I won't fight for you. You talk as though Vasca is evil, but you want her power as much as you want revenge. I can't imagine how your rule wouldn't be more of the same."

The princess's mouth dropped open. Felicity shook her head, full of denial. Nook pitied her. She pitied everyone caught in this blood-drenched world. No wonder Lev wanted to leave it so desperately. Nook stepped forward, dripping arrow at the ready. She addressed the man carrying the bag of coins at his hip. "Our payment."

The bag landed with a heavy thud at Nook's feet.

"Now move."

Felicity stood speechless. Amalia was pulled out of the way by her men. Nook reached back with her clean hand and grabbed Lev's arm. She pushed him up the stairs. At the top, she turned back and held up the arrow. With the room's attention, she let it drop and clatter down the steps. Everyone scrambled out of the way, suddenly no more dignified than scared children. That was the power of the forest.

Amalia recovered first. Skirting the arrow, she stepped onto the bottom stair to see Nook's face. "He'll just go to Vasca," she hissed. "He'll just use you. He's probably been using you this whole time."

"Then you'd better kill her first. That was your plan, right? Another bloody takeover." Nook didn't wait for a response. She nudged Lev out the door, licking the juice from her hand so she would accidentally touch him. He stumbled, still breathing unsteadily. Nook grabbed the front of his coat, forcing him to meet her eyes. "Get me to the trees, Lev."

His eyes focused on her. He drew a deep, sharp breath like he'd just come up for air. He nodded, and he walked, leading them at a brisk pace through the streets. Nook slowly realized no one was paying any mind to them. Something was more exciting than their strange hurry. Nook caught snippets of conversation.

Her blood chilled. Vasca was in Factumn. How had she made it so fast?

Lev only picked up their pace, expression hidden. He moved so easily, ducking out of sight, slipping between buildings, constantly scanning the area around them. Nook had complete trust in him, yet she was still surprised when they reached the wall without encountering any guards.

He hesitated. "You shouldn't—"

"Just keep going, Lev. They're all watching the road while she arrives. The Swords are still with her. I'm sure."

He listened. They didn't stop. His face already covered, they scrambled up the path cut into the wall, out the hole, down its side before Nook could process a flicker of fear with the ground so far away. Once their feet touched the earth, Lev took her hand again. They ran full tilt. A shout echoed over their heads, but the guard spotted them too late. By then, they were jumping into the trees, swallowed by shadow, Coin dropping to their side. They let the darkness of Smuggler's Alley envelope them.

16

THIRST FOR BLOOD

They pushed themselves hard as they fled. Faster than Lev had ever traveled Smuggler's Alley. Coin stayed close, and Nook kept murmuring to the furycat, mimicking his meows. It was like she needed to fill the silence but respected Lev's need for quiet. The sounds were familiar. Nook reverted to her forest presence now that Felicity was gone.

Lev was glad for the darkness. He didn't dare check what Nook's face betrayed. He couldn't even believe she was still touching him, holding his hand. Guiding him along.

But I know when an outsider thirsts for blood.

If she spoke true, she should have seen him for what he was. If she understood outsiders at all, she would have stayed far, far away from him.

Yet she'd done the opposite. She'd given herself and her people away by taking that damn arrow for him—the person who deserved her sacrifice less than anyone else.

He'd deserved that arrow to the chest. His hands felt warm. Wet and sticky. The water at his feet wasn't mud. It was the slick of human insides spilled and scattered along the floors of the palace.

"Stay with me, Lev. Only a bit further."

He struggled to breathe. He couldn't collapse, not in here. "Nook." It was a desperate plea.

Nook halted and turned so fast that he stumbled forward, but she caught him. Arms tight around his neck, she rose on her tiptoes so he could feel the warmth of her cheek pressed to his through his scarf. He bent, making the contact easier for her, but her grip didn't loosen. "We're safe. We're in the forest. We just have a little longer to go, then we can rest. I'm here."

Lev clung to her while his body shook, and his breathing refused to even. He pulled off his gloves and buried them in Nook's hair. He clung to her like a scared child. In the way his child-self had never been allowed to cling to anyone. He was probably hurting her, but Nook didn't feel pain. He couldn't hurt her. She waited patiently, whispering reassurances.

"I don't... you should leave—"

"Stop talking. Just catch your breath and let me know when you're ready to go again."

Lev nodded helplessly and stopped fighting. He let himself sink into the embrace. He listened to her breathing until air filled his lungs. He drew from her steadiness until his shaking stopped. He let the moment linger as long as he dared.

"Better," he sighed.

Nook still didn't let him go for another few heartbeats.

Exhaustion was riding Lev hard when they left the alley, yet still, Nook didn't slow. They hiked until Lev slipped into the distant place in his mind that came with too much physical exertion. They walked until the sunset cast the forest in fiery orange, and Lev no longer needed his mask. Nook pulled it off him as soon as she could. They walked until Lev began to recognize where they were. The birds sang above. Nook whistled with them without seeming to notice she was doing it. He'd never heard the birds so close.

"This is where we met," he said, breaking the silence they'd slipped into for hours. He'd lingered here countless times before, trying to figure out where Nook had come from that day. Trying to recall every detail of the encounter.

Nook smiled. "We only have a bit further to go."

A short time later, Nook turned them from the easy path between trees they'd been following into a difficult batch of bushes and then around a smattering of boulders and felled trees. If Lev were alone, he would have turned from this route long ago, avoiding the climb and scratching branches when so many other trails were available. Very suddenly, they stopped in front of a wall of vines. Woven into trees and covered in thorns, Lev had never seen anything like it.

"Let me hold them aside for you. We coat the thorns with the poison to keep outsiders away. Especially since the murders happened in one of our less protected havens."

Lev thought of Remi, even now hunting for an Unmourned. Would this be enough to protect their vulnerable? They already seemed wary and prepared. Maybe he and Nook hadn't doomed them. As Nook pushed the thorns to give him room to get in, Lev told Nook what he'd heard in the tavern. He couldn't yet admit who the other man in the forest was to him, but he let her know the rebellion was searching the forest with the murderer.

Nook's face was as serious as he'd ever seen it. "I left a few warnings in the trees after seeing that look on Amalia's face. Any of my people in this area will be on guard." Lev was so tired he barely remembered her stopping to mark the trees. "I'll just go leave a couple more. You and Coin will be safe in here until I get back."

Lev sat in the grass, barely taking in the meadow or the flowers closing their petals for the night. All he knew was the wall separating him from the rest of the world. That Nook was the only one who knew where he was. Lev settled in with his pack under his head and wrapped an arm around Coin. It was bliss to feel so protected.

Lev woke with his head on Nook's lap, her fingers in his

hair, and a small fire warming his front. The sky was full dark, and the wall of thorns around them was alive with the singing birds. He didn't move for a long moment, staring into the flames. Unease stirred in Lev's chest. What if the two of them had only worked together with Felicity to fill the silences? Even when the secrets of their group had seemed to hang thick in the air, Felicity had lightened every situation. What if his and Nook's lives were too heavy to bear when shouldered together?

A Queen's Sword falling for an Unmourned. It sounded like a bad joke Jarles would tell when deep in his cups.

Nook's fingers left his hair and traced the scars down his cheek. He shivered. "Who left these?"

"Guess."

"The queen?"

He nodded.

"Why?"

Lev swallowed. He couldn't even remember what he'd done to displease her in that particular incident. "It doesn't matter. You shouldn't have taken that arrow."

Nook rolled her eyes. "No one is going to kill you in front of me, Lev." Her fingers traced his scars again. He shivered. The lines on his face weren't meant to feel so nice. "Did you want to kill the king and queen?" she asked.

He sat up and held her gaze and didn't answer. She waited. And waited.

"No." He dropped his eyes. She saw so much in him. It was too much.

"Did you leave because of it?"

"You don't understand, Nook. *It doesn't matter.* I'm irredeemable. I did so many horrible things. I can't..." He couldn't even find the words. All he knew was a deep sense of wrong. He shouldn't be here. He shouldn't be depending on her and longing for her kindness.

"You were a child, and you grew up surrounded by abuse. You did what you had to in order to survive. Tell me I'm wrong."

Lev swallowed. "I'm a murderer, Nook. It doesn't matter how I was raised. I did that, and now I should suffer for it. You should have let them…" He dropped his eyes and examined the scars crossing his hands in the flickering firelight. So many small nicks from a lifetime of training. So many deeper ones.

"Lev. You were a child. You were wronged. I've seen you fight. I know it isn't you, or your nature, or your choice."

"You shouldn't have shown yourself for me," he whispered.

Nook leaned toward him. Lev stiffened. He was suddenly sure if she touched him again, he would shatter. She refrained for all of a minute before forcing his gaze up with a finger under his chin. The barest, gentle touch made him shudder.

"I see you, Lev. I know you. I'd do it all over again."

It hurt to let her touch him. It hurt worse when he pulled away. "You said when the longclaw impaled you that it would bleed later. Will you hurt for this?" He touched her sternum. She shivered this time.

"When my bleed comes the injury will heal. I'll feel it. I'll bleed what should have been lost, but I've healed worse just from my own recklessness. It's half the reason Bough wants me to hide in High Valley. Fewer opportunities to test my strength."

She should. Hide and be with her people. Far away from him. The thought shot a pang from his chest to his palms. Lev clenched his fists. "What do you mean? How can you heal but not die?"

Nook considered his question, lips pulling to the side. Lev forced himself not to stare at them.

"It's different for all of us. Some have heavy bleeds, some lighter. Some last eight days, some three." Nook swallowed. "Some don't survive their first bleed."

Even with the fire warming his side, Lev felt chilled. "Why not?"

"When we give birth, we believe the blood and pain through the process are enough to make up for the mother's invincibility during the pregnancy and enough to carry the child until they make their first bleed. But the first bleed heals all the injuries of childhood, and those can accumulate. Most of our children grow up protected and watched carefully in High Valley. In my lifetime, I have never known someone to die from their first bleed. But many still take great pains to be careful between bleeds after that first one. This arrow injury could be enough to kill some, but not me."

"How do you know? How do you know it won't kill you?" Now Lev was touching Nook. He'd taken both her hands. He needed to know she was okay.

"Because I have tested my boundaries. Few want to do so, but I know what I can survive, and I believe my people are stronger than their fear lets them explore. When I was thirteen, I fell from a mourning tree. I broke my right arm between two branches on my way down. I'll never forget the sound of that snap. It was the first time I'd really gotten injured. Then I hit the ground. A branch was sticking out through my stomach, and I must have broken both my legs because I couldn't get them to move. With only one functional arm, I couldn't pull myself out of the bushes." Nook smiled wryly. "I was there for four days. By the time they found me, I'd eaten every mourning berry I could reach out of hunger and thirst. My mother sat at my bedside until my time to bleed came. She cried the entire time we waited, convinced I would die from the berries and injuries combined. Bough could barely look at me. She was so scared. Yet I remember being calm. I remember asking them to splint my legs so I could walk around. My mother wouldn't let them; she didn't want to risk any more damage I might have to heal. So, I waited. And when my bleeding came...It was absolutely horrible. But I didn't die."

Nook shrugged. She pulled her hands from his and put them

to his cheeks, tugging his face closer to hers. "If I can survive the forest, I can survive you, Lev. And I believe the same goes for my people."

Lev nearly broke then. He leaned until their foreheads touched. "I'm so scared. All the time."

When Nook tilted her chin until their lips met, he learned that was a lie. With Nook kissing him, he couldn't feel the fear. Her lips consumed him, burning through the cold and hollowness and filling every corner left empty and denied. He clutched her closer, lowering her beneath him. At her encouraging murmur, he deepened the kiss, his body knowing what it needed before his mind could catch up. It needed Nook. Every inch of him always had.

LEV WOKE TANGLED in Nook and the blanket. They'd fallen asleep quickly the night before, even after he'd slept most of the day away. His clothes felt dirty and stale, and he badly needed to bathe. While Nook slept, Lev explored the meadow. It was larger than he expected. Across the small field of flowers was a shelter of thornless and woven vines and, behind that, a stream that ran cool and clear. Lev washed himself and his clothing, pulling out his second set of pants while he dried the first.

As he sat and waited, his eyes slid to the bag of coins Nook ensured he received. He had done it. All he had to do was find Jal again, and he could buy the antidote. When a sound on the other side of the vines made Lev start, he reached instinctually for the sword that hadn't been at his side for years. Maybe, for the sake of his own protection deeper in the forest, he should face his memories and use any leftover coin for a sword.

The thought brought him up short. He winced, realizing the image he'd wanted for his future hadn't changed. He still planned to hide. Despite Nook's kindness and loyalty, he was still alone in his mind. His imagination was so lacking he couldn't even picture a future where Nook wanted to stay with him.

His thoughts continued in a darker, spiraling direction until he forced himself into his damp shirt and found Nook awake and tending the fire. "Nook, if you hadn't met me, would you have gone into the cities?"

Nook considered the question. The tension Lev felt was all of his own making. She was as relaxed now as she'd been while tucked against his chest. Was she this calm every time she was in the shelter of the vines? He thought of the few times she'd seemed nervous. There was never fear on her face during those moments. Just uncertainty. Did her invincibility not allow fear?

For some reason, that chilled his hands even more. If she were fearless, they could never understand each other. She would never get the nightmares that woke him up most nights. Never comprehend the attacks of gasping panic he had to ride through to the end when the memories were all-consuming. She would never be content to run into the forest and hide. She'd said that. He'd known that. But it still hurt to have it repeatedly confirmed.

"I think I would have. I've wanted to for so long. Even if I hadn't, I might have eventually if I wanted to be a mother. We generally spend nights in the cities to get with child, and it would probably have been the only instance in which Bough would have allowed me to leave the forest. Though, she likely would have made me settle for going into Midhaven and someone Jal knows."

"Is it really so simple?" Simple wasn't the word, but it fit. He briefly thought of the families he'd seen over the years, the happy ones that hollowed his chest with longing he refused to dwell on. That happiness wasn't simple. Lev knew little of it, but he knew that much.

"Maybe not, but no one tells me any details. Sometimes, the

connection runs deeper than the night. There are city and Midhaven people living in High Valley, but they aren't allowed to return home. I think Bough told them not to explain how they ended up there. I ask too many questions about the cities as it is."

"Do you want to be a mother?" The question made his cheeks heat.

"I can't imagine wanting to be, but I keep being told that will change." Nook rolled her eyes.

Lev relaxed. His questions persisted, though. "Why, though? Why are you so fascinated by the cities?"

"Do you really hate them so much? What was your life like? As a... Sword?" She seemed to have difficulty naming him as such.

Lev's instinct hushed him. Sharing was difficult, but he forced himself to remember Nook's answers last night. How willing she'd been to talk with him and only him. "It was both painful and mindless. Hard to describe."

"If you hated it, why didn't you leave sooner?"

"I didn't hate it. I didn't let myself think anything of it one way or another. It was all I'd ever known."

"Lev, I know you. You hated it. What kept you from leaving sooner?"

Lev sighed. The memories flowed too quickly to cut off. The urge to protect his brother rose like habit, but Lev trusted Nook. He could trust her with this, too. "I was part of the queen's second generation of Swords. The ones before me were three years older. She had thought they would suffice for a personal army, but she was young when she... recruited them. She learned their loyalty to her and the bloodlust she encouraged weren't enough to keep them completely obedient. I don't know what she did with those Swords, but by the time I have memory, there were only a few left. They were utterly devoted to her. By then, she had discovered another means to keep us in line. We were paired. Given brothers. Until the moment I ran away, all of my memories feature my brother." Lev struggled to draw in air. Coin pressed against his leg, and they waited for Lev to collect himself. He shifted closer to Nook, and she willingly stepped up to his chest, wrapping her arms around his waist and resting her ear over his heart.

Lev spoke into her hair but couldn't bring himself to hold her back. "We were always together. He's the closest thing I had to a friend, to a family. Whenever one of us did wrong, the other suffered the consequences. We were completely loyal to each other and therefore loyal to Vasca to keep the other safe."

They fell silent again.

"So, what happened to your brother when you left?"

"I don't know," he lied.

He could feel her frown and hoped she thought the worst of him for his abandonment. She needed to see him for what he was.

"Was it killing the king and queen? Is that why you left?"

Lev didn't answer.

"They couldn't have been the first people you killed."

He shook his head. They weren't.

"So why did you leave?"

Lev swallowed and forced out the words. A cold sweat broke out on his back and under his arms. He didn't want to lose Nook. He wanted to scare her away. He didn't want her to think less of him. He wanted her to fully acknowledge his horrid deeds.

The pain of war inside him was too familiar.

"I killed them, and I felt nothing, only my queen's approving nod. I knew the significance of my action and how much it would add to her power. I moved to the girl then, and my queen shook her head. I wasn't to kill her also. It was only then that I looked at Amalia's face." Lev swallowed. "I wasn't raised around other people. The most I knew of love was what I shared with my brother. I'd killed but never seen the devastation it left. I'd

228

hardly even seen a family up close until that moment. I *saw* that, though. I'd destroyed her." Lev sucked in a breath. "The look on her face... it wasn't something I could fathom or imagine. Suddenly, death became real, and I knew myself to be a monster. All that feeling that I couldn't access for years came rushing in. I experienced regret, self-hatred, fear... The look on her face haunted me. All the dead we'd left behind, suddenly, I knew there were people screaming over their loss. It was too much. I left. And now I know it's even worse than I thought. That look... it's still there. Amalia was wearing it yesterday. I did that. I broke her. She was just a child. The girl Felicity loves. Someone who is supposed to be the hope for an entire people."

"Lev, what you did was horrible." A shot of pain from his chest to his palms. Lev clenched his fists and made to turn away, but Nook grabbed his arm and forced him to look at her. "But what Vasca did was worse. You deserve to know your family, whoever she took you from. You deserve a real brother without constant fear attached. You deserve a mother who didn't punish you for tiny mistakes. You deserve a childhood of smiles and hugs and love. Not blood and weapons and turning off your mind. The result of you never knowing those good things, that is *not* your fault. But now, what you do from the moment you learned empathy, from this moment forward, that is who you are. And I see it Lev. I see you."

Nook put a hand to his chest and pulled his head down with the other, forcing their foreheads to touch. She kept him there. "It's okay to move forward. It's okay to believe you can be better. To believe in yourself. To acknowledge your potential to do good. To be happy." She paused, a hesitation so unlike her that Lev's heart skipped. "To love."

Lev swallowed and stepped away. Nook let him. He took the hand from his chest and put it to his lips. He didn't want her to hurt because he couldn't breathe. But he needed air. His head was spinning.

The war waged at full force. The one inside. The one in Factumn. Lev only knew that by running into the forest and hiding forever, he'd be losing. He'd be letting Nook down. If he were to be better, to find any semblance of redemption, he'd be ignoring the possibility by hiding. Her world was the forest, but he knew what was happening outside. He'd played a bloody and horrible role. If he continued to ignore it, he'd be nothing.

If he did something, anything to help like Nook was willing to, maybe he'd be that much closer to being like her. To deserving her.

17
LOVER'S MEADOW

Lev was quiet that day. They sat and watched the flowers turn with the sun and enjoyed the peace of the meadow. He kept getting distant, coming back to Nook only when she reached for him. He rarely reached for her. He kept opening and closing his hands, the only real indication of the distress he must be in.

Nook wished she could help. Wished she could find the right words. But some things a person needed to sort on their own, and the trauma of Lev's past wasn't something she could understand.

By the time they sat before the fire to eat dinner, Nook was so tired of trying to make conversation that she found herself missing Felicity. The girl's easy chatter and endless stories filled every silence between her and Lev. Felicity also reminded Nook of the Unmourned. Her absence made their loss even harder.

Nook was comfortable going off on her own. Accustomed to only communicating with her friends and sister through marks on trees for days. But knowing she couldn't go back hurt more in the stillness of the meadow. It ached so deep sometimes she thought she would be sick. Lev was struggling too much already for her to seek comfort from him. The hurts between them were so tall. Frustration pricked at her eyes.

Lev stood. He'd been giving in to restless pacing throughout the day. His hand reached for the sword that no longer hung from his belt. He'd done that so many times without Nook understanding what it meant. Nook shivered, remembering his skill in Midhaven. She'd never seen anything like him. She watched him moving even now, silent and sure and graceful and deliberate. Restless with the energy that propelled him through the forest every day, faster than any other smuggler.

She knew his ability came from a dark place. But it made Lev who he was. And she couldn't look away from him. She hated the distance in his gaze. He seemed so far away; panic flared in her gut.

Nook stood and put herself in his path. "Lev?"

His expression cracked. "Nook."

And he reached for her with a desperation she hadn't seen in him before. Even as her blood rushed and core turned molten, dread pricked the back of her mind. She pushed it away. She would take what he could give her. Take it greedily and savor every second.

Nook pressed herself closer, arms tightening around his neck, she dragged Lev into her space. The heat between them ripped a groan from him that flooded her senses. He responded by shifting, aligning, pressing. Every movement as deliberate and effective as his fighting skills. Every hard curve and soft edge fit together. It was beautiful. It was breathtaking.

Nook gasped his name against his lips and was rewarded with another groan, his body surging over hers, arms tight, lips claiming. She could feel how his heart raged in his chest, and for some reason, it made her want to cry. Instead, she clutched at him, matching his intensity with every breath and heartbeat.

The doubts vanished. If the world burned tomorrow, this

warmth, this heart-racing happiness, it would outshine everything else.

Nook murmured encouragement as Lev lowered them into the flowers. The petals were a soft cushion, the grass between them an itching poke. Lev's presence quickly drowned her awareness of it all.

His head lifted, and she saw everything in his eyes, dark with lust, with tentative happiness. With something she didn't dare yet name. He traced her lips with a shaking finger. Shifting to gentleness and sweetness, he pressed a kiss to her forehead. "I want to stay with you here forever."

Nook knew he didn't mean the words as a promise, more a desperate wish he didn't believe would be granted. A longing that echoed the tugging in her own chest.

"I want you," she whispered, reaching up to cup his cheeks. "I want all of you. Right now."

The distance and pain in his gaze darkened and vanished. He nestled between her legs so that through her clothes, she could feel every answering inch. She loved how he pressed against her, knowing she was strong enough to take his weight.

"Lev," she gasped his name, arching into his warmth, bending her knees to capture him and tilting her hips in invitation.

His answering growl stopped all further thought. Nook would take a thousand arrows to hear it again. They became bodies. Strong and sure. Pleasure and breathing and moans and love they couldn't yet speak. Bodies trained to know their limits, burdened with pain and healing. Covered with scars. Bodies that discovered the pleasure in sharing. They smothered each blemish with kisses, each memory with a smile.

They moved together and learned every inch until they were consumed and breaking.

The sky was black when Nook lifted herself onto her elbows, looking down at Lev as he slept. She traced the scars on his cheeks with gentle fingers and pressed a lingering kiss into his neck, rewarded when he sighed and pulled her close. In this moment, he was sated and relaxed, and every inch of him was hers.

"Lev."

"Nook," he breathed the word into her hair.

"Lev, I wish you wouldn't think so much. I wish you were always with me like you are now. I wish I could help you stop hurting." She couldn't stop touching him. The firm ridges and planes of his bare chest. The wrapped muscles along his arms. She knew if she kept it up, he would rouse again for her.

He was quiet for a long moment, but the press of his arms reassured her. He was still with her.

"I've tried so hard to distance myself from my past. It's easy to focus on day-to-day when you are only trying to survive the forest. Now, because of you, I have to think about it. I have to remember and figure out what it means to who I am now. I can't ignore that I am damaged. That I wasn't made for this." For days spent in a lover's arms. He nuzzled her, nose running along her collarbone. It made her shiver.

Nook nudged in closer, and Lev rolled to hide her between his chest and the circle of his arms. The scars crisscrossing his skin made it impossible to dismiss his words. He'd known far more hurt than she could ever imagine. He'd known swords and courts and battle and death. A world Nook had only glimpsed.

She'd known trees and fear and a different blood. Different battles. Secrecy that wore and smoothed and dulled. That created rifts and distrust and heartbreak. But they were both alive and present, and Nook wanted to make this moment last.

"I never knew it could feel like this." Nook let her hands drift and explore. Goosebumps rose on his skin in her finger's wake. As quiet as he could be, his body was so responsive it assured her and spoke of every need. And he kept it away from everyone but her. She'd seen how quickly he stepped away from Felicity. Even fighting in Midhaven, he kept his distance as he expertly ducked, slashed, and overpowered. He always moved away. Hid himself under layers of fabric.

But he pulled Nook closer. He bore himself for her beautifully.

"You make me happy, Nook." He pressed more kisses on her face, forehead to temple to cheek to jaw. By the time he'd claimed her lips, she had melted. He made her feel everything. Whatever he said, she *knew* they were made to share moments like this. To share the smiles he gave her as they began to move again. To be generous and competitive and laugh at small mistakes. Gentle teasing, gentle words. Careful movements as they reached their end. A breathless laugh. Moans and sighs. When Lev cuddled, Nook felt limp and blissful.

"Stay like you are now," she bid him.

"Hmmm." He kissed her once more before sleep became irresistible.

He was gone when she woke. The bag of coins left behind. Nook couldn't even force surprise.

NOOK SAT BACK, sighing and squeezing her eyes shut. She rubbed at her temples, thinking through the budding headache. It hadn't taken long to find Lev's path. He left it obvious so she would know where he was going, but he'd vanished into Smuggler's Alley long before she'd awoken. Two days later, there was still no sign of him. Not even Coin had reappeared to keep Nook company like he once would have while his owner was in the city.

Nook was alone.

She could follow Lev into the Factumn. She'd even traveled

through a thick cluster of mourning trees to look upon the city wall from the safety of their branches. Not being limited to Smuggler's Alley or the road, she could scale the wall at any point. She could get in. She could explore the city on her own. She had coin, and she would prove she was capable of caution.

But old fears kept her in place. The pangs of longing she'd felt for her mother since their last goodbye hit with a fresh wave. She missed her mother. She missed Bough. She wished going to see them could simply be a visit to ease the pain, but she had been banished. Any return would include groveling and a vow to stay. A promise to give Lev up and return to the High Valley permanently. Nook couldn't do that.

But maybe she didn't have to separate herself entirely from her people. Bough wouldn't have had time to return to Thornwall yet. Maybe she hadn't seen enough Unmourned in her travels with Jal to spread the news of Nook's banishment. It was a slim hope. Trees had likely been marked, and words flew like birds between their people, but Nook could try. She just needed to talk to someone. She needed advice.

She stood and brushed the dirt from her leggings. The weight of decision and direction was welcome, and she straightened her shoulders beneath it. Pausing only to replenish her supply of mourning berries, Nook slipped deeper into the trees.

It took her the day to reach the hunting grounds. A shallow valley where their prey often gathered along the river. It was one of Nook's favorite breaks from the monotony of trees. The birds sang for her, but Nook found herself missing Felicity's labored breathing and attempted jokes. She missed Lev's scent brushing her in the breeze. She missed the sound of him smothering a laugh. She couldn't help but look back toward Factumn. If only she weren't such a coward. He likely needed help. He could be in danger. And she was too scared to leave the comfort of her trees.

Nook couldn't shake the image of the people of Factumn. Every one of them looked like her people suffering their heaviest bleeds. They looked... sick. Hungry. Lifeless. Without even a flicker of hope. Nook shivered just remembering their haunted eyes. She'd never seen people so defeated. Had never seen bones protrude from under the skin. Was that all Vasca's doing?

Or was it her people's? Jal explained before how Factumn couldn't make fields to feed themselves with the mourning trees creeping closer each year. Nook's mother thought the mistreatment of women forced their ancestors into the welcoming safety of the mourning trees. Women had fled here expecting death but found untold power instead. Did that mistreatment justify leaving Factumn to starve? To depend on a power-hungry queen who stole children and did everything she could to form them into mere weapons?

If she could help, what did Nook owe them?

What did it matter if she didn't owe them anything?

Nook knew how to tame a mourning tree forest. She did it even when many of her people were afraid to touch the saplings and berries. Nook could learn to make the antidote and salves that would help the vulnerable who came too close. It was why she was needed in High Valley, to keep the poison away from their people who no longer or never bled or the few lovers brought into the forest to live in secret.

Even Lev, who had only known suffering at the hands of the cities, had returned to help Factumn. Nook knew that with certainty. If Lev still believed he owed something to the outsiders, if he felt he should sacrifice his safety to bring change after everything they'd done to him and made him do, who was Nook to walk away? She could do so much more. According to Amalia, Nook could solve everything.

Nook's pace slowed further, but by then, she'd reached the edge of the grazing grounds. Night had fallen, but Nook had never feared her forest in the dark. She pulled her knife and tested its weight.

She'd been traveling with outsiders enough that it took her

longer than normal to notice the lack of birdsong. The squawk of warning behind her raised the hair on her neck. Nook ran. She reached the small haven that served the Unmourned as a home during hunting season and found a ragged, gaping hole ripped through the side. Vines hung lifeless and shifted in the breeze.

"No. No, no, *no.*" Nook dove inside. The bags, bows, and quivers belonging to Greener, Ash, and Bower had been upturned and cast aside.

Memories of the attack that killed Misty and Harrow flooded Nook. Her mother had described an almost identical scene. Nook's throat was closing. How could this have happened again?

Was it the same killer? The smuggler they saw in Smuggler's Alley? Nook froze. Was it someone who knew there were more Unmourned to find after her display in front of the princess? Had this happened because of her?

Nook fell to her knees, ice flooding her veins. She had smashed those berries in front of the Factumners. Taken an arrow to the heart. She had confirmed her people's continued existence. She'd refused to help and called the princess out for her apparent bloodthirst.

Was this Amalia's revenge?

The sight of a large, bloody handprint brought Nook up short. Misty and Harrow had been bleeding when the attack happened. They'd been followed and tried to fight off the attacker but had been too vulnerable and surprised.

But this was not a haven meant for safety. The thorns weren't poisoned. This was only a shelter for sleep between hunts, a short distance from the cave where they hung their meat. None of the hunters had been bleeding. Ash wasn't meant to bleed again for months, not until her baby was born.

Whoever the attackers were, this was *their* blood. The knowledge brought a rush of relief, quickly followed by anger. If this was Nook's fault, she needed to right the wrong. Nook stood, head spinning. She adjusted her grip on her knife. She'd trained to fight for her right to live in the trees. To defend herself. More so against animals, but Nook could fight off an outsider, too. As former leader of the forest Unmourned, her mother had preached striking first before the outsiders had a chance to realize what they were. Before they could escape and spread more tales of the bleeders in the trees.

Nook quickly found the trail the outsiders had left behind. From her place in the haven entrance, she could see their path had run parallel to her own. It continued toward Factumn, the heavy boots of outsider men and the trail of dried blood unmistakable.

Her own people had left no trail, likely having taken to the trees immediately. They would have gone toward Thornwall.

Nook crouched closer to the men's tracks. One set was uneven, deep in the soft dirt. She quickly found their approaching tracks, a creeping circle around the camp, exposing where they'd hidden behind thick trees and rocks. The tracks had been even and steady before. Nook swallowed. One of the men had been injured badly. The other retreating path marked a long stride, and the heel of his boot sunk deeper. One had run. Nook followed the prints cautiously.

It didn't take long to find the body. It had been there long enough for some animals to pick at, but nothing like a longclaw that would have dragged it away or a furycat that could have eaten large chunks.

Nook felt nauseated, but she knelt closer to examine him. What she found didn't make sense. She marked an arrow wound in the man's shoulder with Ash's fletching. Her cousin hadn't aimed to kill, and there was no evidence of poisoning. It was the only wound Nook could find that was dealt by the Unmourned. The arrow must have been enough to deter the man, or some showing of their Unmourned gift had proved Ash, Greener, and Bower invulnerable, so they ran.

The killing blow had come from the slit between the man's ribs. The wound too large to come from an Unmourned knife. It was a sword wound. Nook frowned at the tracks, reading the running footsteps of the uninjured man. He had doubled back. He'd killed his partner for some reason. It made no sense.

Nook studied the body again, noting a string around the smuggler's neck. Now that she was closer, she recognized him from Smuggler's Alley. She pulled the necklace loose and found a wooden charm with a carving. The little fawn Misty had made for Harrow. Harrow had never taken it off. They'd noticed its absence along with other supplies when they'd found the destroyed haven.

Nook snapped the string of the necklace, freeing it from the man's body before she stood, lip curled in disgust. The forest could have him. It was more than he deserved.

Nook's anger flooded her enough that she nearly left then and there. But something was off about the scene. Nook studied the ground, hair rising on her arms. Whoever had killed the smuggler hadn't left a trail after. The killer *did* know how to hide their tracks. The footprints previously left must have been purposeful.

It reminded Nook uncomfortably of Lev's deliberate trail.

This second killer could still be in the forest. He knew of the Unmourned and was deadly. Fear spurring her forward, Nook ran, frantically looking for evidence of the outsider's direction. She would follow them, and— Nook faltered. Steps and thoughts stumbling. Her mother's warnings and her sister's pleas for caution rang in her head. Her family would want her to seek them first for help even though every moment counted. Every second could be one in which one of the Unmourned was in trouble. In which their secret was revealed. Someone else knew about the havens. Had seen the Unmourned in action.

Thinking of the havens and her people's vulnerabilities brought forth several fast and damning realizations: Greener had been finishing her bleed when Nook last started hers. She was likely back in Thornwall. Ash was untouchable. Nook wasn't certain about Bower, but they were too quick and clever to be caught... so where were Ash and Bower?

Cycle dates whirled through Nook's head. What had the moon looked like last night? The decisions and emotions of the previous few days had been slowly building to a headache Nook only now let herself fully acknowledge. She rubbed at the spot above her left brow and froze. A lack of appetite was usually the first indication she noticed, but with so much happening, she couldn't remember if she'd been eating as much as usual. Next came the headache. Then... Nook pressed her palms into her breasts, going cold at the painful tenderness gathered under the skin there. She'd dismissed it before, thinking her body sore from time in Lover's Meadow. But...

Greener would already be in Thornwall. Nook should be well on her way there, yet she was banished from the haven's safety. She could start bleeding tonight or tomorrow or two days from now. She hadn't been paying close enough attention.

Nook was out of time. The weeks had passed more quickly than ever before. Everything was now so much more dangerous and real. The killer could confirm their secret and knew of their havens. Lev had gone to Factumn, possibly to face the queen who had abused him throughout childhood. The princess was prepared to make desperate choices to avoid marriage. Nook had ruined her relationship with her people. By tonight, Nook might not have her gift to help her make a difference. She had to swallow her pride if she was to help anyone.

Decided, Nook tightened her grip on her knife and ducked into the trees, running through the forest on quick, sure feet from root to rock to tree base as she dodged branches above. She had to make what little time she had count.

She was preparing to swing onto an approaching branch

when a cold snap to her left had Nook whirling, knife swiping out with the motion.

"Nook!"

Nook barely stopped her blade from connecting when she saw who had found her.

1 8
SIMPLE WORDS

Felicity stared down at the new tear in the bodice of her dress. Nook's heart was still racing from nearly killing her. She knelt to greet Coin as she caught her breath.

"I wondered where he ran off to."

"He led me to you. Nook, I came to warn you—Amalia is sending more men into the forest. Or sent them. She wants to capture one of the Unmourned. She...she..." Felicity just shook her head, eyes frantic and apologetic.

"She's even more motivated now that I've proven we exist?"

"Well, yes. I was with her, and it was amazing and just like we used to be, but then she told me she'd just had a meeting with her rebellion leader. She sent him into the forest with a smuggler, but when they found some Unmourned, they fought back, and the smuggler died on the way back to Factumn. She... she's discouraged that the Unmourned weren't willing to fight for her. She's ready to use threats, to do anything to get one of your people to Vasca. Past her tasters and Swords and end the queen. She told the rebel, Pax, to return to the trees and do whatever it took to bring her an Unmourned so she could reason with them. All I could think about was you and how your family helped us. She wouldn't listen to me, not my ideas about using the forest, or when I told her what she was doing was wrong. I kept thinking about what you said. I love her. I love her so much. But she doesn't understand. She's hurting and desperate not to get married and to free her people. I think she'll do anything and I've seen too much of Vasca's willingness to do the same to keep her power. I had to warn you."

"What about what Lev did?"

Felicity chewed her lip. "I served Vasca for years. I've seen how she treats her Swords, even the children. I've done plenty by her command that I could hate myself for." Felicity shuddered. "Maybe I can't forgive him yet, but Amalia was wrong to call for his death so quickly. Where is he?"

"He left. Back to Factumn."

Felicity's face paled. "He went back to Vasca?"

"No." Nook was certain, though he'd told her nothing. "He went back to help. He hates himself for what he did. He wants to make it right. He knew this would happen."

"You knew there were people after you?"

Nook nodded. "One of our camps was disrupted. I knew they would come after us."

Felicity looked miserable. "Amalia's orders were clear. It could happen any minute."

Nook stood and continued the way she'd been going. Felicity followed. She'd gotten better at traveling between the trees, but Nook wished Felicity had the instincts to run like an Unmourned. Time was a crushing weight. She ground her teeth and worked not to take her frustrations out on her friend.

"Where are we going?" Felicity asked. She was already breathing heavily and covered with the dark mud of Smuggler's Alley. Nook acknowledged for the first time how amazing it was she'd come this far without incident and looked gratefully toward Coin. The sight of him brought a pang of longing for Lev's presence, but Nook forced it aside.

"To Jal's path. I need to find Bough."

"Even though you're banished?"

Nook snorted. "I still need to warn her about the people hunting us. She's my sister and our leader; she has to listen."

Felicity nodded and focused on keeping up. Warmth for her friend had Nook slowing only slightly. Felicity would never complain. She'd push as hard as it took to help. Her eyes were still red-rimmed, her lips tugging down. She survived years in Vasca's service, dreaming of the day she could return to her princess. It must have been agonizing to leave Amalia now after so little time together.

"Thank you," Nook said, hoping the two simple words conveyed she knew what Felicity had risked coming to warn her. The forest. Being close to Coin. Her relationship with Amalia after only just seeing her again.

Nook reached for Felicity's hand. She guided her friend to more manageable steps, away from moss-covered or loose rocks. The aid allowed them to pick up the pace. "I don't think it's right," Nook said after a time, "what Vasca is doing. Once my people are safe, I'll help. I can't live with myself knowing I did nothing."

"What if Amalia is right? What if killing her is the only way to end this?"

Nook considered. "I don't know. I just know it has to end."

"Thank you." And Nook heard all Felicity hoped to convey in those two simple words.

The forest dimmed to night. Nook felt the hair on her neck stand on end. The birds were quiet again now with Felicity near, but Coin was walking so close his warmth brushed Nook's leg every other step. She squeezed Felicity's fingers to warn her. The other girl barely seemed to notice. She was exhausted and willing to follow Nook's lead without question. She let go of Nook's hand when they stopped and leaned against a boulder to catch her breath.

Nook edged closer to the nearest tree. She scanned the bark

for a message and found none around her. Tension made breathing hard as Nook waited for the presence to reveal itself. It could be any creature in this part of the forest. It could be the man who killed the smuggler. It could be—

"*Argh!*" Felicity shouted as a form came barreling from the trees and tackled her in a tangle of limbs.

Nook relaxed for the first time in hours as she watched River fall to apologizing and trying to extract himself from Felicity's dress. Nook let out a relieved laugh as Bough followed him, barely stopping herself from tripping over them and making the situation even worse. Nook's laughter was quick to turn into a breathless sob and then Nook was tucked into her sister's arms. Home engulfed her.

"Nook! I was worried sick! Why aren't you at Thornwall?"

"I got banished, remember?"

Bough's arms only tightened. She ran a hand over Nook's hair, and Nook realized she couldn't remember the last time she had fixed her braids or worked through the knots. She ached to cast everything else aside and sit before Bough while she set it all to rights.

But she couldn't do that. Nook pulled away. As she let River pull her into a hug next, she asked Bough, "Have you heard from the hunters?"

Bough nodded. "We saw their marks yesterday. Greener's in Thornwall."

"Are Ash and Bower alright?"

Bough seemed confused by the question. "They aren't bleeding or even close. Unlike some people..."

Nook gulped in a relieved breath, pressing a hand to her sternum. Her heart had only just begun to slow. Felicity was now sitting on the ground, looking as happy to be finished moving as Nook was to hear Bough's words.

"So why were you coming this way?"

"Are you serious, Cranny? I had no idea where you were! You

weren't in Thornwall when you were supposed to be, and I was coming to save you!"

Nook laughed and pulled Bough close, hugging her and River simultaneously. River was silent, clinging as he did when he was worried. His quiet stirred guilt in Nook's chest.

Bough's following words were whispered in Nook's hair. "I'm sorry I banished you."

River let out a shaky laugh. They stepped apart, and River glanced around. "Where is Lev?"

The question brought a sting of pain Nook didn't let herself dwell on. She reached for Coin. "He left. Went back to Factumn without me."

"*You went to Factumn?!* Wait, don't answer that. I just want to be happy we found you," Bough said, pinching the bridge of her nose.

"Bough, we have to help them."

The forest fell silent in the wake of Nook's words.

Bough struggled to place calm in her voice. "We can't. You know that, Nook."

"We are the only ones who can without a bloodbath. Felicity, tell her."

Having caught her breath, Felicity returned to her feet and pled Amalia's case. Somehow, she knew exactly which details to focus on. How Vasca let Factumn stay hungry to keep them submissive, and how desperate Amalia was getting, ready to sacrifice her small rebellion in a fight. She didn't mention Amalia's plan to threaten the Unmourned.

"Why does she want the marriage so badly now? No one even knew she had a son," Bough said.

"It's another means to keep Amalia in line, isn't it?"

"Sounds like she doesn't have a problem with that either way."

They considered the question.

"It's about legacy," Felicity said. "She has power, but what's her future? What's her memory? If she controls Amalia and Amalia's marriage, she controls her grandchildren. There must be something off with her son for us to only now be learning about him. Maybe she's forcing him into this, too."

"Or he's worse than she is," River muttered.

"We truly know nothing about him?" Bough asked.

"Not even Ama has met him yet. Vasca's in Factumn now and said he got delayed."

That was suspicious enough for them to fall quiet again. It made no sense.

"So, how would we help?" River asked.

Bough's eyes narrowed. "We aren't doing anything until we've bled."

"But that could be a week from now! Just for me, not to mention you two," Nook said. "She could have them wed by then. And there's still someone in the trees looking for Unmourned. Someone who killed the smuggler that had this." Nook lifted the necklace with the fawn on it.

There was a weighted beat of silence. Nook didn't know what she wanted to come from this conversation. She just wished the timing weren't so poor.

"What do you think, Felicity?" River asked. "Can Vasca plan and conduct a wedding within a week?"

Felicity shrugged. "I wouldn't put it past her, but like I said, her son isn't even in Factumn yet."

"It doesn't matter. You need to be safe, Nook. We'll go to the haven closer to Factumn so you and River can bleed. I'll leave messages for Fullbloom and Jal so they can protect you while I search for this killer." Bough took the necklace from Nook.

Felicity stepped forward. "It's the smuggler that was bad. Not the man that killed him. Amalia only sent the smuggler because he said he could find the Unmourned. Pax is just supposed to try to get you to talk to Amalia. She's desperate for any help."

Felicity again forgot to mention the threats, but Nook would love to see anyone try to threaten her sister.

Bough gave Felicity a flat look.

Nook was immune to the stare and stepped forward while Felicity faltered. "We need to get to the city. We can help Amalia, convince her she doesn't need to ruin herself and hurt other people to rule."

"If we get involved, we endanger our entire people."

"Lev *is* in danger. He's, he's my people now, too."

Bough placed her hands on Nook's shoulders. She studied Nook for a long moment until acceptance finally filled her blue eyes. "Fine. But Lev is smart. He survived the forest; he'll be safe in the city until you're done bleeding. Then, we can find him together. We have to deal with one threat at a time. This rebel in our trees comes first, but I swear, as soon as everyone here is safe, I'll go to the city to find him."

It wasn't enough. But what could Nook do with her lower abdomen beginning to cramp? "Thank you, Bough."

They camped for the night tucked into an outcropping covered by harmless bushes. The haven was still a couple hours away, but they decided not to risk the dark with such a large party. They would wait for Jal and Fullbloom. River was settled next to the fire, stroking Coin's fur. Bough sat on watch, frowning with the firelight illuminating her profile. She turned her head quickly when rustling in the forest announced Jal and Fullbloom's arrival.

Fullbloom ducked into the outcropping, already bearing a smile. She reached and ruffled Nook's hair. "My goodness, Cranny. You are truly turning into the difficult child, aren't you? Meadow will have a heart attack when she hears about all this."

"My mother will be fine, Wilt."

"When do you start?"

"I think tomorrow," Nook said. Maybe even sooner, but she didn't want to alarm Bough further. Nook rubbed her lower stomach. The space between her hips had pulled into a steady, hot ache that radiated into her core, making her nauseous and slightly lightheaded. It would be a heavy bleed, although Nook expected as much with all the injuries she'd incurred throughout the month. She looked at the sliced skin on her palm. In a few days, the bloodless cut would be nothing more than a thin white line of scar. Maybe not even that. All the blood and pain the poison should have brought was ready to be expelled, the pain gathering deep in Nook's body for the bleed.

Usually, Nook welcomed it. A sign of strength and how much she could survive. She didn't enjoy the pain but considered it worth the price of her reckless freedom. Now, she didn't have time for the weakness. It would take more patience to bear this than she possessed.

Nook drew a deep breath, working to prepare herself. River gave her a small smile, already looking pale himself. He'd received more injuries than she'd realized in Midhaven. They would be suffering together. From the way he sat with his back to the warmth of the flame, Nook could tell the pain was beginning to set in for him, too. She glanced nervously at Bough. Her sister's cycle was about a week behind River's now that he was starting early. Nook would be finished only a couple of days before Bough began, leaving little room for them to face Factumn together. The thought was unexpectedly saddening. Nook used to dream of facing the world at her sister's side, back when she followed her and River around like an adoring puppy. As much as she wanted to believe they had both grown, she hated that, once again, Bough was going forth to face challenges without her.

Quickly, Nook filled Jal and Fullbloom in on the events in Factumn. Whenever she mentioned Lev, she couldn't quite keep the emotion from her voice. Bough sent her sharp glances whenever this happened, but once the story was out, Bough explained how she would search the forest for the rebel tomorrow, then Lev in the city.

Jal was quieter than usual as they debated the best course of action. Fullbloom was frowning at him. The silence and tension between them grew even thicker when Nook asked Jal for his thoughts. He shook his head and glanced at his partner.

"What is it?" Nook asked.

Fullbloom scoffed. "Can't you tell? This idiot is determined to go with Bough tomorrow. He knows Pax."

Jal sighed and reached for Fullbloom, but she shifted away, hiding her face behind her long, curly black hair, shoulders hunched. Fullbloom and Jal had fallen in love hard and fast. They'd spent little time apart since. Bough had already told Fullbloom she'd stay behind to protect River and Nook. They just assumed Jal would remain in the haven, too.

Jal dropped his hand. "I can help. I've known Pax for years now. He's the rebel I usually get updates from. He asks me for help but accepts it when I tell him no. He's a reasonable person and has Princess Amalia's ear almost as much as her surviving Marked Men."

"What will you say if you see him?"

Bough cleared her throat. "I'll offer to go talk to the Amalia."

They all froze, and Bough pressed on. "I'm the forest leader. It's my duty to keep you all safe. To get the threat out of the forest as quickly as possible. Maybe I can talk sense into her. Get her to leave us alone and maybe offer to help in some way that doesn't reveal our people. I'm sure we could think of something."

"I should go with you, then," Felicity said. "She'll listen better with me there. I hope."

Bough frowned at the thought of working with two vulnerable outsiders. Nook was still reeling that her sister had offered to go at all. But when Bough caught Nook's eye, she knew her sister was doing this for her. "I'll still look for Lev, too. Make sure he doesn't do anything stupid. It's the least I can do after banishing you, Nook. You're family. I should never have threatened to take that from you."

Nook had to look away, blinking hard. But Fullbloom hunched her shoulders and angled herself out of the conversation. River watched her, understanding clear on his face, and Nook realized how helplessly terrified he was, too. It wasn't right that they all had to be separated from their loves. It felt like an ominous twist of Fortune.

"Amalia will listen. It'll be okay," Felicity said. The conversation fizzled out, everyone thinking hard, searching for any alternative.

The tension didn't break as Felicity quietly excused herself for a moment of privacy in the woods. She waved off Nook's offer to join her. "I'm fine. The forest doesn't scare me like it used to."

Biting her lip, Nook searched herself for the worried anger Fullbloom wallowed in. Should she have been angry at Lev for leaving her? She was anxious, yes, but she understood why he slipped away. Should she have fought harder to make him stay with her? Did that mean she didn't love him? Well, love might be too fast a word. Except, she missed him so painfully already that it was the only word that came to mind. So, if she did love Lev, if she wanted him near her so badly, why didn't she want to react as Fullbloom was? Why had she woken up unsurprised to find Lev's trail returning to Factumn without her? Where was the sense of abandonment?

Nook knew why, remembering how she'd followed his path to Factumn. In the years before this, Nook had relied on Coin to find Lev's trail through the woods. He was conscious of every footfall in the same way the Unmourned instinctively were. He was nearly untraceable. Yet, he'd carefully left a path, letting Nook know where he'd gone. It was enough to assure her he planned to return. That he hadn't left her, just the forest.

Yet... Fullbloom had to know Jal was coming back. Unless

the worst happened, and the worst could happen to Lev, too. Nook just couldn't find it in herself to be angry he'd taken on the risk alone. It was too in line with his character. The character she'd fallen for. And hopefully, if the time came for Nook to act similarly, he'd understand.

Neither of them had been built to be protected.

Nook was pulled from her musings when Coin jumped to his feet with a hiss, startling River into yanking his hand away. When the furycat bounded into the forest, Nook didn't hesitate to follow. Felicity had been gone too long. Nook should have gone with her.

Panic fueled her as she ran, sprinting to follow Felicity's trail until it abruptly vanished. She stopped reading the forest and hurried after the sound of Coin's growling. But when that cut off with a yelp, Nook's veins flooded with ice. She was only a few paces behind the furycat, but the trees were dense. She found Coin limp in the dirt but breathing and yelled for River, close on her heels, to check him before diving through the trees in what she could only hope was the right direction. But the night was black. The birds were silent. There was no path to follow.

Felicity was gone.

19

STILL JUST PEOPLE

Lev took steadying breaths, more nervous than ever to walk the streets of Factumn. Knowing the queen and his fellow Swords were just on the other side of the city set each nerve abuzz. When he'd entered through his hole in the wall, he'd been stunned by the hush hanging over the streets. The wall had been no more guarded than usual. It would seem all focus was centered on the palace.

Lev waited in the shadows of the alley, a familiar position. He marveled at how quickly he'd readjusted to the art of sneaking through the streets versus the forest. The beginning years of a Sword's training involved mostly slipping through the cracks, blending into shadows, and making oneself easily dismissed. Lev had been one of Vasca's best when it came to spying. When she realized how attached he was to his brother, even compared to the other Swords, she'd exploited this quickly, making Lev do the unspeakable to gather information with force rather than stealth. Lev hated that he knew how it felt to remove skin, nails, and entire body parts. He knew the pitch of a scream right before the truth spilled out. He knew when the truth wouldn't come, and it was best to slit the throat. He knew how it felt to spill blood with a sword versus a knife.

He hoped he wouldn't have to resort to such measures for information. Mathers had done his part. He got Lev another meeting with a rebellion contact. Lev had flashed his marks to her, and she had promised to set up a meeting with someone who could speak to Amalia. But the rebellion was busy and had to be careful. The time had been pushed twice, but Lev had tried for patience. It was finally paying off. Lev needed his questions answered. He needed access to the palace. It was painful, but he could admit he was prepared to do whatever it took to get it.

Lev continued to Nightscape, his stomach a tight knot of dread. They would meet in the neutral area, and both had promised to come unarmed. All Lev could see was Amalia's hatred—the harsh burn of her stare and the echo of it in her men's eyes. Whoever he met would feel the same way towards him. This wouldn't be pleasant.

Lev's contact was waiting in the back corner of the tavern, wearing a cloak with the hood drawn. Lev barely concealed his surprise as he approached and realized who had agreed to meet him. Though, Lev supposed she was the rebellion's true leader. He and Amalia regarded each other for a long moment after Lev sat.

"How dare you use those marks to get this meeting?" she hissed. "My rebel was so excited to have met another Marked Man."

Lev's marks and hood had gained him access to the throne room that day; it felt horrible to use them again to get close to Factumn's royalty. Vasca hadn't been allowed guards or weapons when she sought an audience with Factumn's king and queen. She'd chosen Lev to take the marks. To sneak around and study the Marked Men's habits. Their formations and stances. Chosen Lev to secure her power. He hadn't let her down. He'd been a good Sword. Maybe even the best.

Lev clenched his fists and took a steadying breath. "I needed this meeting."

"So you can tell Vasca what we have planned?"

"I left her service. At first I just wanted out of the cities and away from Queen Vasca. Now I want to help."

"You want to help, then convince the Unmourned to help me."

Lev was shaking his head before the princess had even finished her sentence. "I won't ask that of them. We can figure this out. This is *our* war, not theirs."

"And what do you think *you* can do to help?"

"I can get close to Vasca."

A beat of silence as Lev's intention became clear. Amalia scoffed. "You have no qualms against murdering royalty, do you?"

"Royal people are still just people. She used death to gain power; it may be the only way to remove it. A queen and mother dying. You can't demand more retribution than that. If I can do it, the Unmourned need not be bothered."

"You propose this so lightly." Amalia's words were calm, but the flare of possibility had lit her eyes.

Lev's stomach was twisting, his hands sweating, but he knew none of it showed. "I've killed a lot of people."

The young princess shifted away from the look in Lev's eyes. She was built like a fighter and had carried a weapon comfortably, but the innocence in her gaze belied her lack of experience. She wanted battle but didn't understand its realities.

Lev knew his own eyes hadn't looked so innocent in a very, very long time.

He let the silence carry as the princess considered. "I have a question," she said.

"Yes?"

"Why did you agree to escort Felicity? We were told Jal would be doing the job."

Lev smiled wryly. "Jarles likes to give me the better-paying jobs. He's loyal to Lilstromers. We tend to have worse luck in the trees."

"Why did you hide in the forest? You know Lilstrom. You could have gotten on a boat to go anywhere."

Lev tilted his head, frowning. "What do you know of Queen Vasca's family?"

The look on Amalia's face said just how little. Lev blew out a breath and tucked his hands under his armpits. His finger had felt stiff and cold almost constantly since he'd left Nook.

"King Vasimer, Vasca's father, had six children. All as power-hungry and competitive as Vasca. All with strong kingdoms that they conquered. They have people everywhere, and the scars on my face make me too recognizable. The forest is safer."

"Tell me more about her." Amalia leaned closer. Lev knew she hoped to hear about some weakness, but Queen Vasca's background was only a story of strength.

"Vasca was married into Lilstrom. Her father felt his army was stretched thin enough, so he married her to the king of Lilstrom to gain that port without bloodshed. We know what happened to him." Lev's memories of the Lilstrom king were foggy and sparse. He'd been just a child when the king died. He remembered a kind smile. A smuggled treat. A clap on the back.

A handful of berries Vasca warned Lev not to crush, or his brother would have to eat them, carefully placed in the king's oatmeal as the king ruffled his hair. Vasca's rare, approving smile. The same one she'd given him in the Factumn throne room before he fled.

Royal people were still just people. They died just as easily as the rest. He'd learned that lesson early.

Lev cleared his throat of the memories and pressed on. Now wasn't the time to dwell and fall to panic. "But Vasca always wanted more. She saw the power of the forest but could not conquer it. So she settled for the power bought with the gold from your mountain. Her Swords are better trained than any of her sibling's guards, her income greater, her ambition stronger. This is the first time she's visited Factumn since she conquered it because she's been busy. Lilstrom is flourishing, and she wants her father's attention. Meaning, she needs to tie a knot on Factumn, own it completely, so she can reach beyond the two cities without her grip faltering."

"She thinks she can control me that much better through marriage? I didn't even know she had a son."

Lev nodded, working to keep his face blank. "My point is Factumn is on the outskirts of her mind. You've grown less accommodating as you've gotten older, so Vasca is falling back on what she knows. Likely, she won't want you to last long after the rings are exchanged if you don't behave. Vasca won't bother coming back as long as the gold keeps coming. Her real power is the ocean, the lands her siblings own that will fall to her should anything happen to them or to her father, who grows older by the day."

Amalia drummed her fingers on the table, thinking. Her nails were bitten to the quick. "But we can barely fill her demands as is."

"I've been listening to gossip whenever I can. She plans to send more people here. Enemies, prisoners, traitors. Anyone she doesn't want to deal with."

Amalia's face drained of color. "We can't *feed* ourselves as is. We've had to limit births, trade less selectively..."

Lev nodded. He'd learned of their methods of birth control in the meadow. Nook's people had truly learned every use of the mourning berries. Their bitter taste when he'd swallowed the brew to keep Nook from worrying had been well worth it. She told him Jal was the source of Factumn's birth control along with their access to the antidote. Lev hadn't known the man was so critical to Factumn's survival.

"Queen Vasca doesn't much care as long as the gold continues traveling the road."

Amalia's fingers stilled. "I only met with you because of Felicity. She... had words for me after what happened. She trusts you, and I trust her." Pain tightened Amalia's voice. "She left when she saw how much I was willing to do to be free of Vasca. But I need Vasca gone so Felicity and I can be together. I'll do anything, even meet with my parents' murderer. Even make a plan with you. Do you swear you can do this? Kill Vasca?"

"I can. But it won't be enough," Lev continued. "Vasca's family already wants her gold. They'll fill the void she leaves as quickly as we create it."

"So what do we do?"

"We use the only true weapon we have. We have to use the forest. We have to destroy the road."

"But... we *need* it. We'll starve without it."

"You better form a true alliance with the Unmourned then. No threats. No kidnapping."

Amalia's face went pale. "And if it's too late?"

The tingling chill in his palms grew worse. "What do you mean?" Lev's voice lowered.

"There is an Unmourned in our dungeon now. I had my rebellion leader leave her there. I was going to go speak with her next."

Lev remembered the forest. The path he'd carefully created for Nook to follow.

The path that led directly to her from Smuggler's Alley.

What had he done?

Throat tight with an anger he'd never before experienced, Lev stood, reaching for his knife. Amalia's eyes went wide. She stood quickly and stepped back.

"You'll take me there now. Please." He bit out the last word.

Amalia nodded quickly. They hurried from the tavern. The princess didn't ask when Lev took them on a detour to his apartment. He was good with a knife, but he felt centered and calm when he pulled his sword from its hiding spot. Amalia shied from the weapon. She wasn't the first to do so, and this day, she wouldn't be the last.

They ran to the palace, Amalia breathless beside him. She carried weapons confidently, but Lev quickly saw her training lacked the rigor to keep pace with him and hoped she wouldn't falter.

Lev broke into a cold sweat when the gold-accented palace came into view. His memories shadowed every inch of the lawn. He could practically smell the dead bodies that had been strewn in the wake of his fellow Swords. He could still hear the screams. There was the river, which had run red when Lev stopped in a desperate attempt to clean his hands. Too many bodies bled upstream. He'd ended up getting sick into the water instead.

There were Swords patrolling. Lev could name them all just from their stances and mannerisms. Amalia managed to evade them all, taking a winding path with practiced ease. They paused at a servant's entrance, Amalia oblivious to Lev's struggle to keep his panic at bay. "I'll go first. You won't make it past my guards. If you see a Sword, take care of them."

Lev wasn't sure he'd be able to do such a thing to one of his brothers, but he reached for his sword anyway. Would they hesitate to strike like he would? Or was Vasca's hold too strong?

Amalia eyed the weapon and saw his doubt. She paused with her hands on the door. "I just don't understand. How can you all serve her? Why haven't more of you left? Why haven't you fought her?"

"Because whoever gets caught, their brother dies. And when you are raised to only care for one person, that's enough of a threat."

"So... your brother is dead?"

Lev swallowed. In the days following that glimpse in Smuggler's Alley, Lev had nearly convinced himself he'd imagined his brother's face. There was no doubt Vasca punished his brother, but it wouldn't have been truly effective if Lev wasn't around to witness it. Maybe she hadn't killed him. He didn't know what had happened.

But Lev did know that if his brother was on the other side of this door, he wouldn't be able to fight him.

Seeing he wouldn't answer, Amalia huffed a breath and pushed open the door. Like the city outside, the palace halls were quiet. Servants spoke in low voices but were easy to avoid. "Do you do this often?"

Amalia shrugged. "Vasca keeps guards on me at all times, or outside my doors at least, but I think because she's here, she doesn't think I'll do anything. The Swords have mostly kept to the training yard and upper floors where Vasca is staying. She dismissed a lot of the Factumn servants and guards while she's here."

Lev didn't like it, but he couldn't stop now. Not with Nook in the dungeon. Vasca may not have gone down there yet, but it was only a matter of time before she discovered Amalia's plotting. He had little choice but to shadow Amalia through the dimly lit back hallway behind the kitchens. It had direct access to the stone steps leading to the dungeon for the servants to deliver food to the prisoners. The walls grew rugged, the floor dirt. Not any place Vasca would set foot in.

Everything was fine. He was not going to think about the queen's presence up above.

It was nearly pitch black in the dungeon. Amalia swore as she fumbled with a torch on the wall beside her, struggling to light it. "We kept it dark so Vasca's men wouldn't notice someone down here."

Lev's throat was closed with nerves, so he only nodded and adjusted his grip on his sword as the light flared. Amalia held the flaming torch low as they continued.

"I told Pax to leave her just over—"

Lev stumbled for the first time in years. Even though he'd

261

had that glimpse, the confirmation was too much at this moment. "*Who?*"

Amalia wasn't listening. She'd pulled a key from her belt and thrust it into the door on her right. With a grunt, she awkwardly hauled it open with one hand.

And let out a strangled shout before running inside. It was enough to spur Lev forward, even with the ache in his palms and the roaring in his ears.

"I don't understand! You were supposed to be in hiding... I told you to stay close and that we'd figure everything out. How are you here?"

Lev knew. As soon as he saw Felicity getting to her feet, he knew what was going to happen next. Queen Vasca gained her power through a near-superhuman ability to parse the weaknesses of her enemies. Lev's mind snapped every piece into place even as Queen Vasca's laugh echoed down the hall and light flooded the dungeon's entrance with her arrival. Pax stood expressionless at her side. Lev's grip slackened on his sword at the sight of his brother, at the satisfaction on Queen Vasca's face.

"Finally," she said, glee shining in her eyes. Nothing made her happier than a slow-burning plan coming to fruition. "When they first went to collect the maid, it worried me that the princess let you escape. I thought for certain she would do all the work for me in drawing you from your trees. The second time is the charm, I suppose."

Amalia stood, pressing Felicity behind her. Felicity ignored the princess's arm and stepped to Amalia's side, face ashen even in the orange glow of the torchlight. Lev felt his world spinning. At least he could stop worrying about Nook. She was safe in the forest. Not a witness to this.

It was his only source of warmth as he turned to face the queen, refusing to look at Pax. "You planned for me to escort Felicity?"

"Of course. You think anyone leaves my services without me knowing?"

"What is going on?" Amalia demanded.

The queen turned to her with a smile of poison. "My dear, I would like to formally introduce you to your betrothed. Despite all the trouble he's caused and a complete lack of respect, I must still claim him. This is my son, Prince Lev. I do thank you for returning him to me. I trust now that all the pieces are in place, we can proceed with the ceremony."

The queen's laughter was saturated with wicked delight.

20

CAPABLE

Fullbloom was asleep, forehead wrinkled in worry, even unconscious. Jal and Bough had been in Factumn for hours now. Felicity had become their priority, and Nook hated waiting for the two of them as they asked questions and searched for the girl. Felicity had been gone for over a day. Amalia would soon send the hunter back into the forest for an actual Unmourned and likely be angry at Felicity for leaving her to warn them. All Nook could see was the burning anger, the look she'd given Lev. The desperation for power. Nook wished she were there. She wished she could step in front of Felicity the same way she had Lev. Felicity had come back to warn her. She had left the princess she staked all her hopes and love on and returned to the forest for Nook and her people. It meant something. It meant everything.

Nook paced incessantly. The walking eased some of the biting pains in her lower stomach and allowed her to peer through the vine walls, constantly checking the forest beyond. Kneeling, she checked Coin again. Whoever had taken Felicity had sent the furycat into a tree truck, dazing him long enough for the kidnapper to get away. The furycat seemed fine now, more jumpy but otherwise unharmed. Lev was a painful absence between them. Nook wondered if he'd ever left Coin alone in the forest for this long before.

"Nook, try to get some rest," River gently bid.

Nook scoffed. He'd been sitting stiffly since Bough left. Resting indeed. But she settled herself down next to him. "I don't think I can."

"Then tell me about Lev," River said. "I didn't know you were so familiar with him. Jal says you've known him for years, not just the following around that your mother told us to watch for."

Nook hated that. River and Bough were told to keep tabs on her. They had thought so dismissively about their connection with Lev. Another facet of Nook not taken seriously. She glared into the fire. There was a reason Jal was the only person she talked with about Lev.

"Come on, Cranny. It's me. I didn't even know you kept secrets from me."

"Yes, believe it or not, River, I am my own person capable of thinking for myself. Capable of meeting people without endangering the Unmourned." Here Nook almost stumbled, remembering that damned arrow in her chest. She pressed on, "Capable of feeling romantic things and living a life outside you and Bough. I'm not the kid I once was, following you and Bough around like your attention kept me alive or thinking you could possibly return f—" Nook cut herself off. Cheeks burning, she hugged her middle and stared determinedly into the fire.

"Finish that sentence." River had never used that commanding tone with Nook before.

She shook her head.

"Nook, tell me. Tell me why you're hurting and fighting us so much. What is all this about?"

"Everything changed that day in Lover's Meadow, River. That day I found your message in the dirt and thought you loved me back," Nook's voice was a mere whisper, discomfort making the words almost impossible to get out.

In Nook's periphery, River froze. The same stillness came over him when he drew his bow and prepared to shoot. "Nook—"

"I was a stupid kid. But I've grown up. I love that you have Bough, and Bough has you. I know our mother favors Bough, that the Unmourned trust her more. I know I...I don't have anyone of my own. Except Lev. I met him that day, actually. He stole from me when I ran from Lover's Meadow. Even after that, he's always regarded me as a full person, separate from my ties to the Unmourned. He never once asked why I was in the forest. I never feared him or his knowing about me. And these last weeks, he still never looked at me differently. I thought I could have him in the way all of you have each other."

Nook had rarely seen River so speechless. She couldn't meet the hurt in his eyes. He found his voice. "I didn't know, Nook."

"I know you didn't know. You didn't bother to look close enough. No one did, no one has. No one saw how much happier I was out here by myself. They only saw danger or the child who barely survived that fall from the trees. None of you see me. What I want, how strong I feel because I did survive, how much I want to help and know I can. Everyone only sees Meadow's daughter. Bough's younger sister. An immature Unmourned shirking her duty and refusing to listen. I'm so tired of it. I hated that fight with Bough, but I hated the relief I felt when she banished me even more."

Nook looked to River then. He was always pale and drawn when bleeding. His face was even worse now. The breath he took shuddered. She watched him search for words.

What could he say to fix a childhood of being forced to the outskirts?

"I have Lev now. I'm not letting him go. As soon as I'm able, I'm going to find him."

The fire crackled between them. A cool breeze made its way through the vines. Nook realized how cold she'd gotten.

"I'll help you," River said. "I don't know how much it helps, but I'm sorry, Nook."

"Don't be." Nook sighed. "The worst thing you did was make my sister unbelievably happy. It hurt me at the time, but I can't ever be mad at you for it. I just wish it had been different overall. I won't fault you for being loyal to Bough. She deserves to have someone who only sees her."

River scooted closer, wrapping an arm around Nook's shoulders. "I love you, Nook. You are so brave and smart and determined. I see all that, and I should have admired it, not let it worry me. I'll always be sorry for that. I'll work on being better from now on."

Nook wasn't ready for the tears that closed her throat at his words. She turned her face into his shoulder as she cried. River held her tight. He wasn't Lev, but for a moment, she felt a bit like she was home.

Nook finished scrubbing her under things in the stream steps from the wall. It wasn't nearly as luxurious as soaking in the river at Thornwall, and her fingertips stung from the soap they used to remove blood stains. Still, she was hopeful this would be the last time she'd have to use it this month. She'd barely bled the previous night, and what she had was dark, a good indication she was at the end of her cycle. She knew better than to let her hopes rise. There was usually a time near the end when she didn't bleed for hours, only to lose the last amount in a rush and finally finishing.

Maybe it was close enough. If she was careful and took Smuggler's Alley, by the time she reached Factumn, she could be invulnerable again.

When she returned to the thorns, River was sleeping within. He was over the worst of it, too, but it had been a heavy, painful bleed. The injuries he'd received in Midhaven were as deadly as the longclaw's attack Nook had suffered. She'd healed from so much more than that, but she wasn't sure if River had. For the first time, the worry Bough must feel seeing how battered Nook allowed herself to become made sense. Her people weren't invincible. River may not have survived much more. Nook rubbed her chest where the arrow wound had closed just yesterday, and she flared with pride in her strength.

Nook stared at the scar on her palm. These new marks stirred thoughts of Lev. She sighed. She missed him so much.

The barest rustling announced Bough's return.

Nook whirled, heart frozen in her chest. "What happened?"

Bough was shaking. She barely got out her words between panting breaths. "I finally found Lev and Felicity. They weren't with the rebellion as we hoped. They're being held in the palace."

"What else?" Bough didn't care about Lev and Felicity enough to look this upset.

"He's Vasca's son, Nook. Lev is the prince. The ceremony is tonight. He and Amalia are to be wed."

Nook's hands clenched. Her sister's words refused to make any sense in Nook's mind, but she knew Bough wasn't finished. "What else?"

"The rebellion is no more. When we went to their meeting place, we were captured. Their leader was a Sword in disguise."

"No." Fullbloom lurched to her feet. She'd been watching the thorns for Jal's arrival. Nook felt like she'd fallen into cold water, the roar in her ears making thought difficult.

Bough was nodding miserably. "I... barely got away. They tried to cuff my wrists." Bough looked at her hands, both mangled and broken. Nook swayed. "I have to get to Thornwall. To get help. We'll get Jal back, Fullbloom."

Nook turned away, hands to her temples. She couldn't face

Fullbloom's devastation. This was all Nook's fault. Jal was taken. Her people finally pulled into the fight. Everything Bough hadn't wanted. Nook had brought this on her people.

Fullbloom picked up their water basket and threw it. River's voice was calming, assuring. Nook hadn't even noticed he was awake. She looked up and spotted Coin in the trees above. The sight of the furycat grounded her.

Bough was still talking. "We just have to get there, and the focus won't be on him anymore. With help, we'll get to him. Maybe even just Greener and Ash. The hunting grounds are closer. If I go now, I can get them to Factumn tomorrow. I've already been marking trees—"

"You have to let me go," Fullbloom said.

Nook glanced back to see River nodding. "Nook and I will be fine. You two go; make your plans as you run. You don't have time for this."

Bough threw herself in his arms. Nook looked away again. She'd never felt weaker. More helpless.

As quickly as she'd returned, Bough was gone, and Nook still hadn't found her voice. River lowered himself to the ground, even more pale. He busied himself rekindling the fire. It took him too long with his trembling hands.

"It'll be okay. We'll get Jal, Felicity, and Lev. It'll be okay, Nook."

"You can't. Bough can't. She's supposed to begin her bleed any day now."

"We'll finish first. All of them are useful to Vasca. She won't—"

"How is Felicity useful? Do you think Vasca cares about a maid who betrayed her? She'll kill her if Amalia doesn't do what she wants, and if Amalia does what she wants, an entire city will continue to suffer."

"It'll be okay, Nook."

"You don't know that."

The familiar sensation of the thorn walls creeping too near rose painful goosebumps on Nook's arms. There wasn't time to wait for Bough to return with reinforcements. If Nook could end this, she would. She might even be finished here anyway.

She refused to prick her finger and see if it bled.

She carefully reached for the vines. She snapped off a sapling, the thorn dark and its point curved in wicked sharpness. With River staring with a furrowed brow into the fire, already so tired and drained from his bleed, he didn't notice her move to the baskets holding extra vials and potions. He didn't acknowledge when she dug up a sleeping draught. A powerful one. It wouldn't affect an Unmourned between bleeds, but during... Nook dipped the thorn and crossed to River's side. He put his arm around her readily.

"I know you love Jal and Felicity, but I want you to know I realize how hard it must have been to hear about Lev. That he lied about who he was. Bough might not make it in time to stop the wedding... but maybe it'll be good for the outsiders. I have to believe he'll be a better ruler than his mother."

"She may have birthed him, but he isn't her son. She was never a mother to him. He didn't lie." Nook well remembered the feel of his scars under her fingertips. That wasn't the mark of a mother. "He doesn't want to rule."

"How do you know? He kept it a secret."

Nook shrugged, the motion pressing her closer into River's steadying warmth. "I know him."

"Don't do anything stupid, Cranny."

"I won't, Stream." Then she stuck the thorn into his thigh and caught him as he fell. His face relaxed into an easy sleep. Nook gathered what weapons she could. She pressed a kiss to River's cheek. As she walked toward Factumn, she marked the trees. Her symbol, followed by a triangle to give the direction she went. Another drop, signaling she'd finished her bleed. An underline. Stay safe.

Nook paused before entering Smugglers Alley to carefully gather her last and favorite weapon, using her pouch so she didn't directly touch the berries. Coin stayed close to her side as she lowered herself into the darkness. He remained there when she came out the other side. Together, the creatures of the forest entered the city.

The men on the wall patrolled closer together than when she and Lev passed through it. Even more concerning was the fresh mortar over the gap where she and Lev had found access. Nook paused on the rocks, knuckles white where she gripped them. She'd never asked Bough and Jal how they traveled into and out of the city. Heart sinking, Nook eyed the misshapen wall and knew. It was constructed of large boulders, with cracks and divots and natural recesses enough that it looked like a mountain edge carried and dropped strategically. It jutted into the air, too high and unstable for even the guard to walk. They patrolled it from a wooden boardwalk suspended over the tallest of the rocks.

There was no other option but to climb. Nook glanced at Coin pacing on the ground below. She didn't want to leave him. She wanted to spend time looking for another opening.

She didn't have time.

Nook swallowed back her terror, the memory of falling so close it played on the edges of her mind no matter how hard she fought it. She didn't even know for sure if she was finished with her bleed. But this was worth the risk she'd already committed to taking. She pulled in a breath and conjured every memory she could of Lev's smile.

Without giving herself a moment to think too closely about the height, Nook found the next handhold. Pulling, dragging, even jumping, the sun was just setting as Nook finally reached the wooden walkway. She looked down as Coin turned dejectedly and slipped back into the trees. She ran to the stairs. Going down them was nearly as terrifying as the climb up. Their shape was strange and unfamiliar, and it took her too long to find a rhythm to her steps, but finally, she was in Factumn's silent street. The toll of the palace bells began to clang over the city.

Shaking the tired ache from her fingers, Nook ran. The wedding was about to begin.

21

TRAPPED AND FREE

Amalia came out of her bedroom the second morning of them being locked in her chambers together. The princess had not broken her silence toward Lev the entire time. She only spoke when Felicity delivered their meals. Amalia always left her bedroom and stood right in front of the door at least five minutes before they expected Felicity to enter.

Frowning, Lev glanced at his brother. It was strange how quickly it became natural to have Pax returned to his side. Pax's face had changed over the years. The facial hair was a change, darker brown than his hair, and just long enough to push Vasca's requirements. He'd grown, now taller than Lev. Pax had remained in Factumn, living as the rebels did, and his thin frame standing beside the other Swords betrayed the fact. *Lev* was more filled out from lean forest living. The other Swords weren't sure how to look at either of them, yet Pax was clearly more accepted. He'd lived separately on Vasca's orders.

Lev couldn't tell what any of them thought about him.

Despite all the changes, it was still easy to read the slight shifts in Pax's expression. Vasca had ordered him to remain silent, and so far, Pax had complied. His loyalty stung, but in searching looks, Lev saw the confusion Pax felt. How many questions his brother had. How shaken the trust was. If the trust were still there, they would have already cleared the air, talking late into the night, no matter Vasca's orders.

Pax watched Amalia pace in front of the door, his face blank. But he paid attention. That meant he cared. Lev didn't expect *that* to hurt. Didn't expect the pang of jealousy. For so long, they'd only monitored each other so carefully. Constantly aware of their surroundings, but their focus was on the well-being of the boy at their side. Now, Lev had Nook and Felicity; why couldn't Pax have people? It had to be a good thing. Lev forced the jealousy away. He was the one who fled. Vasca left Pax in Factumn in case Lev returned and positioned him to earn the princess's trust. Pax had survived and made friends. Friends that weren't Lev. If anything, it was a relief he'd remained so far away from the queen.

It was *good* that Pax cared. It meant something that he was bothered by how he'd betrayed Amalia by setting the plan in motion to use Felicity to get Lev back to Factumn. Maybe Pax knew he was in the wrong. Perhaps this would be the first step toward healing. To getting Pax out of Vasca's clutches.

Lev cleared his throat and dropped his voice. He hadn't spoken in a day, the disuse another reminder of the years they spent communicating when Vasca wasn't looking. They could read each other's lips flawlessly. But Pax wouldn't look at him to read his lips. It took Lev shifting closer for Pax to flick his gaze in Lev's direction. "You could help."

A long moment passed. Pax shifted his attention back to the far wall. But then, right when Lev was about to turn away again, there was a crack in the armor. The barest hint of expression that only Lev ever had the privilege of seeing. The room was too still when Pax finally responded. "Not if it means your life."

Lev's stomach dropped, palms twinging. Vasca had already made it clear she would resort to the same punishments and threats they experienced as children. In her eyes, her grip was just as firm as it was three years ago. As soon as Lev had attempted to fight back in the dungeon, she'd nodded to Pax. Lev would never get used to seeing his brother draw his sword and angle it to his own chest. The look in Pax's eyes every time it happened, the determination to be the one to die so Lev would be safe. He would do what Vasca ordered. A death blow was often her most merciful punishment.

Lev whispered, "You've gone this long without me."

Pax's shoulders stiffened. The blankness fell away to a glare as Pax finally, finally turned to him fully. "I've gone this long doing everything I could to keep you alive. You think she didn't know every time you snuck into Lilstrom? Every time you stumbled into Midhaven needing supplies? You think she doesn't know you travel with a furycat and do business with Jarles and —" Pax cut himself off. He'd forgotten himself, and Amalia stared at them with wide eyes. He continued, but loud enough for her to still hear. That said enough about Pax's regard for the princess. He trusted her with this conversation. Lev felt his opinion of her shifting. "I've given far too much to risk you now."

"I've had my taste of freedom, Pax. You know she'll never let me go again. She's claimed me as her own, just like we knew she would one day. Her family will know I'm hers. But I've experienced freedom, and I want so badly for you to have it. She can't kill me, not now. You can leave. Then I could stand against her." Without the threat of Pax's life hanging over him, Lev could do anything.

Pax crossed his arms, his silence chilly.

"You could take Felicity," Amalia said. "Leave through the window like you always have after our meetings. You know how to get out of the palace without being seen, and she can get you to the forest."

Pax glared between them. "I won't take the risk." He stepped closer to Lev, protective, and it felt like Lev's chest was cracking to pieces. How could Pax still be loyal to him after all this? How could he still care when Lev had left him to this world?

Lev grabbed Pax's arms, turning his brother fully to face him. As always, Pax's eyes skimmed the four lines of scar on Lev's face. Pax hadn't felt well that day. He wasn't performing to the best of his abilities right before a mission. What mission, Lev didn't remember. Vasca had been quick to punish. Her nails hot and raking as she held Pax's eyes. *See what you've done?* Her glare had said. But when she left, Pax had been able to rest. The scars were worth that. "Pax. I left you. All I did was thieve and hide. You know as well as anyone I'm not worth risking yourself."

Pax rolled his eyes to the ceiling. "I know exactly why you left. I heard her screaming, too." He flicked a hand in Amalia's direction. "I'm always going to be on your side, Lev. I don't care what happens to me. I've done everything I can to help both of you for the past three years—"

Amalia scoffed. "You gave up every member of the rebellion!" She jabbed a finger toward her desk. "Every paper she sends me are execution orders to sign!"

"I warned everyone I could. Most of them should still be in hiding."

Understanding cleared Amalia's anger. "You did?"

"It's what Lev would have done." Pax glared at Lev to punctuate the words. The look was a reminder of late-night conversations. When Pax would bring up Lev's heritage, would hint that he felt Lev was worthy of more, would float ideas of what it would be like when Vasca was gone... Lev had always cut those conversations short. His brother always possessed a far higher capacity for dreams.

"No, I wouldn't have, Pax. That was all you," Lev whispered. "You did that, and you deserve a chance." He already ached with missing Pax again, but he couldn't stand a true loss. He remembered every instance he'd almost lost his brother. They haunted his nightmares. The accepting look in Pax's eyes each time he was used as Lev's punishment.

The knock on the door jolted them. They fell quiet as Felicity was allowed inside, Brans on her heels. Like all the other Swords Lev had come across since his return, Brans refused to meet Lev's gaze. It saddened him. Brans and Trist had been in the room next to Lev and Pax. While Swords were only close to their brother, Lev hated seeing the others still so lifeless. Stare vacant and listening only to Vasca or the information she needed. But Lev had seen Brans whisper in Trist's ear to make his brother laugh when no one else paid attention.

Lev forced his gaze away. He didn't look at Pax, knowing his brother's face had slipped into an equal lack of expression. Lev refused to let his features become blank. He knew autonomy now. Gentle touches and trust from someone besides Pax. He was human. Not a weapon.

Amalia took the tray from Felicity and set it on the table behind her. The Swords never allowed them long. The princess reached and touched the fading bruise on Felicity's cheek. "Has she..."

Felicity shook her head. She looked Amalia over and glanced to where Lev stood by the fire. Something helpless and akin to jealousy sparkled in her eyes as it had since Vasca forced him and Amalia to agree to the marriage. "I heard a rumor in the kitchen that Jal was captured," she told Lev softly.

Her words brought on a dull roaring in Lev's ears. He crossed the room in a few quick steps, passing Felicity and throwing one unexpected punch. Amalia gasped as Brans fell. Lev flooded with guilt. Brans had time to pull his weapon. Lev hadn't been thinking, but Brans was on duty, alert. He had let that hit land.

Felicity let out a startled laugh that she quickly covered with both hands. She spun and closed the door.

Pax looked thunderous when Lev turned to him and Felicity.

"Please. They're going to come for Jal. You have to stop her. Tell her to leave the city and that I—Just, please."

"What? Who?" Pax demanded. He bent to check his fellow Sword, hissing, "You're going to get us both killed!"

Was it possible Pax didn't know about Nook? Had no one told him about the arrow in the basement? If Pax didn't...Vasca wouldn't either. Hope flared. Lev had to get Nook out of Factumn's walls before she got caught in a war that was in no way her own. Before she thoroughly swept her people into the crossfire.

"He was captured at a rebellion base," Felicity said. "There was a girl with him, but she got away." Felicity gave Lev a significant look.

Amalia caught up, far too sharp. "You think the Unmourned might still come?"

Felicity nodded slowly, glancing at Pax. Lev wanted to quiet them all, but he didn't. That trust in his brother lingered despite everything. "They will for Jal," Felicity confirmed. "I think... I think they were here for me."

Lev glanced at his brother. Pax shifted, still forcing a glare about Brans's still form.

"Pax, what does the queen know about the Unmourned."

There was a long beat. Pax's answer would fully betray the side he fell on. "I left the Unmourned when I took Felicity." Amalia made a noise of outrage. He'd doomed Felicity in that moment. "I didn't say anything of what Remi told me or what I heard in the forest. Vasca still isn't sure the Unmourned exist. She just wanted me to get Felicity back so she would have leverage with Amalia."

Amalia stood still, thoughts whirling. Then, she shifted, settling on a course of action. She turned to Pax, eyes pleading, and anger brushed clear of her expression. Oh, she was good. "She's right, Pax. At this point, all I have is Felicity and my people. I can't save all of them, but if you can get Felicity to safety, I can risk fighting Vasca without worrying about her. No one will be allowed closer to Vasca than Lev and me. We could do something."

Lev jumped right in, matching Amalia's energy. He could taste how close they were. "Pax, as long as Vasca can use you against me—"

"She'll kill you if I leave."

"She won't. You *know* she won't. I'm more important than ever now that she's claimed me. She can't treat me like any other Sword. You have to do this. You have to trust me. Felicity will help you find the Unmourned. If you care about me, you'll make sure they don't get caught in this. And Nook..." Lev couldn't find the words to describe everything Nook had become for him. Couldn't introduce this new, shining facet of his life to Pax in a desperate plea.

Yet, Pax read it on Lev's face, eyes widening. "Lev..."

"I know. I shouldn't have." Pax knew as well as any other Sword how dangerous love could be. "But it's too late. I have to make sure she's safe. You have to do it for me. You'll understand once you meet her."

Felicity's eyes were alight, her smile slightly smug. She seemed to think it was decided as she pulled Amalia close. As always, Lev didn't trust the calculating look in Amalia's eye. "We'll fix this," she said. "Pax and I can ready the rebellion. We'll be there to support you when you make your move."

"No, Felicity. Get to safety. Go with Pax and—"

Felicity cut her off with a kiss. Amalia stiffened, then appeared to melt. She had a dazed look in her eyes when Felicity pulled away. "This is my fight, too, Your Grace," Felicity said. "I'm going to fight for you. We'll win this city together."

One last, quick kiss, and she crossed to the window, glancing expectantly back at Pax. As quickly as that, the situation shifted beyond Lev and Amalia's control. They were supposed to leave to get to safety, to get Nook to safety. Not to stoke her fire...

Pax stared at Lev as though he were a stranger. It hurt, but Lev knew he deserved it. Pax stepped close enough that no one else could hear them. "You and me. That was our promise to each other. It was supposed to be you and me. You left me when you swore to protect me. You're leaving me again."

Lev pulled Pax in for a hug. They didn't have time for this, but he held tight until his brother hugged him back. His exterior was hardened to a sword's edge, but Lev knew Pax's soft core. He'd only ever let Lev see it. Before Nook, Lev hadn't thought he possessed the same qualities. "I'm saving you. This is the only thing left I can give you. It's the only way. Nook will help you, for me. She'll get you wherever you need to go. But I won't marry Amalia. I won't serve my mother any longer." Pax's eyes widened, but Lev pulled him toward the window. "There's an entire world out there. Even just within the forest. You'll learn how little I deserve your loyalty when you meet others. When you let yourself open to them. It's so different than anything you'll experience as a Sword. I want that for you so badly it pains me. Please, Pax. Go. Do this one last thing for me."

"I won't be able to protect you." Pax's voice cracked, his grip on Lev's arm desperate.

"Either way, you can't protect me from her. Let me protect you this time."

"Lev..." Pax searched for words. His eyes dropped to Lev's shaking hands, and he sighed. "Don't die."

Lev's laugh was a broken huff. Brans stirred. With one last look, Pax nodded and climbed over the window. In seconds, he and Felicity were gone.

"Do you think they'll make it?" Amalia asked.

Lev nodded. "Pax will protect them. He'll do what it takes. It won't be easy, though; Felicity will want to stay and help."

"You trust him? To keep her safe? To keep her out of this?"

The question didn't deserve an answer. In the battle of wills, Lev could only guess who would win. He faced Amalia fully.

"We don't have much time. We need our own plan. Do you have anyone you trust inside the palace? It's time to stage your rebellion."

Amalia's gaze turned calculating. "You are still my parents' murderer. A Sword. Vasca's son. Why should I work with you?"

"Because I am all those things. I am the only person you should risk. Shall I tell you my ideas for a plan?"

Amalia considered for a long moment. Brans drew in a sharp breath, the only indication of pain as he woke. A swift kick and Amalia silenced him again. Lev winced in sympathy.

"Very well. Talk."

Lev was still reeling from his brief reunion with Pax. They'd barely spoken, yet Lev felt centered again in a way he hadn't in three years. His brother wasn't dead. Didn't despise him. Had only been punished with a position in Factumn, as far as Lev could see. He'd been here all along, helping in whatever small way he could against the queen. Pax would be there with Felicity and Nook, all three of his people safe together.

Lev's shoulders were surprisingly light as he braced himself to deal with his mother for the first time with no one standing between them. No one he loved for her to hurt in her anger.

Amalia paced, and Lev talked. It wouldn't take long for Trist to realize something was wrong. Felicity should have returned with the dinner tray, and Swords were never apart for long. Likely, Trist had been antsy since the moment Brans left his side. Lev watched the man stir now. He was at least six inches taller than the last time they'd seen each other. It was amazing what three years could do to a person. Like Nook said, they'd been children when Lev left. He'd never seen that so clearly until now.

The sharp click of Vasca's heels in the hall signaled their time was up. Lev was unnerved by the calm that came over Amalia's face as she straightened and turned to meet the queen.

The door opened, and Trist's stoic expression broke until he saw Brans was still moving and cleared his features. Lev experienced a flare of guilt, but at least one thing Vasca ensured was mutual understanding between the Sword pairs. They would understand he'd done what he did for Pax. If the situation were reversed, neither would have hesitated to do the same to him.

Vasca sneered at the fallen Sword only as long as it took her to stalk past him. Trist knelt and quickly checked his brother's breathing. Brans finally regained consciousness enough to rise with Trist's help. He did his best to get in position, hand on his sword hilt and only slightly unsteady. Trist stood a half step in front of him. He was as ready to defend his hurting shadow as he was to follow Vasca.

Vasca glared between Amalia and Lev, finally approaching Lev. He knew a flare of panic. Why did he seem the weaker link to Vasca? What did she have on him?

She grabbed his chin so hard, her nails dug into the base of the scars they had left eight years ago. "*What have you done?*"

"Proved your methods as faulty."

Lighting fast, Vasca released Lev's chin and smacked him so hard Amalia flinched at the sound. He didn't falter, only turned to spit a glob of blood into the fire at his back. The sizzle as it struck burning wood mingled with Vasca's heavy breathing.

"Where is he?"

"Gone. And if you want this marriage to take place, you'll let him leave. Felicity, too."

Vasca laughed. The mocking laugh haunted him from childhood, but as an adult, he faintly recognized it was a slightly ridiculous sound. Too breathy and practiced. Nothing good ever followed it, but it proved she was still just human. Prone to dramatics and thinking too hard about appearances.

They waited. Everything depended on this agreement.

"You think you are in any position to bargain with me? You have nothing."

"I have my promise to cooperate. Do you think dragging Amalia and me to the wedding in chains will gain you any loyalty? Will solidify any sort of alliance in the people's eyes? It'll only get me Factumn's sympathy. They'll learn I'm not your loyal son. I know you want an obedient Sword to marry their princess and keep Factumn in line. I won't be that."

Vasca laughed again. "They won't ever love you. You murdered their king and queen. You earned their city when you drew your sword that day. They'll be happy to see you struggle, but you'll still be their ruler."

"And what power will you hold here after you leave?"

"That is precisely why I will have Pax returned. It won't take much to convince him to stay in my service. I'll always have that power over you."

"Or let him go, and I won't fight you. Never again. As long as he and Felicity are safe."

"No," Vasca shook her head and laughed again. Lev's palms were sweating. "I never thought Pax would betray me. He still won't. Once he starts thinking, he'll realize I have you. I can do whatever I need to get him to return. He's more loyal to you than you'll ever be to him. Shame on you for thinking he's as weak as you. I would never have entrusted him to rally a rebellion if he wasn't completely mine. Well, yours, but I own you both."

Amalia's face had drained of color. Her eyes caught on Lev's cheek, and the imprints Vasca's nails left. "You've barely seen either of them in three years. You don't own them."

"Don't I, girl? How do you think I knew Felicity would make you weak? How did I know when you were going to make raids? Why do you think every move of your rebellion has failed or been caught at the last movement, except the tiniest losses I could afford to give you hope? I own this city. I will have Pax and Felicity returned, and you'll be wed. No more wasting my time."

"You said yourself Pax is loyal to me. He'll do what I asked. It'll be easier for you to let him go."

Another laugh. A second longer to catch her breath. She was *stalling*. Lev tasted victory. His head swam with disbelief.

"I will have them found, or Pax will return by own his free will. You will see. Now, you both have final fittings in an hour. Servants will be in shortly." Vasca turned to leave. She stopped and frowned at the Brans, the bruise blooming on his jaw. "Trist, punish yourself in Pax's stead and for Brans's weakness. Your third finger will suffice and not impair your swordsmanship too greatly."

Lev lunged forward without thinking. Amalia grabbed him. Her eyes were huge as she watched the Sword at the door draw a dagger. He set his hand on the nearest table. In one quick downward jab, he left a finger behind.

Trist's face went white. He swayed, eyes going to Brans for strength. Brans's lips pressed tight together. His accusing stare flicked toward Lev. They waited for Vasca's satisfied nod before leaving the room behind her.

Lev was shaking. The world roaring with numbed pain just like it used to. He couldn't draw in air. His thoughts longed to shut down. He had forgotten what it was like, living like this. His mother's threats constant and all too real. His skin lit with an urgency that he used to live in relentlessly. It had only relaxed when he was safely within the mourning trees three years ago.

All he could do was hope Pax was finally experiencing the same freedom. Lev shook Amalia off. As soon as she detached, she swallowed hard. It wasn't enough. She ran to her room to be sick. Lev's training was returning just as quickly as the panic. He buried every emotion deep as he went to the desk to pick up the finger. With nowhere else to put it, he tossed it in the fire. The smell of burning flesh filled the room.

His mother had to die. No one was safe until then.

22

PREPARATIONS

The streets were abuzz. Murmurs spoke of a stirring rebellion, a wronged young princess, a Sword prince who appeared from the mourning trees. The tension of change was palatable. A wary hope. Stolen glances toward the castle. Because the rebellion persisted, despite the promise of a wedding, despite the Swords on the streets, despite the news they had been smothered. Their survival was proof Vasca wasn't all-powerful. That their princess was ready to lead them.

The hopelessness Factumn had lived under for three years was shifting. Jal, the famous smuggler was captured, and if anything brought the Unmourned rumored to travel with him into the city, it was that.

The air set Nook's nerves alight. It was happening. Things were moving. Jal had followed news of rebellion for years, always carrying it back to Nook. She'd felt so alone in her interest in his tales. Now, she felt like she had barely experienced the thirst she saw on people's faces. She didn't know how to be part of something this big.

Unsure where to start, Nook ran toward the meeting place where they had dropped off Felicity. She was vigilant, knowing this was likely where they discovered Jal and Bough, but with no other leads and the rumors churning, she hoped to find someone to help her. If not, she would go straight to the palace. She couldn't think what else to do.

Nearing the place they had made the exchange, Nook slowed her pace. A tavern across the street had a window facing the rebellion building. She decided to sit for a moment and see how heavily the building was guarded and if anyone else tried to make contact.

It wasn't long before the man serving ale approached her. He took her in, sitting alone amidst the tense atmosphere of the bar. Nook tightened her shoulders, trying to fit in.

"Strange times, huh?" he asked. His eyes were intent, reading. Nook knew she was being tested.

"Very." She paused, drummed her fingers, and decided to go for it. "I tried to get a drink across the street. Didn't realize it wasn't a tavern. Unless it's closed today?"

His left eyebrow twitched, and he rubbed at his chin, considering. "People are scared."

"Are you?"

"Are *you*?"

"I don't have time to be. People need me."

He nodded, a slow smile spreading across his face. But he wasn't amused; it was more that he liked her daring. Nook appreciated that. He slid into the seat opposite and dropped his voice. "Who needs you? Might be I can help you find them."

Nook looked the man up and down. She hadn't grown up in High Valley, where those of her people who didn't bleed lived. She didn't know how to read this man with his bearded face and squared, uncomfortable body. Too much unnecessary bulky muscle made it seem like he couldn't fully relax his arms. He reminded her of gruff, stomping smugglers. Of Remi and the guards in Midhaven.

She missed Lev with a fierce pang that robbed her of breath. His lithe fluidity. His unthreatening touches. His familiarity.

This man's face wasn't changeable and open like Jal's. It wasn't practiced and guarded like Lev, whom she'd learned to read. The man eyed Nook, likely mirroring her own expression.

What would Bough do? Or Jal? Or Lev? Nook wanted to ignore the stirring of caution, just state she was looking for Lev or the rebellion. Maybe she would have if she'd known for certain her bleed was over. She would have risked capture if she knew she could take their arrows and run harder and longer without the pain of working muscles shouting at her.

Nook was saved from answering. An older woman hurried up to the man, leaning down to speak in his ear. His eyes widened, and he stood without another word, following her to the opposite end of the tavern and into a back room. After only a moment's hesitation, Nook followed.

They had locked the door behind them, but something spurred Nook to keep on them. She slipped outside. Rounding the building, she found the back door was barred, too. Sucking in a breath, Nook tipped her head and found a path to climb to the nearest window. She first used the tips of her fingers, gaps between bricks, and the doorknob to get up, then stepped onto the wood holding a large bell that the opening of the door with toll. It was a jump from there to the windowsill. Nook hesitated. Her fear made it hard to think, so she didn't let herself. She was in the meadow, Lev's lips so soft and warm on her skin. She jumped for him.

Nook nearly lost her balance while pulling at the jammed window but managed to open it. Her shoulders barely fit, but Nook had been named aptly and crawled through the tight opening into a lofted space above the back room. It was a storage area, but she didn't recognize the bags or crates. Not the type of supplies they took to High Valley. Over the din of those drinking in the tavern, no one had heard her. She crept until the floorboards ended, a ladder descending into the large, humid back room. Nook listened, a slow smile spreading.

"—told you to go to the forest, then you should go. Hide. They already have Jal and—"

"Felicity knows how to get through the trees, Math." The man speaking was young, with dark hair and a stance too similar to Lev's. He stepped forward, the same fluid grace in his movements, and put his hand on the bearded man's arm. "But I can't leave him behind like that."

"He left you. Mourning trees above, if I'd ever made the connection, I would never have..." The bartender shook his head. "Why not? Why can't you just leave him?"

"Because of the rebellion. Vasca told me to start it, to be her spy and earn Amalia's trust, but how can you think I'd stay loyal to her after all these years? After the bloodbath and seeing his face that day. Hearing Amalia screaming. The wedding is the perfect cover. We go in and free Amalia, and she can rally her people. Everyone with any power left in Factumn will be there. They'll rise. You and I both know it."

"Pax..."

"We can do it. Amalia can do it." Felicity stepped into Nook's view. Her confidence rose the hairs on Nook's arms. Felicity hadn't been so sure when she left the princess to warn Nook about her plans for the Unmourned.

"And what happens to Lev?"

Without another thought, Nook swung her legs over the loft edge and dropped to the floor. A blade was instantly at her throat. Nook slid her eyes to the bearer. "Nothing happens to Lev."

The sword dipped, and understanding lit the man's eyes. "Nook, I presume?" Pax's eyes were as sharp as his blade. His frown doubtful.

Nook raised her eyebrows and tilted her head. She knew her power. She knew she was the reason Lev was even alive for them to discuss today. Nook was the forest and the strength of the Unmourned.

Not even a Sword would look down on her. "Funny. This is exactly how he and I first met, too," she said, using one finger to move the knife away.

Pax snorted and tucked the weapon into his belt. "If we're going to free him, we need a plan."

Felicity's smile was vicious as she skipped forward to hug Nook. "Remember how you wanted to leave him to die in Midhaven?" Nook mumbled into the other girl's hair.

"Shhhhh, Cranny. I have no idea what you're talking about."

Nook laughed.

LEV STARED at the dried blood on the table as the tailor buttoned him into his stiff wedding outfit. The man made an impatient sound, and Lev distractedly nodded his approval, but he couldn't look from Trist's blood.

Trist was alive, though. It was only a useless finger, as Amalia had said.

Lev swallowed as his stomach turned yet again. The room still smelled like burning flesh to him.

The tailor left. Someone else came and readied Lev's hair. Parting it and combing some shiny substance into the strands. They moved to cover the scars marring his cheek, but whatever look he'd turned on to the servant had them scurrying from the room. A pang of self-loathing followed. Imagine scaring someone so much that they disobeyed Vasca's orders.

Too soon, Lev was ready for his wedding.

It took them a long while to get Amalia prepared in her bedroom. By then, Lev was fighting the temptation to approach the table and grab the wine bottle from it. This morning, he thought he was ready. When Pax and Felicity had climbed through the window, he felt he had nothing more to risk.

The blood reminded him otherwise.

So many lives. Swords, guards, citizens. So many lives depended on him walking down the aisle and pledging himself to Amalia.

He'd been foolish to think this would be simple with Pax, Felicity, and Nook safe. He'd been foolish to think it would end with Vasca's death and his demise at the hands of his fellow Swords. He had no idea what would happen after that. Would the Swords rally to continue as Vasca would want? Would they resist Amalia? Would they kill her, too? Who would lead Factumn, then? Who would destroy the road and keep Vasca's family from claiming her crown if they all died in the throne room?

Would he be leaving this place any better?

Lev's thoughts went to Nook as his eyes traveled the line of blood down the tablecloth once again. He hoped she was deep in the forest. That she would see how futile this was. He hoped she'd forgive him. He hoped she'd forget about him.

He hoped she didn't. He hoped she loved him as much as he loved her and that by doing this, he might deserve to live on in her fondest memories.

Amalia was finally released from her rooms. Lev's eyes swam with the gold they'd adorned her with. His attention caught on her pale features, drawn even under the powder and paint.

He looked back to the table—the bloodstain.

With a few sharp clicks of her heels, Amalia crossed the room and gathered up the bloody white cloth. One of the maids who had just spent the better part of the afternoon readying her gasped and ran forward, taking it from Amalia's hands.

"We were told to leave it," the woman protested. But her gaze was full of apology. Good. There were those loyal to Amalia in the palace.

"You can tell Vasca that unless she wants me to wear it down the aisle, you'll burn it now."

The woman ducked her head and left with the evidence of Vasca's cruelty. The other servants followed her out. Cale informed them they had twenty minutes until the ceremony. Lev forced himself to meet the Sword's gaze, then his brother Nic's. He started when they both offered him a nod before they left, locking the door behind them.

Lev's hands felt like ice. The bells of the palace began to ring, summoning the wedding guests to their places.

Amalia crossed the room again, wincing at the pinch in her toes. Her eyes narrowed on Lev's face, and he worked to clear it, but not before she saw his doubt.

"No wonder you ran after killing them," she said. Lev's breath caught. "You don't have the stomach for it, do you? No matter what she did to you, you hate it. The blood, the killing."

Lev looked at his hands. They would be soaked in blood again soon enough. "It doesn't matter. I can still do it."

"At what cost?"

Lev thought of all the times he couldn't breathe. All the nightmares. Every time he rushed to water to scrub at his hands until they were raw. All the tears and vomit and sweat and shaking. The killing he'd done had shattered him.

It didn't matter this time. There was no chance of him leaving the throne room alive. There wouldn't be an opportunity to suffer for this murder. Even if it was what finally broke him, it wouldn't matter.

Amalia grabbed his hands and forced his attention to her face. "Are you still with me?"

"Yes." His voice cracked on the word. He cleared his throat. "Yes. I can do this."

Amalia raised an eyebrow. It was difficult, but Lev gathered himself, breathing deep and slow. He started to slip into that recess of his mind where no thoughts existed. Where he couldn't feel the pain in his body or the weight of his actions.

"You have to get away as soon as you can," he said, voice steadying as he spoke. "When Vasca falls, I don't know what the Swords will do. She never told us what to do in the event of her death. She always believed we would protect her. She told us our lives were only to serve her. If they fail her, they still may turn their swords on Vasca's enemies. You have to leave. The Dagger will be the worst one. He leads the Swords in Vasca's absences. He doesn't need a brother; his loyalty is only to her. He'll strike to avenge her. Get away from him, whatever it takes."

"I won't leave my people right when it is my time to seize power. And you won't give up. You're young and strong. *You* kill the Dagger. I want my throne. You took it three years ago. Now you'll give it back."

Lev frowned, remembering Nook's mistrust of the princess. There was bloodlust in her eyes now. There was judgment for his faltering. For the glimpse he'd shown of his weakness. Amalia would do whatever it took to gain the throne.

But she *was* the better option. She had to be. She was angry and had every right to be. Lev had murdered her family. He owed her a throne if that's what she wanted.

"You're making the right choice," Amalia said.

Lev wished he knew certainty like hers. "You think Vasca's death is really the only answer?"

"What else would stop her?"

"If we could get her from Factumn and close off the road..."

"How would we get her from the city? Scaring her away? How do we do that without fighting? Without death?"

"What if..." Lev searched for the words. "I mean, Pax left. If I can convince the other Swords our loyalty is to each other and not the queen... I could try. Wouldn't it be better to try?"

"Lev. We don't have the time. The only option, the best option for everyone, is to kill her. You don't *know* that the Swords will fight us once she falls. Maybe they won't act. She might be the only death. It's the least amount of risk to everyone."

Lev's eyes slid shut.

"Why did you come here if you aren't sure about this?" Amalia asked, her voice tight with frustration. "You *told* me you could do this."

"I want to be better. What if Nook is right? It *would* be more of the same. What if we imprisoned her? Threatened to kill her if the Swords fought back and give ourselves time to talk with them?"

"You think the Dagger would let that happen? Lev, we have a plan."

"I can fight the Dagger." Lev went to the couch. Last night, Pax had put his knife between the cushions, eyes never leaving Lev's even as he kept silent. Lev drew it now. "I'll try not to kill him, but I can fight him like you asked." Lev pressed the hilt of the knife into Amalia's palm. "You capture the queen. Hold this to her throat until the Swords back down, and I fight off the Dagger. We'll be the only ones close enough to her. It's just us. Can we try? Please?" Lev was so, so tired of death.

Amalia took the knife, maybe a bit too eagerly. Doubt stirred in Lev's chest, but he forced it down. She had to choose correctly. She had to want what was best for her people. "He'll fight to kill, Lev. You can't go into such a duel prepared to hold back. I may not know much about swordplay, but I know that."

"I will slow him down, at least. You just have to get to Vasca and make her surrender. Don't worry about me."

Amalia stared at the blade in her hands. Her eyes were too hungry as they took in the power at her fingertips. They didn't have time for another plan. "Please, Amalia."

"You said you could kill her. You said it was just like killing anyone else."

"I know, but I don't want to be a Sword anymore. I want to di — to do this the right way. I want to deserve this victory."

293

Amalia tightened her grip and nodded. "I'll let you try."

Lev couldn't read her face. He could only trust she would do what was right. He was reminded painfully there were only two people in this world he trusted.

There was little doubt in his mind that Amalia would let him down. There would be bloodshed, and Lev would be in the center once more. At least he would die trying.

23

THE WEDDING

The headache faintly pulsing behind Nook's eyes was not a good sign. She'd been pain-free for hours, but the back and forth between Pax, Mathers, Yalla, and Felicity was getting to be too much.

"We need to go now, get them out of there *before* the wedding and—"

"There is no way they aren't guarded to the teeth. We can't just stroll in there. We need to get in disguised as guests—"

"Once again, there are only three of us. What about the rebellion members—"

"They can wait outside the gates for the signal. Mathers can give it when we—" Mathers nodded along with Felicity.

"There's no way he'll hear—"

"Stop!" Nook couldn't listen anymore. "We're out of time. You all need to rally the people. I go to the wedding. I stop Vasca. It's the only thing that makes sense."

"Nook, she'll capture you as soon as she realizes what you are. As soon as you confirm the Unmourned are real, all she'll want is to go after your people," Felicity said.

"I'm not letting you go in there alone. Lev is my brother. I should go."

Felicity shook her head. It was the same argument. Nook growled with frustration, but Felicity didn't bat an eye as she spoke over the sound. "You can't, Pax. Vasca will just use you to make Lev do what she says."

"And use you to get to Amalia, but Nook is just one person. She can't get Lev and Amalia out alone."

"I'm an Unmourned. I can do it. All I need to do is get close to the queen, which I can do because no one will recognize me."

"You don't have the proper clothing. You think you can just walk in there?"

"And then you'll what?" Pax asked, eyebrows lifting in challenge and ignoring Felicity's protest.

Nook looked at him and didn't need to provide an answer. She would do whatever it took to save her people. Lev included.

"When you get to the palace, someone needs to find Jal. That's all I ask."

There was finally a moment of silence. Pax studied her and sighed. "I know where they'll be keeping him," he said. "I talked to the Swords who captured him. I'll get him out."

Nook turned to him, eyebrow raised. "You won't follow me?"

"If I'm there... Lev will be more worried about me." Pax dropped his eyes. "Felicity is right. He said so himself. I can't risk it, but he trusts you. He loves you. You have to be worth it for him to feel like that after everything we've been through."

Nook's shoulders relaxed, and she grinned. His lips twitched as though fighting off a smile of his own. "You'll save him?" he asked.

"I'll save him. Vasca won't be able to hurt him anymore. You can get Jal?" she asked.

Pax gave her a look in response before turning to Mathers. "Spread the word about what's happening. Gather as much of the rebellion in the crowd as you can. Your princess will not be wed today."

It was the closest they came to any sort of plan. The bells had begun to ring. They were out of time.

Nook left the tavern and went toward the sound, slipping through the crowd ready to gather and see the prince and princess after the ceremony. As she walked, Nook fell into the pace she set when alone. The fast, steady gate that allowed her to travel the forest so quickly. But for once, she wasn't running away, but toward. Nook pushed through the crowd. There was already so much tension no one bothered to grumble.

Outside the palace gate, she faltered. Her head tipped back to take in the castle. Nook had never even imagined anything like it. Not after all of Jal's tales and her mother's warnings. She hadn't known people were capable of building towers and arches and gold-plated décor like that. It was intimidating. Nook didn't have an invitation. She wasn't dressed like those entering. With her stomach clenching again, Nook took off to the left, where a cluster of harmless trees grew outside the palace wall. She would have to climb yet again.

At the base of the tree, Nook paused. It took her a beat to recognize the iciness stirring in her stomach. She was afraid. She was alone, and everything was at risk. Reckless. Her mother's face swam in Nook's mind. She pulled her knife. In the crowd of people trying to get into the ceremony or catch a glimpse of the bride and groom, no one noticed Nook in the time it took her to leave her mark on the tree.

THE HALL WAS CAST in silence. Most faces were Vasca's followers, but some were Amalia's supporters who had only survived this long by hiding their thoughts. Lev felt their eyes. They knew who he was, what he'd done to their late king and queen. His arms and the marks inked into his skin were on display, mocking them all. He half expected one of them to kill him before he could wed their princess.

It bolstered his confidence to know she wasn't alone. Whatever happened to him, she'd be surrounded by people who cared.

Amalia twisted her hands into her shimmering gold skirts. Lev knew she was checking the weight of the dagger hidden there. She would be fine.

Lev barely kept his hands from shaking as they walked side by side to the front of the grand hall. The thrones where Amalia's parents died hadn't moved in the years since. The red cushions hid the blood stains, but Lev had little doubt they hadn't been touched either. The two of them would be expected to sit on those reminders once they were wed.

Lev couldn't stop himself from looking at his fellow Swords. They were all there, lining the room. They'd all known he was Vasca's son. They all knew he was the only one among them who hadn't been taken from a family in Lilstrom. Vasca had been harsher toward Lev than any of them. He was used to snatches of pity in their stares. They eyed him warily now. He was the only Sword who had ever gotten away, even briefly. He saw how they faltered, realizing they may have the skill to run. To hide in the forest. Brother's exchanged looks. Hope blossomed in Lev's chest. He might not survive them, but he could give them a possibility of life beyond Vasca's rule.

He and Amalia stopped on the steps to the dais bearing the thrones and faced each other. The gold washed Amalia out. Or fear paled her skin. But her gaze was steady. They waited for Vasca's approach. She took to the aisle by herself, her dress grander than the bride's, her makeup bold. Her smile poison.

Amalia didn't look at the queen. Her gaze had dropped to the steps they stood on. Traveled to the thrones. They were close enough to make out the pattern of blood. Lev recognized the darkness in Amalia's eyes. A sudden and clear image of his own mother dead on these steps stirred nothing within him. But feeling would come later; it always did.

It was too late to remind Amalia of the plan. Whatever happened next, Amalia's actions were beyond Lev's control.

Vasca was halfway down the aisle, taking twice as long as the two of them had. Holding the attention of her court, squeezing the power. The Dagger at her back. Lev let his focus shift, watching his target without being obvious, as he'd been taught. He forcefully detached from any emotion. Any memory of the hours the Dagger spent training him. How he'd cleaned Lev's cheek after Vasca dragged her nails down it. How, for a brief flicker, pity and anger had lit in the older man's gaze. He'd treated Lev differently because he was Vasca's son, and the Dagger only loved Vasca.

Lev didn't want this fight.

Vasca reached the front of the room. She walked between the bride and groom, taking her place a step above them on the dais. She cleared her throat to begin the ceremony. The world slowed as Amalia's hand moved, fingers diving into the folds of her gown. Lev had shown her how to do this. How to get a good grip on Vasca's arms while holding the knife steady at her throat. The world stilled as Lev watched her, ready to move once she pulled the knife.

But the queen laughed, and the Dagger moved first.

Surprise made Amalia's hand slip, still concealed by her gown. By the time her weapon clattered to the floor, the Dagger had his own knife, the favored blade for which he was named, pressed to Lev's throat. The Swords pulled their weapons. Too fast. Lev was out of practice.

Amalia swallowed, staring between her blade and Vasca. They all knew she wouldn't be fast enough. The queen smiled.

"Give me that," she said, nodding to the fallen knife. Amalia bent slowly and grabbed it. Her grip tightened for the barest second. The Dagger snorted. Seething, Amalia handed it to Vasca. The queen passed it to the nearest Sword and laughed. "Nothing like a bit of drama on a wedding day. Let's carry on, shall we?"

Amalia nodded, eyes sweeping the crowd where the Swords were ready to kill anyone who supported her. The Dagger kept his blade at Lev's throat. He didn't like the cold fury that dulled the brown of Amalia's eyes. What was she thinking?

"Let's not."

Lev nearly sliced open his own throat turning to the sound of Nook's voice. She stood at the center of the aisle. Appearing out of nowhere. A tattered tunic, dirty leggings, belt at her waist, hair in two neat braids, smirking.

Terror like Lev had never known froze his body.

Nook's eyes were only for Lev, and his only for her. She looked tiny, surrounded by billowing dresses and stiff-backed men.

Vasca smiled, showing all her teeth and breathing heavily. Headless of the blade at her son's throat, she nudged him aside as she descended the steps.

"What have we here? Do you wish to explain, Lev?"

Lev didn't move in the Dagger's arms. He couldn't move. His heart beat furiously in his neck, pulsing toward the blade. The Dagger let out a laugh.

"I was curious if any of you would show up. I've heard so much about the famous women of the trees."

Nook's eyes narrowed. She appeared unbothered by the Swords circling her. It reminded Lev of her strength. The power of the forest in her veins. She would survive this. Lev pulled in a shaking breath.

"I wonder," Vasca continued, "are you truly what they say? Would you survive anything?"

"Would you truly like to find out?" Nook's voice was steady, fearless. Almost taunting. He remembered her facing the long-claw, the wildness in her eyes as raw as Coin's.

"What about a beheading?"

Nook only smiled and shrugged. "My cousin lost her arm in a rockslide. It didn't grow back. I wouldn't test it."

"Why not?" Vasca stopped just outside the circle of her Swords.

"Because I see you're skeptical. You can't imagine me being a threat. You want to prove the Unmourned are real. If you behead me and I stay in separate pieces as I just said I would, you prove nothing."

Vasca considered. "So what would be proof?"

Nook reached into her pouch. He knew what was coming next. For some reason, dread still heaved in his gut. He had to keep reminding himself Nook would be fine. He'd seen her eat the berries before. Seen her cut the juices into her palm.

Nook held up her handful of blood-red mourning berries. Slightly shriveled with time spent off the branch, but still just as deadly. The Swords surrounding her didn't flinch at the sight, but the guests gasped and stepped away. Vasca grinned, entering the circle of Swords to stand before Nook, confident in her guards and power.

"Very well. Convince me."

Nook's eyes didn't leave the queen's as she lifted the berries. Lev waited, without breathing, in the Dagger's arms. Nook threw the berries into her mouth and bit down. A small smile. Then, after a sharp inhale through her nose, Nook spat the black juice into Vasca's face. Into the queen's ever-open mouth and smug smile.

Lev stared as Vasca fell, wiping at her face and shrieking until she seemed to lose the ability to force out air. So quickly, she subsided into choking noises and twitches. Veins in her neck turned black, and red froth poured from her mouth. Lev stopped watching. He didn't see the moment his mother died.

His eyes were for Nook and Nook alone. Her face was an apology as she swayed, the juice from the berries dripping down her chin. But this wasn't right. Nook was invincible. She was strong. She ate the berries just to get a reaction from him.

Nook crumpled beside the queen. Chaos erupted in the throne room.

2 4
FINISHED

Nook bit into the berries and felt the drop low in her core as the last of her blood left. The poison took hold. She stopped healing. She stopped needing to heal. Nook felt the two forces war. The life and death, the two great powers of the forest battling for control of Nook's breath.

She wanted Lev to be her last sight. Lev in gold, bringing out the greens and browns of his eyes even from here. Making the lighter shades of his hair stand out. She would never have enough time to memorize him. The freckles and shades and scars. In that moment, she realized that would have been enough. Being with him, it would have been enough. But doing this for him, to save him, it was all she needed. If only the blade weren't at his throat. If only he could hold her through this.

She distantly heard Vasca's screams and knew she should be in the same position, but life was fighting hard.

As Nook fell, she thought she heard her sister's voice.

LEV ONLY KNEW he had to get to Nook. He employed the very maneuvers the Dagger had honed in him since he was a child.

Shock loosened the older man's grip on the blade, and Lev moved. He grabbed the Dagger's hand and twisted it across his body so he could bring the weak joints to his knee with a snap. They were angled in a way that allowed Lev to reach for the sword at the Dagger's belt, but pain had brought the Dagger from his shock. He threw his uninjured fist, connecting with Lev's nose. The sword Lev tried to free slipped from his fingers, skidding to settle just behind the thrones. They threw themselves after it.

The Dagger had nothing left to lose. He snarled as he scrambled for the blade.

But Lev had everything. Nook had held Lev's eyes as she fell. The berries weren't supposed to hurt her, but she struggled to rise from the floor.

The doors at the end of the room burst open. Pax. Felicity. Amalia shouted, and there was movement in the windows. Lev caught a glimpse of Bough freefalling, black braids streaming before she hit the ground and rolled to her feet in the aisle. River was positioned on the window ledge, casting a shadow over the throne room with his bow drawn. Pax made his way to Lev's side, the Swords in the room forgetting Pax's side in this battle and letting him by.

Lev found his feet. His distraction had cost him. The Dagger rose with sword in hand, his smile dead on his lips. They circled the thrones, but it would only be a momentary pause.

Energized. Hopeful. In love. Afraid. Lev had never fought like this. His former mentor stood no chance. When the Dagger rushed him with a roar, Lev ducked and spun, the sword swishing through the air over Lev's head, landing with a thud in the queen's throne, as Lev kicked the Dagger's feet from under him. Pax shouted, and Lev's hand lifted in time to catch the sword his brother threw. He didn't think. His body fell into what it knew best as the Dagger rolled, tugging his sword free and slashing again.

The familiar ring of steel against steel and the dulling rush of battle overtook him. Lev had never truly tested his strength against the Dagger. He had only fought with a sword once in the last three years.

But he'd never tried so hard to win.

Lev saw the moment the Dagger realized this. The moment he saw Lev had always disguised his reluctance to go for the kill as a lack of skill. The moment he realized what it took to survive the mourning forest and how it had strengthened Lev as much as his ruthless childhood. The Dagger's eyes flashed with pride when he realized what a true opponent Lev was. When he realized he had lost.

Lev spun once last time. The Dagger's sword was ripped from his hand. The older man's instinct was to go for his dagger with his opposite hand, but not even the numbing rush of the fight could overpower the pain of his broken wrist. It led to a hesitation.

It led to his death.

As the Dagger's head rolled off the dais, Lev spared the nearest Sword a brief glance, prepared to continue fighting his way to Nook. Ty only stared. When he didn't attack, Lev sprinted down the aisle. The throne room had succumbed to a battle long overdue. Vasca's initial attack on this palace had been subtle, sneaking Lev into position with the marks on his arms and hood over his face, then overpowering the people as they reeled from the loss of their king and queen. It had been quick and bloody, over too fast for the Factumn people to rally a fight.

Anger had built to this point for the last three years. Amalia's people were fighting now, and they targeted the Swords without hesitation. Whether or not Vasca was alive to order her army, brothers were being threatened, and the Swords were fighting back.

Ducking, pushing, and throwing punches, Lev reached Nook at the same time Bough did. Nook was coughing, the berry juice in her spittle spattering the floor. Lev didn't care. He went to kneel at her side, but someone grabbed his arm. Lev turned, sword swinging. He barely stopped himself from slicing through Pax.

"You're bleeding. If you touch her, you'll get poisoned."

Lev tried to shake off Pax's grip. He only cared about Nook.

"Lev," his name on Nook's lips froze all struggle. He turned to her. He felt like he was burning—all the air around him sucked into the flames. "Lev, I won't get worse. My bleed is finished now. You have to stop this. Please. There's been enough death."

The guilt swimming in her eyes was enough to convince him. He used Pax's grip on his arm to get to his feet, understanding what Nook needed. She was kneeling, leaning against her sister, who was immune to the juices Nook still coughed. Bough murmured and wiped Nook's chin gently. The desperation cleared, and the chilling calm of battle returned.

"I love you." The words were so easy to say, so perfect in the air between them. He'd do whatever she asked.

Nook nodded, stained lips tilting up. "I love you."

Bough rolled her eyes, but they held a pleased glimmer as she lifted the antidote to Nook's mouth. Lev was alarmed to see that the blue tinge was not just from the berry juices but her actual lips. She wasn't getting enough air, no matter her assurances. Lev forced himself to look away and do what she needed. He took stock of the room. The Swords were on the defensive yet laying waste to the rebels attacking them. The Unmourned were trying to calm battles where they could, jumping to take hits and looking horrified at the carnage. River crouched in a window above, shooting arms and legs to slow the most aggressive fighters.

He heard Amalia shout and started to relax. Maybe he and Pax could get through to the Swords if she calmed her people, but then he processed her words. "Remember, you only have to strike one in two! They'll stop to help each other!"

She had somehow gotten ahold of a mourning wood staff. She was swinging it with abandon against Ty. When Lev ran to them with Pax at his side, she spun and leveled the staff at his throat. Lev stilled Pax with his free hand, noting his brother's white-knuckled grip on his sword.

"Amalia! It's over. Tell your men to stand down. I can stop the Swords."

Amalia's eyes flashed where she stood a step above him. "I have to end this, Lev. This is my throne."

Pax stepped closer. "Ama, please. You know me. We can figure—"

"You were a spy the whole time, Pax. Why would I trust you?"

Pax tugged at Lev's arm. Lev read his brother's lips. *She's the same.*

Lev didn't want it to be true. He fought the urge to glance back at Vasca's body. He had to reason with her. Opening his mouth to do so, movement to their left caught his eye.

Felicity broke through the mob, hair flying wild, a short sword in her hand, and expression set with angered determination. "Stop this, Amalia! Your people are attacking the Unmourned. We have to—" she went to step onto the raised platform.

Someone in the crowd shouted, "Protect the queen!"

The mourning wood spear was thrown before anyone could react. Not even Felicity. Her gaze dropped to her stomach, and shaft protruding from the front bindings of her dress.

Amalia screamed, the sound wretched enough to still her people and pause the fighting.

"No," Nook's rasped protest made its way to Lev's ears. He'd failed her.

Amalia ran to Felicity's side with a breathless sob, hands fluttering around the injury, unsure how to help. After a moment, she settled for cupping Felicity's cheeks.

"Oh, Felicity..."

But a strange expression crossed Felicity's face. With a puzzled frown, she got a grip on the spear. Amalia shouted and moved to stop her, but Felicity already tugged the weapon free.

A tear was in her dress, but no blood. She didn't even sway. Lev calmed. He'd seen this before.

"It doesn't hurt," Felicity marveled. Above, River let out a relieved laugh.

"You—You're one of them?" Amalia sounded horrified, stepping away.

Felicity smiled. "I guess so."

"But...why you?"

"The forest found her worthy," Bough said, stopping beside Lev. Nook leaned heavily into her sister's side, grinning as she and Felicity met eyes. Her lips were less blue, but she wasn't well. After vigorously wiping off one hand, Nook grabbed Lev's arm for support. With Pax still touching one arm and Nook on the other, Lev's world righted itself. He ducked to press a kiss on Nook's shoulder where she was clean. The Swords around the room stirred as Lev turned to address them.

"This fighting has to stop. Vasca is dead. The Dagger is dead. They can't threaten us anymore. We're free." He glared at Amalia. "We're leaving."

The Swords made no move to continue fighting, but there were so many questions in their eyes. Lev felt the responsibility for them settle in his chest.

The crowd of Amalia's supporters protested but didn't move as they waited for her next order.

"They took everything from us!"

"He killed the king and queen!"

"They aren't even *human*."

Shouts of agreement, yet the people of Factumn waited. They wanted their queen's approval. Lev turned, hands going cold, to see what Amalia would do with the power.

She still stared at Felicity.

"Amalia," Lev drew her attention. "Amalia, you can end this. Let us go. The palace is yours."

She had the power. Yet the gaze she fixed on the hole in Felicity's dress made Lev suspect it wasn't enough. He started to push Nook toward her sister, trusting Bough to get her out.

THERE WAS blood splashed against all the gold in the room. More blood than Nook had known people were capable of bleeding. They called her forest a place of death, yet none of the city dwellers even seemed shocked by the carnage.

Swords were dead. Rebels were dead. Vasca was dead. Nook couldn't stomach the sight of the queen's body. She'd done that. But Lev was here, holding her up. He'd tried to return her to Brough, but Nook wasn't letting go. He'd kissed her shoulder and was still breathing. He was still breathing. The thin line of red on his throat made her heart stutter every time she saw it.

And there was Felicity. Unbreakable. Unmourned. Brimming with the forest's strength. The light in her eyes dimmed as she saw the look on Amalia's face. The jealousy. The bloodthirst. "End this, Ama. Please."

"You don't understand. It's my city. I have to protect them. We can't trust any of them." Amalia swept a hand to encompass Pax, Lev, Nook, and Bough in the statement.

"We can. For this. Look at them, Amalia. They don't want this fight. They never did."

Amalia stared at Felicity as her people waited for her command.

Lev's hand started shaking again where he held her. Nook hated it. She wanted to take him away. Out of the city and to safety with her people and her forest. She wanted to wrap herself around him, but she was still deadly.

Nook knew Amalia was calculating. The princess, now queen, saw the Unmourned noticing Nook's hand on Lev's arm. She'd felt the shift when he kissed her, claimed her. Amalia saw how the Swords looked to him. How many of them stood despite being vastly outnumbered. Amalia's awareness of her current command shifted. She was not in control of the room. Her people were less skilled, more breakable. All she had were a few rebels, two Marked Men, and the mourning wood staff she'd dropped in her haste to reach Felicity. Who hadn't needed her. Who was stronger now than Amalia could dream of becoming.

"Ama, let them go," Felicity bid, reaching for Amalia's hand. Amalia stared at their locked fingers.

"You can't understand. I need stability. I need..." Power. Her eyes went to Vasca's body, her meaning clear even if she didn't want to admit it.

Nook stumbled forward, letting go of Bough to lean entirely on Lev. "If they agree, we will take the Swords with us into the forest. We'll close the road behind us."

"I'll block all the entrances to the city the smugglers know," Lev put in.

"You said you don't lead the Swords. Why should I believe they'll follow you peacefully? As soon as we lower our guards, you could attack again."

Lev turned to the room. Amalia bristled with jealousy once more when, at Lev's nod, the Swords sheathed their blades.

"This is your parents' murderer!" A Marked Man stepped from the crowd to remind Amalia. "He bears false marks—that offense alone is punishable by death. You truly plan to let him walk away?"

Amalia tried to look at Felicity again, but Nook could read the disappointment in Felicity's stance as she frowned at the empty thrones. Amalia's hesitation was enough for Felicity to lose hope for the girl she remembered. She no longer met Amalia's eyes.

"More of the same," Felicity whispered.

Amalia flinched. She stepped back and took a deep breath. She straightened as she turned and delivered her first order as Factumn's true queen through gritted teeth. "Lev has paid the price for his transgressions. For what he did under Vasca's orders the same way I had to follow her directions to keep you all safe. We are not in a position to collect enemies." A significant glance toward Bough and Nook. "I believe Lev will keep the Swords away. I believe the Unmourned will give us control of the road. I believe the fight has gone on long enough, and it would be a misuse of my power to continue it. Step aside and let them leave. It is time to move forward."

Amalia waited, breath held tight in her chest. This was the test of her power, of her right to rule. Yet, she continued to watch Felicity for approval. It took too long for her words to take hold, but take hold they did. As her people lowered their weapons, Amalia released her breath.

Lev looked as if he were afraid to believe her, still angling himself between the queen and Nook.

Felicity's face didn't brighten. Amalia slumped.

So much had been lost today.

EPILOGUE

TWO WEEKS LATER...

The birds sang. Nook smiled at the sound and pressed closer to Lev. He could take the weight. She loved that her forest had finally welcomed him. Even Bough had begun treating him as she did the Unmourned. It made Nook laugh to see her hardened older sister fussing over him, ensuring he'd gotten enough food and checking if she could take a turn helping Nook. Even more amusing was his bewildered response to her attentions. It was beyond reassuring to know Bough had welcomed Lev. He wouldn't be alone.

Lev had been letting Nook use his forearm as they walked, but feeling her snuggle in, he pulled his arm free to snake it around her waist. They'd discovered early on that walking like this slowed them nearly to a crawl, but both drew comfort from the embrace.

They were in no hurry this day. It was just the two of them now. As a group, they had traveled from Factumn to Thornwall. Progress had been so slow, but Nook didn't know if that was her fault or the Swords. Lev had thoroughly explained the forest ways to his brothers, but as they traveled, he had gone quiet to listen to Bough and River's cautions. Lev had never been so deep in the trees. Nook had never traveled with such a large party.

They listened well, but the sight of so many outsiders had made her skin crawl at first.

They left Factumn a quiet, shaken group. Jal had been rescued from the dungeon, and Felicity had looked torn watching their group go. There was a coldness between her and the new queen. Two days into the journey, Coin had vanished. He'd been nearly sewn to Lev's side before that moment, but when he left, Nook knew a stirring of hope. She wasn't surprised when Felicity appeared the next day with the furycat. Felicity's smile shook, especially as she took in Nook's haggard appearance, but she hugged both Nook and Lev before pulling them aside. Pax drifted after them, and Nook marveled again at how Lev relaxed in his brother's presence. He grew more balanced, breathed easier. His hands stilled, and he only checked one half of the forest for threats as Pax was wordlessly entrusted to watch the other.

"What happened?" Lev's voice was low. Nook flushed with pride at how he'd changed. The distant boy who once hid his face from the world looked ready to march back to Factumn on Felicity's behalf.

"It just wasn't going to work," Felicity said, voice breaking. "Amalia's changed. I think she'll be a good queen, but the girl I fell in love with grew into someone so different. She was noble and wanted to be a Marked Man and came to me for comfort. We told each other everything, and it was simple to love her. But now, the way she looks at me...We both changed. And I needed time. I needed to be here, with my people." She ended with a questioning look toward Nook.

"Of course," Nook stepped out from under Lev's arm, ignoring his sharp inhale when she staggered. She wrapped her arms around Felicity. "You can always go back when things are calmer. She'll grow and learn to rule a peaceful kingdom. You both have a lot to get accustomed to right now."

Felicity stepped back and Pax and Lev reached to help Nook

keep her balance. It was so frustrating. Nook heard her teeth grinding before she fully realized how she'd clenched her jaw. The rest of their party had settled down to rest—another new development. Because of Nook's weakness, they had stopped every few hours. Adding days to their trip but using the time to instruct the Swords on forest survival.

Felicity had nodded toward the hushed camp. "They're really all going to go to..." She trailed off. She didn't even know what the Unmourned called their home.

Nook smiled, looking behind her at all the Swords. Though she still called them that occasionally in her mind, she'd worked to pick up their names. "Yes. To High Valley, our city of sorts where those of us who don't bleed live protected in the mountains. There will be a place for everyone there. If they want to stay, they can, or they can make their own way, but for now, it seems crucial to give everyone somewhere to recover. To offer a haven."

Nook's chest tightened as she spoke of High Valley. She still didn't want to go. She knew it would be the last place she would see.

They settled on the outskirts of the camp. Lev and Felicity caught up while Nook rested her head on Lev's lap. Felicity even coaxed a few words from Pax, who remained distant with most everyone. Nook couldn't tell if he was angry at Lev for leaving or if something else was bothering him. He was taking longer than the other Swords to warm to forest life.

Greener drifted over to offer them water and food, eyes lingering on Pax until Nook shot her a look. Greener winked and went to Fullbloom, the two of them breaking into whispers, Jal right there with them.

As the miles slowly passed, Lev eased the tension between the Unmourned and his brothers by walking Nook beside different pairings and sitting with a new set of brothers every break until they'd grown comfortable with her presence. The

Swords were wary of strangers, but slowly, they thawed, going past the boundaries Vasca had maintained, pushing to test their new control over their lives. Two of the pairs now slept soundly in each other's arms and slipped into the forest together whenever they could. Brans began making jokes loud enough for all to hear, humor as honed and stealthy as his skill with a blade. It was amazing to see how Trist had mastered swallowing his laughter over the years of his brother making these cracks under his breath for Trist's ears alone. Now, after a pause, he laughed fully and freely. They all did. The birds hadn't sung for them, but the forest grew lighter.

The Swords started watching over Nook nearly as much as Bough fussed over Lev. It was clear that Lev had always been special among their ranks. That Vasca's treatment toward him and Pax had been worse than any of the others. Lev and Pax were younger, taken into the group as a pair when Vasca gave birth. From the murmured conversations Pax had with the Swords, always looking toward Lev, Nook suspected there was more to their treatment than age and Vasca's remembered cruelty. Either way, the protectiveness extended to Nook when Lev wouldn't let her from his sight. Pax was the only one Lev trusted to keep watch over her while he slept, but another pairing backed Pax without being asked. Bough rolled her eyes every time Lev refused to relax. Nook was too tired to keep arguing about it.

As they had hiked, the Swords nearest moved closer when Nook fell to coughing, watching the forest so Lev could give Nook his full attention. It broke her heart each time his hands shook during these fits. He and Bough told Nook constantly to stop worrying about them, to focus on feeling better.

But she hadn't had enough time.

They were all so careful. Bough preached caution more than ever, telling Nook not to give her body anything else to heal from during the next bleed. Lev said nothing when he saw how

Bough's warnings annoyed Nook, but he was always tense. Always in silent agreement.

River had gone quiet. Nook missed his smile and voice, but she couldn't tell him to stop grieving. He was so pragmatic. He knew, just as Nook did. They were the only two who couldn't lie to themselves about the gravity of Nook's illness.

Lev and Bough told her the next bleed would heal her. She had recovered from so much worse. But she hadn't. Her body had been brought to the brink of death and frozen there. When an Unmourned was injured between bleeds, they didn't feel it. They didn't slow down. This wasn't right.

Nook ached every day. She forgot what it was to move freely. And she was so tired. She wanted to sleep long into the morning and they let her far too often. She stopped to cough and fought for breath at every incline no matter how much Lev supported her. This wasn't a normal poisoning. Her body would succumb to it the moment she became vulnerable again. Pushing away hope of any other outcome was more exhausting than the travel.

They had stayed in Thornwall for Bough's bleed with plans to continue to High Valley as soon as she was safe again. The Unmourned were hesitant to let outsiders into their wall while their leader was vulnerable, but without being asked, the Swords took up guarding Bough and River's home at night. Lev assured them it wasn't necessary, but the need to be needed ran deep. It would take time for them to find a new purpose.

Nook and Lev's tent was guarded, too. It made Lev so uncomfortable that Nook knew there was something bigger at play. Lev didn't want to admit it, but she knew it was because he was Vasca's heir. The Swords had been forged to serve royalty. It would take time to break them of that.

Nook knew Pax was waiting to see how Nook's bleed went before he asked Lev what was next. She wanted to know, too. She wanted an idea of what her love would do for the world without her in it, but it was cruel to ask when Lev put all his energy toward hope of her recovery.

And so Nook understood when Lev asked her if they could go somewhere more private. She knew exactly where she wanted to spend their last moments together. It would be a backtrack, but worth it. Time alone with Lev to rest and marvel at everything they had between them. She wanted to savor their time together. What was left of it.

They had prepared to separate from the group with the plan that Nook would lead Lev to High Valley after—with an unspoken understanding that another Unmourned would come for him if she were unable.

Pax reluctantly bid them goodbye. Nook knew Lev felt guilty for leaving, but she suspected Pax also knew what she and River had accepted. Lev would be all his again soon enough.

Wrapped in each other's arms, they made their way to Lover's Meadow. Out of everyone's eyes, Nook allowed Lev to carry her for stretches, climbing on his back and laughing at the ridiculous situation. They paused to share smiles when they came across the place where they first crossed paths. Coin ran happily in the branches over their heads, immune to the history of the place. He was thrilled to be away from the strangers.

Lover's Meadow was still when they entered. Nook took a deep breath and regretted it instantly when she fell to coughing. Lev held her close, tension stiffening his arms. She knew he gripped her like he did to keep his hands from shaking. Nook turned in his arms once she'd caught her breath.

"I hate this," she said, voice roughened.

"It will be better soon." He was trying to convince them both. Nook attempted a smile.

On her own, Nook carefully shuffled to the center of the meadow. Only once she was on her back did she realize she was crying, tears slipping into the hair at her temples as she stared at the sky.

Lev settled down beside her and held her hand, making no more promises, only giving comfort.

When Nook squeezed his fingers, he rolled closer, kissing her cheek and whispering into her skin. "You are so strong." Another kiss, wetting his lips with her tears as he kissed them away. "You are so beautiful." A kiss on her nose. Nook sniffed and let out a laugh. "You are everything." He kissed the corner of her lips. His eyes were always on her lips; he loved to trace them with his fingertips. She loved how they fascinated him. Nook turned her head, wanting to kiss him back, but he pulled away, leaving inches between them.

"Whatever happens, Nook, you are my everything."

She was going to cry again if he kept talking. Seeming to realize, Lev granted her wish. He kissed her deeply and then made his way over her body. He trailed his fingers and kissed and held her like she wasn't about to break. Like she wasn't broken. Under his attention, she forgot all the pain. She wasn't tired. She felt complete for the first time since she bit down on those berries and stole a life. Lev was magic like that.

"I love you," she whispered into his hair.

He lifted his head. Swallowing, he blinked away his own tears as she traced his scars. "I love you."

It couldn't last long. Nook wasn't strong enough, and Lev was tired from carrying her through the trees. In too little time, he slipped into sleep. Nook forced herself to stay awake and gently extracted herself from the protective circle of his arms. He was so comfortable here in the meadow with her that he didn't wake. Nook sat staring at him as long as she dared before dressing and painstakingly making her way out of the meadow.

She met River not far from the wall of thorns. His features were drawn, eyes dim. "Are you certain about this?"

Nook nodded. "He doesn't need to watch this."

River sighed and offered his arm. He would take her to her mother. To High Valley. There, surrounded by her people, Nook would bleed. River would make sure Bough and the Swords waited in Thornwall for Lev. Nook shooed Coin back to her love's side. Lev wouldn't be alone.

Lev had seen enough death. Nook didn't want to add hers to his scars.

BOUGH HAD COME. Felicity had come. Even Jal had come. They tried to convince him to return to Thornwall for the wait. Pax was the only one who stayed. The two of them waited out the days in hesitant conversation. Lev learned how his brother had come to believe in the rebellion and how Vasca's biggest mistake was leaving him in Factumn to watch for Lev's return. He learned that Pax worried about Amalia and the friendship he hoped could survive his betrayal. Lev began to suspect Pax would return to Factumn. That or travel between cities, as Lev wondered if Nook would still want to do. There was always a pause on Pax's side of the conversation when Lev brought up the future he wanted with her. Pax didn't think Nook would survive. Lev feared the worst, but he couldn't make himself prepare for it.

Coin lounged in the sun beside them. The brothers had fallen into an easy quiet. There was still so much between them that needed to be said, but the waiting overshadowed it.

One day, an Unmourned would come through the wall and tell Lev Nook wasn't in his world anymore. One day, this life would end, and he'd be forced to build himself back up again. Pax was here now to remind Lev that he wouldn't be alone when it happened.

To remind him there was a whole world he was free to wander. His mother was gone. The marks on his arms pardoned. But, whatever chaos reigned in Lilstrom after Vasca's death, Lev didn't want a part of it.

"I don't want to go to High Valley," Pax said, breaking the

319

hush. He had said it before, but there was a real decision in his voice now.

"Where do you want to go?"

They were the only Swords who knew separation that wasn't death. It wasn't that surprising to Lev that Pax considered making his own way.

"Lilstrom. I can help the city. The rebellion taught me how to lead and organize. Maybe I can help them figure out a system that works. The trade there is too important, and pirates likely have their eyes on the place. Should Vasca's father come next...I just think they could use my help."

"They need your help," Lev agreed.

Pax grew hesitant. "They could use you, too. It would be easy to make you their leader. You *are* the heir to the throne."

Lev closed his eyes. "You know I don't want that. They don't want me to rule either way. I killed my fath—"

"Vasca made you kill him. They would consider it a miracle you survived her. And they would also fear you enough to solidify your power."

Lev felt nothing when he considered it. Everything in him was tied to Nook, to waiting. "I don't know, Pax. I don't know anything about ruling or politics. I only know how to kill and survive in the forest." And Nook. He knew her.

"I don't think either of those skills would hinder you as king," Pax said with a half-smile. Lev rolled his eyes even as he cringed at the word. "Just consider the option. It would be a good... distraction. And if the forest grows too painful, maybe it'll offer direction. You could help so much. But you don't have to join me. I just thought I'd suggest it." Pax wanted it. That was all too clear, and a part of Lev wanted it just to keep Pax close. The separation, though survivable, was excruciating.

Lev nodded, and they fell back to their silence. Lev watched Coin chase a mouse at the edge of the clearing. He wouldn't leave the forest. He belonged here with Coin and the memories, no matter how painful. But maybe he could still help the cities. Jal did a lot for them *and* the Unmourned with his trade. Lev could do that. He didn't have to steal anymore. He didn't have to work for Jarles or hide his face. He probably wouldn't even need to pay for the antidote, just ask Bough for a supply. Lev would figure things out.

Once he knew for sure. Once he could mourn or celebrate. Break or be built back up.

His hands twinged with a traveling pang from his heart. He clenched his fists. The days had passed slowly, but any minute now, he'd know.

Lev thought he was prepared, but when the vines rustled, he knew he wasn't. Dread sucked the air from his lungs. Unable to look, Lev watched Pax's face as his brother saw who entered the meadow—watched shock wash over him. Lev couldn't believe it.

Lev thought he'd held on to hope, but when he turned and Nook stepped into the sunshine, he realized he hadn't believed she would return to him.

He stood frozen, and she paused. Pax squeezed Lev's shoulder as he passed. He hugged Nook before making his way out.

She was really there.

Lev walked slowly, his entire body warming in her presence. His hands stilled, and the birds sang.

He was suddenly taken back to the first time they'd met. Her energy and the fire burning in her eyes. His world wouldn't have been the same if that fire had died.

"You can't be serious," she said. He let out a startled laugh. "You've been moping here the entire time?"

"Nook." He'd never been good with words, but her name was his favorite. It was all he needed to say.

"Lev." She smiled, whole and healed and healthy.

He ran and swept her into his arms. "Don't ever scare me like that again."

She stroked his hair, the scars on his cheeks, the outline of his lips. "I won't."

They kissed. They touched each other with wonder. Nook laughed, his favorite sound. "My mother can't wait to meet you," she said. She was so happy. Lev saw how her world was righted. Banishment the furthest thing from her mind. She looked proud of herself.

Yet, Lev couldn't stop his excitement from dimming. "I'm not good with mothers."

"There's no rush. We have all the time to go wherever we want. Whenever we want."

"I'm happy right here."

Nook smiled. She kissed him, and everything fell into place.

ACKNOWLEDGMENTS

I'm so thankful for all the support I have continually received from my family, friends, and even some friends's parents (shout out to Tami!) Thank you for reading the drafts, asking for more content, sharing your favorite books, and lifting me up every day in ways that leave me with space to create. Anna, Allison, Lindsay, Mom, Harley... The list goes on. Special thanks to those who read the early drafts of this book: Ben, Kat, and Tami!

Unmourned was my most intentional piece so far. I wanted to write about something I've known well since I was 10 in a new light. I want to continue normalizing conversations about menstruation. This idea was really inspired by the Deadline City podcast. I don't believe they are making new episodes, but there is hugely valuable content in their archives and I hope the lessons they taught come across in my writing. I am continually working to be better and keep learning and am extremely grateful for those who take the time to teach, especially teach us white authors.

Lastly, I wrote this book shortly after an author I had always admired took to Twitter to spread hate. Anyone who knows me, knows how much I loved growing up with a certain series. I really had to do a lot of reflection and discover my values on the topic of trans rights in the aftermath of this author's actions. This book goes to those who took the time to speak out and educate. The people that stood against a beloved author, especially those belonging to the trans community. I hope that River came across in the loving way I intended. I wanted my anger to become something positive and I'm proud of him, but also always willing to listen to feedback if anyone needs to reach out. It's never too late for me make edits.

Trans rights are human rights.

ABOUT THE AUTHOR

Kelly Cole graduated from the University of Wyoming where she studied English and Creative Writing. Kelly is most active on Instagram and TikTok and enjoys sharing her latest and favorite reads. She lives in Wyoming with her two crested geckos and her dog, Maya. She spends most of her time writing and playing endless hours of fetch (not with the geckos). Visit her website at www.kellycolebooks.com for more information.

Milton Keynes UK
Ingram Content Group UK Ltd.
UKHW041000040324
438885UK00006B/376